D0030822

THE
...RNATIONAL
...LLER

...SAIRE
ADAMSBERG
MYSTERY

"Vargas is such a dazzling
stylist that her unorthodox
plot and eccentric characters keep us enthralled."
—Marilyn Stasio,
THE NEW YORK TIMES
BOOK REVIEW

A
CLIMATE
OF
FEAR

FRED
VARGAS

AUTHOR OF *THE GHOST
RIDERS OF ORDEBEC*

Praise for Fr
Commissaire A

"A wildly imaginative series."

"Spry, ironic, yet fully engaged with the horror of contemporary reality." —*Los Angeles Times*

"It's a full, rich, and strange plate." —*The Seattle Times*

"[A] high degree of intelligence, sophistication, and perversity informs [Vargas'] fiction. . . . It's a tangled web she weaves, and a hard one to escape." —*The Washington Post*

"Vargas writes with the startling imagery and absurdist wit of a latter-day Anouilh, about fey characters who live in a wonderful bohemian world that never was but should have been." —*The New York Times Book Review*

"Bizarre crimes drive Vargas . . . who's won the CWA International Dagger three times, [and] keeps her zany plot under tight control all the way to the surprising finish." —*Publishers Weekly* (starred review)

"Few crime stories are as apt to leave a reader wondering so ardently: Who dunnit? . . . Vargas' characters are like something out of a fairy tale—eternal opposites, ever-renewing archetypes despite their fresh adventures each time. That's why each novel's opening feels new." —*The Philadelphia Inquirer*

"Anyone who enjoys kooky characters and intricate detail will happily follow Vargas along." —*Entertainment Weekly*

A PENGUIN MYSTERY

A CLIMATE OF FEAR

Fred Vargas was born in Paris in 1957. A historian and archaeologist by profession, she is a #1 bestselling author in France and Italy. She is the author of eight novels featuring Commissaire Jean-Baptiste Adamsberg, including *The Chalk Circle Man*, *Wash This Blood Clean from My Hand*, *This Night's Foul Work*, *An Uncertain Place*, and *The Ghost Riders of Ordebec*, also available from Penguin. Her books have been published in forty countries and have sold more than ten million copies.

Fred Vargas

A Climate of Fear

Translated from the French by
Siân Reynolds

PENGUIN BOOKS

PENGUIN BOOKS

An imprint of Penguin Random House LLC
375 Hudson Street
New York, New York 10014
penguin.com

First published in Great Britain by Harvill Secker,
an imprint of Penguin Random House, 2016
Published in Penguin Books 2017

Originally published in French with the title *Temps glaciaires*
in 2015 by Flammarion, Paris

ISBN 9780143109457 (paperback)

Printed in the United States of America
1 3 5 7 9 10 8 6 4 2

Set in Minion

I

ONLY ANOTHER TWENTY METRES, TWENTY LITTLE METRES TO reach the postbox, it was harder than she had expected. That's ridiculous, she told herself, there aren't little metres and big metres. There are just metres, that's all. How curious that at death's door, even from that privileged position, you should go on having such futile thoughts, when anyone might think you would come up with some important pronouncement, one that would be branded with red-hot iron in the annals of human wisdom. A pronouncement that people would repeat now and then in days to come: 'Do you know what Alice Gauthier's last words were?'

Even if she had nothing memorable to declare, she nevertheless had an important message to deliver, one that would certainly be inscribed in the most despicable annals of humanity, which are infinitely larger than those of wisdom. She looked at the letter, held in her shaking hand.

Come on, just sixteen little metres. From the door of her building, Noémie was watching over her, ready to intervene at the slightest stumble. Noémie had done everything she could to stop her patient venturing out on to the street alone. But Alice Gauthier's imperious character had been too strong for her.

'And let you read the address over my shoulder?'

Noémie had taken offence, she didn't do things like that.

'Everyone does things like that, Noémie. I had a friend – an old rogue he was too – who always said: "If you want to keep a secret, well, keep it." I've kept this secret for a long time, but it's going to hinder my getting to heaven. Although I'm not sure if heaven's where I'm going, whether or no. Just get out of my way, Noémie, and let me out.'

Alice, get a move on for God's sake, or Noémie will come running. She leaned on her Zimmer frame, and forced herself forward another nine metres, well, eight anyway. Past the pharmacy, then the launderette, then the bank, and she'd be there, by the little yellow postbox. And just as she was starting to smile at her approaching success, her sight clouded over and she lost her grip, falling down at the feet of a woman in red, who caught her in her arms with a scream. Alice Gauthier's handbag spilled open on the ground and the letter fell from her grasp.

The pharmacist came running out of her shop, and was quickly feeling her everywhere, asking questions, applying first aid. The woman in red was meanwhile putting the scattered objects into the handbag, before placing it back at its owner's side. This bystander's brief role was coming to an end, the emergency services had been called, she had no further part to play, so she straightened up and moved away. She would have liked to go on making herself useful, to be more important at the scene of the accident, or at least to give her name to the paramedics who were arriving in force, but no, the pharmacist had now taken complete charge, with the help of a distraught woman who said she was the nurse-companion: this one was talking loudly, on the verge of tears, protesting that Madame Gauthier absolutely refused to be accompanied, she lived just a stone's throw away, at number 33a, and she, the nurse, had not been the least bit negligent. They were putting the old woman on to a stretcher now. On your way, Marie-France, it's none of your business any more.

But it is, she thought, as she went down the street, yes, she really had done something. By catching the woman as she fell, she'd prevented her striking her head on the pavement. Perhaps she had saved her life, who could deny that?

The first days of April, and the weather was milder now in Paris, but there was still a nip in the air. A nip in the air. If there was a 'nip', where in the air did it lie? In the middle somewhere? Marie-France frowned in irritation at the silly questions that flew at random through her head like gnats. Just when she had saved someone's life too. Or was the nip scattered everywhere in the air? She fastened her red coat more tightly and pushed her hands deep into her pockets. On the right, her keys and her wallet, but on the left her fingers met a thick wad of paper that she had not put there. Her left-hand pocket was the one she used for her travelcard and the forty-eight centimes for bread. She stopped under a tree to think. And there in her hand was the letter belonging to the poor woman who had fallen down in the street. *Turn your thought over seven times in your head before you act*, her father always used to say to her, though he had never in his life taken his own advice. No doubt he barely managed more than four times. The writing on the envelope was very shaky, and the sender's name on the back, Alice Gauthier, was printed in big wobbly letters. Yes, this was certainly her letter. Back there, Marie-France had returned everything to the handbag, and in her haste to pick up the papers, purse, pills and tissues before the wind whisked them away, she had stuffed the letter into her pocket. The envelope had fallen on the other side from the bag, the woman must have been holding it in her left hand. *That's* what she had set off to do all on her own, Marie-France thought: post a letter.

Should she take it back to her? But where? She must have been taken to the emergency department of some hospital or other. Should she give it to that nurse or whatever she was at number 33a? Watch it, little Marie-France, watch it. Turn your thought over seven times. If this

Gauthier woman had taken the big risk of going out to post a letter, it must mean she hadn't meant it to fall into anyone else's hands. Turn your thought over seven times, but not ten, or twenty, her father would say, otherwise it gets worn out and you'll never find the answer. There are people like that, who go on thinking in circles for ever, it's sad, just look at your uncle.

So no, not the nurse. It must be significant that Madame Gauthier set out on an expedition without her help. Marie-France looked around to see if there was a postbox nearby. Over there, the little yellow rectangle across the square. Marie-France smoothed the envelope out against her leg. She had a mission, she had saved the woman and now she'd save the letter. It had been intended for the postbox, hadn't it? So she was doing no harm, on the contrary, in fact.

She slipped the envelope into the slot labelled *Paris suburbs*, after checking several times that it was to an address in the Yvelines *département*, postcode 78, to the south-west of the city. Seven times, Marie-France, not twenty, or this letter will never get sent. Then she slid her fingers inside the box to check that it had fallen down inside. Yes. Last collection 6 p.m., it's Friday today, the recipient will get it first post Monday.

A good day that was, my girl, a very good day.

II

DURING THE MEETING WITH HIS OFFICERS, COMMISSAIRE bourlin from the 15th arrondissement of Paris was chewing the inside of his cheeks, looking undecided, hands clasped over his large paunch. He had been a handsome man once, older colleagues remembered, before he had put on an enormous amount of weight in a few short years. But he still had plenty of presence, as the respectful attitude of his listening staff indicated. Even when he blew his nose noisily, almost ostentatiously, as he just had. It was a spring cold, he had explained. No different from an autumn cold or a winter cold, but it was airier, less commonplace, more light-hearted, somehow.

'We should close the file, sir,' said Feuillère, the most eager of his lieutenants, summing up the general feeling. 'It'll be six days ago this evening that Alice Gauthier died. Suicide, an open-and-shut case, surely.'

'I don't like suicides when there's no note.'

'The man in the rue de la Convention a couple of months ago didn't leave a note either,' said a junior officer who was almost as fat as his chief.

'Yes, but he was drunk out of his skull, lonely and penniless, not the same at all. Here we have a woman of very orderly habits, a retired maths teacher, having lived an extremely conventional life, we've checked her out. And I don't like suicides who have just washed their hair that morning, and who are wearing perfume.'

'That's just it,' a voice said, 'some people like to look their best when they're dead.'

'So one evening,' the commissaire said, 'Alice Gauthier, wearing perfume and a tailored suit, runs a bath, takes off her shoes and gets into the water, fully dressed, before slitting her wrists?'

Bourlin took a cigarette, or rather two, since his thick fingers prevented him taking one at a time. Consequently, there were always lone cigarettes lying alongside his packets. For the same reason, he never used a lighter, because he was too clumsy to roll the wheel, but had a large box of outsize matches bulging from his pocket. He had declared this office in the police station a smoking zone. The nationwide smoking ban was driving him to distraction, at a time when the world was bombarding beings – all beings, not just human beings – with 36 billion tons of CO_2 a year. *36 billion*, he would say. And you can't even light up a cigarette on a station platform in the open air!

'Commissaire, this woman was dying, and she knew it,' Feuillère insisted. 'Her nurse told us: the Friday before she died, she had tried to go out and post a letter, she was absolutely determined, wouldn't hear a word against it, but she didn't manage it. Result: five days later, she slits her wrists in the bath.'

'A letter that may have contained a farewell message. That would explain why there wasn't a note in her home.'

'Or her last wishes.'

'But who was she writing to?' asked the commissaire, taking a deep pull on his cigarette. 'She had no direct heirs, and her savings didn't amount to a huge fortune, anyway. Her lawyer hasn't received any change to her will, and her twenty thousand euros will go to saving polar bears. And in spite of this vital letter going astray, she kills herself instead of writing again?'

'Because the young man called to see her,' replied Feuillère. 'On the Monday and then again on the Tuesday, the neighbour is sure about that. He heard him ring the bell and say he'd come by appointment. At a time when she was alone every day, between seven and eight in the evening. She must have *told* him about her last wishes, so the letter would be beside the point.'

'A young man whose name we don't know, who's now disappeared. At the burial, there were only some elderly cousins. No young man. So? Where did he go? If he was a close enough acquaintance for her to call him in urgently, he must have been a relative or a friend. In which case, he ought to have come to the funeral. But no, he's vanished into thin air. Carbon-dioxide-laden air, let me remind you. And the neighbour heard him say his name from behind the door. What was it again?'

'He couldn't hear clearly. André or Dédé, some name like that, he can't be sure.'

'André is a rather old-fashioned name. So why did he say it was a young man?'

'Because of his voice.'

'Commissaire,' called another lieutenant, 'the examining magistrate wants us to close this one. We're still getting nowhere with the schoolboy who was stabbed, or the woman who was attacked in the Vaugirard car park.'

'I know,' said the chief, grabbing the second cigarette lying by the packet. 'I had a conversation with him last night. If you can call it a conversation. Suicide, suicide, close the file, move on, never mind if you bury some facts, small ones, I grant you, by trampling on them like dandelions.'

Dandelions, he thought, the poor relations of the flower world, no one respects them, you tread on them or feed them to rabbits, whereas no one would tread on a rose. Still less feed it to a rabbit. There was a silence, each of the men in the room torn between the impatience of their new examining magistrate and the negative mood of the commissaire.

'All right, let's close it,' sighed Bourlin, as if physically surrendering. 'On condition we have one more stab at finding out about the sign she drew by the side of the bath. It was very firm and very clear, but incomprehensible. *That* was it, her last message.'

'But we don't know what it means.'

'I'll call Danglard. He might know.'

Nevertheless, Bourlin reflected, pursuing his train of thought, dandelions are tough plants, whereas a rose is always delicate.

'Do you mean Commandant Adrien Danglard?' asked a junior officer. 'From the Serious Crime Squad in the 13th?'

'The same. He knows things that you won't learn in thirty lifetimes.'

'Yes, but behind him,' murmured the officer, 'there's Commissaire Adamsberg.'

'So what?' said Bourlin, standing up almost majestically, fists on the table.

'So nothing, sir.'

III

ADAMSBERG PICKED UP HIS PHONE, PUSHED ASIDE A HEAP OF FILES and put his feet on the table, leaning back in his chair. He had hardly slept at all the night before, since one of his sisters had gone down with pneumonia, out of the blue.

'The woman in 33a?' he asked. 'The one who cut her wrists in the bath? Why the hell are you bothering me with this at nine in the morning, Bourlin? From the internal report, it was a straightforward suicide. You've got suspicions?'

Adamsberg liked Commissaire Bourlin. A man with a large appetite for food, drink and tobacco, perpetually on the boil, living life at full tilt, skirting precipices but solid as a rock himself, with a shock of curly hair like the fleece of a newborn lamb, he was someone to respect, and would still be at his post when he was a hundred years old.

'Our new examining magistrate, Vermillon, he's keen as mustard, and on to me like a tick,' said Bourlin. 'You know what they do, ticks?'

'Yes indeed. If you find a beauty spot with legs, it's a tick.'

'And what do I do with it?'

'You extract it by using a very tiny clawhammer. You're not calling me for that?'

'No, because of the magistrate, who is one enormous tick.'

'So you want us to use a huge clawhammer, the two of us, and extract him too?'

'No, but he wants me to close the file on this woman, and I don't want to.'

'Any reason?'

'This suicide, a woman who had washed her hair that morning and was wearing perfume, didn't leave any note.'

Adamsberg listened, eyes closed, while Bourlin filled him in on the case.

'An incomprehensible sign? Alongside the bath? And what do you want from me?'

'Nothing from you. I want you to send me Danglard's brain to have a look. He might know what it means, he's the only person I can think of. Then at least I'll have a clear conscience.'

'Just his brain? What am I supposed to do with his body?'

'Get the body to come along as best it can.'

'Danglard isn't in yet. As you may know, he keeps different hours depending on the day. Or should I say the evening before?'

'Haul him out of bed, I'll be expecting both of you over at her apartment, 33a. Just one thing, Adamsberg, my trainee, the brigadier, is something of a young brute. Needs a bit of polish.'

Sitting on Danglard's old sofa, Adamsberg drank a strong coffee, while the commandant got dressed. It had seemed the quickest solution simply to drive over to Danglard's, wake him up and take him off directly in his car.

'I haven't even had time to shave,' Danglard grumbled, as he bent his large ungainly body to look in the mirror.

'You haven't always shaved when you come in to the office.'

'That's different. I'm being consulted now as an expert, and experts shave.'

Adamsberg was registering reluctantly the two wine bottles on the coffee table, the glass lying on its side on the still-damp carpet. White wine doesn't stain. Danglard must have dropped off to sleep on his sofa without needing to worry about the keen eyes of his five children, whom he was bringing up as a single parent, like cultured pearls. The second pair of twins had in fact now left to go to university, and the empty-nest feeling didn't help. The youngest one was still there though, the one with blue eyes who was not Danglard's own, and whom his wife had left with him, as a baby, when she walked out down the corridor, without a backward glance, as he had told everyone at least a hundred times. Last year, at the risk of a serious quarrel, Adamsberg had become his torturer, hauling Danglard off to the doctor's, and Danglard had waited for his test results in a zombie-like alcoholic daze. The tests had shown he was in perfect shape. There are some people who manage miraculously to escape everything that life throws at them, this was such a case, and it was not the least of Danglard's talents.

'And we are expected for what, exactly?' asked Danglard, adjusting his cufflinks. 'What's this all about? Some kind of hieroglyph?'

'The last drawing made by someone who committed suicide. A sign nobody can decipher. Commissaire Bourlin is very worked up about it, he wants to understand it before closing the file. The magistrate is on his back like a tick. A very big one. We have just a few hours.'

'Oh, if it's Bourlin,' said Danglard, relaxing, but smoothing down his jacket. 'He thinks the new magistrate's going to burst a blood vessel, does he?'

'Since he's a tick, he's afraid he'll spit poison at him.'

'What you mean, if we're talking about a tick, is that Bourlin is afraid it will inject the contents of its salivary glands into him,' Danglard corrected him, as he tied his tie. 'Nothing like a snake or a flea. Actually a tick isn't an insect, it's an arachnid.'

'Yeah, right. So what do you think about the contents of Vermillon's salivary glands?'

'You don't want to know. But I'm no expert on obscure signs. I'm just a miner's son from Picardy,' the commandant reminded him with pride. 'I only know a few bits and pieces.'

'Well, he's placing his hopes in you, in any case. For his conscience's sake.'

'If it's to act as someone's conscience for once, I certainly wouldn't want to let him down.'

IV

DANGLARD HAD PERCHED ON THE EDGE OF THE BLUE BATHTUB, the same one in which Alice Gauthier had slit her wrists. He was looking at the side of the white washstand, on which she had drawn the sign with an eyebrow pencil. In the tiny bathroom, Adamsberg, Bourlin and the latter's young officer were waiting in silence.

'Talk among yourselves, dammit! I'm not the oracle of Delphi,' said Danglard who was annoyed that he had not been able to identify the sign at once. 'Brigadier, would you be good enough to get me a cup of coffee? I've been fetched straight from bed.'

'From bed or from an early-morning bar?' the young man whispered to Bourlin.

'And my hearing's perfect,' said Danglard, still poised elegantly on the edge of the old bath, without taking his eyes off the drawing. 'I didn't ask for any comment, I just asked you, very politely, for some coffee.'

'One coffee, you heard,' said Bourlin, gripping the arm of the young officer, his large hand easily encircling it.

Danglard took a battered notebook out of his back pocket and copied the drawing. It looked like a capital H but the central bar was slanting, and then entwined with the bar was a concave line.

'Anything to do with her initials?' Danglard asked.

'Her name was Alice Gauthier, maiden name Vermond. But she had two other first names, Clarisse and Henriette, so H could be for Henriette.'

'No,' said Danglard, shaking his heavy jowls, just now shadowed with grey stubble. 'It's not an H. The line across is clearly oblique, it goes up. And it's not a signature. Any signature always ends up changed, it absorbs the writer's personality, it gets deformed, contracted, fixed. Nothing like the straight lines in this letter. This is a faithful, almost childlike reproduction of some sign or emblem, with which the writer isn't familiar. If she wrote it once or five times, it would be a maximum. Because it looks like the work of a pupil trying hard to get it right.'

The brigadier came back with some coffee, provocatively offered in a boiling hot thin plastic cup directly to Danglard's hand.

'Thank you,' the commandant said without reacting. 'If she killed herself, she might be pointing her finger at the people who drove her to it. But why draw a coded sign in that case? Out of fear? But fear on whose behalf? Her relatives? She's invited us to search, but without wanting to give anything away. If someone killed her – and that's your worry, isn't it, Bourlin? – no doubt it indicates whoever attacked her. But then again, why not something more direct?'

'It must be a suicide,' grumbled Bourlin, looking beaten.

'May I?' asked Adamsberg, leaning against the wall and deliberately pulling a crushed cigarette out of his jacket pocket.

This was the magic word, allowing Bourlin to strike a huge match and light his own cigarette. With the tiny bathroom suddenly full of smoke, the brigadier stalked out, to stand in the doorway.

'What was her occupation?' Danglard enquired.

'She taught maths.'

'That's not it either. It's not a mathematical or physics symbol. It's not the zodiac or a hieroglyph. It's not a Freemason's sign or a satanic cult. Nothing like that.'

He muttered to himself for a moment, looking annoyed and concentrating hard.

'Unless,' he went on, 'it's an Old Norse letter, some kind of rune, or a Japanese or even Chinese character. There are various characters like an H with an oblique bar. But they don't have that concave loop underneath. That's the tricky bit. So we're left with the hypothesis that it's a Cyrillic character but badly drawn.'

'Cyrillic? You mean the Russian alphabet?' asked Bourlin.

'Russian but also Bulgarian, Serbian, Macedonian, Ukrainian, plenty of choice.'

With a meaningful glance, Adamsberg cut short the learned disquisition he sensed Danglard was about to launch into on Cyrillic characters. And indeed Danglard regretfully abandoned his story of the disciples of St Cyril who had invented that alphabet.

'There is a Cyrillic character Й not to be confused with И,' he explained, drawing them on his notebook. 'And you can see that it has a little concave sign like a cup over the top. It's pronounced "oi" or "ei" depending on context.'

Danglard intercepted another look from Adamsberg which stopped him taking this further.

'Well,' he went on, 'supposing this woman was having difficulty drawing the sign, given the distance between the bath and the washbasin, which meant she had to stretch her arm out, she might have misplaced the little cup sign, putting it in the middle, not on top. But if I'm not mistaken, this character isn't used at the start of a word in Russian, only at the end. And I've never heard of an abbreviation that uses the end of a word. Still, you might look through her address book to see if any of her contacts might have used the Russian alphabet.'

'I think that would be a waste of time,' said Adamsberg quietly. It was not to avoid upsetting Danglard that Adamsberg had spoken in an undertone. Except on very rare occasions, the commissaire never raised his voice, taking his time to enunciate, and sometimes running the risk of lulling his interlocutors to sleep with his gentle intonation, hypnotic to some, attractive to others. Results of an interrogation might be very different depending on whether he or one of his officers was conducting them, since Adamsberg could either make the suspect drop off, or else provoke a sudden flow of confessions, as if a magnet had attracted a set of obstinate nails. The commissaire didn't attach great importance to it, admitting that he sometimes sent himself to sleep without realising it.

'What do you mean a waste of time?'

'What I say, Danglard. It would be better to try and find out whether the concave line was drawn before or after the oblique line. And the same for the two vertical strokes of the H, were they drawn before or after?'

'What difference would that make?' asked Bourlin.

'And,' Adamsberg went on, 'whether the oblique line was drawn upwards or downwards.'

'Yes, obviously,' Danglard agreed.

'The oblique line looks as if it's crossing something out,' Adamsberg continued. 'As if to negate it. But only if it was drawn upwards, firmly. Then, if the smile was drawn first, it was struck out afterwards.'

'What smile?'

'I mean the convex curve, it looks like a smile.'

'Concave,' Danglard corrected.

'If you like. But that line, on its own, looks like a smile.'

'A smile someone wanted to cross out?' suggested Bourlin.

'Something like that. As for the two uprights, they could be framing the smile, like a sort of simplified face.'

'Well, very simplified,' said Bourlin. 'Far-fetched. I'd say.'

'Yes, too far-fetched,' Adamsberg agreed. 'But check all the same. What order do they use to write the Cyrillic character, Danglard?'

'You'd write the two uprights then the slanting line, then add the little curve on top. Like we put accents on last.'

'So if it seems the curved line was drawn first, then it couldn't be a failed attempt to write the Cyrillic letter,' remarked Bourlin, 'and we don't need to waste time looking for some Russian in her address book.'

'Or a Macedonian. Or a Serb,' Danglard added.

Put out by his failure to decipher the mystery sign, Danglard dragged his feet as he followed his colleagues into the street, while Bourlin issued orders on his phone. In fact, Danglard always dragged his feet, which meant he wore out his soles very quickly. And since the commandant was deeply attached to English-style elegance, to make up for having nothing beautiful about his looks, renewing his London-made shoes was a problem. Anyone crossing the Channel was implored to bring him back a pair.

The brigadier had been impressed by the glimpses of Danglard's knowledge, and was now walking docilely alongside him. He had started to get 'a bit of polish' as Bourlin had said. The four men parted on the Place de la Convention.

'I'll call you when I get the forensic results,' said Bourlin, 'it shouldn't be long. Thanks for your help, but I think I'm going to have to close the file tonight.'

'Since none of us understands it,' said Adamsberg with a wave of his hand, 'we can say anything we like. It reminds *me* of a guillotine.'

Bourlin watched for a moment as the two colleagues walked away.

'Don't worry,' he said to his junior. 'That's just Adamsberg.'

As if that statement was enough to clarify everything.

'Still,' said the brigadier, 'what does he have in his brain, that Commandant Danglard, to know so much stuff?'

'White wine.'

Less than two hours later, Bourlin telephoned Adamsberg. The two vertical lines had been drawn first: left, then right.

'Like when you write an H then,' he went on. 'But next, she drew the curved line.'

'So not an H.'

'And not the Cyrillic alphabet either. Pity, I liked that theory. Then she added the crossbar, which was drawn upwards from the bottom.'

'So she struck out the smile.'

'Precisely. We've got nothing here, Adamsberg. Not an initial, not a Russian. Just some unknown symbol, addressed to some person or persons unknown.'

'Whom she's accusing of driving her to suicide, or alternatively that she wants to warn of some danger.'

'Or,' suggested Bourlin, 'she simply killed herself because she was terminally ill. But first, she wanted to leave a record of someone or something, some event in her life. A final confession perhaps, before leaving this world.'

'And what kind of confession does one make at the very last moment?'

'A secret you couldn't bring yourself to tell before.'

'For instance?'

'A secret child?'

'Or a sin, Bourlin. Or a murder. What sin could this dear old Alice Gauthier have committed?'

'I wouldn't call her "dear old" Alice. She was authoritarian, a very firm character, tyrannical even. Not a very nice woman.'

'So did she have some problems with her former pupils? Or with the education authorities?'

'No, she was very well regarded professionally, she was never censured for anything. Forty years in the same school, in a difficult area. But according to her fellow teachers, the kids, even the toughest of them, dared not open their mouths during her lessons, she wouldn't put up with any nonsense. So you can imagine that head teachers clung on to her like a sacred treasure. She just had to appear in the doorway of a classroom for the din to stop immediately. Her punishments were dreaded.'

'Did she go in for *corporal* punishment?'

'No, no, nothing like that.'

'What then? Writing out three hundred lines?'

'Not even,' said Bourlin. 'The punishment was, she would withdraw her affection. Because she loved her pupils. That was the big threat. Losing her affection. Lots of them went to see her after school, on one pretext or another. Just as an example of how tough this little woman was, she got hold of one young drug pusher in the school and, I don't know how, he gave her the names of a whole gang within the hour. So that's the kind of woman she was.'

'Pretty sharp then?'

'Still thinking about your guillotine?'

'No, I was thinking about the lost letter. To this unknown young man. Perhaps one of her former pupils?'

'So the sign might refer to the pupil? A gang's emblem? A secret symbol? Don't get me started again, Adamsberg, I've got to close this one down tonight!'

'Look, find an excuse to hang on to the case. Just one more day. Say you're still working on the Cyrillic possibility. But whatever you do, don't tell them we're involved.'

'Why should I hang on? You've got something in mind?'

'No, nothing. I'd just like to have a think.'

Bourlin sighed in discouragement. He had known Adamsberg long enough to realise that 'thinking' didn't mean much where he was concerned. Adamsberg didn't think. He didn't sit down at a table with paper and pencil, he didn't stare in concentration out of the window, he didn't draw up a table of facts with arrows and figures, he didn't even put his chin in his hand. He pottered about, walking silently, weaving in and out of offices, passing remarks, pacing slowly round a crime scene. But no one had ever seen him thinking. He seemed more like a fish, swimming along aimlessly. No, that's not right, a fish does have an aim. Adamsberg was more like a sponge, drifting with the currents. But what currents? And some people said that when his vague brown eyes looked even more distracted, it was as if they contained seaweed. He belonged to the sea more than to dry land.

V

MARIE-FRANCE GAVE A START WHEN SHE READ THE DEATH
announcement. She had missed a few days, so she had dozens of
notices to catch up on. Not that this daily ritual gave her any morbid
satisfaction. No, the reason – and this was an awful thing to say, she
thought, not for the first time – was that she was watching out for the
death of a first cousin who had once been fond of her. And on that side
of the family, which had plenty of money, they published a notice in
the paper if anyone died. It was in this way that she had learned of the
deaths of two other cousins and of the husband of the cousin in
question. Who was therefore alone in this world, and rich. Her
husband had made his money from balloons, of all things. Marie-
France was forever wondering whether there was any chance that the
manna of this cousin's wealth might perhaps descend on her. She'd
tried calculating the size of the manna. How much would it be? Fifty
thousand? A million? More? After tax, what would there be left? Would
her cousin have thought of leaving it all to her? What if she left it all to
the Society for the Protection of the Orang-utan? She'd been pretty
keen on orang-utans, Marie-France could quite understand that, and
was ready to share it with the poor creatures. Don't get carried away,
my girl, just read the announcements. The cousin was getting on for
ninety-two, it couldn't be long, could it? Although in that family, they

bred centenarians, the way other families bred large numbers of children. In her family, they produced old people. And they didn't do a great deal with their lives, which, she thought, probably preserved them. This cousin, though, had got about a bit, to Java, Borneo and all those scary islands – because of the orang-utans – and that might wear you out sooner. She went on reading chronologically.

Régis Rémond and Martin Druot, cousins of the deceased, along with her friends and colleagues, regretfully announce the death of Mme Alice Clarisse Henriette Gauthier, née Vermond, in her sixty-sixth year, after a long illness. The funeral will leave her home, 33a rue de la . . .

33a! She heard again the nurse calling out: 'It's Madame Gauthier from 33a . . .' Poor woman, she'd saved her life – by preventing her head striking the pavement, she was convinced of that now – but obviously it hadn't been for long.

Unless, that letter . . .? The letter she had decided to post? What if it had been the wrong thing to do? What if the precious letter had triggered some disaster? Was that why the nurse had been so opposed to it? Well, the letter would have been posted anyway, Marie-France consoled herself, pouring out a second cup of coffee. That was fate.

No, it wouldn't! The letter had fallen to the ground when the woman collapsed. Think, girl, think it over seven times. And if Madame Gauthier, in the end, had committed a . . . what did he used to call it, my old boss? He was always talking about it – an *acte manqué*, a Freudian slip. Something you don't mean to do, but you do it all the same, for reasons hidden beneath other reasons. Had the old woman's fear of what might come from posting the letter made her suddenly feel dizzy? And had she then lost the letter as an *acte manqué*, abandoning the idea for reasons hidden under other reasons?

In that case, it was *she*, Marie-France, who had played the role of fate. She had taken the decision to carry out the old woman's intention. And yet she had thought it over several times. Not too little, not too much, before she had crossed the road to the postbox.

Forget it, you'll never know anything about it. And there's no reason at all to think the letter might have had lethal consequences. That's just your imagination running wild, my girl.

But by lunchtime, Marie-France had still not forgotten it, as was proved by her getting no further in her reading of death announcements while still being none the wiser whether the cousin who loved orang-utans had died yet.

She walked towards the toy shop where she worked part-time, her mind troubled, her stomach aching. And that, my girl, means you are chewing it over and you know quite well what Papa used to say about that.

It wasn't that she had never noticed the police station on her way – after all she passed it six days a week – but this time it shone out to her like a lighthouse in the dark. *A lighthouse in the dark* – that was her father's expression again. But the problem with a lighthouse, he would say, is that it switches on and off. So your plan may come and go all the time, and it goes out anyway in daylight. Well, it was daylight now, and the police station nevertheless seemed like a lighthouse in the dark. Proof that you could modify the biblical pronouncements of your father, no offence intended.

She went in timidly, registered the gloomy-looking lad in reception and, in the background behind him, a very large, very heavily built and rather scary woman, talking to a small fair-haired character who didn't seem of any account, alongside a balding man who looked like an ancient bird huddled on its nest waiting for a last clutch of eggs that would never arrive, while over there was someone reading – she had good eyesight – a magazine about fish, plus a huge white cat sleeping on the photocopy machine, and a tough guy who looked ready to tear people limb from limb. And she almost walked straight out again. No, she told herself firmly, it's just that the lighthouse goes on and off and just now it's off. A tall man with a paunch, elegantly dressed, but no oil painting, came over dragging his feet, and gave her a sharp look with his blue eyes.

'Were you wishing to report anything in particular, madame?' he asked with perfect diction. 'Here, we don't receive complaints about thefts or muggings. This is the Serious Crime Squad. Homicide and murder only.'

'Is there a difference?' she asked anxiously.

'A very great one,' the man replied, leaning towards her in an attitude of old-world courtesy. 'Murder is premeditated killing. Homicide may be unintentional.'

'Well, yes, in that case, I'm coming about a maybe-homicide, a not deliberate one.'

'Do you wish to bring a charge, madame?'

'No, no, but it might have been me that did it, the homicide, without meaning to.'

'In some kind of disturbance?'

'Oh no, monsieur le commissaire.'

'Commandant, not commissaire, madame. Commandant Adrien Danglard at your service.'

It was a long time ago, if ever, that anyone had spoken to her with so much courtesy and deference. This man was far from good-looking – he seemed rather ill-assembled to her gaze – but my word, his beautiful way with language won you over. The lighthouse switched on again.

'Commandant,' she said, with a little more assurance, 'I'm afraid I may have sent a letter that caused a death.'

'A letter containing a threat? Anger? Vengeance?'

'Ah no, commandant' – she liked repeating this word which seemed to give her more importance – 'I don't know anything about it.'

'Anything about what?'

'Anything about what was in the letter.'

'But you said you sent it.'

'Yes, I sent it. But I thought about it first. Not too little and not too much.'

'But why did you post it – that's what you did, was it? – if you hadn't written it yourself?'

The lighthouse had gone off.

'Well, because I picked it up off the ground, and then after that the lady died.'

'So you posted a letter for a friend, is that it?'

'No, no, I didn't know her at all. But I'd just saved her life. That must count for something, though, mustn't it?'

'It counts for an *immense* amount,' Danglard agreed.

Hadn't Bourlin said that Alice Gauthier had set off to post a letter that had disappeared?

He drew himself to his full height, as far as possible. Danglard was actually very tall, much taller than little Commissaire Adamsberg, but people tended not to notice this.

'Immense,' he repeated, being conscious of the distress of the woman in the red coat.

Lighthouse on again.

'But then, later, she died,' she went on. 'I read it in the deaths column this morning. I look at the deaths from time to time,' she explained, a little too quickly, 'to check I haven't missed the funeral of someone close to me, an old friend, you see.'

'That is a concern which does you great credit, madame.'

Marie-France cheered up immediately. She felt a kind of affection for this man who understood her so well and who washed away all her sins so promptly.

'So I discovered that Alice Gauthier, from 33a, had died. It was *her* letter that I posted. And oh dear, monsieur le commandant, what if I set something off? Like I said, I thought it over seven times, not more or less.'

Danglard had received a jolt on hearing the name of Alice Gauthier, and at his age, receiving a jolt and having his fast-fading curiosity about the minutiae of life reignited meant that he felt gratitude to the woman in the red coat.

'Which day did you post this letter?'

'Friday of last week, when she collapsed in the street.'

Danglard moved smartly.

'Would you be so good as to accompany me to see Commissaire Adamsberg?' he said, ushering her by the shoulders, as if he were afraid that the unknown elements she possessed might spill out on the way, like the contents of a vase.

Obediently, Marie-France allowed herself to be guided. She was going to the big chief's office. And the big chief's name – Adamsberg – was not unknown to her.

She was disappointed though, when the gentlemanly commandant pushed open the door of the chief's office. Inside, a drowsy-looking character wearing a shabby black cotton jacket over a black T-shirt was nodding off, his feet up on the desk: he had nothing in common with the social graces of the man who had greeted her.

The lamp in the lighthouse was flickering out.

'Commissaire, madame says she posted Alice Gauthier's last letter. I thought it was important for you to hear what she has to say.'

Although she had thought him practically asleep, the commissaire opened his eyes at once and sat up properly. Marie-France stepped forward awkwardly, irked at having to leave her friendly commandant for this odd-looking man.

'Are you the chief?' she asked, expressing disappointment.

'Yes, I'm the commissaire,' Adamsberg smiled, being both accustomed and indifferent to the disconcerted faces he often met. With a wave of his hand, he invited her to sit down opposite him.

Never believe in the authority of the authorities, her father used to say, *they're the worst*. And in fact he would add: 'bastards, the lot of 'em'. Marie-France clammed up. Aware of her retreat into her shell, Adamsberg motioned to Danglard to sit down beside her. And indeed it was only after prompting by the commandant that she decided to open her mouth.

'I'd been to the dentist. I don't live in the 15th arrondissement. It just happened, she was coming along with her walking frame, she took ill and she fell over. I caught her in my arms, so her head didn't hit the pavement.'

'Very good reflexes,' said Adamsberg.

Not even a 'madame', which the commandant would have added. No 'immensely' either. Just a cop making an ordinary remark and, anyway, she had no great love of the police. While the other man was a real gentleman – though one who'd strayed into the wrong job – this one, the boss, was a run-of-the-mill cop, and in a couple of minutes he'd be accusing her of something! *Go to the police and in no time you're guilty of something.*

Lighthouse out.

Adamsberg glanced at Danglard again. No question of asking her for her ID papers, as they normally would, or they'd lose her completely.

'Madame happened to be there by a miracle,' the commandant explained with some insistence. 'She saved Madame Gauthier from a blow that could have been fatal.'

'Destiny must have set you on her path,' Adamsberg took over. No 'madame', but still, it was a compliment. Marie-France turned the anti-cop half of her face towards him.

'Would you like some coffee?'

No answer. Danglard stood up, and from behind Marie-France, he mouthed at Adamsberg *'ma-da-me'*, in three syllables. The commissaire took the hint.

'Madame,' he said, more pressingly, 'may we offer you a cup of coffee?'

After a slight nod from the woman in the red coat, Danglard headed upstairs to the coffee machine. Adamsberg had caught on, it seemed. This woman had to be reassured, treated politely, and her wavering narcissism had to be cultivated. The commissaire would have to alter his manner of speaking, which was too casual and natural. But of course he'd been born like that, natural, straight out of a tree or a rock or a stream. He was from the mountains of the Pyrenees.

Once the coffee had been served – in cups, not plastic beakers – the commandant took charge of the conversation.

'So, you caught her as she fell,' he began.

'Yes, and her nurse came running to help at once. She was shouting, she said that Madame Gauthier had absolutely refused to let her come along with her. Then the lady from the pharmacy took over, and I just picked up her things that had fallen out of the handbag. Because who else would have done it? The emergency people, they don't think of that. But in your handbag, well, everything's in here, your whole life.'

'Very true,' Adamsberg said encouragingly. 'Men stuff everything in their pockets. So you picked up a letter?'

'She must have had it in her left hand, because it was the other side from the handbag.'

'You are most observant, madame,' said Adamsberg, smiling at her.

The smile suited him. It was gracious. And now she felt that she was of interest to the big chief.

'Yes, but I didn't realise at once. It was only afterwards, when I was on my way to the metro, that I felt the letter in my coat pocket. Now don't go thinking I pinched the letter, will you?'

'No, of course not, one does this kind of thing inadvertently,' said Danglard.

'That's right, inadvertently. I saw that it was marked with the sender's name, Alice Gauthier, so I realised it was the old lady's letter. After that I thought it over, seven times, not any more.'

'Seven times,' Adamsberg murmured.

How could you count the number of times you thought something over?

'Not five, and not twenty. My father always said you should think something over seven times in your head, before you act, not less, because you might do something silly, but especially not more, or you'd go round and round in circles. And end up corkscrewed into the ground. Then you're stuck. So I thought: this lady went out on her own to post this letter. So it must have been important, don't you think?'

'Yes indeed.'

'That's what I thought,' said Marie-France more confidently. 'And I checked it was her letter, she'd written her name in big letters on the back. First, I thought I'd better return it to her, but she'd been taken off to hospital, and which one would it be? I didn't know, the paramedics never even spoke to me, or asked my name, or anything. Then I thought I should take it back to number 33a, because the nurse person had said that's where she lived. That was the fifth time of thinking. But then I said to myself, no, absolutely not, because the lady had stopped the nurse coming with her. Perhaps she didn't trust her or something. So at the seventh turn, I decided to finish what the poor lady hadn't been able to do. And I posted it.'

'And did you by any chance note the address, madame?' asked Adamsberg with a note of anxiety.

Because it was quite possible that this woman, with all her elaborate precautions, tormented by her conscience, could have refrained from reading the name of the addressee, in order to respect the old woman's privacy.

'Well, of course I did, because I looked at it for so long, while I was thinking. And you have to know the address, because the postbox has all these different slots: Paris, Suburbs, Provinces, Abroad. You mustn't get it wrong, or the letter will go astray. It was Yvelines, Paris suburbs, *département* 78, then I posted it, and now, since I found out that the poor lady died in the end anyway, I'm worried I might have made a terrible mistake. Perhaps the letter started something. Something that might have killed her. Would that be unintentional homicide? Do you know how she died?'

'We'll get to that, madame,' said Danglard, 'but your help is very valuable to us. Anyone else might have forgotten about the letter and never come forward to see us. Apart from the address being in Yvelines, did you notice to whom it was addressed, and do you by some miracle remember it?'

'No need for a miracle, I have a good memory. Monsieur Amédée Masfauré, Le Haras de la Madeleine, route de la Bigarde, 78 491, Sombrevert. So I was right to put it in the "Suburbs" box, wasn't I?'

Adamsberg stood up, stretching his arms out.

'Absolutely magnificent!' he said, coming over to her and grasping her shoulder rather familiarly.

She put this inappropriate gesture down to his feeling of satisfaction and felt happy too. *Very* good day, my girl.

'But what I'd like to know,' she said, looking serious again, 'is whether what I did might have somehow caused that poor lady's death, by some consequence or other. Do you understand, that worries me? And when I see that the police are involved, it means she didn't die in her bed, isn't that so?'

'No, you can't have been the cause of anything, madame, you have my word on it. The proof of that is that the letter will have arrived on the Monday, or Tuesday at latest. And Mme Gauthier died on the Tuesday evening. And she didn't receive any letters or visits or phone calls in that time.'

As Marie-France breathed deeply in relief, Adamsberg shot a look at Danglard, indicating: *we don't tell her the truth.* We don't mention the visitor on Monday and Tuesday. We tell her a story, we don't want to ruin her life.

'But she died peacefully didn't she?'

'Well, not exactly, madame,' Adamsberg said hesitantly. 'She committed suicide.'

Marie-France gave a little cry, and Adamsberg patted her shoulder, consolingly this time.

'We think that this letter, which had disappeared, contained her last words, which she wished to send to a close friend. You have nothing to blame yourself for, on the contrary.'

Adamsberg did not wait for Marie-France to have left the building – duly escorted by Danglard – before he was on the phone to the commissaire in the 15th.

'Bourlin? I've got a name for your man. The one Alice Gauthier's letter was addressed to. Amédée something or other in Yvelines *département*, don't worry, I've got the full address.'

Adamsberg certainly didn't have a good memory for words, in that respect, Marie-France was way ahead of him

'How did you get it?' asked Bourlin eagerly.

'Didn't do a thing. The nameless woman who helped Alice Gauthier when she collapsed had picked up the letter, and she had it in her pocket without realising it. And luckily, after long and due thought – seven times, I'll spare you the details – she posted it. And the best of it is, she had memorised the full address it was going to. She recited it to me, just like you might be able to recite a La Fontaine fable you learn at school, "The Fox and the Crow", say.'

'And why would I recite "The Fox and the Crow"?'

'Don't you know it?'

'No, apart from some line about being "the phoenix of these parts". Couldn't make head or tail of that bit. So you see, it's the stuff we don't understand we remember best.'

'OK, enough about the crow, Bourlin.'

'Well, you started it.'

'Sorry.'

'So let's have the address.'

'Here we are: Amédée Masfauré, I don't know exactly how that's pronounced, M A S F A U R É.'

'Amédée, eh? Like the Dédé the neighbour heard. So he came running as soon as he got the letter. Carry on.'

'Le Haras de la Madeleine – that must mean it's a stud farm – route de la Bigarde, 78 491, Sombrevert. That do you?'

'Yes, it does, except I'm supposed to close the case tonight. The magistrate was cross about the Cyrillic hypothesis, I only managed to get a day's extension. So I'm going to jump in my car and go right away to see this Amédée.'

'Mind if I come along too, incognito, with Danglard?'

'Because of the sign?'

'Yes.'

'OK,' said Bourlin after a brief pause. 'I know what it feels like to have a puzzle going round in your head. But tell me, why did this woman come to see *you*, instead of coming over to me?'

'Animal magnetism, Bourlin.'

'Really?'

'No, what really happened was that she goes past this station every day. And today she walked in.'

'And why didn't you send her straight over to me?'

'Because she was entirely captivated by Danglard's charm.'

VI

COMMISSAIRE BOURLIN HAD DRIVEN FAST. HE HAD BEEN WAITING for his colleagues for fifteen minutes, stamping about outside the high wooden gates that barred the entrance to the stud farm, the Haras de la Madeleine. Unlike Adamsberg, who was oblivious to the symptoms of impatience, Bourlin was an impetuous man, always rushing ahead of things.

'What the fuck were you up to, Adamsberg?'

'We had to stop twice,' Danglard explained. 'Once for the commissaire to view a rainbow that was almost complete, and once for me to look at an amazing Templar granary.'

But Bourlin had stopped listening, and was pulling the bell at the gate.

'*Carpe horam, carpe diem,*' Danglard murmured, standing two paces back. 'Seize the hour, seize the day, Horace's advice.'

'Big place,' commented Adamsberg, looking at the estate through the hedge which, in this month of April, had few leaves. 'The stud farm must be down on the right, I suppose, those wooden buildings. Plenty of money. A pretentious house with a gravel drive. What do you think about it, Danglard?'

'It will have replaced an old chateau. The two lateral pavilions or lodges either side of the drive are seventeenth century; they must be dependencies that were once attached to a more impressive building. Probably knocked down during the Revolution. Except for that tower, over there in the woods, that must have survived. See its top? A watch-tower, much older. If we went over to take a look, we might find its foundations date back to the thirteenth century.'

'But we're not going over to take a look, Danglard.'

A woman opened half the heavy gate, after a lot of clanking of chains. Over fifty, small and thin, but as Adamsberg noted, her face was rosy and she had plump cheeks rather out of keeping with the rest of her body. Round cheeks but a skinny frame.

'Monsieur Amédée Masfauré?' Bourlin asked.

'Down at the stables, you'll have to come back after six. And if it's about the termite inspection, it's been done.'

'Police, madame,' said Bourlin, taking out his ID card.

'Police? But we've already told you everything! Haven't we had enough trouble? You're not going to start all that palaver up again, are you?'

Bourlin exchanged a look of incomprehension with Adamsberg. What had the police been doing here? Before him?

'When were the police here, madame?'

'Nearly a week ago now! Don't you people talk to each other? On Thursday morning, right after it happened, the gendarmes were here in a quarter of an hour. And again the next day. They questioned everyone, we all had to take our turn. Isn't that enough?'

'After what happened, madame? What do you mean?'

'No, obviously you don't check with each other,' said the little woman, shaking her head in a manner more irritated than worried. 'Anyway, they said they'd finished, and they gave us back the body. They kept it for days. Maybe they did a post-mortem and found nothing.'

'Whose body, madame?'

'Why, the boss's, of course,' she cried, detaching each syllable. 'He killed himself, poor man.'

Adamsberg had taken himself outside the group and was walking in circles, hands behind his back, kicking pieces of gravel in front of him. Watch out, he remembered, go round in circles and you'll corkscrew yourself into the ground. Another suicide, dear God, the very day after Alice Gauthier's. Adamsberg listened to the difficult conversation now taking place between the thin little woman and the bulky commissaire. Henri Masfauré was Amédée's father. He had killed himself on Wednesday night, with his shotgun, but his son had only found him next morning. Bourlin wouldn't let go: offering his sympathies, he was very sorry, but he was here about something completely different, nothing so serious, he assured her. What was that? A letter from a Madame Gauthier to Monsieur Amédée. This lady was now dead, and Amédée must have received her last wishes.

'We don't know any Madame Gauthier.'

Adamsberg pulled Bourlin a few paces away.

'I'd like to take a look at the room where the father shot himself.'

'It's the son, Amédée, I want to see, Adamsberg. Not some empty room.'

'We need to see them both, Bourlin! And contact the gendarmes to see what they think about the suicide. What gendarmerie would that be, Danglard?'

'Here, between Sombrevert and Malvoisine, I think it must be Rambouillet. Captain Choiseul – like the statesman of the same name under Louis XV – is a competent chap.'

'Just do it, Bourlin,' Adamsberg insisted.

His tone had changed, more imperious, more urgent, and Bourlin acquiesced, though pulling a face.

After ten minutes of confused conversation with Adamsberg, the little woman finally opened the gates wider and went ahead of them along the drive, and up to her employer's study, on the first floor. Her confident round cheeks had partly recovered the ascendancy over her frail body. That said, she couldn't see the slightest connection between the boss's study and the letter from some Madame Gauthier, and it seemed to her that this cop, Adamsberg, couldn't either. He was just getting her mixed up in it, that was all. But the policeman, with his voice or his smile, or something, reminded her of her old teacher in primary school, long ago. That teacher, he could have persuaded you to learn all your times tables in one evening.

Adamsberg now knew the woman's name – Céleste Grignon – and that she had joined the household twenty-one years earlier, when the 'little one' was five years old. The 'little one' was Amédée Masfauré, who was sensitive and fragile, didn't have good health, and it was important not to touch a hair of his head.

'Here we are,' she announced, opening the door to the study and crossing herself. 'Amédée found him here in the morning, sitting on his chair, at his desk. He had the shotgun wedged between his feet.'

Danglard went round the room, examining the book-lined walls and the magazines piled on the floor.

'Was he a professor?' he asked.

'Better than that, monsieur, he was a man of science, and better than that, he was a genius. He was a genius at chemistry.'

'And what did he do, as a genius at chemistry?'

'He was researching how to clean the air. Like putting a vacuum cleaner in the sky and collecting all the pollution in a bag. A huge bag, of course.'

'Cleaning the air?' said Bourlin abruptly. 'You mean getting rid of CO_2, carbon dioxide?'

'Stuff like that, yes. Getting rid of the black bits, the smoke, all that rubbish they make you breathe in. He put all his money into it. A genius and a benefactor to humanity. Even the minister asked to see him.'

'You'll need to fill me in about that, it's fascinating,' said Bourlin with a tremor in his voice, and Céleste changed her mind about this man.

'You'd be better off talking to Amédée about it. Or Victor, the secretary. But please lower your voices, the body is still in the house, you understand. In his bedroom.'

Adamsberg was walking round the dead man's chair and his desk, a heavy piece of furniture, with an old-fashioned green leather panel on top, worn out where elbows had rested, and covered with scratch marks. Céleste Grignon and Bourlin had their backs turned to him, discussing carbon dioxide. He tore a page from his notebook, and did a quick rubbing with a pencil over the leather surface, while Danglard continued to explore the walls, examining the books and pictures. A single canvas struck a strange note in this scholarly retreat. It was a crude daub, the only word for it, of the valley of the Chevreuse, in three shades of green, spotted with little red dots. Céleste Grignon went over to him.

'Not very good, is it?' she whispered.

'No,' he agreed.

'Not at all good,' she went on, 'and you wonder why Monsieur Henri would have a thing like that in his study. There's not even any air in the landscape, and he loved the air. It's blocked, so to speak.'

'Yes, you're right. Perhaps it's a souvenir.'

'Not at all. I know, because I painted it! Don't be embarrassed,' she added immediately, 'you have an eye for what's good and bad. No need to be ashamed of that.'

'Perhaps if you practised,' said Danglard tentatively, for he was indeed embarrassed, 'perhaps if you worked at it.'

'I do work at it. I've painted hundreds like that, all the same, it amused Monsieur Henri.'

'And the little red dots?'

'If you look closely, you get to see that they're ladybirds. They're what I'm best at.'

'Is it a message of some kind?'

'No idea,' said Céleste Grignon, with a shrug, moving away as if completely uninterested in her work.

Having melted somewhat – since these cops were actually more polite than the gendarmes, who had treated them brusquely, as if they were machines – Céleste took them to the large drawing room on the ground floor and fetched them a tray of drinks. It would take her about twenty minutes to go and fetch Amédée from the stables. Before leaving, she repeated the admonition to keep their voices low.

'And the gendarmes?' Adamsberg said to Bourlin, as soon as she had left. 'What did they tell you?'

'That Henri Masfauré had killed himself, and that the evidence was indisputable. I got Choiseul himself. Everything was carefully examined. The man was sitting down, he'd wedged his shotgun between his feet, and shot himself in the mouth. His hands and his shirt were entirely covered in powder.'

'Which finger did he use?'

'He pressed the trigger with both hands, right thumb on top of left thumb.'

'When you say "entirely" covered, you mean his thumb as well? Was there powder on the top of the right thumb?'

'That's *exactly* what Choiseul meant. This isn't a fake suicide. It isn't a case of a murderer putting the victim's hand on the gun and then pressing his finger. And there was a motive. A terrible row between the father and son, that night.'

'Who says so?'

'Céleste Grignon. She doesn't live up in the house, but she came back for her cardigan. She didn't hear what they were saying, but they were shouting. According to the gendarmes, Amédée wanted his independence but his father kept him trapped here, insisting that he should be ready to take over as his successor at the stud farm. And they parted on furious terms, both of them were upset, and the father went out for a ride on horseback in the night to calm his nerves.'

'And the son.'

'He went to bed, but couldn't sleep. He lives in one of the pavilions by the gate.'

'Can anyone confirm that?'

'No, but Amédée didn't have any trace of gunpowder on his hands. Victor, the boss's secretary – he lives in the other pavilion opposite Amédée's – saw him come back at night, and his light went on, and stayed on. It wasn't like Amédée to sit up late, and Victor hesitated to go and see him. The two young men get on well. So, long story short, suicide. Nothing to do with our investigation either. What *I* want to see is this letter from Alice Gauthier.'

Adamsberg, who found it hard to sit still for long, walked from the window to the wall and back, not in a circle.

'And Choiseul had some analyses done?'

'All the basic stuff. Alcohol level, 1.57. A lot, yes, but they didn't find a glass or bottle. He must have drunk something to steel himself, but apparently cleared it away. Tests for the common drugs – negative. And for all the usual kinds of poison.'

'What about that drug GHB?' Adamsberg asked. 'And what's the other stuff, Danglard?'

'Rohypnol.'

'That's the one. Very useful if you want to get someone to hold a shotgun between his legs without protesting. A few drops in his glass, which would explain why it's disappeared. But it's too late in any case, because there are no traces after twenty-four hours.'

'You could try testing a hair,' said Danglard. 'It can stay up to seven days in hair.'

'We don't even need to do that to be certain,' said Adamsberg with a shake of his head.

'Jesus,' said Bourlin, '"Confirmed suicide". What are you thinking of? Choiseul isn't a beginner.'

'Choiseul didn't know about the sign at Alice Gauthier's place.'

'Adamsberg, we came here about the letter.'

'Even before reading the letter, you can call your big tick and tell him you're *not* closing this file.'

Bourlin was not one to ignore such a laconic piece of advice from Adamsberg.

'Explain what you mean,' he said. 'They'll be back here in a few minutes.'

'No fault attaches to Choiseul. You had to know what to look for to find it. This,' he said, holding out a piece of paper to Bourlin. 'I picked it up by rubbing the leather on the desk, which was covered with scratches. But here,' he went on, tracing certain lines with his finger, 'you can make it out quite well.'

'The sign,' said Danglard.

'Yes. The leather was cut in order to draw it, and these scratches are quite fresh.'

The door opened, and Céleste came in, panting for breath.

'I did *tell* you the little one was delicate. I told him you just wanted to see him about a letter from this Madame Gauthier, and he started shaking all over. Victor spoke to him, but he jumped on Dionysos, and galloped off into the woods. So then Victor got on Hecate and went after him. Because Amédée went without his hard hat, and without a saddle. And on Dionysos as well! He's not strong enough to do that. He's sure to have a fall.'

'And he's sure not to want to talk to us,' said Bourlin.

'Madame Grignon, please take us down to the stables,' said Adamsberg.

'You can call me Céleste.'

'Céleste, will Dionysos come when he's called by name?'

'He obeys a special whistle, but Fabrice is the only one who can do it. Fabrice is the stud manager. But look out, he's a tricky customer.'

*

There was no doubt about the identity of the thickset man who came to meet them as they neared the stables. Short but strong as an ox, bearded, with the sullen face of an old bear confronting an enemy.

'Monsieur?' said Bourlin, holding out his hand.

'Fabrice Pelletier,' said the man, folding his short arms. 'And you are?'

'Commissaire Bourlin, Commissaire Adamsberg and Commandant Danglard.'

'Nice gang of three. Don't go in there, you'll spook the horses.'

'Well, while we're standing here,' Bourlin interrupted, 'you've got two spooked horses already, charging through the woods.'

'I'm not blind.'

'Would you please call Dionysos back?'

'If it suits me. Suits me fine anyway if Amédée's got out of your clutches.'

'That's an order!' Bourlin snapped. 'Or you can be charged with failure to help a person in danger.'

'I don't take orders from anyone, except the boss. And he's dead,' said the man, keeping his arms firmly folded.

'Whistle up Dionysos, or I'll arrest you right away, Monsieur Pelletier!'

And at that moment, Bourlin looked no more ready to parley than the brutish stud master. Two old males, facing each other, claws out and jaws set in a snarl.

'Whistle him up yourself!'

'Let me remind you that Amédée went off without a hard hat, and riding bareback, no saddle.'

'Bareback?' cried Pelletier, unfolding his arms. 'On Dionysos? But he must be crazy, the stupid kid!'

'You see, you *are* blind. Now whistle up that bloody horse!'

*

The stud master strode heavily over to the edge of the trees, and gave several long whistles. They were complicated and tuneful, unexpected, coming from the lips of a man like him.

'Fancy that,' said Adamsberg simply.

A few minutes later, a youngish man with a shock of curly fair hair approached them, head bowed, leading a mare by the reins. Pelletier's sophisticated whistles could still be heard echoing through the woods.

'This is Victor? The secretary?' Danglard asked Céleste.

'Yes. Oh my God, he hasn't found him!'

Apart from his remarkable hair, this man, who looked in his mid-thirties, was far from handsome. He had a melancholy, brooding expression and unprepossessing features: a large once-broken nose, wide mouth, low brow over small close-set eyes, and a short bull-like neck. He shook hands with the three police officers without paying much attention, looking only at Céleste.

'Céleste, I'm so sorry,' he said. 'He wasn't far ahead of me, I could hear the hooves, he'd gone off like a fool into the brushwood towards Sombrevert. Just where the storm brought all those trees down. Hecate knocked her leg on a branch, and now she's lame, so Pelletier'll have it in for me, won't he?'

The distant sound of hooves made them all turn towards the woods. Dionysos appeared, riderless.

'Holy Mother of God!' cried Céleste, her hand to her mouth. 'He's been thrown!'

From further back, Pelletier was making reassuring signs to her. Amédée was following in his wake, arms dangling, looking like a shamefaced teenager caught after running away.

'Oh,' said Céleste, taking a deep breath, 'Pelletier's good, you have to admit. He can bring any animal back. You should see him when they do dressage. The boss used to say' – and here she crossed herself – '"with his character, I'd have got rid of him long ago. But you can't do without someone like him. Got to take the rough with the smooth.

Like for everyone, Céleste, the rough with the smooth." That's what the boss used to say.'

Amédée allowed himself to be hugged by Céleste without reacting. Then he turned to the three cops, with an expressionless face. He, by contrast with Victor, was a rather good-looking young man, with a straight nose, finely shaped lips, long eyelashes, curly dark hair. He was sweating and his cheeks were flushed from his escapade. There was something feminine about him, a romantic delicacy and charm, no sign of a beard.

'I'm really sorry, Pelletier,' said Victor to the stable master, who was feeling Hecate's hock anxiously. 'I wanted to catch him.'

'Well, you didn't manage it, lad, did you?'

'He'd gone off towards Sombrevert. She caught her leg against a low branch.'

Pelletier stood up and pressed his cheek against that of the mare, ruffling her mane.

Fancy that, Adamsberg said, once more, to himself.

'Nothing broken,' said Pelletier. 'Bloody lucky for you, or I'd have let you have it. You shouldn't take Hecate to go chasing off like that, Artemis would be the one, she sees a branch, she jumps it, and you damn well know that. Now Hecate's in pain, I'm going to put a poultice on her.'

As he started to lead the mare away, he turned towards the policemen.

'Oh, and while we're at it,' he shouted back, 'you needn't waste any of *your* precious fucking time looking up my record, I'll tell you all about it. Yeah, I've done four years, for beating up the missus. Broke her arm, knocked her teeth out an' all. Twenty-five years ago. Seems she's got herself dentures and married again. So now you know. It's no secret, everyone here knows, I've never pretended it didn't happen. But I didn't do the boss in, if *that's* what you're wondering. I only go for women, and only my own, got no woman any more anyway.' And Pelletier stalked off with dignity, leading the mare tenderly by the neck.

VII

CÉLESTE HAD MADE SOME MORE COFFEE — 'TO MOP UP THE emotions', she said, as she might have spoken of mopping up a spill – with tea for Amédée. She had augmented the refreshments with some biscuits and a little fruit cake. Danglard helped himself without waiting to be asked, followed by Bourlin. It was past seven in the evening, and he had had hardly any lunch. They were back in the large room on the ground floor, with its tall windows, its layers of carpets, its statues and pictures hung cheek by jowl round the walls.

But without their shoes.

'Nobody's allowed in here with horse manure on their soles,' Céleste had announced. 'I'm sorry, I must ask all these gentlemen to take off their shoes.'

So they were all sitting in their socks, creating a rather incongruous atmosphere which somewhat detracted from the authority of the forces of order. Adamsberg had preferred to take off his socks as well, on the principle that it is always more elegant to be naked than half dressed – but Bourlin reacted by protesting that he had no manure on his soles. To which Céleste had replied, in a tone that brooked no dissent, 'Everyone always has horse manure on their soles.' Adamsberg thought she was quite right, and persuaded Bourlin to comply. This was not the moment to lose their recent ally. She requested them once more to keep their voices down.

'All right, yes, it's true,' said Amédée, after crossing and uncrossing his legs several times, one thigh over the other, his red socks emerging from his torn jeans. 'It's true. I didn't want to talk to you. So I ran away. That's all.'

'To talk to us about your father, or about Alice Gauthier's letter?' asked Bourlin.

'About Alice Gauthier. And the letter. It's between her and me. And I don't think I've any right to show it you without her permission. I don't know why you're so interested in it, it's just her business and mine.'

'But we can't get her permission,' said Bourlin, stretching his big hands out on the tablecloth and hiding his feet under the table. 'Because Madame Gauthier died last Tuesday. And it was the last letter she wrote.'

'But I saw her on Monday!' said Amédée naively.

The instinctive, almost animal reaction that people always have, as if the fact that you saw someone on a Monday means it is impossible for them to have died on the Tuesday. Sudden death is always incomprehensible.

'But the doctor said she had months to live yet,' the young man went on. 'That's why she was settling her affairs, big and small. I'm quoting her own words.'

'She slit her wrists in the bath,' said Bourlin.

'She can't have!' said Amédée firmly. 'She'd just begun this big jig-saw puzzle, a painting by Corot. And she was hoping to finish the sky before she died. The sky's the hard bit. The heavens are "hard both to work out, and to get to", I'm quoting her again.'

'She might have been lying to you.'

'I don't think so.'

'Because you knew her well?'

'Monday was the first time I ever met her.'

'And it was her letter that made you go to see her?'

'What else? And now I suppose you want to see it, the letter?'

Amédée Masfauré spoke quickly with a sharper manner than his mild features would lead you to expect. He took an envelope from his inside pocket and passed it to the large commissaire, with a stiff, awkward gesture. Adamsberg and Danglard leaned over to read it.

Cher Monsieur,

You don't know me, so this letter will surprise you. It's about your mother, Marie-Adélaïde Masfauré, and her tragic death on that terrible rock in Iceland. You'll have been told she died of exposure. That is not true. I was on the same trip, I was there, I know. And for ten years, I haven't found the courage to speak about it, or the peace of mind to get a good night's sleep. Very egotistically, because I am an egoist, now that I am at death's door, I would like to tell you the truth you have the right to know, which has been kept from you, by me and by others. I would ask you to come and see me as soon as you can, one day between 7 and 8 in the evening, when I am alone, without my nurse.

Yours faithfully,
Alice Gauthier

33a rue de la Tremblay
75015 Paris
Staircase B, 5th floor facing the lift

PS Take care no one sees you, come into the building by the back entrance, which is at 26 rue des Buttes. The lock is easy to operate with a small screwdriver unless it is broken again, which it is all the time.

Bourlin folded the letter again with a serious expression.
'We didn't know you had lost your mother.'

'Well, it was ten years ago,' Amédée said. 'I didn't get to go with my parents on the trip to Iceland, I was just seventeen at the time. She had this sudden urge to go and "purify herself in the eternal ice". I'll always remember those words and her enthusiasm. My father let himself be persuaded, in fact he got fired up about it. The eternal ice wasn't really his thing, but it was hard to resist my mother, she was so full of energy. She was funny, optimistic, irresistible really. Other people may tell you she was a bit overpowering, but that was because everything amused her, she wanted to do everything. So they went on this trip. Her, my father and Victor. Victor was very excited by the holiday, he'd never been out of the country before. And they came back alone, just my father and him. She'd frozen to death, was what they told me.'

Amédée sniffed, and not knowing how to go on, massaged his toes, wriggling them about.

'Yes, I remember now,' Danglard intervened. 'Was it that case of a dozen French tourists, marooned for two weeks in the fog? On some island in the north? They survived only by eating seals that had come ashore.'

'You said you didn't know about my mother,' Amédée reacted. 'But it looks like you've already made enquiries.'

'No, no, I just remember seeing about it in the papers, that's all.'

'The commandant remembers everything,' Adamsberg explained.

'That's like Victor then,' said Amédée, changing knees and twisting his other foot in his hands. 'He's got a fantastic memory. That's why my father employed him. He doesn't need notes for writing up the minutes of a meeting. And yet he knows nothing about chemistry.'

'So,' Adamsberg continued gently, 'Madame Gauthier gave you a different version, did she, about your mother's death?'

Amédée abandoned his foot and put his arms on the table. He twisted his fingertips like spiders' legs. He was one of those people who can bend the last joint of their fingers backwards or forwards. It made a kind of little dance, rapid and intriguing, on the tabletop.

'She said in the letter she was an egoist, and that was too true. She didn't give a *damn* about me, and what her fucking revelations might do to me! She just wanted to go to heaven with wings and a precious white robe and that was all. Well, she doesn't deserve a white robe. It's because of her that my father's dead now. And because of me. Because of what that *bloody* woman said.'

Céleste had left the room, and came back to put a box of tissues down alongside her little one. He blew his nose and left the tissue crumpled on the table.

'Thanks, Nana,' he said in a softer voice.

'Do you mind if we record this conversation?' asked Bourlin.

Amédée seemed not to hear, or not to care. So Bourlin switched on his small recorder.

'So what did this bloody woman say?' Adamsberg pursued.

'That my mother had been *murdered* on the island! And that everyone had hushed it up.'

'Murdered? Who by?'

'She refused to give me a name. She explained that she had to keep it secret for my own protection. Protection, my foot! She said this man was terribly dangerous, evil, ruthless. Abominable, a monster. He'd already bumped off another member of the group before that, some sort of Foreign Legion guy, who wouldn't obey him. This man had got out his knife, and he'd killed the legionnaire, just like that. Everyone else was horrified, except the killer. And he dragged the body away and chucked it into the sea, in the middle of the ice floes.'

Amédée blew his nose again. They were getting to the crucial point, his mother's death, and he was reluctant to go on.

'Go on,' whispered Adamsberg.

'So, three days later, or four, I don't know, when they were even weaker, because of the cold and hunger, and the fog still hadn't lifted, this monstrous man said "he wanted to screw someone before he croaked". The others didn't dare say anything, because since he'd killed the legionnaire everyone was scared stiff of him. He'd become their leader, he was terrorising them. But the doctor – because there was a doctor in the group, they called him "Doc" – did stand up to him a bit, and said something like, "You wouldn't have the energy to do that, this is no time for boasting," and that enraged the guy, and he said to my father: "You think I can't screw your missus?" And my father staggered to his feet, and the others all intervened then to stop the fight.'

Amédée picked up another tissue.

'We're really sorry about this,' said Bourlin.

'So that night, my mother cried out, and everyone woke up. This man, he was on top of her and his hands were already . . . well, his hands were groping . . . My mother had enough strength to push him away and he fell backwards into the fire. Actually, that doesn't surprise me,' said Amédée, smiling briefly. 'The man leapt up, and he had to slap his backside to put out the flames, he looked ridiculous, you see, humiliated. And the worst of it was my mother laughed, and called him all kinds of names, she said he was a pig, a bastard and a lot more, she had a big vocabulary, my mother, But she didn't keep her mouth shut, more's the pity. Because this guy went mad, he fell on her, and stabbed her, one blow to the heart. And he dragged her away, and threw her into the ice too. And my father didn't make a move. Not him, not anyone else either.'

The young man picked up two more tissues. There was a little pile growing round his constantly moving fingertips.

'So, I asked, why didn't they kill him?' Amédée went on. 'There were ten of them! Ten against one! What Alice Gauthier said was "leadership, domination". See, this guy was the only one left with strength enough to go and forage around the island for something to eat. In case a puffin or razorbill or something might land there. So they all shut up and waited, they were exhausted, couldn't raise a finger. And one day, stinking of fish and covered with blood, he appeared with a seal. He'd broken its spine with a stick. My father and the doc got up to help him pull in the beast and cut it up. The man told them to put stones on the fire to heat, and they grilled the meat on that.'

This time, Amédée wiped his nose with the back of his hand.

'Alice Gauthier, when she told me this, her gimletty little eyes were shining, like it was the best gastronomic treat of her life, like it was some giant *salmon* or something. They made the seal last a few days. Actually, you have to admit the man could have killed the lot of them and kept the seal for himself, but no, he brought food for the whole group. We have to recognise that, Gauthier said. And when the fog did lift in the end, that's how they had enough strength left to hike across the frozen ice and get back to Grimsey Island. But here's the thing.'

Now that he had finished telling the atrocious story about his mother, Amédée's voice had become more audible and less choked with tears.

'This is the scary thing. The man told the others: "Those two died of cold. Is that clear? We found them frozen to death in the morning. If one of you squeals, I'll kill you, like I did the seal. And if that isn't enough, I'll kill your children, your wife, or if you don't have a wife, your mother or brother or sister, or anyone I can find. You let slip a syllable of this, and it's curtains for you. You might say to yourself: 'I'll tell the police, he'll go to jail.' Big mistake! I've got men devoted to me, they're like slaves. They'll get a message as soon as we get to Grimsey by the. . ."'

At this point, Amédée frowned, searching in his troubled memory.

'Alice Gauthier, she said some strange word. Yes, he'd tell his men via the "tölva". The *tölva* means computer, she said. Because in Iceland, they make up these new words so as not to have Americanisms, and *tölva* in Icelandic means the "witch that counts", so it's a computer, see. My mother would really have liked that, the "witch that counts". She couldn't cope with computers.'

And the young man smiled, for a moment oblivious to the presence of the three cops.

'Sorry,' he said, returning to them. 'So then this man said, more or less: "If I'm in prison that won't change anything. You know what I'm capable of. And you all owe me a huge debt. I saved your pathetic lives, you bunch of losers, not one of you was capable of finding stuff to eat, not one of you put in any effort, not one of you came out in the fog with me. No, you just gave up, and stuck around the fire like a lot of wimps, but you were glad enough to eat my seal." And that was true, Alice Gauthier said. Just as it was also true that they were all terrified of him. Herself included, she insisted on that. And that's why for ten years, nobody has denounced the man who killed my mother and the legionnaire. Not even my father! He kept his mouth shut as well, he was so scared. He wasn't afraid to tackle the planet's air, but he was frightened of this man.'

Amédée was getting distraught: standing up, he banged his double-jointed hand on the table, scattering the paper tissues.

'Yes, that's why I yelled at him. After I left Alice Gauthier's flat, I hung about in Paris for a couple of days, I was shattered, furious, and I never wanted to see my contemptible father again. In the end, I came back here on Wednesday night and I went for him. That's not what I told the gendarmes, I gave them some story about how I wanted my independence and so on. I called him everything under the sun. He was broken, my father, I was glad, really glad, to see him on his knees, wallowing in his shame. The great genius, who'd let his wife's murderer go free. So without even finishing his whisky – '

'Excuse me,' said Bourlin, 'he was drinking whisky?'

'Yes, like every night, two glasses. He went dashing out like a coward to ride one of the horses, and before that, with his hand on the door-knob he said: "He'd told us that he'd kill our *children* with us. So yes, I protected myself, but I was protecting you too. Put yourself in my place." And I just shouted, "I'd rather be dead than in your place!" I went back to my lodge, feeling mad. I heard the horse come back, and I was still wishing my father would roast in hell. Then after about three hours, I began to see reason again. Yes, of course, my father had wanted to protect me. So in the morning, I went over there to have a calmer talk with him. I went up to his study, and I found him, dead. He'd killed himself, because of me.'

Amédée pulled his fingers until they cracked, another thing he could do. Céleste was weeping silently in a corner. Adamsberg poured out the rest of the coffee, the cake was finished, half past eight was striking from some village clock somewhere, and it was getting dark.

'That's all,' said Amédée. 'Maybe I'm not giving you the exact words she said, the dialogues and all that, I don't have a memory like Victor's. But that's pretty much what happened. Well, at least my mother pushed him arse first into the fire, and she was the only one there with any spirit. Will you have to tell anyone about what happened in Iceland?'

'No,' said Bourlin.

'Can I go now?'

'Just one thing,' said Adamsberg, pushing a drawing across to him. 'Have you ever seen this sign?'

'No,' said Amédée, in surprise. 'What is it? An H? For Henri?'

'So there we are,' said Bourlin, once Amédée had gone, and rubbing his stomach to calm the hunger that was beginning to torment him. 'After making her confession, Alice Gauthier put her conscience in order and slit her wrists in the bath. Amédée's right, she was only telling him this for her own peace of mind, without worrying about the consequences for the young man. If this "monster" kills everyone who gives him away, Amédée'd better keep his mouth shut from now on.'

'Don't put it in the report that he's been speaking to us.'

'What report?' said Bourlin.

The three men walked slowly down the dark drive. Danglard was walking on the edge of the gravel, so as not to damage his shoes, and Adamsberg on the verge, since he never missed a chance to walk on grass. Proof according to his divisionnaire, who admired Adamsberg's intelligence but didn't like him, that the commissaire had never reached a normal level of civilisation. Since the Paris authorities had allowed plants to grow between the grids round the city's trees, Adamsberg often went out of his way to walk on the grids, tiny patches of wild nature. Just now, as he trod on the plants on the verge, one of them left on his trousers some tiny sticky balls you had to pull off one by one. He lifted his right leg, saw through the dark a dozen or so of these clinging on to the cloth, and plucked one off. They attached themselves quickly, clever little things, and didn't give up easily, although they didn't have legs. The name of this plant, known to every child, he had quite forgotten.

As for Bourlin, any other preoccupation went to the back of his mind when he was driven by hunger. They had to make an end of this quickly.

'Any problem, Adamsberg?' he asked.

'No, none.'

'Dramatic consequences of Alice Gauthier's confession,' Bourlin summed up. 'Amédée yells at his father, and when next morning he goes back to tone down his words, it's too late. Henri Masfauré, in despair at being abandoned by his son, kills himself.'

'Keep on straight ahead,' said Adamsberg, as the others were preparing to turn left. 'We need Victor's account of what happened in Iceland, before he has a chance to communicate with Amédée. Céleste says he's in his lodge, he doesn't dine up at the house.'

'What more could Victor add?' said Bourlin, shrugging his massive shoulders.

'And what about the sign?' asked Danglard.

'It must be a sign known to the Iceland group,' said Bourlin, getting more grumpy with every minute that passed. 'We'll never know.'

'Yes, we will,' said Adamsberg treading deliberately on another tuft of dried burdock.

Burdock! That was it! He'd remembered the name of the plant that clung to you: burdock, and the little balls were burrs.

'Two suicides,' said Bourlin. 'We close the files and we go and eat.'

'You're hungry,' said Adamsberg with a smile, 'and that's blinding you. What would you say to Amédée coming back next day to the Gauthier woman, and drowning her in her bath because he's furious with her? He said himself he spent two days in Paris. Remember what he called her? "That bloody woman." Who hadn't had the guts to try and save his mother, or the courage to speak up afterwards. No more than his father. And what did he say about his father?'

'His *contemptible* father,' said Danglard.

'And as soon as he's back, he confronts the father and kills him. Why not two false suicides, Bourlin?'

'Because Choiseul knows his job. No powder on Amédée, hands or sweater.'

'You're hungry, that's why you're not thinking. Amédée puts on gloves and an overall, and comes out of the study clean as a whistle. Or if you don't like that idea, what about the Icelandic monster, the "abominable" one? He first kills Alice Gauthier, then Henri Masfauré.'

'But how would this killer know that Gauthier had talked?'

'He might be capable of guessing who *might* talk, Bourlin. Which one would crack first. There could be several triggers. For instance, having a terminal illness – the Gauthier woman's case – and he knew it. So many people confess something on their deathbed. As for Henri Masfauré, remorse, his son rejecting him after he heard Gauthier's revelations. The killer said he'd keep an eye on them, didn't he? Perhaps he was particularly vigilant with those who were ill or depressed, or heavy drinkers repenting their sins.'

'Or believers,' added Danglard. 'What if there was a priest in the group? It happens, priests going on trips to the pure expanses of the north.'

'Well, there's been no mention of a priest so far,' said Bourlin, patting his stomach. 'It's night-time now,' he insisted.

Adamsberg had hurried ahead and was knocking at the door of Victor's lodge. The clock was striking quarter past nine, echoed by another in a nearby village.

'I understand about police procedure,' Victor said, 'but I can't come to Paris now, the burial is tomorrow morning, nine o'clock. Remember? You can sleep in your cars in front of my door if you're afraid of me speaking to Amédée, lock me in till nine, and we can meet at ten thirty tomorrow. No, wait, I've got a better idea,' he said, looking at Bourlin. 'If I'm not mistaken, the commissaire is hungry. Since I'm not a suspect – and I take it I'm not, is that right?'

'No, just a witness,' said Adamsberg. 'All we want is for you to tell us what happened in Iceland. Whatever it was, it has now caused four deaths, two there ten years ago and two this week.'

'You don't believe they were suicides?' asked Victor, looking somewhat anxious.

And if the Iceland killer was on the prowl, there was some cause for anxiety, thought Adamsberg.

'We don't know,' he said.

'All right. If I'm only a witness, in fact simply telling you what I know, is it legally permissible for us to have a meal together?'

'No objection,' said Bourlin impatiently.

Victor put on a corduroy jacket and ran his hands through his fair hair.

'About eight hundred metres from the gates,' he said, 'there's a family-run inn. Parents, son and daughter. I often eat there. But there's only one menu in the evening, no choice, and only two sorts of wine, a white and a red.'

Victor locked his door and pulled a folded newspaper from his inside pocket.

'Come close to the gate so I can read under the street light. The menus for the week are in the local paper. Tuesday – it's Tuesday today, isn't it? Tuesday. Starter: chicken gizzard salad.'

'I won't eat gizzards.' said Danglard.

'I'll eat yours,' said Bourlin.

'Main course: Steak au poivre and *pommes paillasson*. Know what they are?'

'You bet I do!' said Bourlin. 'Straw potato cakes. Let's stop wasting time, Victor, I'm with you.'

The four men walked quickly through the darkness, three on the asphalt, Adamsberg on the grassy verge.

'You're not a townie?' asked Victor.

'From the Pyrenees.'

'And you haven't got used to Paris?'

'I can get used to anything. Perhaps I misheard earlier, when some one mentioned your surname.'

'Misheard? I don't believe you. Yes, it's Masfauré, Victor Masfauré, and no, I'm not Henri's son, or cousin or anything else like that.'

Victor was smiling broadly in the night. A generous smile, show-ing regular white teeth which briefly transformed his plain features.

'And it isn't a coincidence,' he went on, almost laughing. 'Because it was precisely *because* of my name that I met this Masfauré family. It's such a rare surname that Henri wanted to prove I was related to them. He had a very full family tree. But he had to give up, I'm not from the same branch.'

'Masfauré,' Dangard reflected, irresistibly attracted by the slightest intellectual puzzle. '"Mas" means a little farm in Provençal. And "fauré", probably from Faurest, Forest, Forestier: the farm in the forest. Were your ancestors from Provence?'

'Henri's were, yes, but I don't have any.'

Victor spread his hands, obviously used to explaining this.

'I was abandoned at birth and fostered,' he said. 'Here we are at the Auberge du Creux,' he went on, pointing to the light at the roadside. 'Will this do?'

'Let's just get a move on,' said Bourlin.

'The Inn in the Hollow,' mused Danglard, 'an odd name.'

'You do put your finger on things, commandant,' Victor said, smiling once more. 'I'll tell you about it. After Iceland,' he went on, pushing open the door with its small panes of glass. 'Once we've finished with fucking Iceland.'

There were still customers sitting at three tables, even at this late hour by village standards, and Victor asked the proprietress – after greeting her with a kiss – for the most isolated table, near a window at the back.

'There are always more people in when it's straw potato cakes,' he explained for Bourlin's benefit.

VIII

THE CHICKEN GIZZARDS PASSED FROM DANGLARD'S PLATE TO Bourlin's, and the commandant filled the glasses. Adamsberg put his hand over his own glass.

'We're going to hear a witness statement, so one of us should keep a clear head.'

'I always have a clear head,' Danglard declared, 'and in any case, we're recording it, if Victor Masfauré agrees.'

Delighted to have a double helping, Bourlin passed the recorder to Adamsberg, with a gesture signifying that he was handing over responsibility as well, just let him get on with his dinner.

'Victor, how many people were there in this group?' Adamsberg asked.

'Twelve.'

'Was it an organised tour?'

'No, not at all. People had come individually. We three had chosen our itinerary, stage by stage, from Reykjavik to the north coast. We arrived one evening at the little island of Grimsey, the most northerly in Iceland, and we were having dinner in the inn at Sandvík. It smelled of herring, it was warm inside. Sandvík is the village with a harbour, the only one. Madame Masfauré absolutely wanted to go to Grimsey, because the Arctic Circle runs through the island. She wanted to set foot on it. The restaurant was full. And the three of us, Henri, his wife, and I, had a few glasses of *brennivín* after dinner – that's the hooch they have there. We were certainly making a lot of noise, especially Madame Masfauré who was delighted at the idea of treading on the Arctic Circle and her enthusiasm was infectious. Gradually various other French tourists who happened to be there gravitated towards us and sat at our table. You know what people are like. They go off to the ends of the earth to get away from home, but the minute they hear a compatriot's voice, they're on to it like a camel heading for an oasis. And of all the women who were dining there that night, Madame Masfauré was by far the most beautiful. She was incredibly attractive – I think it was because of her that people clustered around us, women included.'

'She was irresistible, according to Amédée.'

'Yes, that's the word for it. So there were nine other French people at our table, in the end, very varied, a bit of everything. We didn't know anything about each other, some people mentioned their professions. There was the ever-present ornithologist, a specialist on little auks, I remember his big red face. Well, that's how he looked that night. Once we got stuck on that little island across the strait, nobody's face had any colour. There was someone in business too, he didn't say what, he seemed to have forgotten it. A woman who worked on environmental issues, and her companion, also a woman.'

Bourlin moved his hand to one side, without dropping his fork, and pulled a photo out of his leather briefcase.

'On this photo, she's ten years older – and she's dead,' he said. 'Was this the companion?'

Victor examined the macabre photograph and nodded.

'Yes, no question. She had very large ears, that wouldn't change after death. Yes, it's her all right.'

'This is Alice Gauthier.'

'So she's the one who wrote to Amédée? I didn't know her name, back then. She seemed like a domineering character, bold, an astonishing woman. And yet she kept her mouth shut, like all the others, she was afraid, like all the others.'

'So who were the others?' Adamsberg asked.

'There was one big man with a shaved head; there was a doctor – his wife had stayed back in Reykjavik. There was a vulcanologist too, and he was essential.'

Bourlin had pressed his index finger on the straw potato cakes to appreciate the texture. Satisfied, he now looked at Victor, who was counting on his fingers, thinking, while his meal got cold.

'There was a sporty character,' said Victor, 'a ski instructor or something. And then there was the mad guy. But that first night, there was no sign of anything alarming about him.'

'Eat up,' Bourlin almost commanded. 'So what *was* there a sign of?'

'Nothing. He seemed ordinary, neither antisocial nor particularly friendly. Medium height, ordinary face, about fifty, small goatee beard, round glasses, no particular expression. He had a lot of hair, thick pepper-and-salt hair. He was well off, perhaps in business, or a professor, we never found that out. He had a stick with a metal point, like people have in Iceland, it's normal, to test the ground. He would bounce it up and down on the ground. And then the vulcanologist, whose name was Sylvain, told us about this local legend. From the way the doctor shook hands with him, showing great respect, Sylvain must have been someone at the top of his profession. But he was very straightforward, not pretentious. And that's when it all started. Unless it was the *brennivín*. But anyway, that's when it all went wrong.'

The daughter of the house now brought them a second bottle of wine. She had a lovely face, plump, but clear-skinned. Adamsberg eyed her. She reminded him of a younger version of Danica, and the night he had spent in her room at Kiseljevo.

Danglard had adopted as his mission, among many others, responsibility for bringing Adamsberg back to earth when he sensed him wandering off to distant places. He laid a finger on his wrist and Adamsberg blinked.

'Where were you?' whispered Danglard.

'In Serbia.'

The commandant glanced at the girl who was now back by the bar.

'Yes, I see,' he said. 'Apparently that was not to everyone's liking, you may remember.'

Adamsberg agreed with a nod, smiling vaguely.

'Sorry,' he said, turning back to Victor. 'Why did it go wrong?'

'Because of the story the vulcanologist told us.'

'Would that be Sylvain Dutrémont, by any chance?' asked Danglard thoughtfully. 'Very dark hair, beard, very blue eyes. A burn scar on one cheek.'

'I don't know,' said Victor hesitantly, 'we didn't exchange surnames, only first names. But yes, he had a scar on his cheek, where the beard didn't grow.'

'Well, if it was Dutrémont, he died a few years ago, during the eruption of Eyjafjallajökull, the one that caused all that ash over Iceland.'

'Well, that makes five gone, out of twelve,' said Victor quietly. 'But that was an accident, I presume?'

'There was some talk about it,' Danglard explained. 'Because his body was found quite a distance from the erupting crater, with bruises. Possibly from a fall, as he tried to escape the lava flow. But the inquest recorded an open verdict.'

Bourlin broke the thoughtful silence that followed.

'So what did Sylvain say?'

'That off the coast of Grimsey, among the many uninhabited islets there, just a stone's throw away, one was very special, both feared and fascinating. It was said that on this islet, there was a rock that was still warm, about the size of a gravestone, covered with ancient inscriptions. And if you lay down on the warm stone, you became invulnerable, you'd live for ever, or some such. Because you would be penetrated by waves coming from the centre of the earth. That kind of stuff. Well, it seems there are quite a few people on Grimsey who've lived to be a hundred and that's how they explain it. Sylvain said he was going to go there the next day, to examine it from a scientific point of view, but on no account should we tell the locals he was going, because they don't want anyone to set foot on it. They say it is inhabited by a demon, an "afturganga", a sort of zombie. The doctor laughed, we all laughed. But within an hour, everyone in the group had decided to accompany the vulcanologist, even the doctor. Everyone made out they were sceptical, but in the end you might be tempted by a stone that promises you eternal life. Although everyone pretended it was just to challenge the tradition, or a bet made when we'd all been drinking. It was only three kilometres away, about an hour on foot across the pack ice, we'd get back in time for lunch. Well. As for getting back . . .'

Bourlin ordered another batch of *pommes paillasson* and everyone watched him indulgently. The Rabelaisian appetite of the commissaire helped to lighten the atmosphere somewhat as they approached the epicentre of the story.

'So we set off at nine in the morning, from the pier in the harbour. Sylvain had warned us again, not a word to the locals, because as well as the *afturganga*, they would be horrified if some ignorant tourists defiled their stone by putting their irreverent backsides on it. The sky was blue, it was freezing cold, but a perfect day, not a cloud in sight. Still, in Iceland, they say the weather changes all the time, in five minutes if it's in the mood. From the harbour, Sylvain discreetly pointed out the rock: it was black, and had a distinctive shape, like the head of a fox, with two little cones like ears and a long dark stretch like a muzzle. Well, we got there without any problem, dodging the cracks in the ice. It was a tiny island, we had quickly explored it, and it was the civil servant, Jean his name was, I think? Not sure. Anyway, he soon found the stone.'

'I thought you were supposed to have a phenomenal memory,' Danglard observed.

'Oh, I only remember things I'm asked to remember, then I wipe them to make room, don't you?'

'Absolutely not. Anyway, this Jean?'

'He lay flat out on the stone, laughing, he was quite uninhibited. And as each of us took our little turn on the stone – it was warm, that was true – time was passing. The guy with the shaved head had lain down on it very seriously and without a word, closing his eyes. Then suddenly, Sylvain called out: "Time to go, we've got to move!" and he pointed to a mountain of fog moving towards us. It came on so quickly that we had hardly gone twenty metres across the ice before Sylvain decided we should turn back. You couldn't see six metres ahead, then four then two. He told us to hold hands, and guided us back to the island. He reassured us, saying that it could move away in ten minutes, or an hour. But it didn't. We ended up staying there for two weeks. Fourteen days in the freezing cold, with nothing to eat. The island was quite deserted, a place of death, just this *afturganga* living there. Black rocks covered in snow, not a tree, not an insect, not a –'

Victor stopped speaking suddenly, his knife suspended in mid-air. His terror was so obvious that they all froze along with him. Adamsberg and Danglard turned round, following the direction of his gaze. There was nothing to see but a wall and two glass-panelled doors. Between them was a clumsy painting of the Chevreuse valley. Another by Céleste, a copy of the one in Masfauré's study. Victor remained in the same position, hardly breathing. Adamsberg motioned to his colleagues to start acting naturally again, without comment. He removed the knife from the young man's hand and gently brought his arm down on to the table, as if manipulating a puppet. Taking hold of his chin, he turned it to face him.

'It's him,' Victor whispered.

'The man behind us, that you can see reflected in the glass?'

'Yes.'

Victor shook himself, like one of the horses, drank off his wine and wiped his face.

'I'm sorry,' he said, 'I didn't think telling this story would make me panic. I've never told anyone before. It can't be him. It was the reflection that confused me. That man looks younger than he was ten years ago.'

Adamsberg examined the man who had come into the inn soon after them. He was dining alone and looked absent-minded, the local paper spread out on his table, as he glanced wearily round the room. He seemed tired out by his day and was simply ready to go home to bed.

'Victor,' said Adamsberg, 'this man doesn't have a small beard or white hair, except some greying at his temples. Think. What was it made you imagine it was him?'

Victor frowned, twisting one of his curls in his fingers.

'I'm sorry,' he repeated.

'Think,' said Adamsberg quietly.

'His eyes perhaps,' said Victor hesitantly, as if suggesting a hypothesis. 'Eyes that look quite ordinary, watch everything and then get fixed when you're least expecting it.'

'And he fixed them on us?'

'On you, yes.'

Adamsberg stood up and shambled over with his aimless gait towards the proprietress. After a few moments, she came to sit at their table.

'You're not the first,' said the large woman with a laugh, 'and you won't be the last, even if you are a commissaire. The big restaurants, they've all been out here to try and find out. No,' she said, waving a tea towel, 'it belongs to us and that's where it's going to stay. So put that in your pipe and smoke it.'

Adamsberg poured her a glass of wine.

'Oh, try as hard as you like that way,' she went on, taking a sip, 'I'll only tell anyone when I'm on my last legs, and then I'll only tell my daughter!'

'A deathbed confession,' murmured Danglard. 'Come on, madame, we won't tell anyone else, gentleman's honour.'

'I've never heard of any gentleman's honour that was worth a bean, for this or anything else. This woman I know in Brittany was tortured to get her to reveal the secret of her pancakes. In the end, she said she put beer in the mixture. And they let her go. But it wasn't beer.'

'What on earth are you talking about?' asked Bourlin in a drowsy voice (whereas Danglard, by contrast, became more lively the more he drank – alcohol seemed to do him good).

'The recipe for *pommes paillasson*,' said Danglard.

'But we also want to know who that customer is, sitting on his own near the door,' said Adamsberg. 'Just three words about him and we'll let you go.'

'Oh, I don't know him. And I don't know if I've got any right to talk about my customers. And talking to the police is something else again, isn't that true, Victor?'

'Too right, Mélanie.'

'We can agree about that,' said Adamsberg, smiling, with his head on one side.

Danglard was observing the commissaire at work, as he unconsciously transformed his bony face with its irregular features into a trap as charming as it was unexpected.

'You don't *know* him, but you don't want to say anything about him? So you *do* know a little something about him, all the same?' said Adamsberg.

'Well, just three words,' said Mélanie, pretending to pout.

'Five,' Adamsberg negotiated.

'I just thought he was odd, that's all.'

'Why?'

'Because he asked me if I knew the shoemaker.'

'What?'

'If I knew the shoemaker, in Sombrevert village. I didn't under-stand. I said yes of course, here everyone knows everyone else, so what? I don't like this kind of thing. Then he brought out his business cards, and I saw "Inspector of Taxes". So I said, "Well, what about it? Do you think he's hiding something, our shoemaker? Shoelaces perhaps?"'

'Well said,' remarked Victor.

'Ah, but they get on my nerves these people, always poking about in the shit – oh pardon me, commissaire.'

'Not at all.'

'Making poor folk sweat blood, when the big money's being made somewhere else. I thought, what he really wants is just to show me his card. To impress me. And that's the worst of it, they do, even if you've got nothing to hide. In the kitchen, you pay extra attention to how you cook the meat. See what I mean? Sooner he goes away, the happier I shall be.'

'Mélanie,' said Victor, 'your little back room, could you open it up for us? It's just that these gentlemen and me, we need a quiet corner, you understand?'

'I understand, but it hasn't been heated, I'll have to put a match to the fire. Is it about poor Monsieur Henri's death?'

'That's it, Mélanie.'

She shook her head slowly.

'A good man,' she said. 'And where's the ceremony tomorrow, Victor? In Malvoisine or Sombrevert?'

'Neither – the Mass is going to be in Le Creux, in the little chapel. Well, you know, he wasn't a believer, it's so as not to give offence.'

'Here, in Le Creux? Not sure if that would be proper,' said Mélanie, her jowls quivering. 'Well, I suppose we're all right in Le Creux, so long as they don't go near the tower.'

Danglard restrained himself, it wasn't the moment to have a chat about the superstitions of Le Creux, the hollow place. Mélanie lit the fire in the next room, and the men sat down close to the warmth, on a blue-painted school bench. Except for Adamsberg, who paced up and down behind them.

'I dream about it often, you know,' said Victor. 'Funny thing, not about the stabbing, or about her. I dream about the way we managed to light a fire, thanks to the legionnaire, that's what we called him, the guy with the shaved head. The first day we just stayed as if stunned on the bank, waiting for the fog to lift. But *he* gave orders: fetch wood for the fire, see if you can find any edible wildlife. He ordered us about like an officer, and we obeyed like soldiers. "Where are we going to find wood?" the civil servant moaned. "There's nothing growing on the island!" And the legionnaire was on it at once: "Look over there, you dope! Didn't any of you notice anything? There are remains of a shed, about thirty metres long, must have been for drying fish. Take it apart plank by plank. And some of you pack snow together in blocks. Work in threes, and hold hands if you move away. And hurry, before it gets dark!" He was a real dynamo, the legionnaire. You had to wonder if lying on the warm stone had worked some magic for him.'

Victor held out his hands to the fireplace.

'My God, I'm telling you, if we hadn't had a fire, what would have become of us? And that was thanks to this character. He was a brute, but an efficient one. At night, it burnt up well, we'd built our snow-block walls a little distance from the heat and stuffed the entrance with our bags.'

Bourlin lit a cigarette, thinking of the frozen wastes of Iceland and warming himself by the fire. Here, they were in a private room, and Mélanie had brought them ashtrays and coffee, plus a glass of something stronger for Monsieur Danglard.

'So that was our shelter,' Victor went on. 'It was about zero inside, but at least six or seven below outside, with the wind. We were still very cold, and the legionnaire made us get up every hour, day and night, with a slap if need be, we had to move around and talk, say the alphabet out loud, for instance, so that our limbs or faces didn't get frostbite. There was nothing to eat, and sitting down, we tended to get sleepy. Shaved-head didn't want us to lie down in the snow. He was a bastard, that man, but he saved our lives, those first days. Until the monster with the beard got rid of him. You see, *he* couldn't stand the legionnaire giving orders. There was a quarrel, we hadn't eaten for three days, and suddenly the monster exploded with anger, he pulled his knife, just one blow, and that was it, he killed the legionnaire. His blood was all over the snow, it was horrible. All the man said was: "He was a pain in the ass." That was his epitaph.'

Victor looked up at Adamsberg.

'I'd like to go quicker through the next bit now. Or else I'll have a glass of pick-me-up, like the commandant.'

'You can do both,' decreed Adamsberg, as he leaned on the mantelpiece. 'Does this sign mean anything to you?' he asked, opening his notebook.

'No, nothing. Why? What is it?'

Victor was expressing the same perplexity as Amédée.

'Nothing,' said Adamsberg. 'Carry on, we're listening, Victor.'

'So then he dragged the corpse away on to the ice, so that seabirds wouldn't peck out its eyes or eat it in front of us while it was warm. And then three days later, he said, looking at Madame Masfauré, if he was going to die, he'd like to screw someone first – his words. Henri Masfauré and me, we stood up. And there was another fight.'

Victor touched his nose.

'He punched me so hard he broke my nose. It used to look normal, now it's like this. He pushed Henri over backwards, no bother. He seemed to be made of iron, this man. And then, waving his knife, he made us all sit down. Cowards? Yes. But we hadn't eaten anything for six days, we were freezing cold, we had no strength left in our bodies. He must have got his energy from that damn stone too. But in the night, we heard cries. It was Madame Masfauré screaming, because this monster was assaulting her, he had his hands inside her anorak and trousers, I'll skip this bit, commissaire, it's painful. Henri and I got up again, we were like frozen zombies. The others did too, and then Madame Masfauré pushed the guy over backwards and he fell in the fire.'

At this point, Victor actually smiled, as Amédée had.

'So his trousers were on fire, he had to try and beat out the flames from his backside, you could see through to the skin, by the firelight! And someone, I think it was Jean, the civil servant, he shouted out, "You *murderer*, your arse is on fire, go burn in hell!" and at the same time Madame Masfauré was yelling, calling him everything under the sun. And the guy pulled the knife out, and he stabbed her, just like that. Madame Masfauré. Right in the heart.'

Victor took the brandy Mélanie had brought for him.

'So that night we were all terrorised. While the guy went away with the body, Henri was sobbing. And we said we'd kill the guy. But at dawn, he wasn't back. Every day, he used to go off round the island, he never gave up. He was looking for something to eat, so we all kept quiet. He reappeared one night, soon after that, and ordered us to put stones in the fire, then chucked this meat on to it. Kilos of fish – we were stunned. He said, "If any of you know how to set seal traps, put up your hand. Five days, I've been setting traps. And if you want to eat, there it is. But if you eat, you bloody well keep your mouths shut after that. Open your mouth, and you're dead." So we ate. This seal was a large male, but there were ten of us, so it wouldn't last that long. In the morning he went off again to set his traps and walk round the island with his stick. I have to say, there were the rest of us, huddled round the fire, like a lot of losers, chanting the alphabet to keep awake, but he kept going. He kept on hunting, searching. And later, he brought in another seal, a young one this time.'

'Excuse me,' said Danglard, 'Amédée mentioned just one seal. Perhaps Alice Gauthier got it wrong.'

'No, that's impossible. Amédée has never paid much attention, least of all just now. Two seals, a big male and a young one. That guy saved our lives, you have to admit that. After all, he could have eaten it all himself without telling us. But he shared it. I discussed it later with Henri. Here was a guy brutal enough to kill at the drop of a hat, but humane enough to share his food. After all, if he had killed the lot of us with his knife, which he could have, and eaten his seals himself, he could have survived, waiting for the fog to lift. Well, in the end, that fucking mist did lift, in the space of ten minutes. We held each other's shoulders, and we set out across the ice. We could see the roofs of the village again. They took us in, fed us, washed us – we smelled of seal blubber and rotten fish from head to foot – but all of us kept our mouths shut. Well, not quite. We all told exactly the same story, how we had lost two of our companions out there, frozen to death, that was the official version, imposed on us. Or else we'd be for it too, or so he said. Ourselves, or our friends, children, parents, anyone close to us. I didn't have a child, or parents, or friends. But because of his son, Henri begged me to button my lip. So we left the murderer alone, and I promise you he was a dangerous man, and still is.'

'Names?' Adamsberg asked. 'The surnames of the other people in the group?'

'No one knows them. Except him.'

'That's impossible, Victor. Two deaths, there must have been an inquest of some kind, on your return to the village. They must have taken notes of your IDs, as well as witness statements.'

'Well, the police meant to do it, the ones in Akureyri, that's across on the mainland. But that man forestalled them. He gave us no time to recover, made us get the ferry for this small town called Dalvík. Avoiding Akureyri. I thought Henri was going to die during the six hours the crossing took, then we went on to Reykjavik, and then to

Paris. The Akureyri authorities hadn't dreamt for a moment that we would just run away. Why would anyone run away, after all that? So they took their time. And we slipped through their fingers.'

'But Masfauré must surely have had to declare his wife's death?'

'Yes, of course. But the killer didn't mind if the names of the dead were known, the two "frozen to death" tourists. But he didn't want anyone to know his name or ours. The legionnaire was identified because his sister gave evidence. He was called Eric, Eric Courtelin I think. You can check that in the news reports of the time. Hush!' he said, suddenly standing up.

'We weren't saying anything,' objected Danglard, as Bourlin raised half-shut eyes.

This time it wasn't so much fear on Victor's face as an anxious kind of animation. Adamsberg heard coming from outside a kind of howl and a plaintive, sad cry.

'It's Marc!' said Victor, opening the window with a swift movement.

Adamsberg started to walk over, wondering what kind of person would produce such an inhuman and blood-curdling whine. Without a word of explanation, Victor put his leg over the windowsill and jumped on to the road, as if driven by great urgency.

'I'll be back,' Adamsberg said to Mélanie. 'Would you have somewhere, an armchair, a sofa, anything, so that the commissaire can lie down? I'll be back.'

I'll be back. These three words, which Adamsberg repeated a thousand times, as if he were constantly reassuring those around him, since he was himself afraid he might never come back. You take the path into the forest, you look at the trees and then who knows?

IX

ADAMSBERG WAS ALREADY IN PURSUIT OF VICTOR, WHO IN TURN was chasing after the mysterious Marc, following the whining anxious cries, when he heard Danglard's characteristic footsteps behind him.

To see Commandant Danglard run was a surprising experience, the first time one witnessed it. Mélanie watched from the doorway, as his figure moved in the strangest fashion, the unshapely torso bent forward, followed, far behind it seemed, by two long but uncoordinated legs that reminded her of melting candles in the church at Sombrevert. Heaven protect him!

'What kind of animal is he after?' puffed Danglard, as he caught up with Adamsberg.

'It's not an animal, it's a person.'

'Making a noise like that? I'd say an animal!'

Adamsberg had now reached Victor's side, and grabbed him by the collar.

'Dammit, let me go!' Victor yelled. 'It's Céleste! Marc came to fetch me!'

'Who the hell is Marc?'

'Her wild boar of course, for chrissake!'

Adamsberg turned to Danglard, who was lagging several metres behind by now.

'You were right. It is an animal. Taking us to Céleste, but don't ask me how or why.'

Instead of taking the path towards the house, Victor had headed off westwards into the woods, evidently knowing the trail by heart. Adamsberg was close behind, while Danglard, puffing and panting, doggedly brought up the rear, holding a torch, and trying to protect his shoes. They had gone a good kilometre into the forest, Adamsberg calculated, as he came to a halt with Victor, in front of a ramshackle wooden hut, where a very powerful-looking wild boar was indeed standing facing the door and grunting.

'Watch out,' said Victor. 'Marc doesn't like strangers, especially if they get near Céleste's place. Take my hand, I'll guide you, we have to mix our scents together. Pat his head. You'll see, his muzzle is as silky as a duckling's back. That's special about him, his snout is still a baby one.'

Victor took Adamsberg's hand and put it on the so-called baby snout of the impressive long-haired beast, one metre sixty in length, Adamsberg guessed, with a massive head, much larger than its girth.

'Friends, Marc, these are friends!' Victor was saying, as he fondled the animal's neck, while banging with his other hand at the heavy door made of logs.

'Céleste! It's me, open up.'

'It's not locked!' called a piping voice from inside, sounding annoyed.

Victor pushed the door and bent double to enter this cramped and miserable hut. The boar rushed inside and over to Céleste, then turned round and stood defending her with its white tusks. As large and white as Victor's teeth.

'It was nothing,' said Céleste, wringing her hands.

'Marc came to fetch me at the inn. So tell me what happened.'

'He was scared.'

'He's not easily scared. Only if *you're* scared.'

'He can have his own troubles, can't he? What would you know about a boar's troubles?'

Adamsberg, after walking round the outside, entered the cabin.

'Smells of horses,' he remarked.

'Everything smells of horses round here,' replied Céleste.

'But not outside, not in the woods. And what's more, it smells of liniment in here. A mixture of mint, camphor and hyacinth. They used to put it on donkeys' hooves where I come from. Did *he* come here?'

'Who?'

'The man who whistled for Dionysos.'

'Oh, Pelletier,' said Céleste casually, almost innocently.

'He did come here?'

'That would surprise me,' said Victor. 'Marc can't stand him, and he knows that.'

'All the same,' Adamsberg insisted, 'was he here this evening?'

'It was nothing but the door rattling and Marc was startled,' said Céleste, frowning grumpily. 'He's just an animal after all.'

'No, that isn't it,' said Victor. 'Marc has very sensitive reflexes. He came because he thought you were in danger.'

The little woman, sitting down on the only stool in the cabin, brought out a pipe from her overall pocket, and started packing it. A short pipe with a large bowl, quite masculine-looking.

'Céleste,' Victor pressed her, 'we're going to bury Henri tomorrow morning. This isn't the moment to hide the truth. Suicide or murder, they're different, a person doesn't go to heaven the same way.'

'God knows all,' said Céleste, lighting the pipe and waving away large clouds of smoke. 'But what are you talking about murder for, Victor? Aren't you ashamed of accusing folk?'

'I'm talking about it because the police are. So perhaps God knows, or perhaps you do, what Pelletier was doing coming round here at night.'

'It smells of horses and liniment in here,' Adamsberg repeated quietly, rather fascinated by this little woman with her teeth clamped round the pipe stem. 'But I like the smell of liniment,' he added, turning his face in the dark – the cabin was lit only by two candles.

'All right,' Céleste admitted. 'But he just rattled the door.'

'No he didn't, he broke it open,' said Victor, pointing to splinters of wood. 'What did he smash that log with, an axe?'

'He was drunk, it wasn't his fault. I should get it made of oak, not pine, you can see it isn't very strong, I did mention it to Monsieur Henri.'

'Céleste, just stop this. What did he do to you?'

'Nothing.'

'Nothing. And that's why Marc came rushing to the inn?'

'He's just an animal,' she repeated.

'Who? Pelletier?' said Victor, raising his voice.

'No need to get in a state, all he did was shake me a bit by the shoulders.'

'A bit? Show me.'

'Don't touch me!' she ordered.

And Marc took up his guard-dog position again, gnashing his tusks.

'Céleste,' Adamsberg interrupted gently, 'Henri Masfauré didn't kill himself. What did Pelletier say to you?'

And Céleste had the feeling that the commissaire would not take his vague eyes off her, any more than her old schoolteacher would have when he was waiting for her to finish her homework. And curiously enough, Marc had calmed down, to the point of moving slightly towards the commissaire, offering up his snout. Adamsberg carefully stroked the duckling-like fur on his nose. This meeting seemed to decide Céleste.

'He just said that since Monsieur Henri's death, I've been giving him dirty looks,' she said. 'And he said it's got to stop.'

'And why were you giving him dirty looks?'

Céleste took out a pipe tamper from another pocket, pressed down the tobacco and took a long pull.

'Oh, he was drunk, he's making things up. And then Marc went for him, and after that he chased him through the forest. I had no idea he'd go and fetch Victor.'

'When did he get here?'

'Nine years ago. He lost his parents when he was small, they were killed just like that, and his brothers and sisters died of neglect.'

'That might mark your character,' said Danglard. They had forgotten him, and he was standing outside, leaning against the upright of the damaged door.

'I meant *Pelletier*, not Marc,' said Adamsberg. 'When did he come to *live* here?'

'Oh, him? Soon after I did. What's that got to do with it?'

'Everything's got to do with it when there's a death,' said Danglard.

'Because you're thinking he killed Monsieur Henri? Who was his benefactor! And all because Marc panicked just now? It's the rutting season, if you want to know. He hasn't got it out of his system, he's got to start again, and he gets nervous, you have to understand.'

'We've come across plenty of people who've done in their benefactors,' said Danglard.

'After he'd gone,' said Céleste, in a changed voice as if she was making chit-chat in the big drawing room, 'I heard a viper hissing outside.'

She frowned, looking concerned and puffed at her pipe.

'I should block the cracks with wood pulp,' she said, 'or they'll get in.'

Victor glanced across at Adamsberg. They wouldn't get another word out of her, not tonight at any rate.

'What you can do is spread bird droppings, especially crows' droppings,' suggested Adamsberg. 'It's known to repel vipers.'

'Tons of that in the tower,' said Victor.

'I don't want anything from the tower, as well you know, Victor.'

'Céleste, why didn't you want to tell us all that? To protect Pelletier?'

'Now that Monsieur Henri has left this world, we none of us know what's to become of us, in the household. Me, Victor, Pelletier. So I wasn't going to get him into trouble, just because he'd had too much to drink.'

She got up from her stool and started pottering around the cabin, pouring water from an old jug into an enamel basin, then meticulously spreading a blanket over her foam mattress, which had been laid on the ground with a blue plastic undersheet to protect it from damp. Adamsberg was contemplating this desolate home, with its old coal-burning stove and beaten earth floor, when a dark circular patch about twenty centimetres across caught his eye. He crouched down and felt it with his hand. Just a little circle, damper than the surrounding earth.

'Does Marc piss on the floor in here?' he asked.

'Yes,' said Céleste firmly.

'No, he doesn't,' said Adamsberg, 'he marks his territory outside the cabin.'

He began grubbing up the cool earth with his fingers, watched with alarm by Céleste.

'You have no right to do that,' she said, raising her voice. 'That's where I hide my savings.'

'You'll get them back,' said Adamsberg, continuing to move the loose soil.

He did not need to dig very deep before his fingers met the edge of a thick drinking glass with a flat base, which he pulled out of the little hole. Standing up, he shook it, then waved it under his nose.

'Whisky,' he remarked calmly.

'Henri Masfauré's glass?' asked Danglard.

Must have been poisoned, was what the commandant was now thinking. Céleste must have been in love with the great clean-air genius! Perhaps Masfauré planned to marry again, who knows? So she killed him. But if so, why not destroy the glass?

'Marc will see you to the drive,' Céleste suddenly announced, as if she was talking about her butler at the end of a social evening.

'After Amédée discovered him,' Adamsberg said, 'you went up to the study. And you put away the bottle, and took the glass.'

'Yes. Marc will see you to the drive.'

'Why, Céleste?'

Céleste sat back down on the stool, and rocked to and fro for a moment, with the boar coming and going, rubbing up against her legs enough to make them pink. Then he went towards Adamsberg and lifted his snout. Without feeling apprehensive, Adamsberg stroked his head.

'The master had killed himself. The police and journalists were going to tell people. That he drank whisky every night. They were going to sling mud at him. That's why I took the glass.'

'Why did you bury it?'

'It was his last glass, it was in memory of him. You don't throw away the last glass of someone who's died.'

'I'll have to take it away to get it analysed,' said Adamsberg, slipping it straight into his pocket. 'But I'll bring it back to you.'

'Yes, I understand. But don't clean it, please. Marc will see you to the drive.'

And this time, the men obeyed. Adamsberg motioned to Victor to stay behind a little while with her. Marc trotted docilely ahead of them to the drive, as his mother Céleste had ordered him – without showing any animosity.

'A man and a woman, eh?' said Danglard, who was using his torch to follow the path at their feet.

'But which man, Danglard?' asked Adamsberg.

'Henri Masfauré, who else?'

'I don't think so. You're forgetting Pelletier's visit. Céleste knows something, he's afraid of her and, worse, he's threatening her. And yet she's protecting him. How old was she when he got here? Thirty-five?'

'So?'

'So, a man and a woman.'

The two men walked along in silence, with Marc rootling along in front of them.

'Who does the tower belong to?'

'The parish of Le Creux.'

'What's the matter with it?'

'According to Céleste, it's got an evil reputation. She said it was used as an oubliette in the olden days. They locked prisoners up inside and left them to rot.'

'Ah, so obviously. . .'

'So obviously, you can still hear their groans and their ghosts calling for vengeance.'

'Understandable.'

'Quite.'

Marc did not stop at the drive, but led them through the trees to a hole in the fence.

'Obviously,' Adamsberg said, 'he knew that we could only get through this way. The gates are triple-locked.'

'Céleste told him "to the drive".'

'I wouldn't want to offend anyone, Danglard, but Marc may be brighter than she is. Why? Because he adapts, whereas Céleste is stuck.' Adamsberg patted the boar's muzzle.

'I'll be back,' he told Marc.

Bourlin was fast asleep, flat out on the blue school bench which had vanished under his bulk. Adamsberg shook him awake.

'I'm going back to Paris with Danglard now.'

'Pity,' said Bourlin, sitting up. 'I like it here. Mélanie would have made those potato cakes for me every night.'

'Yes.'

'Never eaten any as good as that. I've been stood down on this case, of course. Just got the message. Obviously, the 15th arrondissement doesn't extend to the Auberge du Creux. So you *will* have to take it on now.'

'Yes.'

'What was all that noise about?'

'It was a wild boar, or rather a tame boar, coming for help. Pelletier had been manhandling Céleste. She lives in this tumbledown hut in the woods and smokes a pipe. Like a witch.'

'A hut? What on earth was her employer like? A philanthropist or a slave trader?'

'Might be useful to find that out. Don't forget to get a photo of the sign on the leather desktop.'

'That bloody sign.'

'Like a guillotine.'

'As you said before. Have you ever seen a guillotine with two blades?'

'No, never.'

X

ADAMSBERG WAS BACK ON THE ROAD, AFTER DROPPING THE WHISKY glass off at the Rambouillet gendarmerie. With formal instructions that it should be returned to Céleste after analysis. The patter of rain on the windscreen woke Danglard, who was dozing.

'Where've we got to?' he asked.

'Just went through Versailles.'

'I meant the investigation. Murders or suicides?'

'Two suicides, both leaving the same sign behind them, Danglard. Two suicides connected to the same rock in Iceland. Something's not right. And Amédée is the link between them, going to and fro.'

'Difficult to see that boy as a frenzied killer, committing two murders in two days. He looks more like a poet, pale-cheeked and wielding a pen. Rather than a shotgun or a razor.'

'Yes, but he's hard to work out. A changeable character, a nervous temperament, his eyes can be absent-minded, then change to furious.'

'He's liable to take fright too, given he ran away on horseback.'

'If he'd really wanted to, Danglard, the best way would have been to jump in his car.'

'The best way for idiots, if you'll forgive me, commissaire. On horseback, we couldn't have followed him. He might have ridden to

Rambouillet, taken a train to Paris, and then on anywhere, Lisbon, Naples, Copenhagen. Faster than we could catch up with him.'

'If that was his plan, he wouldn't have chosen Dionysos, or ridden bareback, come to that. No, he must have been thinking of something else,' said Adamsberg, putting down his window and stretching his arm outside the car.

He always did this, enjoying the feel of the rain on his hand.

'Or perhaps he wasn't thinking at all,' said Danglard.

'That would be even more worrying, but possible, I suppose. An empty brain behind that handsome face. The opposite of Victor. A very sharp mind behind an ugly face.'

'What about Victor anyway? *He* could have read Alice Gauthier's letter and rushed in to Paris.'

'To stop her saying any more, yes. But Victor had no reason to kill his boss. And for the others, it's the opposite.'

'Quite,' said Danglard. 'Pelletier, or any of the neighbours might have wanted to kill Henri Masfauré. According to Bourlin, he was sitting on a fortune. The family had accumulated a thousand or so works of art between 1870 and 1950. Lots of money there, enough to excite envy and disputes. But on the other hand, no motive to go and drown Alice Gauthier.'

'Still less to draw that sign.'

'We keep harking back to the sign.'

Danglard sighed and leaned back in the seat.

'It really irritates you, that you couldn't decipher it, doesn't it?' said Adamsberg.

'It's worse than that. Why did you talk about a guillotine though? It doesn't look anything like a guillotine.'

'I talked about it, Danglard, because that's what it is, a guillotine.'

The commandant shook his head in the dark. Adamsberg slowed down and pulled in on the verge of the highway.

'What the heck are we doing now?' groaned Danglard.

'I'm not getting out for a leak, I'm going to draw a guillotine for you. Or rather *that* drawing of a guillotine. So I'm going to redraw a drawing.'

'Right.'

Adamsberg switched on his hazard lights and turned to Danglard.

'Remember the Revolution?' he asked, while detaching a burr from his trousers.

'The French one? I wasn't there, but yes, I'm acquainted with it.'

'That's good, because I'm not. But I do know that at some point during the Revolution, this engineer suggested adopting the guillotine as a means of carrying out the death sentence on criminals, so that they would all be executed in the same way, and with minimum suffering. At the time, it wasn't meant for the Terror.'

'He wasn't an engineer, he was a famous doctor, Dr Guillotin.'

'Right.'

'Joseph-Ignace Guillotin.'

'I'm sure you're right.'

'He'd been the personal physician of the king's brother, the Comte de Provence –'

'Danglard, do you want me to do this drawing, yes or no?'

'Go ahead.'

'This was some time at the beginning of the Revolution, when the king was still on the throne. And you needn't tell me it was Louis XVI, I do know that. And at some meeting or other, Guillotin came along to present his machine. Apparently, the king was present.'

'Must have been before August 1792, then.'

'No doubt, Danglard.'

The commandant frowned and Adamsberg lit one of his crumpled cigarettes, offering another to his colleague. The two lit ends glowed in the silent interior of the car.

'We could be the only people in the world,' mused Adamsberg quietly. 'Where is everyone? All the other people?'

'They're out there, they're just not doing drawings at the side of the road, that's all.'

'Well, it's said,' Adamsberg went on, 'that the doctor brought plans showing a classic beheading machine. Because in fact, some such thing already existed.'

'Yes, it had, since the sixteenth century. But Dr Guillotin improved the mechanism.'

'So what did it look like, the earlier version, Danglard?'

'It had a curved blade.'

'Like this then,' and Adamsberg drew with his finger on the misted-up windscreen: two uprights and a curved line between them.

'Yes, like that. Or with a straight blade. Guillotin thought that the straight blade would be more efficient and do the job faster.'

'Well, that's not what I was told. I was told that the *king*, who was a lot better at mechanics than he was at politics, looked at the plans, thought about them for a bit, then crossed out the curved blade with an oblique straight one, to suggest his own modification. So it was him that transformed the machine, improved it in fact.'

Adamsberg now drew a transverse line on his sketch.

'Like this.'

Danglard put his window down too, and tapped away his cigarette ash. Adamsberg removed another burr from his trousers. If they were seeds, he might plant them in his little garden. He put it on the dashboard.

'Oh, what sort of story is that?' asked Danglard.

'It *is* a story, exactly, I didn't say it was *true*. I just said that people have said this. That Louis XVI designed the perfect instrument, the one that would later cut his own head off.'

Danglard looked grumpy, blowing out smoke between his teeth.

'Where did you read that?'

'Didn't read it at all. Do you remember that old guy who knew lots of history, used to sit about in the Place Edgar-Quinet? He told me this one day, and he drew the picture with his finger on a wet tabletop in the Viking cafe. I'm sorry,' said Adamsberg, starting the car, 'it's not humiliating not to know things. If it was, I'd be covered in mud.'

'I'm not humiliated, I'm astounded.'

'But what do you think now, about his sign?'

'It's not revolutionary anyway. Or there wouldn't be that allusion to the king.'

'To a king who was executed, Danglard. Not the same. You could see it as a sign of the supreme Terror, the supreme punishment.'

'If that's what the killer wanted to represent.'

'It could be a coincidence. But it would be a very strange one.'

'You mean a killer who's interested in history?'

'Not necessarily. After all, *I'd* seen the image. It could just be a killer who remembers everything he's heard.'

'A hypermnesiac.'

'Like Victor, for instance.'

Adamsberg drove on in silence, as they approached the outskirts of Paris.

'We're not the only people in the world,' he said, as he overtook a lorry. 'It's surely someone who's *thinking* about the Revolution.'

'No doubt about that.'

XI

UNLIKE DANGLARD, ADAMSBERG DID NOT NEED MUCH SLEEP. HE opened his eyes at 7 a.m., and started fixing the coffee while his son, Zerk, cut the bread. Zerk was as casual as his father, and the slices came out thick and uneven.

'Was there some trouble last night?'

'A death out in the Chevreuse valley. We were called in to question people: there's a son who's pretty as a girl and very edgy, a secretary with a phenomenal memory, a stud farm, a brute of a man who runs it, a woman who lives in a hut in the forest, a wild boar, a local inn, Louis XVI's guillotine, a haunted tower full of bird droppings, and all this out at some place called Le Creux, which isn't on any map.'

'Got off to a bad start then?'

'Well, let's say it's very concentrated.'

'The pigeon dropped in yesterday. You missed him.'

'He hasn't been for a couple of months. Was he looking well?'

'Yes, very, but he crapped on the table again.'

'Think of it as an offering, Zerk.'

By nine o'clock, Adamsberg had gathered almost all his colleagues in the largest room in their headquarters building, the one that Danglard had pretentiously baptised 'the council chamber'. That was as opposed to the smaller 'chapter room', used for meetings of limited size. The names had stuck. Danglard was present at the council this morning, but only half awake, and he reached for the coffee which Estalère was serving. In the council, as everywhere else, the young officer had voluntarily devoted himself to fetching the coffees, a function he fulfilled to perfection – the only one, according to some ill-wishers. Otherwise, his wide green eyes made him look perpetually startled. Estalère venerated two idols in the squad, Commissaire Adamsberg and the imposing and powerful Violette Retancourt, to whom her parents, failing to realise that she would grow to 1m 84, and weigh 110 kilos, all of it solid muscle, had given the incongruous name of a fragile flower. The fundamental dissimilarity of his twin gods left Estalère in a state of rueful perplexity, unable to choose between such divergent paths.

Adamsberg had no gift for organised presentations and syntheses, and on this occasion, he turned the task over to Danglard, who provided a summary of events, from the woman in her bath – fully clothed, he added, for the benefit of Lieutenant Noël, the most tabloid-minded officer in the squad – through to the chase in the forest after the boar. He recounted it all in chronological order, while introducing the main thematic points, in a skilful narrative which Adamsberg admired. Everyone knew of course that from time to time Danglard would launch into some scholarly digression, which would make his speech longer, but they were used to that. The woman in the log cabin and the haunted tower attracted the interest of Commandant Mordent, whose head jerked up on his scrawny neck, giving him the weird aspect of an old heron, watching gloomily for a fish. Mordent was a specialist on fairy tales, which was of no great use to the squad's usual work, any more than Voisenet's encyclopedic knowledge of ichthyology – the study of fish, as Adamsberg had had to learn. Particularly freshwater fish. Voisenet's passion extended to other forms of wildlife, and he was already wondering which species of corvids lived in the tower: jackdaws, crows, rooks – ravens, even?

The slight and discreet Justin, sitting next to Retancourt who looked as if she could blow him away with one puff of breath, was the only one taking continuous notes.

While Adamsberg was still pulling burrs off his trousers, Danglard passed the drawing of the sign round the table and they all shook their heads as they saw it, except for Veyrenc de Bilhc, a Pyrenean who came from the same mountain range as Adamsberg. Veyrenc held on to the paper for a moment, under the attentive gaze of the commissaire, who knew that his fellow countryman had been a history teacher in another life.

'Mean anything to you, Veyrenc?' asked Adamsberg.

'Not sure. Are those burrs you're pulling off?'

'Yes, but they're old, from last year. They're dried up, so they cling like hell. Well, it reminds *me* of a guillotine. Go on, Danglard, explain this bit, but don't get too carried away about Joseph-Ignace Guillotin.'

A general air of uncertainty followed Danglard's next explanation, delivered without much conviction, about Louis XVI, the convex blade, and the change to a straight, oblique one. Veyrenc alone sent a quick smile to Adamsberg, that charming smile of his, with a curl of the lip indicating discreet satisfaction.

'The French Revolution?' said Retancourt, folding her arms. 'I think we can rule that out, can't we?'

'I didn't say it *was* that,' Adamsberg replied, 'I just said it reminded me of a guillotine. And the analyses that have been done seem to show that this was the way the sign was drawn: first the two uprights, then the curved line, then the oblique one.'

'It's a nice idea,' intervened Mercadet, who was for once wide awake and with his mind operating at maximum sharpness.

Mercadet suffered from narcolepsy, which meant he had to have a nap every three hours, and the squad had managed to protect him from the divisionnaire discovering any hint of this.

'But if it's true,' he went on, 'I find it very hard to see what a guillotine – half-royal and half-revolutionary – has to do with this business in Iceland.'

'Not just hard to see, impossible,' Adamsberg agreed.

'Especially since we still don't know if these *were* murders,' growled Noël, stuffing his fists into his leather jacket. 'Maybe those two – Alice Gauthier and Henri Masfauré – were secret lovers, and they had some kind of suicide pact?'

'But there's no record of any phone calls between Gauthier and Masfauré,' said Danglard. 'Bourlin checked back a whole year.'

'Perhaps she wrote to him. They both kill themselves, and the drawing's a sign of their collusion. There's nothing to prove they were murdered.'

'There is, now,' said Adamsberg, taking out his mobile, 'the lab has worked fast. Danglard has told you that both Henri Masfauré's hands were blackened with gunpowder. Whereas a possible killer, wearing gloves, and covering up Masfauré's thumb to pull the trigger, would have left the thumbnail free of residue. But no, that wasn't the case, the gunpowder was everywhere. Conclusion, suicide. But I asked for a more detailed examination.'

'I see,' said Estalère seriously, this remark being followed by a moment of consternation all round.

'And,' Adamsberg went on, 'there are indeed gaps in the residue on the wrists, where the killer would have had to hold on to Masfauré's hands. And a quite unequivocal clue on the right thumb. A line, a white stripe about three millimetres wide. So the killer *did* press the victim's thumb down on the trigger, but with the aid of a piece of string, or rather something more solid, like a leather shoelace. Conclusion: Masfauré was murdered.'

'So if it is the same sign,' Estalère persisted, rubbing his brow, 'the woman must have been *deliberately* drowned in her bath.'

'Exactly, and it must have been the killer who drew the sign, not her.'

'But that doesn't hold up,' interjected Retancourt. 'If he wanted to disguise these two murders as suicide, why draw the sign at all? If it hadn't been for the sign, the two deaths would have been registered separately, and no one would have been any the wiser. So?'

'Because he wanted to *claim* the murders?' suggested Voisenet. 'He's drawing a sign of power. With this so-called guillotine?'

'That's just banal pop psychology,' said Retancourt.

'Still,' said Mordent, 'life is always banal. Just now and then a pearl, a grain of sand, a shining particle, falls on our shoulder. And in the ocean of ordinary waves, power is the most banal vice among mankind. So why not draw a symbolic guillotine to indicate your power?'

'Is it royalist?' asked Adamsberg. 'Or revolutionary? It may not matter in the end. It's a sign indicating the supreme form of execution.'

'Why supreme?' asked Mercadet.

'Because of Iceland. He had had eleven people under his thumb, he is still holding them there, and he's turned on by it. Only there are just six of them left now.'

'All in mortal danger,' said Justin.

'Only if they talk.'

'But the wall of silence is starting to crack,' said Adamsberg. 'Two deaths in two days. Reported in the press. The other six will have understood. Will they keep quiet, or go to ground, or will they panic?'

'It's impossible to protect them,' added Danglard. 'Apart from Victor, we don't know any of their names. We have a civil servant called "Jean", a "Doc", the ecologist who was Gauthier's woman companion, an expert on little auks and a sportsman. That's all. And we can add Amédée to the list of those in danger.'

'If Amédée isn't the killer himself,' objected Mordent. 'He had plenty of motive. I'm wondering why we don't just put the screws on him at once.'

'Because at the moment, the screws would be turning in a vacuum,' said Adamsberg. Who had gathered a little pile of burrs, and was letting a long pause go past.

'Right, eight of you will leave for Le Creux after lunch,' he ordered. 'That means you too, Estalère.'

'Estalère could hold the fort here,' said Noël mockingly.

'Estalère makes the people he's questioning feel at ease,' said Adamsberg, 'unlike most cops, starting with you, lieutenant. I want you to collect all the gen you can out there. Gossip, lies, truths, suspicions, grudges, . . . Interview the villagers, the local bigwigs, the mayors of Sombrevert and Malvoisine, anyone you can. Who was Henri Masfauré? What do they say about his wife? Or about Céleste, Pelletier, Amédée, Victor? Everything there is to pick up.'

'Funny thing,' observed Danglard. 'The very first person to be executed with the new guillotine in 1792 was a thief called Pelletier.'

'Danglard, please,' said Adamsberg resignedly, 'they're all hungry and they've got to leave at 1400 hours. You too, by the way. I'd like you to go and see Henri Masfauré's lawyer, take Mercadet with you, he's good with figures. The inheritance is huge, apparently. Mordent, take anyone you like and find out about the past of his wife. Noël, you can concentrate on the tough guy who runs the stud farm, he's an ex-con, right up your street. Take Retancourt. When you meet him, you'll see that won't be overkill. And don't stand behind the horses, he's quite capable of ordering them to kill you, just by whistling. Veyrenc, I want you to stick to the son, Amédée. Froissy, stay here please, and concentrate on Alice Gauthier, question the nurse again, the neighbour, her ex-colleagues, everyone.'

'Can we go and take a look at the tower?' asked Voisenet, still thinking about the birds.

'What for?'

'To get a general idea.'

'Well, go there if you like, lieutenant, and while you're about it, collect a bucketful of bird droppings and scatter them around outside Céleste's cabin. Don't tell her they come from the tower, she's scared stiff of it. She's difficult at first, but she's OK.'

'Why?' asked Kernokian.

'Why is she difficult?'

'No, why the droppings?'

'To keep vipers away. There are some in the wood. Or she imagines there are. And her cabin isn't well insulated. You need to make a ring round it.'

'Yes, fair enough,' agreed Voisenet, 'they don't like the smell. But what about her? Difficult but OK? What's that supposed to mean?'

'It can often happen with someone who's been protecting a child through thick and thin. And why is she defending him anyway? Dig deep, all of you. And have a meal at the Auberge du Creux, the cooking's excellent, as Bourlin will confirm.'

'The Inn in the Hollow?' asked Mercadet, looking surprised.

'Yes, lieutenant, that's what they call it, a piece of land between two villages, but not marked on the map. There's an inn, a chapel and the medieval tower.'

'Medieval tower? Fucking waste of time,' muttered Noël.

'No, Noël, nothing is a fucking waste of time. Not the tower, not the pigeon and not Retancourt. Remember?'

Noël gave a grudging nod. It was true that once, during a past emergency, he had turned up to give blood to save the life of Retancourt, with whom he was normally at daggers drawn. Adamsberg hadn't quite despaired of civilising him one day.

Giving out orders like this – it came with his wretched job and he couldn't delegate it to Danglard – unsettled him. He finished as quickly as possible and the team split up to go for lunch. Some went to the decadent and rather pricy Brasserie des Philosophes and the others to the little cafe called the Dice Shaker, where the owner's wife, imperfectly repressing her fury, carried out her authoritarian husband's orders without a word, but made very good sandwiches. Their nickname for the husband was 'Glass-of-white', though actually they didn't call him anything, because he didn't like talking to the customers. Social warfare thus existed between the two establishments located opposite each other. It would lead to murder one day, Veyrenc always said.

Adamsberg watched him go out. Veyrenc had understood that the sign could be a guillotine. The sun was now shining into the large room, and in its light the lieutenant's fourteen strangely coloured locks showed up auburn, against the rest of his jet-black hair.

'I thought of something when I woke up,' Danglard murmured before leaving, in a conspiratorial tone which did not promise well. 'Just one of those thoughts you have in the morning.'

'Hurry up, commandant, you'll hardly have time to eat.'

'Well, it's about the Comte de Provence.'

'I'm not with you.'

'I told you that Guillotin was his personal physician.'

'Yes, you did.'

'In my half-sleep, the Comte de Provence led me, through one thing after another to the nobility, the counts and the dukes.'

'You're lucky, Danglard,' said Adamsberg with a smile. 'Waking thoughts don't usually take us into exalted company.'

'Then I thought about the first names of Amédée – which is an unusual one, you have to admit – and Victor. They have both been the names for hundreds of years of the dukes of Savoy. I'll spare you the list of the Amédées of Savoy.'

'Thank you, Danglard.'

'But between 1630 and 1796, there were three dukes of Savoy called Victor-Amédée. Victor-Amédée III opposed the Revolution, and consequently his duchy was invaded by the French revolutionary army.'

'So what?' said Adamsberg, sounding tired.

'So nothing. But it tickled me that we're dealing with a Victor and an Amédée.'

'Oh please, Danglard,' said Adamsberg, detaching another burr from his trousers, 'don't get in the habit of saying something without good reason. Or we'll never get very far together.'

'OK, understood,' said Danglard, after a pause.

Well, Adamsberg was right, he thought as he pushed the door. His influence was subtle, like rising flood water, and it's true that he should watch out. And keep away from the slippery banks of his river.

XII

ADAMSBERG HAD KEPT JUSTIN BACK TO MONITOR THE REPORTS coming in from Le Creux. They were on a speakerphone and Justin could use a computer keyboard faster than Adamsberg, who was a two-finger typist.

'The dead man married the irresistible Adélaïde twenty-six years ago,' Mordent told them in his flat voice. 'But their *son* only came to live with them when he was five years old. The boy's arrival surprised everyone else. They learned that he had been placed in some specialised home for the first few years, because of psycho-motor problems. That wasn't the term they used, but it's what they meant. That the little boy wasn't "normal" in some sense.'

'But Amédée has almost no memory of that time, or of the institution,' came the deeper voice of Retancourt. 'He can just remember some ducks having their heads chopped off, that's all.'

'What?' asked Justin, looking up, pushing back a stray lock of blond hair, which made him look like a model schoolboy from the thirties. 'You did say "ducks"? Not "bugs" or something?'

'Ducks,' Retancourt said firmly. 'Heads chopped off.'

'Guillotine,' Adamsberg murmured.

'Commissaire,' said Retancourt, 'with respect, that's what people do to ducks. Cut their heads off. Perfectly normal on a farm.'

'It does sound more like a farm than an institution,' Justin remarked.

'Perhaps it was one of those places where they have animals around for therapy,' said Mordent. 'It's quite fashionable. Contact with animals, responsibility, little tasks in the farmyard, feeding them, changing their water.'

'For a child, chopping duck's heads off isn't a "little farmyard task", is it?' said Adamsberg.

'Perhaps he just saw it happen by chance. And in any case, he was a disturbed little boy. Perhaps he still is.'

'What else does Amédée remember?'

'A cold bed, and a woman shouting. That's about it.'

'Any other children with him?'

'He remembers one big boy, who took him for walks, and he idolised him. Probably one of the helpers. The family doctor lives in Versailles, so I'm going there now with Veyrenc. Retancourt is going to tackle Pelletier, looks a tricky one.'

Danglard was calling on the other line.

'The lawyer was in Versailles, I've just left him.'

'They did everything in Versailles, these people.'

'Well, it would be a better place to go than the village of Malvoisine. Given the kind of sums we're talking about. Masfauré had gone for a large legal firm. Very elegant building, old panelling, Aubusson tapestries on the wall, there's a hunting scene with a few delicious, slightly risqué details, that –'

'Danglard, please,' Adamsberg cut him off.

'Sorry. The lawyer hasn't finished calculating the value of the whole estate but it's getting on for 50 million euros. No less! There was even more before, but Henri Masfauré had put a lot of his own money into his research into pumping CO_2 out of the atmosphere and the reconversion of residues. The prototype factory that was supposed to test the technology is nearing completion, it's down in the west in the Creuse *département*. A philanthropist and a very important scientist, according to the lawyer. There's a will, made a year and five months ago.'

'Go ahead,' said Adamsberg, pulling a crumpled cigarette out of his jacket pocket. Although in theory he didn't smoke, the commissaire abstracted cigarettes from his son's packets, and stuffed them into his pockets loose, where they twisted and fell to bits, as they enjoyed their new life of freedom.

'Everything goes to his son Amédée, on condition he gets the factory finished and sees that it starts working. There's a legacy of a hundred thousand euros to Victor, and five hundred thousand to Céleste.'

'I can understand in Céleste's case,' Adamsberg said, 'but it's unusual to leave as much as a hundred thousand to your secretary. One wonders what he'd done to deserve a sum like that.'

'No, commissaire, it's just that these people don't view money the way you and I do. But they're certainly large enough sums to be a motive to cause his death.'

'To kill Masfauré, maybe, but not Gauthier, the maths teacher in Paris.'

'Unless,' said Danglard. 'Perhaps the idea was to commit a previous murder, accompanied by the same cryptic sign, to throw people off the scent. In which case, we'd have a classic case of a red herring.'

'Shall I keep on noting all this?' asked Justin. 'It's not the report now, just speculation.'

Justin's meticulousness was precious, you could always count on the excellence of his minute-taking, though the downside of that was his extreme pedantry.

'Yes, Justin, get it all down,' Adamsberg ordered. 'But how could Victor or Céleste have known about the existence of Alice Gauthier?'

'Well, Victor had known in essence that she existed, ever since the Icelandic events. And Céleste, well, she's had every opportunity of poking around the house, so she could have chanced on some kind of correspondence between Alice and Masfauré. Then if the cops conclude they both committed suicide, fine. And if they start going off on the Iceland trail, even better. But if not, there's always the weird sign, invented to throw us off the scent. A well-planned sequence, anticipating what the logic of any police inquiry might be.'

'It's possible.'

'I agree,' Justin put in. 'Though I won't write that down,' he said to himself.

'But how could they have known about the will?' Adamsberg went on.

'There was a copy of it in Masfauré's house,' said Danglard. 'Which hasn't been found. I'll ring off, commissaire, because I need to book our tables at the inn. By the way, I found out why this place is called the Hollow. Nothing to do with our inquiry but it's interesting. Oh, sorry, forgot Pelletier, very important. He doesn't get anything. Or rather he doesn't *now*. In a previous will, he got fifty thousand. And according to the lawyer, who's a stickler for form, but with an easy manner – this lawyer behaves as if he's an old aristocrat, but actually, I think the "de" in his name is invented, because all the Des Mar . . .'

'Danglard!'

'I didn't note that,' said Justin, non-committally.

'Yes, well, Pelletier gets nothing at all.' Danglard picked up the thread. 'Because Masfauré suspected he was exaggerating the prices of horses and their stud value. If you have a stallion from a good line, it can be worth thousands of euros and that's not counting the ones with really illustrious ancestry.'

'No, don't count them, please, commandant.'

'Masfauré suspected that Pelletier was in cahoots with the dealers, preparing false accounts and splitting the difference in cash.'

'That must have been what Céleste suspected too,' said Adamsberg.

'No doubt. And if it's true, you can just see how much money he could have made. So Masfauré changed his will.'

'This lawyer whose name doesn't really start with a "de", does he know why Masfauré didn't take Pelletier to court over this?'

'He wanted to complete his investigations before taking any action. Pelletier is an absolutely irreplaceable stud master, he could do anything he liked with the horses, make them dance on one leg by whistling a waltz. So Masfauré wanted to be quite certain of his facts before getting rid of him. That gives Pelletier a good motive for murder too.'

'What's Voisenet doing now?'

'He's looking into the wife who died in Iceland.'

'Put him on the line.'

'That is, er, he's actually just made a quick visit to the tower of haunted spirits.'

'Excellent,' said Adamsberg. 'At least then we'll know one thing for sure in this fog of uncertainty.'

'Yes, whether they're jackdaws or hooded crows,' Danglard agreed.

All that evening, Adamsberg pored over his colleagues' reports. He hadn't put the heating on, so he lit a fire in the grate after supper. Feet up on one of the firedogs on the hearth, with his laptop – or *tölva* – resting on his thigh, he went through the information that Justin was emailing to him from home, or rather his parents' house, where he was still living at the age of thirty-eight. Since he had no household of his own to look after, Justin was always available for consultation, unless he happened to be out playing poker.

Noël had opted to use kid gloves when he began questioning Pelletier about the real stud value of his horses, thinking he would get a result by roundabout questions. But Retancourt, not one to use kid gloves as a rule, had waded straight in, saying there was some talk that he had been cheating on his employer. Pelletier had flown into a rage, and in a reflex action had hurled himself at the large policewoman, not realising that he would make less impression on her than on a concrete pillar. Retancourt had angled her shoulder and thrown him to the ground without striking a blow. Her rough childhood among four brothers who liked fighting had enabled little Violette to acquire formidable combat skills. But once he was on the ground, Pelletier had whistled in a special way and two aggressive stallions had come racing towards them, panting through their nostrils. Back on his feet, Pelletier got the horses to stop fifty centimetres short of the two officers, and they had understood very clearly that these huge males, with powerful hooves, might charge again at a sign from their keeper. Noël had pulled his gun.

'Stop right there!' Pelletier ordered. 'That horse is worth half a million. More'n *you'd* be able to pay for in compensation, eh, you piddling little cop!'

This last exchange had been reported by Retancourt, not by Noël. Adamsberg could imagine how furious and humiliated that had made Noël feel. No one had ever called him a piddling little cop before.

'See, if *you* died,' Pelletier went on, eyeing Noël like a horse dealer sizing him up, 'the compensation'd be ten thousand, mebbe, and that's being generous. *She'd* be worth more,' he said, pointing at Retancourt and spitting on the ground. 'Ten times as much. I do *not* cheat on the sales, so get that into your thick heads. I hear any more about that, I'll sue.'

As for Amédée, the commissaire could now better understand the nervous, withdrawn but sensitive nature of the young man, who had been ready to run away. And his possible mental disturbance. He had been isolated for five years from birth. In a 'cold bed'. Cold, in some luxury psychiatric establishment? Had he had regular visits from his parents? There was no way of knowing. According to the family doctor in Versailles, Amédée suffered not only from persistent chest infections and earaches, which were indications of stress, but from some form of 'repression'. That is, he had deliberately repressed any memory of his early years. 'Too painful?' Adamsberg scribbled. 'Abused? Abandoned.' And he added: '*Decapitated* ducks.'

Amédée's mother, irresistible though she might have been, did not have a good reputation in the neighbourhood, whether Malvoisine,

Sombrevert or even Versailles. Opinion on that score was unanimous, apart from the mayor of Sombrevert, who was counting on Amédée's vote. There were sixteen separate witness statements, all in agreement, and expressed in every kind of register – from the mayor's deputy, who had taken coffee with Estalère: 'Let's say she acted as if she was to the manor born', to the lady at the dry cleaner's, whose words were 'thought she was Lady Muck', Justin reported. Other descriptions were 'built like a Greek goddess', 'oh, she looked down on other people', 'you never got a please or thank you out of her'. She was seductive all right, but a gold-digger, 'who didn't look after her kid at all', 'lucky for him Céleste was there'. She was interested in money most of all, 'tight with her money, she was', and 'never had enough of it, poor Monsieur Henri'. As for the high society of Versailles, they had always regarded her as a vulgar upstart.

Voisenet and Kernorkian had managed, from a few letters discovered in boxes in the attic, to reconstruct the circles Marie-Adélaïde Masfauré (née Pouillard) had moved in before her wealthy marriage. The picture was incomplete but seemed to point to working-class parents without resources, of whom she had quickly become ashamed, her early days employed at a Paris hairdresser's, then an apprenticeship as a make-up artist, followed by a modest stage career. Her beauty and combative vivacity had taken her to the casting couch of at least three theatre directors.

Adamsberg looked up at his son, who was padding quietly about in the kitchen.

'Danglard's coming round,' he said, which immediately brought a smile to Zerk's face, and prompted him to fetch another glass from the sideboard.

'Isn't he staying out there with the others?'

'No, Danglard sleeps back home with his children. In his lair.'

'I thought the children had left the nest.'

'Even so. He sleeps near their beds.'

The gate squeaked and Zerk opened the door.

'He's stopping in the garden,' he said, 'and Lucio's offering him a beer.'

The commandant had put a bottle of white wine down in the grass and was chatting to Lucio, the old Spaniard who shared a small communal garden with Adamsberg. Worldly-wise and ceremonious, Lucio always drank two beers outside in the evening, whatever the weather. Then he pissed against the beech tree before going inside, and this was the only point of disagreement between the two neighbours. Adamsberg claimed he was destroying the base of the tree, while Lucio argued that he was providing it with beneficial nitrates. Danglard had sat down alongside the old man on a wooden packing case under the tree, and did not look as if he would budge any time soon. Adamsberg took two stools outside, followed by Zerk, who was carrying a glass for the commandant, two beers wedged between his fingers, and a corkscrew. When Adamsberg had first encountered his previously unknown son aged twenty-eight, Zerk had called it a 'cork-hook', and used various other odd terms. Adamsberg had wondered whether this young man was intelligent and original, or, on the contrary, slow and limited. But as he sometimes wondered the same about himself, without letting it assume much importance, he had abandoned the enigma.

'How many cats have you got here now?' asked Danglard as some graceful shapes went past in the shadows.

'The little one has grown up,' Adamsberg said, 'and she's very fertile. Six or seven, I don't know, I get them mixed up, except for the mother who comes and rubs against my legs.'

'Well, you brought her into the world so she's attached to you, *hombre*,' said Lucio. 'We've had two litters, there are nine of them now. Pedro, Manuel, Esperanza,' he started, counting on his fingers.

As Lucio went on listing them, Adamsberg passed a sheaf of papers across to Danglard.

'I just printed out these reports. Seems she was a greedy wife more than a mother. And we know nothing at all about the first five years in the life of little Amédée.'

'. . . Carmen and Francesco,' Lucio concluded, having accounted for all the cats.

'Céleste only entered the picture when the boy was five,' said Danglard, reaching out his glass to Zerk.

'Where did *she* come from?'

'A village near Sombrevert, with good references. Reading between the lines, because she doesn't like to speak ill of people, she let us understand that the boy would never have received any real affection, or comforts, even material ones, if it hadn't been for her. The mother waltzed off whenever she felt like it, to Paris or elsewhere, while the father worked from dawn to dusk in his study. Everything depended on Céleste, right up to today. One way and another, she said, apart from the natural shock and sorrow, his mother's death didn't actually change Amédée's daily life, he was a teenager by then.'

'How did Amédée react when he was told his father didn't commit suicide?'

'He was relieved that he couldn't have been responsible. But he immediately realised that he'd make "a fucking good suspect", as he put it. He's expecting to be arrested at any moment. Everything seems to have come to a standstill out there, except for Victor, who's sorting out Masfauré's papers and Pelletier, who's carrying on working, because murder or no murder, the horses have to be fed and watered. Amédée is mooching around the woods and fields, with burrs sticking to his trousers. Now and then he sits down on a bench and pulls them off.'

'Point in his favour.'

'Not what I think,' said Danglard, 'he just has no idea what to do with his ten fingers.'

'That,' Lucio interrupted, 'is an existential question. What should you do with your ten fingers? I've only got five, but I still ask myself that. At my age.'

Lucio had lost an arm as a child during the Spanish Civil War, and this amputation had left him with an ongoing, unabated and recurrent obsession. Just before the incident, he had been bitten by a spider and hadn't finished scratching the itch. For Lucio, 'finishing scratching' had become a determining concept in an individual's lifetime behaviour. You have to finish scratching an itch, or you will suffer from it all your life long.

'Amédée only cheers up when Victor stops working and comes to see him,' Danglard went on. 'Amédée doesn't seem to have any other anchor in his life besides Céleste and Victor. No girlfriends. Victor protects him, that's obvious. You'd think he'd done it all his life. Every couple of hours, he leaves the study and goes for a stroll with him.'

'What about Victor himself?'

'Well, like everyone else, he's wondering who killed his employer. And Alice Gauthier. Voisenet dared to suggest it could be Amédée, and Victor's brows came down like thunder and he turned his back on Voisenet, as if restraining himself from hitting him. Then he came back and said. "For Christ's sake it must be the Iceland business. What *else* could it be? I told you about that mad killer! Who else can it be?" Voisenet replied rather tactlessly that there was no way of identifying the man he meant, or any other members of the group. "So that's why you're homing in on Amédée, is it," Victor said, 'because you can't find anyone else? So you need a scapegoat." Talking of wildlife, they're hooded crows. Voisenet was disappointed, he'd been hoping for ravens. I think it was because of the tower that he was a bit off form when he was doing the questioning. But he did take the trouble to put a ring of bird droppings round the cabin without Céleste noticing.'

'Good. At least that's something we've accomplished.'

'This Amédée,' Lucio butted in, 'is he the one who says he can't remember anything about the first five years of his life?'

'Yes.'

'Not surprising then if he looks at his fingers as if they don't belong to him. He hasn't finished scratching, that's all.'

'It's more that he doesn't *want* to scratch, Lucio,' said Adamsberg. 'He's deliberately wiped out all his memories, he's incapable of telling us where he was, who with, or why.'

'He must have had a really nasty bite then.'

'The suggestion is he was in some kind of care home, and not a cheap one, because his father was very rich.'

'Care home, my foot,' said Lucio. 'He was put somewhere where he went through hell. You have to make him scratch, that's the only way. Where was he as a kid? The parents must have known. Means the pair of them were assholes. Good motive for killing, isn't it? Bang, bang, a nice clean shot in the head, debt paid.'

'Lucio, someone else was murdered, a woman in Paris, and she's got no connection with Amédée's childhood.'

'At the same time?'

'Day before.'

'Well, that's just to put you off the scent. If you've got dogs chasing after you, chuck them a piece of meat and carry on.'

'That's what I said this afternoon,' said Danglard, 'though I put it differently. At any rate, Henri Masfauré wasn't a slave-driver to Céleste. Not only did he leave her half a million, but it was *her* choice absolutely to go and live in that cabin in the woods, no question about that. Amédée explained to Estalère. By the end of the day, Estalère was the only one he would talk to.'

'So what's this bit about, *hombre*?'

This was the first time that Lucio had called him *hombre*, which Danglard took to be an honour. He had rather thought the old man tended not to rate too highly his roundabout way of talking.

'She'd had her eye on the cabin for a long time – it's an old apple store. But she waited until Amédée was twelve before she asked the boss. Every evening of her life – I'm trying to report her words as Amédée told it – when she went to sleep, she would "go off to her cabin", to chase away her troubles. A make-believe cabin in her head, of course, she said, surrounded by dangers, the wind, the storm, wild beasts. She imagined it over and over again, the cabin, never finding total security or the perfect cabin, until she found this old hut in the woods. Masfauré refused at first, he said it was too dangerous. But that was exactly what she liked about it. No feeling of security unless there was a threat of danger. She never sleeps so well as when the rain is beating on the roof and the wild boar is rubbing against the wooden walls.'

'It must have changed when Marc arrived, then?'

'To some extent. He sleeps outside and protects her. She took him in as a stray orphan, starving and whining outside her door.'

'*Who* was this that was whining?' asked Lucio.

'A young wild boar,' Adamsberg explained. 'She called him Marc. And he defends her better than a regiment of soldiers.'

'The cabin's a womb substitute,' said Lucio. 'Once we're out of it, idiots that we are, we just have to fight, as we used to say in Spain, you need to get yourself a new one.'

'Out of what?' asked Zerk.

Adamsberg asked his son for a cigarette, possibly to cover up his naivety, and muttered to him quickly: 'The mother's womb.'

'Well, in that case,' said Zerk, giving his father a light for the cigarette, 'we should all be living in cabins.'

'We all certainly try to,' Lucio agreed. 'So this woman, Céleste, did she have some problem with *her* mother?'

'They quarrelled when she was a youngster,' said Danglard. 'But the mother died before they could be reconciled.'

'There you are then, what did I say?' remarked Lucio, opening a bottle of beer with his teeth. 'She couldn't bury the quarrel, she hasn't finished scratching. And that takes you straight to a log cabin. You shouldn't try to winkle her out of it, that woman, no way.'

The mother cat came to rub up against Adamsberg's leg, picking up a few little burrs as she did. Adamsberg stroked her head, which sent her to sleep for a few minutes. He had the same effect on his very young son, Tom. Adamsberg's fingers, like his voice, seemed to contain some soothing and soporific quality, more effective than any log cabin. But he wasn't about to try and scratch Céleste's head.

'Right, I'm off to my own cabin,' he said, standing up. 'Time to go, it's coming on to rain. Lucio, don't piss against the tree.'

'I'll do as I please, *hombre*.'

XIII

COMMISSAIRE BOURLIN WOKE ADAMSBERG AT SIX IN THE MORNING.

'I've got another suicide on my hands, commissaire. Got a pen handy? 15th arrondissement again, or it wouldn't be on my plate.'

'Bourlin, are you going to call me every time someone dies in your division?'

'417 rue de Vaugirard, third floor, door code 1789B.'

'1789! Ah, the Revolution, always the Revolution!'

'What are you muttering?'

'Nothing, I'm trying to get dressed with one hand.'

'The code doesn't work anyway, they don't use it.'

'Signs of a break-in?'

'No. Perfect suicide. Well, I should say ghastly suicide, Japanese-style, knife in the belly. Probable motives: he ran an art publishing house, went bust, lots of debts, financial ruin.'

'Any prints on the knife?'

'Only his own.'

'So why am I putting my clothes on for this, Bourlin?'

'Because on his bookshelf there are three books on Iceland. And he wasn't a big traveller. Something on Rome, a map of London, a guide to the Camargue, that's it. But *three* on Iceland. So I looked for the sign. Well, I sweated blood trying to find it, believe me, because white on white, it was't easy, you had to be looking for it.'

'Get to the point.'

'The sign's there all right, carved with the tip of the knife on a skirting board, right down by the floor. But done recently, there are flakes of paint on the ground.'

'Tell me the address again, I wasn't listening properly.'

The man had been killed in his kitchen, which was now awash with blood. Stepping platforms had been brought in for the police to walk across. The crime scene people had finished, and they were, with some difficulty, removing the body. The victim was small, but overweight and heavy, and their gloves slipped on the blood-streaked dressing gown.

'What time?' Adamsberg asked.

'2.05 this morning, exactly,' Bourlin replied. 'The neighbour heard an awful cry and the sound of someone falling. He called us. Look, here's the sign.'

Adamsberg crouched down and opened his notebook to copy it.

'Yes, that's it. But it looks smaller, more hesitant.'

'Yes, I noticed that. You think someone's imitating it?'

'Bourlin, for now we're floating around like bubbles in the wind. Better not think too hard.'

'As you like.'

'Have you got photos of the victim on your laptop?'

'In my witch that counts? Yes. Victor might be able to identify him. His name is Jean Breuguel, B R E U G U E L. Not like Bruegel the Elder, as Danglard would say, just Breuguel.'

'OK,' said Adamsberg who had no idea what Bourlin was talking about. 'Send the pictures to Victor. Explain to him in brief what's happened. Here's his email address,' he said, passing his notebook over.

A notebook full of sketches, either in the margins or taking up whole pages, Bourlin noticed, as he prepared to send the photographs to Le Creux.

'Did you do those? All the drawings?'

Adamsberg was looking down at the platform, bending under Bourlin's weight, surrounded by a sea of blood.

'Yeah,' he said with a shrug.

'That's Victor, there, under his address?'

'Yes.'

'And that's Amédée, Céleste, Pelletier,' said Bourlin, riffling through the pages.

'By the way, Masfauré had written Pelletier out of his will, on suspicion of cheating over the price of horses for the stud.'

But Bourlin wasn't listening, instead turning over the pages of the notebook, suspended twenty centimetres over the pool of congealing blood. Finally, he typed Victor's email address into his phone, and handed the notebook back to Adamsberg, looking suspicious.

'Did you do a picture of me too?'

Adamsberg smiled and turned to the first page.

'Actually, this was done from memory,' he said, 'on our first visit to Le Creux.'

'Oh, you haven't made me look bad at all,' said Bourlin, who was actually rather pleased with the image of himself in the drawing.

'Here,' said Adamsberg, tearing out the sheet, and handing it to him. 'Keep it if you want.'

'Could you do my kids?'

'Not now, Bourlin.'

'Yes, but one day?'

'Yes, OK, one day when we all go back to have a meal at the Auberge du Creux.'

'Right, the pictures have gone off,' said Bourlin, closing his laptop. 'Come and look at the books on Iceland. They're in here,' he said as they went into the sitting room. 'I put them on the coffee table. You can pick them up, there weren't any prints on them.'

Adamsberg shook his head.

'No, naturally, because these are brand new. All three of them. No dust, no pages turned down, impeccable condition.'

He opened one of the books and sniffed it.

'They even *smell* new.'

'Wait a minute,' said Bourlin, sitting down beside Adamsberg on a ramshackle grey sofa. 'Wait a minute. You mean he's *put* these books here to send us chasing off on the Iceland trail? But because they're brand new, it's a false scent?'

'Exactly. We were wrong, Bourlin.'

'He slipped up, then. He should have bought some second-hand ones.'

'Didn't have time, maybe. Three murders in a week, think about it, he's moving fast. But the books did at least make us look in one direction, and we found the sign.'

'But why is this wretched sign everywhere, if he wants us to believe these are suicides?'

'He knows we don't think they're suicides any more. Or else he doesn't really want us to. A murderer who signs his work is bursting with pride, just banal pop psychology, as Retancourt would say. Some day or other, when we've closed the files, he'd have made it clear that these were indeed murders, committed by him, his work. So that these deaths are not consigned to the oubliettes of the tower in Le Creux.'

'But perhaps the sign hasn't been drawn for us, but so that the other people should know about it. The rest of the Icelandic group?'

'But look, we think this one here never set foot in Iceland, Bourlin.'

'Shit, no, I forgot,' said Bourlin, shaking his head. 'And this time the sign's a bit different too. But who else would know the link between the first two murders and the sign? Victor and Amédée – and only them. You showed them the drawing.'

The two men thought for a moment in silence. That is, Adamsberg was dreaming, but Bourlin was thinking and indeed ruminating, turning his thoughts over twenty times in his head, while he blew his nose, still affected by his spring cold.

'Unless it's not the same killer,' said Adamsberg. 'Unless there's someone who knows about the other two murders and the sign, and used them in order to commit this one. Then slipped in the books on Iceland. But wasn't very used to drawing the sign.'

'You're thinking that could be Victor?'

'Yes, could be. In order to lift any suspicion from Amédée, who will surely have a cast-iron alibi for last night. But who could watch Victor coming and going? At night, Céleste is in the woods, and Pelletier's a long way off, in the stables.'

Bourlin clasped his head between his two enormous hands.

'Not that I want to dodge out of anything, Adamsberg, but I wouldn't be at all sorry to hand all of this over to you. I'm completely lost.'

'That's because you haven't slept.'

'You're not lost then?'

'I'm used to it, it's not the same.'

'I'll get the Thermos.'

Bourlin poured them both some coffee in cut-glass goblets, the only receptacles he could find without going back into the kitchen.

'Used to what?' he asked.

'Used to being lost. Bourlin, just imagine you're walking on a beach, with sand and rock pools.'

'Yes, OK.'

'And you see a lot of seaweed all tangled together, making up a sort of Gordian knot. A big heap, maybe a very big one.'

'Yes.'

'Well, that's what we've got here.'

'A heap of *shit*, you mean.'

'Alas, no. Is there any sugar?'

'No, it's in the kitchen, I don't dare go in there to fetch sugar. Question of respect, Adamsberg.'

'I don't mean the sugar, I mean the ball of shit, that's what the "alas" was about. Because shit is a coherent kind of matter, easily analysed, whereas a tangle of seaweed is made up of thousands of different strands, all coming from dozens of different kinds of algae.'

The two men drank their unsweetened coffee, looking tired. It felt sad, in this small sitting room as the pale dawn came up: the surroundings looked as if they had remained unchanged for twenty years. Barely illuminated by fitful gleams of sun, the room was redolent of decline and neglect. It felt odd, what was more, to be drinking coffee out of cut-glass goblets.

'Take a look at your *tölva* to see if Victor has replied,' said Adamsberg without moving, plunged deep as he was in the old sofa pitted with cigarette burns.

Bourlin had three goes at typing his password, as the keys were small for his large fingers.

'You can add another strand to your seaweed,' he announced finally. 'Victor says he's never seen this one before. And he's supposed to be, what did Danglard call him, a hypermnasiac?'

'Hypermnesiac I think. Not sure though.'

'So it's like you said. This Breuguel wasn't one of the group. But someone wants us to think he *was*.'

'Have you established how the killer got in?'

'The kitchen door opens on to the service staircase,' Bourlin explained, 'but in particular on to the rubbish chute. Every night, this is according to the downstairs neighbour, Breuguel went out on the landing to throw his bin bag down the chute before he went to bed. All the killer had to do was wait on the landing and follow him into the kitchen to attack him.'

'And to know his habits.'

'Or to have watched him for a while to find them out. Like the others, this man must have been likely to talk. Ruin, depression, factors that would combine to make him confess.'

'Confess what?'

'About Iceland.'

'But this guy never *went* to Iceland,' said Adamsberg.

'Oh shit,' said Bourlin, plunging his head in his hands again.

'It's like I said. The tangle of seaweed. Hard to escape. What time is it?'

'You're wearing two watches. Why don't you look at them?'

'Because they don't work.'

'So why wear them, and anyway why two of them?'

'I don't know, it goes back a long way. But can't you tell me the time?'

'Eight fifteen.'

Bourlin poured more coffee into the glasses.

'Still no sugar,' he moaned in a desperate tone, as if the lack of sugar summed up the alarming state of the investigation so far. 'And I'm hungry.'

'You can't go nicking food from the kitchen, you said so yourself, Bourlin. You don't rob the dead, when it means treading in their blood.'

'Well, fuck that.'

Adamsberg hoisted himself out of the old sofa and walked round the shabby sitting room. Bourlin had returned with some sugar and a can of ravioli, which he was eating cold from the tip of his penknife.

'Feeling better?' Adamsberg asked.

'Yeah, but this stuff's disgusting.'

'What we have to do,' Adamsberg started slowly, and almost scientifically, 'is to imagine that this big tangle we were talking about' – and he spread his arms wide – 'is even bigger than we thought.'

'How big?'

'Big as you.'

The two men considered this possibility in silence. Then Bourlin attacked the ravioli once more.

'In that case, we're fucked,' he announced. 'We'll never find the killer.'

'That's quite possible. When someone sends thirty billiard balls down towards you, it's hard to spot the right one. The one you need to start.'

Adamsberg took a bit of ravioli from Bourlin's knife.

'What do you think of this cold ravioli?' Bourlin asked.

'You're right, it's disgusting.'

'Well, that's one thing we've established.'

'And the birds in the tower, they're hooded crows.'

'Two things, then.'

'So faced with this situation,' said Adamsberg, coming to a halt, 'we have to throw our own billiard ball into the game. However futile it might be. Go back to the old tried and tested methods.'

'Put out a press release, you mean?'

'Yes, press and social networks. It'll go round the world in less than six hours.'

'To tell the killer that we know these are not suicides?'

'He'll certainly appreciate that. But we shouldn't try to provoke a character who's obsessed with the guillotine.'

'If it is a guillotine.'

'If it is. I'm not forgetting, Bourlin. We should be concerned with protecting the surviving members of the Icelandic trip. Now that he's opened the floodgates, we can't be sure he isn't already thinking of eliminating them, one after another, to have done with them once and for all.'

'Are you pulling my leg? You said we should *forget* about Iceland. Because of this man and his new books.'

'And what if Victor's lying? What if he really *did* know him?'

'So we go back to the Iceland business?'

'How can we afford to ignore anything, when we have no idea where we are with this?'

'Do we mention the sign in the press release?'

'No,' said Adamsberg, after a moment. 'We'll keep that to ourselves for now. We'll publish something along the lines of . . . oh, Danglard will draft it – "Three murders in a week". With names and photos.'

'Three?' asked Bourlin. 'And what if number three has absolutely no connection with Iceland?'

'Too bad. What we say is: "The police have reason to believe that the French people who were involved in the dramatic events in Iceland, etc., etc., might be at risk from this killer. Anyone who feels they might be concerned should report as soon as possible to a gendarmerie or police station, for the sake of their own protection, etc., etc." With the address and telephone number and email of our squad.'

Bourlin finished his impromptu breakfast, crushed the can in his huge paw, closed the laptop, and hauled himself up out of the sofa by leaning on the arm.

'So send down the ball,' he said.

XIV

BY TEN THIRTY, ADAMSBERG, UNSHAVEN AND WITH HIS T-SHIRT
on inside out, had finished telling members of the squad the circumstances of the third murder. And that the whisky glass found under
Céleste's floor contained no suspicious substance – which might exon-
erate her, unless there was some secret love story, as Danglard had
suggested. She might have wanted to keep the last trace of Henri
Masfauré's lips.

The press release had been composed and Lieutenant Froissy would
be responsible for circulating it any minute. Almost all the officers had
come back this morning from their mission in the Yvelines.

The council chamber was emptying when Adamsberg caught
Froissy by her sleeve.

'Lieutenant,' he said, 'after putting out the release, can you find me
something to eat? I haven't had a bite since last night.'

'I'll do that right away,' said Froissy with concern.

Food was Hélène Froissy's weakness, some said a pathological one.
Far from stuffing herself as Bourlin did, Froissy ate little and remained
slim and elegant, but was seized with panic that she would not be able
to find food when she needed it. The filing cabinet in her office had
been converted into a kind of survival cache in case of war, and members of the squad knew they could go and forage there for something

to eat if they were working overtime. These depredations scared Froissy enough to prompt her to replace them immediately, making up unconvincing excuses to leave the station and go shopping. The commissaire's pangs of hunger reflected her own anguish as if in a mirror. She would have dropped anything to feed someone else. Despite this painful obsession, Froissy was a valuable member of the team, by far their best computer expert, ahead of Mercadet. But Mercadet just now was asleep upstairs in the coffee-machine room.

'It's not urgent,' Adamsberg assured her. 'Do the release first. Quick as you can. Then while I eat, you can tell me anything you've found out about Alice Gauthier.'

Within ten minutes, the expeditious Froissy had put out the press release which was now on its way round the world, and brought some rations for Adamsberg to eat at his desk. They came on a plate with a knife and fork, since the lieutenant did not neglect the proper way to serve food. Adamsberg guessed why there was no fresh bread. Froissy had been afraid that if she took the time to go out to a baker's, she would find the commissaire fainting from starvation. An eating emergency always came first.

'So go ahead,' said Adamsberg, cutting himself a slice of pâté.

'That one's wild boar pâté with armagnac. I've also got some thin-sliced Parma ham, in a packet, so it's not so good, or some smoked duck, or – '

'It's perfect, Froissy,' said Adamsberg holding up his hand. 'Now tell me. Did you find out any more about Alice Gauthier's visitor, the one on Tuesday 7 April, the day *after* Amédée called?'

'The neighbour thinks it was the same person both times, because he heard that Dédé in the name again. And it was the same time of day too, when she would be alone. But he can't swear to that.'

'And what do Gauthier's colleagues say about her?'

'I saw two of them and the head. When she got back from that Iceland trip, they all greeted her as a sort of heroine, but she wouldn't have any of it. She refused all their commiserations. Like we already knew, she was a tough cookie. She insisted they never raise the subject, and they obeyed. They didn't know anything about her private life. One of her colleagues thought she was a lesbian, but she wasn't sure, not that it matters anyway. Nothing from that, then. I asked the head if there were perhaps any of her former pupils who had a grudge against her and might have taken revenge. But he said that even if they *had* had a row with her, they wouldn't step out of line.'

'Even the drug dealers she pursued?'

'Same thing apparently. They were all young, underage, and they got off lightly, not even suspended sentences. You don't go killing someone years later on account of something like that. No, the only hot event, well, cold event, in her life is this Icelandic business.'

'She didn't have some friend or confidante, man or woman, whom she might have spoken to about it, before she saw Amédée?'

'Nobody that we know of. The two colleagues say that after that drama, she became more reclusive. The woman they had seen sometimes meeting her from school disappeared. I guess that must have been her friend, the "environmental expert". So presumably they quarrelled. As for the twice-yearly dinners for the staff, she stopped coming to them. Her pupils' homework was always marked and returned next day, which suggests she didn't go out at night. The concierge in her building confirms that – she didn't go out or receive visitors. And then two years ago, she became ill. And stopped leaving the house altogether.'

'So that's a blank,' said Adamsberg. 'We've either got dead ends or a hundred contradictory theories that twist and turn and leave us more confused.'

'Don't worry, commissaire, the press release will get us out of this. When we manage to question all the survivors from Iceland, the fog will lift in ten minutes, like it did there.'

Adamsberg smiled. Froissy had a way of coming out with naively optimistic remarks, as if she were speaking to a child. Feed, reassure, comfort.

'Don't leave your computer, Froissy, don't miss a single message, I beg you.'

'Night and day, sir,' said Froissy, taking away the empty plate. 'I've arranged a targeted alert, in case there's any reply to the release.'

And she was indeed capable of carrying out instructions night and day. She would doze off in her armchair, waiting for the alert. A special alert tailored to a single message. Adamsberg didn't even know that existed in the 'witches that count'.

XV

AND NOW A PERIOD OF SILENCE, AT FIRST BEMUSED AND THEN anxious, gradually overcame the squad.

By the evening of the day the press release had gone out, not one of the surviving members of the Icelandic expedition had contacted anyone. Adamsberg had removed the last burrs from his trousers and was wandering from one room to another, surrounded by his puzzled officers, whose activities were slowing down from hour to hour, everyone waiting for Froissy to appear from her office and invigorate them. A small discussion group had gathered in the corridor.

'Even if they don't all go on to social networks,' said Voisenet, 'or even if none of them do, *someone* will have told them. A friend or a family member.'

'They're scared,' said Retancourt.

She was carrying over her arm the squad's large white cat, a shapeless creature that liked to rest like a folded towel, paws dangling, relaxed and confident. Retancourt was the favourite human of this cat, known as the Snowball, a 'ball' of eighty centimetres when at full stretch. She was on her way to feed it, that is to take it upstairs to its dish, since the cat – which was in perfect health – refused to walk upstairs on its own and eat, unless it had company. So you had to wait alongside it while it finished its meal, then carry it back down to its favourite perch on the warm photocopy machine.

'More afraid of the killer in the abstract than of being murdered tomorrow?'

'They're obeying the rule of silence. If they show up and talk to us, they'll be executed. So why trigger that? They think they're safe as long as they keep quiet.'

'After three deaths, you'd think one of them at least would be looking for refuge.'

'Victor was right when he said this guy frightened them out of their wits.'

'Ten years down the line?'

Adamsberg joined them.

'Yes, ten years down the line,' he agreed. 'And if he's got a hold like this over them, it must be because he doesn't let them forget. He must see them, or write to them. He's watching them and exerting constant pressure.'

'But why, in the end?' asked Mordent. 'This group met pretty much by accident one night at an inn, they don't know each other's full names. What could they say that would endanger him?'

'We might get an identikit of him, a profile,' suggested Voisenet. 'Some of them might know what kind of work he did. Or perhaps they actually know much more than we think.'

'You mean Victor?' asked Adamsberg.

'For example. He had no choice, he had to answer our questions. But perhaps he only told us the minimum. It would be too risky for him, and for the others, if he gave us any precise details about this man. Same goes for Amédée. Perhaps Alice Gauthier told him a lot more than he's let on. So he's keeping his mouth shut too, in order to survive.'

'What are we going to do?' asked Estalère, who was shaken by the squad's apparent paralysis.

'Feed the cat,' said Retancourt, going upstairs.

'Mercadet's asleep,' said Estalère, counting on his fingers, 'Danglard's having a drink, Retancourt's feeding the cat, Froissy's watching her screen. But what about the rest of us?'

Adamsberg shook his head. There wasn't a single strand of seaweed emerging from the tangle that one could pull without its breaking.

He spent the weekend more or less glued to his phone, with the sound turned up, so as not to miss a call from Froissy. But he had lost hope. They were all terrified, had gone to ground, and were keeping their mouths shut. As for police protection, no one believed in that. Who would think that having a couple of policemen outside your door would dissuade the murderer from reaching them? They knew what to expect, they knew *him*, they had seen him in action. And how long would protection last anyway? A couple of months? A year? Could the police mobilise fifty men to protect them for ten years? Of course not. The killer had warned them: even prison wouldn't prevent him from eliminating them. Themselves, their partners, children, brothers and sisters. So what was the point of turning up like idiots at a police station? They would be like lambs to the slaughter.

That is, if Iceland was the right lead . . .

It was warm, that Sunday evening. Adamsberg was pacing round the garden, mobile in hand, followed by the mother cat. As if he had been watching from the window, the old Spaniard joined him, carrying two bottles of beer.

'Not getting anywhere, eh, *hombre*?'

'And I'm not going to, Lucio. Three people die in a week, and others are in danger, four of them that I can't even identify. They will be murdered tomorrow, or in a year, or in twenty years, who knows?'

'Have you tried everything?'

'I think so. Even making a mistake.'

Because in the end, the press release would only have managed to put the killer on the alert. Without bringing in a single piece of evidence. It had been a blunder, and that was all. Perhaps he hadn't thought hard enough. Perhaps he hadn't turned his thoughts over seven times.

Lucio took the top off the bottle with his teeth.

'You'll ruin your teeth, opening bottles like that.'

'They're not my own teeth.'

'Yeah, right.'

'This isn't like an investigation where you just stop in the middle,' said Lucio. 'It's a story that's come to an end. It ought not to be itching.'

'It's not itching. But it's not over. Another day, another death. That's where I am now, waiting for someone to die and hoping he'll leave a clue. Which he won't, believe me.'

'There must be some pathway you haven't explored.'

'No, there aren't any pathways. Just a big tangle of seaweed. Dried up. No way through. And he's constructed all this. And just when you think you see a light, he confuses everything again, tangles it up.'

'He's enjoying himself, isn't he, this guy?'

Lucio scratched his empty arm in the air at the place where the spider had bitten.

'You're like this because there's been no woman in your life for months.'

'What do you mean "like this"?' said Adamsberg, opening his bottle of beer sharply by tapping the top against the beech tree.

'That damages the tree too. "Like this", moaning to everyone about your tangled seaweed.'

'And how do you know I don't have a woman in my life? I've always got a woman somewhere.'

'No you haven't.'

XVI

HE DIDN'T GET INTO WORK UNTIL 9.20 ON THE MONDAY MORNING.
A bad night, haunted by tangled seaweed. A dozen or so squad members were gathered round in reception, dominated by the large figure of Retancourt, who seemed to balance the composition of the whole, giving a high point to this rather pictorial scene. They were waiting, silent and tense, all eyes on the desk, as if Gardon, the duty officer, held in his hands either a providential gift or an explosive device. Gardon had never found himself the centre of attention before, and he was at a loss what to say or do. Everyone knew that Gardon was not the sharpest knife in the box, but no one was thinking of taking the letter out of his hands. That would have been to insult the man at the desk. He'd received it, it was his job to deal with it.

'It came by special courier,' he explained to the commissaire.

'What did, Gardon?'

'This letter. It's addressed to you, sir. But it's on thick paper, with fancy writing, it looks like a wedding invitation, and it says this on it –' and he pointed to the top left-hand corner of the envelope. 'I showed it to Lieutenant Veyrenc, and then they all came to take a look.'

Gardon handed the letter to Adamsberg on the flat of his hand, as if on a silver salver. Everyone else stayed stock-still, fixed to the spot, all eyes now on the commissaire. 'They know something you don't know,' Adamsberg said to himself, hearing Lucio's husky voice in his head.

The address had been written with a fountain pen, not in biro or felt pen, and the writing was almost calligraphical, while the envelope was a luxurious lined one. He hesitated to look at the top left-hand corner to decipher the name of the sender, in small print, which seemed to have turned his whole squad to stone.

ASSOCIATION FOR THE STUDY OF THE WRITINGS OF
MAXIMILIEN ROBESPIERRE.

His fingers tightened their grip on the envelope and he looked up.

'The guillotine!' whispered Veyrenc, summing up everyone's thoughts – everyone's single thought – as the others nodded, indicated agreement, shrugged their shoulders or stroked their chins.

Adamsberg's original interpretation of the sign as a guillotine had amused some people and irritated others; either way, they had considered it a distraction, a speculative wander off the beaten track, such as they had come to expect from him, and they had attached little importance to it – with the exception of Veyrenc. Adamsberg met his gaze, and saw that he was smiling.

'*Its shining blade must flash, as dawn begins to break,*' Veyrenc began in a low voice. '*The darkened planks stand tall, reaching to the sky. / The cold steel severs now the life that it will take / To view this deathly image is to prepare to die.*'

'Oh for heaven's sake, Veyrenc, get the metre right,' said Danglard.

Veyrenc shrugged. He had an ingrained habit, inherited from his grandmother, although she was no poet, of speaking in twelve-syllable alexandrines. Sometimes he got the syllabification wrong, which annoyed his learned colleague. Alone among the others, Danglard was now staring at the floor, shoulders hunched. Adamsberg could guess what he was thinking. His deputy was suffering again, both over his inability to decipher the sign and his sarcastic dismissal of Adamsberg's suggestion. Like the others, he hadn't wanted to view the 'deathly image'.

'Well, if it's a letter, we should open it, shouldn't we, sir?' asked Gardon, without meaning to be impertinent, and his words prosaically interrupted the moment of collective tension that had transported them all to some threatening, or perhaps poetic, universe.

'A paper knife,' said Adamsberg, holding out his hand. 'I don't want to tear this envelope. Council chamber,' he added, 'and fetch the others from their offices or the coffee room.'

'Mercadet's feeding the cat,' said Estalère.

'Well, get both Mercadet and the cat down here.'

'I'll go,' said Retancourt and nobody objected, since bringing down the Snowball, plus the lieutenant, who would be half asleep, was no easy feat, especially with the uneven step on the stairs that regularly tripped people up.

Adamsberg read the letter to himself, while Estalère busied himself serving coffees in the council chamber. Adamsberg was no good at reading out loud with fluency, and he stumbled over words or mispronounced them. Not that he was embarrassed at doing so in front of his colleagues, but he wanted to present them with a clear text, foreseeing that the prose written by this refined correspondent might not be the simplest in the world.

Froissy was last to enter the room, her eyes tired after three days and nights in front of her silent screen.

'We've got an answer finally, but it's come the old-fashioned way,' Adamsberg told her.

He waited for the noise of coffee spoons to die down before starting to read.

'This is from François Château, who is president of the Association for the Study of the Writings of Maximilien Robespierre.'

Monsieur le commissaire,

It was only late last night that I was informed by one of my colleagues of the communiqué your service has released, concerning three recent murders within a few days: those of Mme Alice Gauthier and of MM Henri Masfauré and Jean Breuguel. Your statement informed me of their names, which were unknown to me. However, I immediately recognised the photographs of all three unfortunate persons, which you had circulated to the press.

I regard it a duty of the utmost importance to inform you that all three of them were members of the above mentioned association, of which I have the honour to be president. Although they attended only occasionally, they had been present at our assemblies during the last seven to ten years – I fear I cannot be more precise – joining us once or twice a year, in early autumn or in the spring.

Their 'non-appearance' might not necessarily have concerned me unduly, before I read the contents of your statement to the press. We do not insist on regular attendance, and members are free to attend or leave meetings as they wish. Nevertheless, the coincidence of these three deaths, and the fact that they had participated in our study group, seemed to me a matter of legitimate anxiety. All the more so, since I have become aware of the conspicuous absence of another member, one who was far more assiduous in his attendance, and who appeared to have some kind of contact with the deceased. They certainly greeted each other on meeting, of that I am sure.

I must ask you to forgive the length of this letter, but I feel certain that you will readily understand my fear – to use an expression perhaps more associated with the police – that a murderer is 'at large' in our association, something which might lead to further tragic deaths, and would undoubtedly put an end to our activities.

*It is for these reasons that I would be extremely grateful if you could
agree to meet me without delay, if possible at 12.30 on the day that
you receive my letter. In view of the alarming nature of this affair, it
seems highly preferable that I should not be seen entering your headquarters. I should therefore be much obliged – while apologising for
these unusual conditions, dictated by circumstances – if you could go
to the Cafe des Joueurs, rue des Tanneurs, and introduce yourself to
the proprietor, mentioning my name. He will let you out through the
back door, into a lane leading to an underground car park. Taking
staircase 4, you will find yourself outside the rear entrance of a restaurant called La Tournée de la Tournelle, on the embankment of the
same name. I shall be sitting well inside the room, at an inconspicuous
table, reading a motorcycling magazine. I would be obliged if you
would bring this letter with you, so that I may be certain of your
identity.*

*With respect, monsieur le commissaire, I remain your faithful
servant, etc.*

Adamsberg had stumbled over only a few words – as who wouldn't? –
he asked himself. A disconcerted silence followed his reading of the
letter, possibly prompted more by its tone than by its content.

'Could we hear it again?' Danglard asked, noting the startled expression of Estalère, who was obviously quite lost.

Adamsberg automatically consulted his two non-functional
watches, asked someone else the time – it was 10.10 – and acquiesced,
without anyone objecting.

'So it's goodbye to Iceland,' Voisenet commented, as the commissaire put the letter down.

'Yeah, right,' said Noël. 'No chasing off after fish in the frozen north
for *you*. But if I've got this straight, we're on to some weird fish right
here. A tank full of nutty fans of Robespierre and the French
Revolution? That'll be worth a look!'

'Equally chilly climate,' said Voisenet.

'It wouldn't be correct to call them "*fans* of Robespierre",' Mordent intervened, with the condescending tone he regularly took towards Noël. 'They're historical researchers who study Robespierre's writings. That's a big distinction.'

'Yeah, well, even so,' Noël answered, 'they've got a thing about the guy, haven't they? This is a Serious Crime Squad. We're not in the business of defending mass murderers, are we?'

'That'll do, Noël,' said Adamsberg.

Noël shrugged back inside his heavy leather jacket, a virile armour that made him look twice as tough as he really was.

'Could it be a trap?' asked Justin, pointing at the letter. 'He's asking you to go through a real labyrinth to get to see him.'

'Amazing what people will get up to to lose the cops,' said Kernorkian.

'That's rather reassuring in one way,' Adamsberg remarked.

'Look,' said Justin, 'even if the lane and the car park aren't death traps, they're asking you to go and meet a guy who talks like a book, and we have no idea if he's telling the truth, or even if he really is the president of this association. It all sounds very conspiratorial, like an old-fashioned ambush.'

'I won't be going on my own, Justin. Danglard and Veyrenc will come along, they'll help me to work out the historical ingredients of this conversation.'

'Cook up the sauce, you mean,' said Voisenet.

'History is not a sauce,' protested Danglard.

'Apologies, commandant.'

'And as protection,' Adamsberg went on, 'because, indeed, you never know, I'll need five officers as backup. In other words, just you, Retancourt. Wait for us in the car park, and see us out. That's the riskiest moment. Then just go round through the main door of La Tournée de la Tournelle, like an ordinary customer coming for lunch. Make yourself inconspicuous.'

'That'll be difficult,' remarked Noël sarcastically.

'Not as difficult as for you, lieutenant,' said Adamsberg. 'Anyone can see from a hundred metres you're a gung-ho cop. Retancourt can look either threatening or reassuring when she feels like it.'

Adamsberg could read on Retancourt's calm features that Noël would pay for the insult; it wasn't the first time.

'This association *does* exist, I've just checked it out,' said Froissy who rarely took her eyes off her laptop, and who had missed the last exchanges. 'It was founded twelve years ago. But on its website, it doesn't give the names of its officers.'

'We can check that in the *Journal Officiel*, they're obliged to name them by law,' said Mercadet, 'I'll do it.'

'Their website is very sober,' Froissy continued. 'Reproductions of classic eighteenth-century engravings, a few texts by Robespierre, some photos of their meeting place, dates of the assemblies, and an address. It looks like an ancient guildhall or something.'

Danglard leaned over to look at the screen.

'Probably a former granary,' he said. 'The rib vaulting at the top of the windows suggests late eighteenth century. Where is it?'

'Northern Paris, on the edge of Saint-Ouen, 42 rue des Courts-Logis,' Froissy told him. 'They say they've got 687 enrolled members. They have a big debating chamber, with a speaker's rostrum, a cafe, a lounge and cloakrooms. Their meetings, which are either "ordinary" or "exceptional", take place once a week, on Monday evenings.'

'Tonight then,' said Adamsberg with a slight shudder.

'And tonight's an "exceptional" one,' Froissy added.

'What time?'

'Eight o'clock.'

'You'd have to have a lot of money to hire a place like that. Can you find out, Froissy? Who owns it, who rents it, etc. Don't forget that we've been strung along ever since the beginning of this case. We've been sent to Iceland, prepared for the guillotine, yes, but through a sign that was too obscure to work out at first sight. Then with the murder of Jean Breuguel, we're taken back to Iceland, *wrongly*, let me point out, and back again to the guillotine, but this time the sign has been drawn differently, more hesitantly. We've been bounced between apparent suicides and real murders, and between suspects: Amédée, Victor, Céleste, Pelletier, or the "killer on the island". And now we're faced with Robespierre. Or rather with a murderer inside this association, assassinating people who appear to be enthusiastic about Robespierre.'

'He's infiltrated their club, has he?' said Kernorkian.

'Or perhaps more than one person has infiltrated the assocation? Political murders, perhaps?'

'Or some personal vengeance,' suggested Voisenet. 'Because for Robespierrists, our three victims don't seem to have been very assiduous at the assemblies.'

'If the president is telling the truth.'

'And if he exists.'

'Or else,' said Mordent, 'like this guy says – what's his name?'

'Château, François Château.'

'Well, like this François Château suggests, someone is out to destroy the association. Who'd want to stay in a club when some crazy killer is eliminating its members? It would have to shut up shop in less than a year. The reason could be political, or it could be personal.'

'But then,' said Justin, looking down at his notes, 'why were we sent off at the start into that Icelandic business?'

'I don't know that we were actually "sent" off there,' said Adamsberg, pacing back down the room. 'Perhaps I made a mistake, or expressed myself badly, or lost my way. It's this wretched tangle of seaweed – a cat couldn't find its kittens inside that.'

'Not even Snowball,' said Estalère.

'Nobody directed us anywhere,' Adamsberg went on. 'We went off in that direction on our own. Even at the scene of the first murder, the killer left a sign that was nothing to do with Iceland. But there was that letter that Alice Gauthier had written to Amédée, then there was that second murder out at Le Creux, and the hot rock in Iceland was the link. So we all went off to Iceland on our own.'

'Where the fog comes down in five minutes and swallows us up,' said Mordent. '*Why do you carry / Your load of mist / witch of the rain / on the fields?*'

Danglard looked at him in some astonishment.

'Sorry for interrupting,' said Mordent. 'I didn't make it up, Veyrenc, it's an Icelandic poem.'

And Mordent stretched out his long neck, a sign that the old heron was embarrassed and concerned.

'That doesn't alter the fact,' he insisted, 'that the first two victims *had* both been to Iceland. Coincidence? But we don't like coincidences, do we?'

'Not necessarily,' said Adamsberg, doing an about-turn. 'These two victims might have met up *after* the Iceland drama. Let's suppose that one of them was already a member of this association. And let's suppose that the first one, for the sake of argument, Henri Masfauré, initiated the other, let's say Alice Gauthier, to the meetings of the Robespierre society.'

'But we found nothing to suggest any activity like that by either Masfauré or Gauthier.'

'No, but if this president is telling us the truth, they really were members of the society, Mordent. Jean Breuguel too. It's not the kind of thing you would shout from the rooftops: Robespierrist studies? That might not have pleased the head of Madame Gauthier's school, or Masfauré's industrialist contacts.'

'Yes, it *is* still a subject with a whiff of sulphur about it,' Danglard confirmed.

'But if the killer had nothing to do with Iceland,' said Mercadet, 'why did he take those books to Jean Breuguel's flat?'

'Just to fool us, lieutenant, to encourage us along the false trail we'd started on, and keep us away from the association. That would explain why the drawing of the guillotine was so weird. He needed to draw it, but he didn't want us to identify it.'

'Got it,' came Froissy's high-pitched voice.

'What?'

'The hall, it's called the Grange aux Blés, yes, it's a former granary, and belongs to the municipality of Saint-Ouen. They hire it out to various groups and the Robespierre association has it one night a week. The name of the person who hires it for Mondays is Henri Masfauré,' she added calmly, 'at a rent of . . . 120,000 euros a month.'

'*What?!*' said Adamsberg, breaking off from pacing up and down. 'A whole new side of the mountain suddenly comes to light, the invisible philanthropist.'

'A philanthropist and Robespierre, that's like day and night!'

'No, Kernorkian,' said Danglard, and his voice had an acid edge. 'Robespierre had a genuinely philanthropic turn of mind, believe me. He was in favour of the happiness of the multitude, he wanted everyone to be able to earn a living, the abolition of slavery, the abolition of the death penalty – yes, that's true, he did speak against it early in the Revolution – universal suffrage for men, and honourable citizenship for all the groups excluded from society, blacks, Jews, illegitimate children. And he wanted "sublime" perfection on this earth.'

'Danglard,' Adamsberg interrupted, 'let's try and keep to the point. Which is: there's a murderer inside the Robespierre association, who's started killing its members. Stick to the point.'

A surprising command, coming from Adamsberg, who was more like a sponge floating in the water than a limpet sticking obstinately to its rock. He asked the time again. It was 11.15.

'Needs to change the batteries in his watches,' Froissy whispered.

'Let's return to the subject in hand,' said Adamsberg more firmly. 'Veyrenc and Danglard, get ready to come with me, but no arms.

Mordent, check out the business of renting that hall with Masfauré's lawyer. Was it official, above board, or was it paid in cash? Get hold of Victor, and ask if Masfauré had any history books in his library, works on the Revolution. Or do you think he concealed his hobby?'

'At 120,000 a month, I'd call it more than a hobby,' remarked Mercadet.

'True. Froissy, I want you to send out an urgent internal memo now to all the police and gendarmerie stations in the country. We're looking for any apparent "suicide", accompanied by a drawing of the guillotine. Send them pictures of the drawing, in the three versions we've got.'

'Who's the apparent suicide?' asked Estalère.

'Don't you remember,' Adamsberg explained, with the protective patience he always used towards Estalère, 'that François Château told us *another* of his members had disappeared, and that he had been acquainted with the victims we already have? Whether that's true or not, we should start looking. The police could have missed a fake suicide.'

'And not noticed the sign,' said Mercadet. 'After all it was almost invisible in the case of Masfauré, and Bourlin only looked for it at Breuguel's flat because of the books on Iceland.'

'Get them to start with any reported suicides in the last month. Have them send officers out to check the scene for the sign. And if that doesn't turn something up, they'll have to go back to the previous month and so on. Tell the divisionnaire we're extending our inquiries. Justin, can you draft the memo? And, Froissy, imitate my signature. We'll be leaving in ten minutes. Retancourt, you get ready and go first, as our vanguard.'

'Danglard,' Adamsberg said, as they went out, 'what's the saying "If the mountain doesn't come to you, you have to go to the mountain"?'

'I thought we were supposed to be sticking to the subject,' said Danglard somewhat curtly.

'Yes, indeed. But Mordent wasn't obliged to recite that Icelandic poem to us. You're infecting them, commandant, one by one. In the end, there won't be a single cop concentrating on the central issue in this squad. And right now, I need cops who can concentrate.'

'Because *you* can't.'

'Precisely. So, this thing about the mountain?'

'It's not a "thing" exactly, commissaire. It's a saying from the Koran, and indeed it's about Mohammed. "If the mountain won't come to Mohammed, then Mohammed will have to go to the mountain."'

'Well, in my case, and more modestly, I should say "Although I didn't go to the mountain, the mountain came to me", because I couldn't see the way ahead.'

'Yes, you did. You understood the sign.'

'But I didn't go anywhere with it, Danglard. I just couldn't get past the guillotine.'

'Best not to, indeed.'

'And if that letter hadn't arrived this morning, we'd still be stuck.'

'But the letter *did* come. And it came because you put out the press release.'

'Commandant, you're being very kind to me today,' said Adamsberg with a smile.

XVII

ADAMSBERG CALLED COMMISSAIRE BOURLIN FROM THE CAR.

'We're leaving Iceland, Bourlin,' he said. 'For good.'

'And going where?'

'To the Association of Robespierre Studies.'

'You mean the Association for the Study of the Writings of Maximilien Robespierre,' Danglard corrected him, loudly enough to be overheard.

'Well, shit!' said Bourlin. 'Your guillotine!'

'The president wrote to us personally – three of his members had gone missing.'

'Our three so-called suicides?'

'Exactly. And there's a fourth one missing now, he says.'

'How many members have they got?'

'Getting on for seven hundred.'

'Shit!' Bourlin repeated.

'That's what I wanted to tell you.'

'Do you think the killer's going to chuck a bomb in among them? To cut a corner?'

'No. He's enjoying himself too much. For the moment.'

The owner of the Cafe des Joueurs was waiting when they arrived.

'They didn't tell me there would be three of you.'

'There was nothing to say there shouldn't be,' said Adamsberg, taking the letter out of his pocket.

The mere sight of the elegant handwriting reassured the cafe proprietor, who led them to the back exit, through into a small courtyard, and then to a further one, before they reached the lane and a metal fireproof door.

'You go down there to the car park of La Tournelle. I presume they told you which staircase to take?'

'Yes.'

'Well, be quick,' the man added, looking left and right. 'And don't draw attention to yourselves. Although with him –' and he indicated Veyrenc's hair – 'I guess that's a waste of breath.'

Then he turned on his heel, without a further word. Justin was right. It smelled of old-fashioned plotting and conspiracy thrillers.

'This is all a bit ridiculous, don't you think?' said Veyrenc.

'I suppose it is,' said Adamsberg. 'Mind you, he was right about your hair.'

'And whose fault is that?'

Adamsberg pulled a face. It was true that people wouldn't forget Veyrenc when they saw him, with his heavy, handsome features and his two-tone hair, rather like leopard skin in reverse. He would be the last officer anyone would send on surveillance duty or into an eighteenth-century conspiracy. Some other boys had tortured him when he was a child, cutting his scalp with knives; the hair had grown back over the scars, but now it was auburn. It had happened back home, where both of them came from, in the high meadow at Laubazac, behind the vineyard. Adamsberg could never remember this without a pang piercing his chest.

They emerged from staircase 4, and pushed the back door of the Tournée de la Tournelle, finding themselves in a rather grand restaurant, with white table linen, full of customers at this time of day. Danglard spotted Retancourt sitting in a corner, with a pink Alice band on her blonde hair and wearing a tailored suit to match. On the table in front of her was a magazine about baby clothes. The imposing lieutenant was knitting without looking at her needles, only stopping now and again to eat a mouthful from her plate, and pulling the white wool out of a large basket at her feet.

'Retancourt knitting?' whispered Veyrenc. 'Who knew? Looks like an expert too.'

'I didn't know, I have to say.'

'You wouldn't think she was an assault tank in camouflage, would you? Impeccable. Her gun must be under the balls of wool.'

'Our man's over there,' said Danglard, 'by the coat stand. White shirt and grey waistcoat, cleaning his nails.'

'Can't be,' said Veyrenc. 'I don't see President Château cleaning his fingernails in a restaurant.'

'He's picking up the magazine,' Adamsberg said. '*Motorbikes Past and Present*. He's looking over at us. And hesitating because there are three of us.'

They went over to the table and the man half rose to shake hands.

'Gentlemen. So you read my letter.'

Adamsberg pulled open his jacket to show the envelope tucked in his inside pocket.

'You are Commissaire Adamsberg, aren't you?' said François Château. 'I think I recognise your face from the press. And these gentlemen are?'

'Commandant Danglard and Lieutnant Veyrenc.'

'We are pooling our expertise,' said Danglard.

'Please sit down.'

Reassured, Château put away his polished steel nail file in his waistcoat pocket, and asked them to choose from the menu, recommending the mushroom and sorrel vol-au-vent, followed by liver Venetian-style. He was quite short and slim, with narrow shoulders, a round face and pink cheeks. His ash-blond hair was going thin on top, and his small blue eyes were inconspicuous. There was nothing striking about his appearance at all, except for the nail file and his upright posture, very deliberate, as though he were sitting in church. Adamsberg was quite disappointed, as if the president of the Robespierre association ought to have been more intimidating.

'Will you have something to drink?' said Danglard, who was looking at the wine list.

'Just a little, but willingly in your company,' said Château, with a more relaxed smile. 'White for me, preferably.'

'That'll do me,' said Danglard, ordering some immediately.

'I do beg you once more to forgive me for this cloak-and-dagger stuff. But I am, alas, obliged to go in for it.'

'You've been threatened?' asked Veyrenc.

'For a long time,' said the little man, his lips tightening once more with tension. 'And it's getting worse. Please forgive me for cleaning my nails,' he said, showing them his hands, with black under the finger-nails. 'I have to do this.'

'You're a gardener?' asked Adamsberg.

'I've just been planting three orange trees from Mexico, hoping for some good blossom. As for the threats, gentlemen, you need to know that managing an association centred on Robespierre is not like being in charge of a ship in the merchant navy, if I may say so. It's more like commanding a destroyer, forced to face enemies and storms, because the mere *name* of Robespierre provokes passions which are always ready to rise up and overwhelm you. I confess that when I started this study group, I was not expecting it either to be so incredibly successful, or to trigger such strong feelings, both for and against. And sometimes, if I may say so,' he added, playing with the tip of his knife on the plate, 'I'm tempted to resign. Too many complicated reactions, hot tempers, people who either worship him or damn him, and in the end what was supposed to be a research association has become an arena for people's fantasies. I deplore it.'

'That bad, is it?' asked Dangard, filling all the glasses except Adamsberg's.

'I anticipated your suspicions, because of course it's absolutely understandable. Look, I've brought with me two recent letters, which prove that the threats, so to speak, are not light-hearted. I have plenty more back in my office. Here's one that arrived about a month ago.'

You think yourself a great man, and you believe you have already triumphed. But will you be able to predict, will you be able to avoid the blow from my hand? Yes, we are determined to take your life, and to deliver France from the serpent seeking to tear her apart.

'And here's another,' Château went on. 'Posted on 10 April. Just after the murders of Alice Gauthier and Henri Masfauré, if I'm not mistaken. As you see, the paper's ordinary, the text has been printed from a computer. Nothing to give away the writer, except that it was posted in Le Mans, which doesn't help us in any way.'

Danglard pounced eagerly on the second letter.

Every day I am beside you, I see you every day. At every hour, my arm is raised to strike your breast. Oh, most wicked of men, live a few more days to think about me, sleep so as to dream of me! Farewell. This very day, as I watch you, I shall enjoy your terror.

'Unusual, wouldn't you say?' said Château, with a nervous laugh. 'But, gentlemen, please eat up.'

'Very unusual,' said Danglard seriously, 'and all the more so because these two texts are exact copies of actual letters sent to Maximilien Robespierre, after the vote of the terrible law of 22 Prairial, 10 June 1794, the one that extended the powers of the Revolutionary Tribunal and became the instrument of the Great Terror.'

'Who are you?' exclaimed Château, pushing back his chair. 'You're not policemen at all! Who are you?'

Adamsberg held the man back by the arm and looked at his pale face. Château was breathing rapidly, but seemed to calm down a little on seeing the expression of the commissaire – if he really was a commissaire.

'Yes, we are, we're all cops,' he reassured him. 'Danglard, show him your badge, discreetly. The commandant just happens to know a lot about the revolutionary period.'

"I don't know *anyone*,' said Château dully, and still on the defensive, 'who would know the text of those letters, except historians.'

'Well, *he* does,' said Veyrenc, pointing at the commandant with his fork.

'Commandant Danglard's memory,' Adamsberg confirmed, 'is a supernatural chasm, into which it would be unwise to venture.'

'I'm sorry,' said Danglard, shaking his large and unthreatening head, 'but these letters are actually fairly well known. Do you think that if I was one of the people threatening you, I would have revealed myself so stupidly?'

'Well, yes of course, you're right,' said Château, pulling his chair back in, and looking somewhat reassured. 'But all the same . . .'

Danglard served more wine, and gave a slight nod to Château, indicating reconciliation.

'Who were these letters addressed to?' he asked. 'On the envelope, I mean.'

'Believe it or not, to "Monsieur Maximilien Robespierre". As if he were still alive! As if he were still threatening people. That's what I told you, some really crazy people are coming to our assemblies, and now attacking our members. With the aim, or at any rate that is what I believe, of creating a climate of terror, which will reach me in the end. You read that sentence: "*This very day, as I watch you, I shall enjoy your terror.*" I created the association, it was *my* concept, and as such I've been its president for twelve years. So it would be logical, wouldn't it, if the writer of these letters, or some other maniac, ended up aiming for the head, don't you think?'

'Isn't there anyone else alongside you?' asked Adamsberg.

'Yes, we have a treasurer and a secretary, who also act as my bodyguards. The names listed in the *Journal Officiel* are not their real ones. Mine is genuine. Because at first, I wasn't on my guard.'

'And there's a financial backer.'

'Perhaps.'

'A wealthy patron, indeed.'

'Yes.'

'Henri Masfauré.'

'Yes, that is the case,' said Château. 'Who has just been murdered. He paid the rent for the hall. When he joined us nine years ago, our finances were not in good order, and he took charge. By killing him, the murderer has cut off the sinews of war, money.'

Adamsberg watched as the little man carefully sliced up his vol-au-vent with his earth-stained hands, searching for some kind of explanation for this contrast in such a well-mannered person. The soil of the earth makes hands noble, dirt cheapens them. Or something like that.

'If Masfauré was enthusiastic enough to finance you, why didn't he attend more often? You said in the letter that he, like the other two victims, turned up only occasionally.'

'Henri was engaged on a famous scientific project – revolutionary in fact, that isn't putting it too strongly – and his work was what absorbed his time entirely. He chose not to risk being too closely identified with the association. It wouldn't have pleased some of his collaborators, I gather. And indeed the same problem does arise for all of us. I am the chief accountant of the Grand Hôtel des Gaules, 122 rooms. You know it perhaps?'

'Yes,' said Veyrenc. 'But I thought you were a gardener.'

'Well, if you want to put it like that,' said Château in a weary voice, looking at his dirty fingernails. 'I look after the hotel gardens, because nobody else knows how to. That said, if the manager were to find out that I am president of this association, I would be out on my neck. Because anyone with anything to do with Robespierre is immediately suspect, it's as simple as that in most people's minds. Henri was just satisfied that the association could continue existing. He came along twice a year.'

'In your view,' asked Adamsberg, 'was it Masfauré who invited Alice Gauthier, the murdered woman, to come to some of your sessions?'

'Yes, quite probably. Because they often sat next to each other. I must have seen this Madame Gauthier, and the other man, Monsieur Breuguel, about twenty times, not more. I recognised them from your photos, because they didn't wear any disguise. They attended sessions from behind the barrier, standing back from the deputies.'

'Disguise?' asked Adamsberg.

'I don't get it,' Veyrenc interrupted. 'There are other groups in France who do research on Robespierre, actual historians who study archives, read texts, analyse them and publish their results in scholarly journals. But *your* association provokes troubles, passions and hatred.'

'Yes, true,' said Château, sitting up straight to allow the waiter to serve the liver Venetian-style.

'There is a reason for that,' Danglard said. 'Monsieur Château has told us of his concept, which required a large building to be hired, at some expense. With exceptional sessions. I would think this takes us to the heart of the matter. Your society doesn't spend its time leafing through the archives, does it?'

'You are quite right, commandant, and I have brought along some photos which may help you more than my description. Because I real- ise,' he said, reaching into a briefcase to take out some documents, 'that on account of listening to eighteenth-century rhetoric for years on end, I have acquired the tiresome habit of expressing myself in a pompous fashion, which does not always communicate itself easily to others. Even at the hotel, would you believe.'

A dozen photographs now went round the table. In a very large hall, lit by chandeliers with false candles, about three or four hundred people, dressed in the costume of the late eighteenth century, were gathered round a rostrum, some in the centre, others on the steps, some sitting, others standing or striding forward with raised hands and outstretched arms, seeming to shout at or applaud the orator on his platform. Around them, in side galleries, were about a hundred other men and women, in modern clothes but discreetly dressed, so that they melted into the shadow, some of them leaning over the balustrade. Tricolour flags were draped here and there. But one could almost hear the sounds in the room, the voice of the orator, the murmurs, the bursts of clamour, the insults.

'Amazing!' said Danglard.

'Do you like it?' asked Château, with a genuine smile, and a hint of pride.

'It's a theatrical performance?' Adamsberg asked. 'A production?'

'No,' said Danglard, passing from one photo to another. 'It's a very faithful re-enactment of the sessions of the National Assembly during the Revolution. Am I right?'

'Quite right,' said Château, his smile even broader.

'I presume that the speeches being declaimed by the orators and the other deputies are the actual historical texts?'

'Of course. Every member receives a full text of the session for that evening ahead of time, with his own interventions marked, depending on who he is playing. It's done via a website that you need a code to access.'

'Depending on who he's *playing*?' asked Adamsberg.

What was the point of playing at the Revolution?

'Yes, necessarily,' replied Château. 'One member will play Danton, another Brissot, Billaud-Varenne, Robespierre, Hébert, Couthon,

Saint-Just, Fouché, Barère and so on, all the leading politicians of the time. He has to learn by heart the speech he will deliver. We function over two-year cycles, from the sessions of the Constituent Assembly of 1789 to the Convention of 1793–1794. We don't do them all of course! Or the cycles would last five years, would they not? We choose particularly representative or memorable dates. In short, we are scrupulously reproducing history. The result is rather impressive.'

'So what do you describe as "exceptional" sessions?' asked Adamsberg. 'One like tonight's?'

'Sessions where Robespierre is present. Those evenings attract a large crowd. He only attends twice a month, because his part is very long and exhausting. And he can't be replaced. But at the moment, he's on every week, because we've fallen a bit behind.'

Château looked anxious again.

'There's a "but" about this success,' he said.

'Uncontrollable passions,' suggested Danglard.

'It was something we hadn't foreseen at all,' Château agreed. 'It wasn't in the plan, don't you see? Is there a little wine left, commandant? At first, we assigned roles according to the physiognomy and temperament of our members. We had a splendid Danton, very ugly, with a stentorian voice. And we had excellent talents for Couthon, he's the one confined to a wheelchair, for Saint-Just, the exterminating angel, and for Hébert, the crude journalist. But by the end of the first year, all of the deputies, even those in very minor roles, had become totally committed to their character, and to the cause of their group – whether they were the centrists in the so-called "Plain", the moderate Girondins, the radical members of "The Mountain", the Dantonists, the Robespierrists, the Enraged or the Extremists – it was a real free-for-all. Members didn't stick to their texts any more, they shouted at each other, or insulted each other during the sessions: "Who do you think you are, citizen, to dare to cheapen the Republic with your hypocritical words?" that kind of thing. We had to put an end to it.'

Château shook his head sadly, the wine making his cheeks rosier.

'How did you do that?' Danglard asked.

'Every four months now, we insist that members change their political group: a centrist has to join the Mountain, an *enragé* has to become a moderate and so on. And believe me, these compulsory conversions don't always take place calmly.'

'Interesting,' said Veyrenc.

'So interesting, actually, that we have embarked on some innovative research. To explore a phenomenon that no historian has yet explained: how was it that Robespierre, with his pale face and his glacial manner, totally lacking in charisma and empathy, with a high-pitched voice and an insignificant physique – how was it that he inspired such adoration? With his serious expression, and his blank eyes blinking behind his spectacles? Well, we observe this and we take notes.'

'And how long have you been conducting this research?' asked Danglard, who now seemed more fascinated by this association than with the investigation in progress.

'About six years.'

'With any results?'

'Yes, indeed, we already have thousands of pages of notes, observations and analysis. Our secretary is in charge of the project. Take women, for instance, the thousands of women who were such fervent admirers of Robespierre, in love with him indeed, whereas he wasn't interested. We have women members who are allowed in the public galleries, commandant. And they do seem to fall for him, you wouldn't believe.'

'I'd like to stretch my legs,' said Adamsberg. 'Can we take a turn along the embankment?'

'Willingly, gentlemen, I have been too long sitting here.'

The four men walked along the bank of the Seine, ending up by way of contrast near the equestrian statue of King Henri IV. They sat down on a bench in the sun, in the little park named after him, the Square du Vert-Galant on the Ile de la Cité.

'These photos,' Adamsberg said, 'do you have any close-ups?'

'No, our rules forbid that,' said Château, who was busy cleaning his fingernails again. 'Our members enrol anonymously, and all snapshots are forbidden. For reasons of confidentiality, as I mentioned earlier. And everyone has to leave their mobile in the cloakroom, switched off.'

'So you can't give us the name of the fourth man whose absence has worried you, nor provide us with a photo of him?'

'That is correct. And in any case, he wears theatrical make-up, and takes on a role. He didn't at first. But after a while, he caught the bug so to speak, like so many others. That's why his absence concerns me. He should have been there two weeks ago, he was due to speak. And he wouldn't have missed it, because he enjoyed it too much. But in that throng of people, whose faces are all in some way masked, I couldn't possibly suggest a suspect. I *can* tell you that the ones who get most excited when Robeslpierre appears number about fifty. But the murderer might equally well be a man of the shadows, as stealthy as a predator, not letting his hatred appear on the surface.'

Château was now working hard on his ring finger.

'And what about this?' said Adamsberg, showing him a drawing of the sign. 'Have you ever seen this? It has appeared at the scene of all three murders.'

'No, never,' said Château, shaking his head. 'What is it supposed to represent?'

'That's what we wondered. What does it suggest to you? In context?'

'In context?' said Château, rubbing his bald patch.

'Yes, in *your* context.'

'The guillotine?' said Château, a little like a schoolboy, hesitating to answer in class. 'But which one? The one before, or the one after? Or the two mixed up? That doesn't make any sense.'

'Very true,' said Adamsberg.

Who now thrust his hands deep in his pockets. He couldn't see either how they were to track down one man among seven hundred anonymous and disguised members of the association. Another mass of tangled seaweed had appeared on his horizon, one even more tentacular than his previous obsession, but now moving towards it, and getting mixed up obscenely with it.

'Did you say that people can take part in your sessions as occasional members?'

'Yes, three times a year.'

'Like tonight for instance?' asked Adamsberg.

'Who? The three of you?' asked Château, surprised, dropping his nail file.

'Why not?'

'But what do you hope to get from that?'

'An impression,' said Adamsberg with a shrug.

'It's an important session tonight. His very long speech of 5 February 1794, or 17 Pluviôse, year II, if we go by the revolutionary calendar. It will be cut down though, I assure you.'

'I'd like to see that,' said Danglard.

'Very well. Come along at 7 o'clock this evening to the back door of the building, number 17, I'll arrange for you to have costumes and wigs. That is, if it does not inconvenience you. Because if you remain in ordinary modern dress, you would have to stay in the public gallery at the back, and you would then see very little.'

'Your Robespierre impersonator,' said Adamsberg, 'why can't you replace him with someone else?'

Château fell silent for a moment, looking thoughtful and out of countenance.

'Gentlemen,' he said, 'if you come along tonight, you will understand.'

XVIII

ADAMSBERG, WITH LONG, STRAIGHT BLACK HAIR, TIED IN A PONYTAIL and reaching halfway down his back, was looking at himself in the tall mirrors in the association's cloakroom: he was wearing a dark grey, double-breasted riding coat, a white shirt with a standing collar and a white stock knotted at the throat. 'Elegant but sober,' Château had decided for the commissaire. 'We won't add anything, because I don't believe it would suit you. You will be the son of a modest provincial notable, let's leave it at that. For your Commandant Danglard on the other hand, I suggest a cream waistcoat, a dark purple frock coat and a lace jabot, as he could be the slightly more worldly descendant of an illustrious military family. As for your colleague with the auburn streaks, a wig, of course, and a dark blue waistcoat, coat to match, white breeches, son of a Parisian lawyer, brilliant but more austere.'

Dozens of men were going past them, looking preoccupied, dressed in silk, velvet and lace, and all hurrying towards the great chamber of the National Asssembly. Some had gone into corners to reread the text of their speech. Others were chatting in period dialogue, addressing each other as 'citizen', and talking about the miller who had been stoned for hoarding flour, a woman who had died of a stomach complaint, or a cousin who was a priest and had escaped into exile. A little lost in the midst of what seemed to him a huge and somewhat infantile masquerade, but all the same distracted by his own appearance, Adamsberg almost failed to spot his two colleagues.

'Hurry up, "citizen", ' said Veyrenc, putting a hand on his shoulder, 'the session starts in ten minutes.'

It was only by his upcurled lip that Adamsberg had recognised his lieutenant, and then with a slight shock. Yes, indeed, it would be easy for a murderer to infiltrate these surroundings, where all these men were unrecognisable, and their names unknown – and to observe any-one as much as he pleased.

Danglard, looking quite jaunty in his purple silk coat, was leaving his mobile with one of the staff.

'Pity we don't wear these clothes any more,' he commented cheer-fully. 'I don't appear to advantage in boring modern dress. How did we get to this age of totally unimaginative clothing?'

'On stage, Danglard,' said Adamsberg, pushing him towards the massive wooden doors and forgetting for a moment, in this strange theatre, that he had only come here because he needed to try and pen-etrate the slippery heart of the bundle of seaweed.

They positioned themselves in the 'Plain' of centrist deputies, a few feet away from the rostrum, from which an unknown speaker was boasting about the recent victories of the patriotic Republican armies. It felt cold inside these stone walls, hung with tapestries, and under the huge barrel-vaulted wooden roof. There was no central heating, the conditions of the revolutionary era were being respected. By the light of the large candelabra, Danglard was watching the crowd, par-ticularly the tiered seats on the left, where the deputies of the so-called Mountain sat.

'There! That's Danton!' Danglard whispered to Adamsberg. 'Third row down, sixth along. He will be guillotined in two months exactly, and he already senses it.'

'Of the 8th Squadron,' a nearby deputy was complaining, 'only twelve horses and nine men were left standing!'

The presiding officer of the assembly now called upon Citizen Robespierre to speak. There was silence and a man walked straight up the steps of the rostrum, then turned round. There was frenetic applause, women called out from the galleries, and flags were waved.

The actor, straight-faced, his complexion pallid under his white wig, his thin, stiff torso tightly buttoned into a striped frock coat, looked over the assembled deputies then adjusted his small round spectacles before looking down at his text.

'He looks deathly pale,' said Adamsberg.

'He wears powder, he always does,' muttered Danglard, signalling to Adamsberg to keep quiet, as the assembly now fell quite silent, at a near imperceptible gesture from the actor.

His voice rose up in the air, high-pitched and without resonance. He went through his speech, sometimes repeating sections, sometimes showing extraordinary talent, sounding vicious, reassuring, aggressive, by turns, punctuating his delivery with a few broad declamatory gestures.

'It is time to state clearly the aim of the Revolution and the destination at which we wish to arrive: it is time to give ourselves an account of it, and of the obstacles which still keep us from that aim.'

After about fifteen minutes, Adamsberg felt his eyelids closing. He turned towards Danglard, but the commandant, leaning forward, was watching the speaker, fascinated, mouth open above his lace jabot, as if he were observing an animal of some unknown species. It looked to Adamsberg as if it would be impossible to snatch his commandant out of this state of bemusement.

'...We desire an order of things when all base and cruel passions will be in chains, and all generous and benevolent passions will be awakened by the laws...'

*

In his boredom, Adamsberg sought some complicity on his other side, from his compatriot and son of a vineyard owner, Veyrenc. Less mesmerised than Danglard, but just as amazed, Veyrenc was staring intently at the small, intense and pale-complexioned man who was declaiming from high above them, not missing a detail of the scene. Adamsberg looked again at the actor, seeking to discover how he was thus able to subjugate his colleagues. Strikingly elegant, subtle and precise in each of his gestures, the man might inspire interest through his incantatory declarations, astonishment by his austere demeanour, or alarm by the fixed stare directed from those pale blue, repeatedly blinking eyes, or by the tightly compressed lips which did not seem capable of a smile. It was living History, the president had warned them, the actor was embodying the Sea-Green Incorruptible. And totally succeeding.

'. . . *In our country, we wish to value morality over egotism, the reign of reason over the tyranny of fashion, scorn for vice over scorn for misfortune, pride over insolence, love of reputation over love of money, good people over polite society, genius over wit, the charms of true happiness over the staleness of pleasure* . . .'

'Citizen Robespierre,' a voice interrupted from the right-hand side of the assembly, 'what demon drives you to think Man is so perfectible? Are you seeking to force virtue on the "good people" to make them lose the very reason you talk about so much?'

'That's not in the texts!' Danglard whispered with annoyance in Adamsberg's ear. 'The speech of 17 Pluviôse was not interrupted.'

Adamsberg realised that Danglard was genuinely shocked by this departure from the official record. As was Robespierre, who took off his glasses, and whose relentless gaze now turned on the interrupter, to whom he directed a mere twist of his lips. The man sat down at once, all passion extinguished.

'Christ Almighty,' murmured Veyrenc.

The orator had resumed his speech, imperturbably.

'. . . and we desire that by sealing achievements with our blood, we should at least see the dawn of universal felicity. That is our ambition, that is our aim.'

The entire chamber rose in a standing ovation, and the space was filled with the sounds of chairs grating on the floor, benches creaking, applause, shouts, insults exchanged between deputies, while from the public galleries the revolutionary tricolours were frantically waved.

Feeling shamefaced, Adamsberg had discreetly slipped out of the building. He waited for his colleagues, leaning against a tree, smoking one of Zerk's cigarettes. This extraordinary evening had irritated him as much as it had troubled him, and he looked in near-amazement at the ordinary people and objects around him, the tree, the metal grille round its roots, the passers-by wearing jeans, the darkened window of a chemist's shop, a newspaper kiosk. It had taken no more than an hour for that other century to draw him inside its margins, for him to become accustomed to the costumes, lights, declamations and sounds of the assembly. As for Danglard and Veyrenc, they were quite lost for the evening, fascinated, spellbound by the fever of the period. So yes, he did understand. What an admirable, yet dangerous object that little François Château had created! What unpredictable passions might overcome these men, who had for years now been carried away by the enchanted atmosphere of these evenings – and what terrifying assassin might they engender?

An hour and a half later, the three men were driving back into central Paris without exchanging a word. Seeing their shocked faces, Adamsberg decided to let them return gradually to the present day. Only when they had crossed the Seine and were waiting at a traffic light, did he say calmly:

'Pedestrians, asphalt, traffic fumes, the twenty-first century.'

'You didn't understand,' said Veyrenc.

'Well, as long as you're not calling me "citizen", there's still hope.'

'No really, you didn't understand,' Veyrenc insisted.

'Do you remember,' said Danglard from the back seat, 'what Château told us? That they couldn't find a replacement for Robespierre. And that we'd understand why tonight.'

'Yes,' said Adamsberg, 'because that actor is quite fantastic.'

'No, commissaire, because it's him.'

'Him, who?'

'Robespierre. The actor, as you call him, is HIM. He *is* Robespierre, the Incorruptible.'

Adamsberg sensed that it would be pointless and unbecoming, almost vulgar, to remind his colleagues that Robespierre had died by the guillotine. As was confirmed for him, when he heard Veyrenc murmuring, as if to himself, face turned to look out of the car window.

'Nothing more to be said. It was HIM.'

XIX

'A RESULT, COMMISSAIRE,' SAID MORDENT, STRIDING INTO ADAMSBERG'S office.

His long legs made Mordent look more than ever like an old heron.

'What?' asked Adamsberg, without looking up.

He was standing at his desk, but that wasn't what annoyed Mordent, because the chief almost always worked standing up. It was that he wasn't working at all. He was drawing. Whereas the rest of the squad was anxiously monitoring calls from police stations all over France, because of the call Adamsberg himself had sent out about the fourth 'false' suicide. Worse than drawing, he was painting in watercolours! He had borrowed paints from Froissy, who did landscapes as a hobby.

'You're drawing,' said Estalère, who had come in on Mordent's heels.

Estalère was always following on someone's heels, for some reason. He was like a lost duckling, attaching himself to another brood. Whoever he came across in the corridor, Mordent, Voisenet, Noël, Justin, Kernorkian, Froissy or anyone else, he wheeled round and started following, so that all the officers had got used to finding the young man just behind them, and delegating to him some task or other.

'Last night, Estalère, I woke up at four o'clock with an idea in my head,' Adamsberg explained. 'I scribbled it on a piece of paper and went back to sleep.'

He pulled a crumpled sheet of paper from his pocket and held it out to the young policeman.

'It just says "draw", ' said Estalère. 'Was that your idea, sir?'

'Yes. So I'm following instructions. You should always follow instructions that come in the night, Estalère, not the ones in the evening, which are often overblown and harmful.'

'And the ones that come at night? What are they like?'

'They don't tell you,' said Adamsberg, shaking his head and dipping a very fine paintbrush into a bowl of water.

'Commissaire,' Mordent interrupted, 'I just told you something when I came in.'

'I know, commandant. But you didn't go on. You said "A result", and I said "What?" As you see, I'm listening.'

'We've found our dead man,' said Mordent with emphasis.

'The fourth? With the sign?'

'Yes. Only we don't know yet if he's the right one.'

'Who's the *right* dead man then?' asked Estalère.

'We don't know,' said Adamsberg, standing back to look at his picture, 'whether he is the man missing from the Robespierre association, as reported to us by the president. Or whether perhaps we have come across yet another one, someone else. In the Icelandic case, which isn't our case any more, we were afraid of a potential six deaths once the murderer got going. In this case, there are six hundred potential victims. Forgive me,' he said, putting down the paintbrush and looking at Mordent, 'but with watercolours, there are some strokes that you can't let dry before you've finished them. So who? Where? How? Everyone to the council chamber.'

Estalère hurried out of the office, this time without following anyone. Council chamber meant a meeting, and a meeting meant coffee to fetch. With sugar, without sugar, with milk, without milk, just a spot of milk, espresso or americano, he knew it all, having memorised everyone's order. He never drank coffee himself. Adamsberg looked at his stationary watches and Mordent indicated to him that it was eleven o'clock.

'The call was from the gendarmerie at Brinvilliers-le-Haut, near Montargis,' Mordent announced, once everyone had gathered in the chamber.

'In the Loiret *département*,' Danglard added.

'They didn't exactly have a suicide, but a fatal accident, nineteen days ago, in a village called Mérecourt-le-Vieux.'

'That was four days *before* Alice Gauthier's murder,' Veyrenc calculated.

'So why did they answer our call?' asked Justin. 'We didn't say "accidents", we said "presumed suicides".'

'Because one of the gendarmes, when called to the scene on the evening of the accident, got some bright blue chalk on his sleeve, from a wall. After our call – he was a bit excited on the phone, so I'm just trying to give you what he said – he wondered what blue chalk might be doing on the wall of some stairs down to a dark old cellar. It was a narrow staircase, that's how he came to brush against the wall.'

'Because the accident happened in a dark old cellar?' asked Voisenet.

'Yes.'

'Man or woman?'

'A man, aged about sixty. Every evening, he went down to the cellar after dinner, so it was night-time, to fetch two bottles of wine for next day, so that they would be the right temperature. And he always carried them laid flat, so as not to disturb the sediment. That's what his sister said, because he was living with his sister's family. He must have tripped on one of the steps as he came up, and fell backwards. Because his hands were occupied with the bottles, he couldn't reach out to grab anything, and he fell all the way down the steps. As did the bottles, though one of them didn't break, the gendarme said.'

'There's no justice in this world,' said Kernorkian.

'So what did the inquiry find?' asked Adamsberg. 'Could a member of the family have pushed him?'

'They were all still at table when he fell. They were drinking the wine he'd fetched the day before,' said Mordent, consulting his notes.

'And this gendarme?'

'A real old-timer, stickler for detail. So he went back this morning, to take a look, because of the chalk mark.'

'He's got a good head on him then,' said Veyrenc.

'Yes. And he found the little blue drawing, about fifteen centimetres high, on this dirty old wall. The drawing is smudged from his jacket, but the sign is clear enough.'

And Mordent circulated the photo taken by the gendarme.

'This killer isn't fussy about his methods,' said Danglard. 'Chalk, eyebrow pencil, scissors, knife. Just so long as he can leave his mark, that's what matters to him. And as we've already noted, he's not setting out to make it conspicuous. But he can't *help* drawing it, and in certain murderers, that is a sign of pride. Not uncommon, in fact,' he said, with a glance at Retancourt.

'I think,' said Adamsberg, considering the blue graffiti, 'that in the case of Jean Breuguel, the killer carved the sign with his left hand. That might explain why the drawing was clumsy.'

'Why the left hand?'

'Because his right was covered in blood.'

'And that gets us where?' asked Noël, who for all that he was unreconstructed, misogynist and aggressive, was no fool.

'Where it gets us, lieutenant, is to the possible conclusion that Breuguel, not to be confused with Bruegel, is *not* an exception to our series after all.'

'What do you mean, Breuguel, not to be confused with Bruegel?'

'Ask Bourlin, he's the one who said it.'

'When someone says the name "Breuguel",' explained Danglard, 'people are inclined to think they mean Bruegel the Elder, the sixteenth-century Flemish painter.'

'No,' said Noël, 'people are *not* in the least inclined to think that.'

'I agree with you there,' Adamsberg admitted. 'Mordent, what was the name of this victim, his occupation, do we have a photograph?'

'Angelino Gonzalez. He was formerly professor of zoology in Laval University in Quebec, then he taught at the Jussieu Faculty in Paris. Since retiring, he's been living with his sister, while trying to find a flat somewhere in Brittany, because he's a Breton.'

'He's a *Breton*, with a name like Angelino Gonzalez?' scoffed Noël.

'Oh, shut up, Noël,' said Adamsberg calmly, and it was on the tip of his tongue to say, 'And where are you from?' because he well knew that his lieutenant had been an abandoned child, left outside the social security office one Christmas morning in the snow, hence his name, which, as Mordent would have said, was the stuff of fairy tales. Except that it had not been much like a fairy tale in reality.

'What kind of zoologist?' asked Voisenet.

'Birds.'

'Victor said there'd been a specialist on little auks in the Iceland group,' said Kernorkian.

'We don't know that Gonzalez was a specialist in northern seabirds,' said Mordent.

'And anyway, we've decided Iceland is irrelevant,' said Mercadet firmly.

'Absolutely,' Adamsberg agreed. 'But all the same, Justin, get a check on his passport.'

'It's been done,' said Mordent, 'but his passport was only eight years old. Two return trips to Canada, that was all.'

'We decided Iceland was irrelevant,' repeated Mordent.

'How many times do we have to say that?' said Danglard with some irritation.

'Look,' said Adamsberg, 'it's quite natural that we've still got memories of the Icelandic business running through our heads. Send the photo of Angelino Gonzalez to the president of the association. And send a copy to Victor as well.'

'Oh, for heaven's *sake*,' said Danglard. 'Why Victor?'

'Why not, commandant?' said Adamsberg, standing up. 'Don't worry, I think we have left the icy rocks behind. And indeed I fear our new trip into Robespierre's Arctic Circle might be even chillier.'

The team broke up to go for lunch, some to the Dice Shaker cafe, others to the Brasserie des Philosophes, and the rest eating a sandwich at their desk, which was Adamsberg's choice, since he had 'things to do', in other words a drawing.

The replies arrived quickly. First came Victor's, saying he had 'never seen that guy at all, he didn't look remotely like the worshipper of little auks who was with us', and one from François Château, who said, yes, he did fancy he recognised him. But did they have any other photos to show him?

They arranged to meet him at 3 p.m. at his office at the association's headquarters. A sign of confidence, but with express instructions that if Veyrenc was coming along, he should wear something on his head. Which he did, a black baseball cap with *Paris* written on it in golden letters.

'It was all I could find in our cupboards,' said Veyrenc, 'and I got this khaki bomber jacket from Retancourt. Good, isn't it? I'll keep my distance behind you.'

'Why is it,' asked Adamsberg, 'that whatever we do, people always guess we're cops?'

'Because of our perverse expressions,' said Danglard. 'Because we look as if we're always on the alert and suspicious for no reason. Because of the power we think we have, and because of the aggressive aura we give off, so people think we're ready to pounce. It's a matter of pheromones, not a matter of what clothes we're wearing.'

'Talking of clothes,' said Adamsberg, 'was it you, Danglard, that took photos of us last night dressed up as eighteenth-century politicians? And then sent them to everyone's mobile in the squad?'

'Yes, indeed. I thought we looked splendid.'

'But everyone laughed at us.'

'Laughter is a defence mechanism when you're impressed. They all thought you looked terrific, let me tell you. Froissy fell in love with you at 9.20 this morning. It changes their usual view of you. Men and women both.'

'All very well, Danglard. And what do I deduce from that?'

'Ambiguity.'

Adamsberg was accustomed not to reply to the remarks of his deputy.

XX

'MY WORD, I THINK SO, YES, I THINK I HAVE SEEN HIM HERE,' SAID
François Château, looking through the four photographs that
Adamsberg had brought. 'You may take the cap off in here, lieutenant,'
he said with a smile.

'His name was Angelino Gonzalez,' said Veyrenc, as he obeyed, and
shook out his multicoloured hair.

'Lieutenant,' Château went on, still smiling, 'it's not the National
Assembly you should have been in, but the Roman Senate. You're the
very image of a bust from antiquity! But I'm sorry, I'm losing the
thread, I was making up a role for you. Angelino Gonzalez, you say?
But as I told you, I don't know people's names.'

'But you do observe them,' Adamsberg said.

'We need to know the *kind* of people who attend, so to speak. After
the session – you left too early last night, you know – a buffet supper is
served in the annexe alongside. You have to pay, but most people stay for
it. And that is the time when they can not only eat and drink, but chat
among themselves. I go along sometimes, I take part, I overhear conversations. I could almost give you an undertaking that seventy-five per
cent of our members are actually professional historians, which doesn't
prevent them getting carried away, as I said before. Another fifteen per
cent are, let's say, amateur historians, from every walk of life, people who

are eager for knowledge. So, for instance, if you'll forgive me for saying so, we might find a policeman among us, someone like your Commandant Danglard. And the other ten per cent are all sorts, professionals, civil servants, psychologists, psychiatrists, businessmen, teachers, and some people who do actually work in the theatre. There are one or two artists, but I have noted that there is only a slight correlation between a taste for history and practising the arts. And over the last twelve years, you might say I've got to know all of them. And all of them, whoever they are, are won over by the costumes, the faithful reproduction of official texts, the period atmosphere, and, I think I may say, the fact of wearing an eighteenth-century frock coat. It lends one aplomb.'

'I noticed that,' said Danglard.

'You see. And that's not counting the fact of playing a part, even a non-speaking one. Here, commandant, everyone exists, every voice counts. We vote in the assemblies. We participate in the creation of ideas and laws. In short, we become significant.'

'What about the "occasionals"?' asked Adamsberg.

'I certainly don't neglect them. Because it's among such members that one might find people "infiltrating" or spying, or enemies. They don't pay the annual subscription – which is high, because you can imagine how much it costs simply to acquire and maintain the costumes – but they have the right to come to three sessions a year, as if going to the theatre. We couldn't do without them – all our full-time members started off as occasionals. But some insist on remaining visitors. Which was the case for Henri Masfauré, and Alice Gauthier, and the third man, the one with the name of a painter.'

'Jean Breuguel.'

'That's the one.'

'But if you don't ask for people's names or identity papers, how do you know your occasionals only come three times?' asked Veyrenc. 'Or for your full-time members, how do you know somebody else doesn't come in their place?'

'We ask for a pseudonym, and we photograph the palm of every-one's hand. At reception, we compare the lines with our photo. It's quite quick and accurate, and it's not like a fingerprint.'

'Good idea,' said Veyrenc.

'Well, no, it's not bad,' said Château with satisfaction. 'Certain other people thought perhaps we should use the back of people's identity papers, but that carries too much information. You'd quickly get to the person.'

'Who are these "other people"?' asked Adamsberg.

'My two co-founders, I told you about them, the secretary and treasurer, who are also anonymous, and who act as my bodyguards.'

'Are they accountants too?'

Château smiled again. Once past his initial distrust, the man was on the whole agreeable, and with a sharp intelligence.

'Don't ask, please, commissaire. Let's just say that they're both very keen on history.'

'Keen, you say,' said Danglard. 'So not professional historians, then?'

'I didn't say that, commandant. They are in fact in charge of the research side of our enterprise.'

'The study of the "Robespierre effect". '

'Well, not only that. The therapeutic effect too. We only discovered that after a while. Many people who were suffering from depression, or from extreme timidity, or were in other ways scared of life, have found some help here. They are able to re-enter real life and face it again, after having taken part in this reality at one move. Do you see what I mean? You must meet my associates – let's call them Leblond and Lebrun if you will agree to that – because they know the members better than I do, especially the stranger or more unusual ones. And perhaps they also know the "occasionals", who are loyal attenders, yet still wish to stay on the margins. That's a bit of a worry.'

'But an obscure point,' said Veyrenc. 'Why are you worried about them, if they are the least representative people?'

'Maybe it's just an unfortunate coincidence, since the fourth victim – Gonzalez you called him? – wasn't one. But then I can't be sure about him. Because if he *is* the man I'm thinking of, he always wore a wig and frock coat. So it's hard to identify him from this photograph after death. But he did have a long nose, drooping eyelids and thick lips, so I think I'm right.'

'One moment,' said Adamsberg, getting up. 'Do you have a piece of paper?'

'Of course,' said Château, a little surprised, passing him a sheet of computer paper.

Adamsberg chose a photo of Gonzalez and did a rapid and accurate sketch of it.

'That's good,' said Château. 'You probably don't go in much for history, do you?'

'I don't have a good memory for the written word, I remember better what I've seen. Now, watch carefully.'

And with a few deft strokes, Adamsberg added to Gonzalez's face a wig, a high collar and a stock knotted at the throat.

'And now?' he said, passing the sketch to Château. The president nodded and stroked his bald patch, looking impressed.

'Yes, of course,' he said, 'I *do* know him. I can see him perfectly now.'

'An occasional?'

'No. He liked strong emotions, He often came to the special sessions. He always volunteered to take speaking parts. He made an excellent Hébert, for instance, the man who yelled insults at everyone, an extremely crude journalist – the editor of the paper *Le Père Duchesne*, as you will know.'

'No, I don't know,' said Adamsberg.

'I'm sorry,' said Château, reddening, 'I didn't mean to offend you.'

'No offence taken.'

'Hébert was famous for writing "fuck this" and "fuck that", every two lines in the paper, and Gonzalez liked imitating him, they were stirring sessions. "Let those toads in the Plain go and sneeze into the sack," he would say. Robespierre was very shocked by Hébert's vulgar language.'

'Sneeze into the sack?' asked Adamsberg.

'A contemporary expression for being sent to the guillotine. Gonzalez was also successful at playing Marat, the wild one. My word, the trouble he took over his make-up, to get his eyes to look hooded. We have three make-up artists here,' said little Château, cheering up, as usual when he was describing his 'concept'. 'And in a completely different style, he also played the unforgettable Couthon. Yes,' he finished, passing the portrait back to Adamsberg, 'he really loved it. Coffee?' he asked, standing up.

Adamsberg looked at his two watches, then at the clock on the panelled wall.

'We're taking up a lot of your time,' he said.

'It matters even more to me than to you to discover who is killing our members. My time is entirely at your disposal,' Château went on, over the sound of the coffee machine. 'Four murders in three weeks. But it will be terribly hard to identify a killer among our large membership.'

'Well, I have to say,' Adamsberg commented, 'we would have a much greater chance of doing so, if everyone spoke the truth.'

And he saw once more the infernal knot of seaweed whose tentacles gripped him, even in the night. He didn't like what he had to do next.

'What do you mean, and to what are you referring, commissaire?' the president asked him calmly.

'I'm referring to Robespierre.'

'Exceptional performance, don't you think?' said Château, putting the cups down on the desk. 'I didn't conceal that from you, did I? That 17 Pluviôse speech is certainly a choice example, don't you agree? Though in places it gets really rather boring, as was often the case with the Incorruptible. But he manages to get it across.'

'Like him.'

'Him? Who?'

'That's what my colleagues said when we went home last night. They came out of your session more or less in a state of shock.'

'So soon?' smiled Château, passing round the sugar.

'"It was HIM," they said. "*Himself*. Robespierre."'

The president glanced in some surprise at Danglard and Veyrenc, who were both looking at Adamsberg uncomprehendingly, at a loss as to why the commissaire was revealing their reactions of the previous night.

'And they were right,' Adamsberg went on. 'It *was* Him, and that of course is why you can't find a replacement for him.'

'What are you getting at, commissaire?' asked Château with a shake of his head. 'Your colleagues themselves are looking a bit mystified, if I'm not mistaken.'

'Do you mind if I smoke?'

'Not at all,' said Château, taking an ashtray out of a drawer.

Adamsberg took out a cigarette, while with the other hand he placed a folder on the desk. From it he took a watercolour painting on stiff paper, and passed it across to Château.

'What do you think of this?' he asked.

'The sitter isn't handsome,' said Château, after a moment of silence during which he clamped his mouth shut, 'but the portrait is excellent. You really are talented.'

'And is it a good likeness?' asked Adamsberg, passing the picture to his colleagues.

He lit his cigarette, leaned back, and for once in his life tried to feel calm without succeeding.

'Yes, it is,' said Château. 'It's of me.'

'Yes, absolutely,' said Danglard, looking rather stunned and carefully putting the watercolour back on the desk, so as not to harm it.

'Is this perhaps a present, commissaire?' asked Château warily.

'You may have it with pleasure, but not just yet. Do you remember the experiment we did just now with Gonzalez's face, when we added the wig and costume? I took the liberty of choosing for you the exact costume in which Robespierre appeared last night. He wore a striped coat in two shades of golden brown, his jabot was cream-coloured and made of plain lace, the wig was a dazzling white, the spectacles were round, and of course his face was powdered and pale.'

Adamsberg showed the second painting to his colleagues before passing it across to the president. All three men stiffened, and Adamsberg let his ash fall on the floor, without intending to.

'The face is without the natural rosy complexion that you normally have,' he added.

All said and done, Adamsberg stood up to pace the room for a moment, stretching his arms discreetly downwards.

'It's Him,' whispered Danglard, while Veyrenc, bemused, simply stared at the portrait.

'Him? Who?' Adamsberg asked gently. 'Him, Maximilien Robespierre, whose head was cut off in 1794? Or *you*, sitting opposite us, Monsieur François Château? Robespierre returned from the shades of the dead? Or François Château, who knows him so well, so intimately, that he knows how to give his fixed smile, blink his eyes repeatedly, maintain his impassive expression, make the delicate gestures with his hands, imitate his voice, stand very erect, with his back like a ramrod? And indeed,' he went on, turning back to the desk and leaning towards Château, 'you do naturally hold yourself very straight, your movements are very delicate, your voice is naturally quite weak, your eyes are pale blue, and your smile is rather strained.'

Château was suffering, and his pain communicated itself like a toxic aroma inside the small room, reaching each of the others. In his distress, and now that Adamsberg's drawing had revealed his alter ego, it was possible to recognise in him yesterday's Robespierre. He had shrunk in his seat, his lips had become thinner and the pink had left his cheeks. Adamsberg slumped back in his chair, as if exhausted and regretful about his own attack. He placed his burnt-out cigarette end in the ashtray, and shook his head rather sadly.

'But you, Monsieur Château, you really *do* know how to smile, whereas He couldn't, more was the pity for him. You don't have his pallor, you don't wear glasses, you don't have any facial tics. Any more than you have ulcers on your legs, or suffer from nosebleeds. As you see, I did a little research yesterday.'

'Well,' said Château in an expressionless voice, 'it's just that I'm a very good actor. But once more, I must congratulate you, commissaire. I'm an experienced observer, but I was convinced that no one would ever guess my own very ordinary face was detectable behind his. Your colleagues themselves did not recognise it, as far as I can judge.'

'And as a consequence,' said Adamsberg, 'you are right to fear that you are in danger. If I was able to detect François Château behind Robespierre, someone else could have. No one can replace you at the rostrum. No one else would be capable of it. If *you* were to die, the association would collapse. And more than that, if you weren't there any longer, Robespierre himself would disappear, he'd be returned a second time to oblivion. And yet they took the precaution of covering his corpse with quicklime to be sure of destroying it. But what about his soul? Where did his soul go?'

'I don't believe in stories about souls, commissaire,' said Château, in a more hostile tone.

'We will leave you now, Monsieur Château. I will take the liberty of returning in three hours.'

'May I ask why?'

'Because you are not merely "a very good actor". You're Him, as my colleagues said. Or to put it another way, you are an excellent actor, *because* you are Him.'

'You are leaving the realm of reason, commissaire.'

'I'll be back at –' Adamsberg glanced at the clock – 'seven thirty this evening. Meanwhile take care, it's more important than you think.

XXI

NO SOONER WAS HE OUT OF THE ASSOCIATION'S OFFICES – WHICH meant going with a porter through two iron gates fitted with security locks and electronic codes, since the president was protected as if in a fortress – than Adamsberg phoned Retancourt, instructing her to lay on round-the-clock protection for François Château. The killer had eliminated Masfauré because without his money the association would not be able to carry on. That first blow was already lethal. And it could be presumed that after that murder, Robespierre was the future target. Arrived at by gradually instilling suspicion, then fear, and finally terror, as Robespierre had, before striking at the heart. *Live a few days longer to think about me, sleep, to dream of me. Farewell. This very day, as I watch you, I will be enjoying your terror.* How many members had he planned to kill? Enough for a rumour to start and begin thinning the ranks of the association, before aiming at its centre? Enough to leave Robespierre-Château standing alone, devastated by the collapse of his concept? The sign was, yes, certainly anti-Robespierrist, because it was a design for the guillotine, as amended by Louis XVI. The mark of the king's last power, referring to the very machine that would decapitate him.

'Stick close to him, Retancourt, take little Justin with you, he's inconspicuous, and use Kernorkian on a motorbike. Take turns for shifts with whoever you like except Mercadet, Mordent or Noël.'

Retancourt filled in the reasons for herself: one too sleepy, the second too arthritic, the third too impulsive.

'Leave Froissy at her desk though, I need her for computer searches. Do you know if she's got anywhere?'

'Not yet. She's looking for a more direct channel, i.e. an illegal one.'

'Excellent. I'll be leaving the association headquarters at about eight thirty. Have Justin and Kernorkian in position by then, because I think our man's in real danger. Though not necessarily today. It could go on for weeks,' Adamsberg warned her, knowing that a mission to watch someone without any certain end point could be a strain on one's nerves. 'Danglard and Veyrenc are returning to base, and they'll explain the situation to the team.'

'You hit the bullseye, all right,' said Veyrenc. 'François Château *was* the actor playing Robespierre. But why are you going back to harass him again?'

The three men were standing by their car. Adamsberg intended to go for a walk, as was obvious without the need to mention it. He had given his folder of drawings to Veyrenc to help explain matters to his colleagues, and was preparing to stroll away, hands in pockets.

'Because now,' he said, 'the man's under threat of death.'

'We understood that,' said Danglard. 'But yes, why are you still after him?'

'Danglard, have you ever left a bottle of wine half full, once you've opened it?'

'What's that got to do with anything?'

'You know quite well. We haven't emptied the François Château bottle yet. You could look at it two ways. François Château is Robespierre and he's under threat. Or François Château is Robespierre and he's dangerous. Or it could be something much less simple.'

Veyrenc, his hair once more tucked away under the tourist baseball cap, frowned and lit a cigarette, automatically passing the packet to Adamsberg.

'You think Château feels so closely identified with Robespierre that he has somehow *become* him?' he said. 'So he might reproduce the death sentences during the Terror? No sooner destroying one enemy than he discovers another?'

'It would be a never-ending process,' Danglard commented, 'since the enemy Robespierre was pursuing was inside him. But in that case, why would Château have written to us in the first place?'

'I don't know,' said Adamsberg, shifting from one foot to another, indicating that he was eager to be off. 'We have to get to the bottom of this bottle. To find what's there.'

'The dregs,' said Danglard.

'Not quite,' said Adamsberg. 'It's a bottle with two corks. We have emptied the first chamber. If Froissy finishes her research in time, I hope to be able to extract the second cork.'

'What did you ask Froissy to do?'

'An identity check on François Château.'

'You think he's given us a false name?'

'No, not at all. When you get back, can you send me a photo of Victor.'

'What's Victor doing back again in the case?' asked Danglard.

'He was Masfauré's secretary, he may have accompanied him to the association, he may have heard something, might know something. Tell me, Danglard, did Robespierre have any descendants?'

'Total blind alley, commissaire. They said that Robespierre had an empty sack. As in empty balls.'

'Yes, I got that.'

'I don't mean physical impotence, but a psychological block. A remarkable symptom of the extensive pathology of the man –'

'Zerk is cooking a leg of lamb tonight,' Adamsberg interrupted. 'It'll be too much for two.'

'Let me bring the wine,' said Danglard hastily, since the white wine Zerk bought at the corner shop was rotgut, as far as he was concerned.

'It's not so much for your company,' smiled Adamsberg, ' but I need to pick your brains some more.'

'When this case is closed,' said Danglard, 'can I keep those drawings?'

'You want them as well? Why?'

'It's just that it's a marvellous portrait of Robespierre.'

'It's a portrait of Château,' Adamsberg corrected him. 'You're mixing them up yourself now. So what must it be like for him?'

The Seine was too far away for him to get there and back in time, especially at his leisurely pace. His best bet was to go to the Saint-Martin Canal. It was still water. It wasn't the Gave de Pau, his native stream, of course, but it was quite like a river with seagulls overhead. The buildings along its banks were not the rocks of the Pyrenees, but they were still made of stone. Stone and water, leaves on the trees, seagulls, even rather bedraggled ones, were never to be despised.

His mobile vibrated as he reached the canal and its smell of wet clothes that the dirty water of cities always gives off. He was desperately hoping for a reply from Froissy and looked up at the shrieking gulls to offer them a pagan prayer. But they weren't listening, and the text was merely to send him a photo of Victor. All this, although far from Iceland, did still concern the young men at Le Creux. Because if Victor knew about his philanthropic boss's parallel hobby, he might well have told Amédée about it. And who knows what Victor and Amédée would have made of Henri's enthusiasm for Robespierre? Dangerous? Expensive? Victor had apparently reported that Masfauré's bookshelves contained nothing about the Revolution. That was logical enough, if he wanted to keep his links to the association a secret. And he certainly seemed to have done that. Mordent had reported that the lawyer had no record of any payments to any cultural association. So the money must have been handed over in cash.

Stone, water, birds. He leaned back on the bench he had chosen, hands clasped behind the nape of his neck, looking up at the sky, watching for any particularly leisurely gulls. It was easy to choose one, climb on its back without hurting it, and guide its flight, gently manipulating its wings, sending it away over the fields to the sea, and there play at flying in the face of the wind.

After travelling six hundred kilometres like that Adamsberg sat back up, asked someone the time, and hailed a taxi. The idea of returning to Château's dark office did not appeal to him. Still less the prospect of emptying the bottle. That is, if he had the wherewithal to remove the second cork.

At 7.25, the porter opened the clanking gates once more for him and asked him to wait for Monsieur Château in his office, he wouldn't be long. Having no more of the crumpled cigarettes scrounged from Zerk, Adamsberg had had to buy himself a new packet. Pacing up and down while smoking in the panelled office of the little president would not be excessive behaviour, if he was to pull that second cork. Froissy's latest reply had reached him seven minutes earlier. How brilliant Froissy was! Having guessed right on this point made him feel slightly dizzy, as if he had ventured into the realms of unreason, realms where the mechanisms were unfamiliar and, worst of all, the future was hard to predict. Whereas, alone in the high Pyrenees at night, he felt as much at ease as a mountain goat. But the world of François Château, which had just become even more murky, was not at all his territory. He thought about the story Mordent liked – the one where as you entered the forest, the branches closed behind you and the way back was no longer possible or visible.

Adamsberg had not dared to open the desk drawer to take out the ashtray, and was looking at the books on the shelves without reading the titles.

'Good evening, commissaire,' came a rasping voice from behind him.

A voice he had heard the day before. François Château had entered the room, or rather this time Maximilien Robespierre had. Adamsberg stood stunned, faced with the person he had not seen from close up the previous evening. Arms folded, back rigid, this man, now bewigged, his face powdered and wearing a sky-blue coat, was looking at him with that smile that was no smile, blinking his eyes behind the little round spectacles with tinted lenses. Adamsberg was transfixed, as the others had been earlier. Talking to Château was one thing, discussing matters with Maximilien Robespierre quite another.

Without a word, the person opened the drawer and put the ashtray on the desk.

'That's a handsome costume,' said Adamsberg, for want of anything better, sitting down on the edge of a chair.

'I wore this at the Feast of the Supreme Being which was my apotheosis,' the man replied drily, taking up his stance again. 'The only morning when I was seen to have a genuine and open smile, people who are fond of anecdotes like to say, because of the celestial sunshine that had dawned on Paris that day. You have never seen that unique brightness, and you never will. I was wearing this same coat again on 8 Thermidor in front of the assembly. But it was powerless to avert my death two days later, bringing an end to the Republic.'

Adamsberg opened his cigarette packet and proffered it without response towards Château (or whatever he should call this man). He, who had detected the little president behind Robespierre that night, should not have been overcome by his appearance now. But with his outfit, the man's whole personality seemed to have changed, as if Robespierre's impassive face had replaced, even brutally blotted out, the smiling and rather childish features of François Château. Almost nothing of the modest president remained, and Adamsberg wondered what was behind this excessive and indeed ridiculous performance, which nevertheless disturbed him. Did Château expect to be able to draw from Robespierre the strength he feared he would not have himself for this interview? Did he mean to impress the commissaire with this icy demeanour? But there was something else, he concluded, observing him through the cloud of smoke. Château had been weeping, and did not want it to be noticed at any price. Under the face powder, Adamsberg could distinguish, in spite of everything, the red edges of his lower eyelids and the pouches forming underneath his swollen eyes. Adamsberg instinctively pitched his voice at its lowest and gentlest.

'Is that so?' he said, still perched uneasily on his chair.

'How can you doubt it, monsieur le commissaire? After me, Reaction swept through France, and she fell like a careless and easy woman into the arms of a tyrant. And then what happened? A few brief attempts at rebellion, memories of our glorious efforts, quickly swallowed up in a cheapened republic where corruption and greed destroyed our ideals, although the words Liberty, Equality, Fraternity still echo nostalgically round the world. The motto may be carved on buildings, but no one nowadays shouts it out with heartfelt enthusiasm.'

'Did you make it up? That motto?'

'No. The words were around everywhere at the time, but I combined them in a single cutting phrase: "Liberty, Equality, Fraternity or Death".'

Château, his nostrils flaring, suddenly interrupted himself and leaned towards Adamsberg, putting his delicate hands flat down on the desk.

'Will that do, monsieur le commissaire? Have we amused ourselves enough now? Because that's how you wanted to see me, wasn't it, to see me as "Him"? Did you like the show? And are we finished now?'

'What will become of all this?' asked Adamsberg prosaically, gesturing broadly to indicate the whole building.

'What does that matter to you? We still have enough money left to finish our research.'

The biting, icy-cold tones of Robespierre persisted in the president's voice, and were still disturbing Adamsberg.

'This man,' he said, 'do you know him?' and he held out his phone with the photo of Victor.

'Is he dead too? Is he another contemptible traitor?' asked Château, taking hold of the phone.

'Have you ever seen him here?'

'Of course. He's Henri Masfauré's secretary, his name's Victor, he's a foundling and a son of the people. Has he been eliminated too?' he asked coldly.

'No, he's still alive. So he came along with his boss to the assemblies?'

'Henri couldn't do without his secretary, and Victor obeyed. He memorised everything. Question him.'

'That's my intention,' said Adamsberg, conscious that in his imperious role Château had just given him an order.

It didn't embarrass him, but it struck him forcibly. He stood up, took a few steps, and then put his phone down on the table, after pressing 4, which would communicate directly with Danglard, so that his deputy would be able to follow the rest of the conversation from headquarters. In this extraordinary situation, his deputy's opinion would be valuable.

'How does it come about that you look so like Robespierre?' Adamsberg asked, without sitting back down.

'Make-up, monsieur le commissaire.'

'No, you really do resemble him.'

'A freak of nature, or the intervention of the Supreme Being, take your pick,' said Château, sitting down and crossing his legs.

'A resemblance that prompted you to go looking for traces of Robespierre and to found the association, the "concept"?'

'No, not at all.'

'Until the character of Robespierre took you over entirely.'

'Perhaps because it's getting late and you've had a hard day, monsieur le commissaire, your subtle mind is losing its sharpness. You're going to ask me next if I have become "identified" with him. By some kind of aberrant mental quirk, or because I am suffering from a split personality, or some other completely grotesque idea. I'll stop your ridiculous assumptions right there. I play the *part* of Robespierre, as I have just demonstrated to you, and that is all. And indeed, I am very well paid to do so.'

'You're quick off the mark.'

'It's not hard to be one jump ahead of you.'

'He's beaten,' said Danglard out loud, in the anxious tones of a man watching a match of some kind.

All the squad had gathered round, leaning together over the table to hear better the voices coming from the phone.

'You are indeed François Château, I do know that,' said Adamsberg.

'Exactly. End of discussion.'

'And you are the son of Maximilien Barthélémy François Château. Who was himself the son of Maximilien Château.'

Château-Robespierre stiffened, and at the other end of the line so did Danglard and Veyrenc.

'What?' said Voisenet, expressing what the others felt.

'Those were the first names of Robespierre's own father and grand-father,' Danglard whispered quickly. 'The Château family gave its sons the same names as the Robespierre family.'

President Château now entered upon one of the rages which were known to overcome the Incorruptible, banging his fist on the table, his fine lips trembling as he shouted at Adamsberg.

'Is he in danger?' asked Kernorkian.

'Shut up, for heaven's sake,' said Veyrenc. 'Retancourt's on hand.' Knowing that the lieutenant was nearby reassured them, even Noël. Their heads moved closer to the speaker.

'You damnable traitor!' Château was yelling. 'I called on your assistance in complete confidence, and you have used that, like a contemptible hypocrite, to go snooping like a rat into my own family!'

'"Contemptible hypocrite", one of Robespierre's favourite expressions,' Danglard commented quietly.

'And anyway, what of it?' Château was going on. 'Yes, the entire family was fervently pro-Robespierre, and believe me, I wouldn't wish that on anyone!'

'So why didn't you inherit these sacred names?'

'Thanks to my mother!' Château shouted. 'She did all she could to protect me from these Robespierrist fanatics, but she drowned in front of my eyes, when I was twelve years old. Are you satisfied now, monsieur le commissaire?'

The little man had stood up, pulled off his wig and thrown it violently on the floor.

'The mask's off,' Danglard said, 'the second cork is out of the bottle.'

'Can a bottle have two corks?' asked Estalère.

'Obviously,' said Danglard. 'Now be quiet. We can hear water running. He's got a basin in the office by the coffee machine, he's washing the make-up off.'

Château was rubbing his cheeks fiercely, as a white stream of water rolled off them. Then spitting and sniffing shamelessly, he wiped his face, now regaining some of its natural rosy colour, and came to sit down, caught between pride and distress. He extended an elegant hand, this time to ask for a cigarette.

'You are a skilled fighter, monsieur le commissaire, I ought to have had you guillotined earlier,' he said, finding his smile once more, though it was a rueful one now. 'You should have been beheaded first of the lot. I know what you're thinking. That my family somehow made me think I was a "descendant" of Robespierre. That they tried to stuff this into my child's brain. Well, it's true. My grandfather was responsible, he was an impossible old man, and he'd been raised in the same cult. My mother was against it, but my father was a weak man. Shall I go on?'

'Yes please. My own grandfather was nothing to boast about, he'd been shell-shocked by the Great War, and he was a tyrant.'

'The old man started on me from the age of four,' Château said, slightly calmer now. 'He taught me Robespierre's speeches, but also his posture, his voice, how to imitate the delivery, and most of all he taught me about Robespierre's distrust of potential enemies, distrust in fact of everyone, with purity as his rule for life. The old idiot was pumped up with pride at the idea that he was descended from the great man. My mother helped me to resist. Every evening, like Penelope with her web, she undid for me what the old man had done in the daytime. But she abandoned me. I always thought the old man must have sabotaged the boat she was drowned in. Like Robespierre: eliminate any obstacle in your path. After that, he became even more dictatorial. But by then I was twelve and the shield my mother had given me was more effective. So the old man was faced with another obstacle: me.'

Adamsberg stopped walking up and down, and both men took another cigarette. Château, with his face now half washed, still bearing traces of powder, without the same presence, his bald head ringed round with tousled fair hair and his eyes swollen, but still wearing Robespierre's famous sky-blue coat, was as splendid as he was touching. He could have looked grotesque. But his distress, his graceful posture and the extraordinary sight he made both disturbed and moved Adamsberg. He, Adamsberg, had worked for this defeat, indeed this debacle, because it was necessary for the investigation. Pull the second cork, empty the bottle down to the dregs. But at a cost.

The squad was thinking much the same; people held their breaths, and there was a perceptible emotion in the room, which only Estalère expressed.

'Sad, isn't it?' he said.

'My father was mad about Napoleon,' said Voisenet, 'but he didn't try to get me to invade Russia. Still, he hated me getting involved with fish.'

'Silence!' said Danglard.

'Nevertheless,' Château was saying, breathing out cigarette smoke, 'your suspicions go further, don't they? You think the old man must have twisted my personality, like a blacksmith with a piece of iron. That I've absorbed the "Chosen Role" he assigned to me, and that now, I'm reproducing Robespierre's own destructive tendencies. That *I'm* the one who's killing members of my own association. That's what you're thinking. And in that respect, monsieur le commissaire, you are quite mistaken.'

Château was twitching his fingers open and closed, against his damp lace jabot, as if he wanted to feel or caress something. Adamsberg had noticed this compulsive gesture the previous day. Some kind of medal or pendant, a talisman, he supposed, or perhaps a locket containing his mother's hair.

'So if your mother had provided you with a shield as you put it, what drove you, all the same, to found this association and to take on this hated role?'

'I could imitate Robespierre to perfection with my eyes shut, from the age of fifteen. Even after my old grandfather died, I was haunted by Robespierre, he was walking beside me, following me everywhere, never letting me go. So I decided to turn round and face him. *Face up to him*, commissaire. With the aim of finishing with him, settling his hash for good. So I grappled with him, I got hold of him, and I played him. He's my creation now, not me his. *I'm* pulling the strings now.'

Adamsberg nodded.

'We're both tired,' he said, sitting down and crushing out his cigarette. 'Your associates, your co-founders, what did you call them?'

'Leblond and Lebrun.'

'OK, Leblond and Lebrun, do they know all this?'

'No, absolutely not. And can I beg you, if we are allowed to beg things from the police, that they should remain in ignorance?'

XXII

ZERK WAS NOT YET A GOOD COOK, BUT HE WAS MAKING PROGRESS. His leg of lamb was roasted exactly right, and the tinned haricot beans were acceptable. Danglard poured out generous glasses of wine, and Adamsberg gave himself time to finish his dinner before tackling the case once more. His companions understood as much and made small talk about other things, which greatly pleased Zerk, who was as unskilled as his father at verbal jousting. And it allowed Adamsberg to forget briefly about the knot of seaweed, which had not yet lost any of its density and darkness.

They carried their coffee over to the fireplace, Danglard taking his usual position on the left, Adamsberg on the right, feet on a firedog, and Veyrenc in the centre.

'So, what was your impression?' asked Adamsberg.

'He sounded genuine,' said Danglard.

'Well, he sounded genuine when we had lunch with him on the Tournelle embankment,' said Veyrenc sceptically, 'when he concealed from us the fact that he was going to play Robespierre. Though, of course, he wasn't under any obligation to tell us that.'

'Perhaps there's a third cork in this bottle,' said Adamsberg.

'There are some bottles with nine corks, apparently,' said Danglard, pouring himself another glass.

'Not for you, commandant.'

'No, corks don't bother me. They come out in my hands like obedient insects.'

Zerk had already had too much to drink and had nodded off at the table, head on his arms.

'He claims to be pulling the strings of his character,' Adamsberg said, 'performing at the rostrum, and therefore being in control. But when he came in as Robespierre this evening, when he fell into a rage at me, and started using expressions like "damnable traitor", "contemptible hypocrite", "foundling and son of the people", it didn't seem to me that little Château was running the show. As if once he was in costume – he was wearing a blue frock coat, the same one, he said, that he wore for the Feast of God –'

'Not God, the Supreme Being,' said Danglard.

'Well, anyway, as if little Château had become permeable, absorbent, filled full of the character without controlling him. Robespierre can get inside him whenever he wants, and at those times, François Château doesn't exist. Nothing left. Contrary to what he tried to make me think. There again, he wasn't telling the whole truth. And yet he was obviously suffering. His smile was painful to see.'

'*That smile is painful to see,*' Danglard began quoting. '*The passion which has visibly drunk all his blood and dried out his bones has left in place his nervous energy, like a cat that has been drowned and then resuscitated by galvanism, or perhaps a reptile that stiffens and rears up, with an unspeakable gaze, frighteningly elegant. The overall impression though, make no mistake, is not hate: what one feels is a kind of painful pity, mingled with terror.*'

'Is that a description of Him?'

'Yes.'

'Where did you get the idea of looking into his family names?' asked Veyrenc.

'Since Château was so obsessed with the man, I thought perhaps he might be descended from him. That was before I knew that Robespierre had no children.'

'No, no children,' Danglard confirmed. 'Women, anything to do with sex, terrified him. It was on this fear that he based his notion of "vice", unconsciously no doubt. He lost his mother when he was six years old, and since she was almost permanently pregnant for those six years, she hardly had time for little Maximilien before she died in childbirth. After her death, his previously impeccable father, a respectable lawyer in Arras, abandoned the household and disappeared, deserting the four children. Aged six, Maximilien, the eldest boy, was left feeling responsible, without having known an ounce of love. They say that the child became rigid after that and they never saw him laugh or play again.'

'Sounds a bit like Château,' said Veyrenc.

'Yes, more than a bit, in fact.'

'When stripped down – what I mean is,' said Adamsberg, 'when he's without the covering of Robespierre – he does seem rather asexual.'

'If Robespierre hadn't got involved in the Revolution,' said Danglard, 'and had remained a small-town lawyer in Arras as he started off, he might well have been like our Château. Talented but petrified, full of exaltation, but gagged. Unable to approach a woman. And yet women fell for *him* in large numbers. But no, there are no descendants. None of the four Robespierre children ever had any. It's always possible of course that Maximilien might have had the odd affair, or even just one, before he became "Robespierre". But the historians doubt it.'

At this point, Danglard stopped speaking, and looked thoughtful, knitting his brows. He stiffened like a hesitant animal, suddenly in a state of alert.

'Oh my God!' he said. 'Château! No, don't say anything, I'm trying to get there.'

The commandant pressed his glass against his mouth, half closing his eyes.

'Got it!' he said. 'There was this rumour. I had completely forgotten about it, it nearly slipped through my fingers, like the cats in your garden.'

'We're listening, commandant,' said Adamsberg, taking a cigarette from his own packet. He would leave it for Zerk tomorrow and steal some more from him, because he preferred his son's. But you don't rob a sleeping man.

'There was a persistent rumour about a secret son of Robespierre,' Danglard said, 'born in about 1790. And called . . . yes . . . Didier Château.'

'Château!' said Adamsberg, sitting up.

'Like Château.'

'Carry on, commandant.'

'Indeed, he was called *François* Didier Château, François like our François. But the only "proof" of this relationship is one letter. In 1840, so when this François Didier Château was about fifty, the president of the Paris Appeal Court, no less, made a strong plea for him to be given an official position. And yet he was only a simple provincial innkeeper at the time. So how did François Didier Château, bastard and son of the people, manage to get to know the all-powerful Parisian lawyer? That's the first puzzle. Anyway, in a letter to the prefect of his *département*, the president asked that this innkeeper should be made the postmaster of . . .'

Danglard rubbed his forehead, sat up and drank some white wine.

'. . . of Château-Renard, in the Loiret,' he said finally, sounding relieved at retrieving the name. 'But better than that, the president said that his protégé was also recommended by various respectable people in the area, such as the justice of the peace, the mayor, the local landowners. So how did this innkeeper come by such advocates in high places?'

'His reputation?' said Veyrenc.

'Exactly. Because in his reply, refusing to give him the job, the prefect – remember we are under the July Monarchy now . . . Can you pass me your laptop please, commissaire?'

'Right,' Danglard went on after a few minutes, 'here we are: *I have to tell you that the sieur Château whom you have recommended to me is the natural son of Robespierre.* Note how firmly the prefect states this, without the shadow of a doubt. *He is not responsible for his birth, I know, but unfortunately his origin has had a bad influence on his opinion and his behaviour, and he is extremely radical in both respects.*'

Danglard put down the computer, and folded his arms, smiling and satisfied.

'Is there any more, Danglard?' asked Adamsberg, stunned, leaning towards his colleague as if towards Aladdin's magic lamp.

'There isn't much else, but still. After Robespierre's death, the mother of this François Didier had taken refuge in Château-Renard with her four-year-old son. Were there rumours? Was she afraid for the child? Was his life in danger? Quite possibly. After all, a few years earlier, people had been afraid that the child in the Temple was a threat. The threat of blood calling for vengeance. Like the prisoners in the tower at Le Creux.'

'What do you mean, the child in the Temple?' asked Adamsberg.

'The dauphin, Louis XVI's young son. The royal family were imprisoned in a building called the Temple.'

'So what else do we know about this supposed child of Robespierre?'

'There is a physical description of him when he was serving in the Napoleonic army. Nothing very conclusive, but it doesn't actually contradict any link with the supposed father. What I mean to say is, he wasn't six feet tall with a Roman nose and dark eyes. No, he was less than one metre sixty, had blue eyes and fair hair, a small nose and a small mouth.'

'Yes, that's vague.'

'But there's another puzzle. Five years after failing to get a job as postmaster, our innkeeper becomes director of public coaches. The state stagecoaches! A big deal,' said Danglard, clicking his fingers. 'Friends in high places again. That's all, no more left to say.'

'That's a lot, Danglard. The prefect's letter is very striking.'

'Actually,' Danglard said, 'I don't believe a word of it! I don't believe Robespierre ever slept with a woman. What's to say that this Denise Patillaut – that's the mother's name, it's just come back to me – being pregnant and unmarried, didn't boast of the famous father to deflect the opprobrium normally attached to an illegitimate birth? And then the Château family preserved the legend. Down to our François. If he really is a descendant of François Didier.'

'We do have another element,' said Veyrenc. 'His extraordinary resemblance to Robespierre.'

'Well, we'll never know,' said Danglard, 'and nor will the Château family. No DNA testing's possible, because Robespierre's remains were finally dispersed in the catacombs under Paris.'

'But the most important thing isn't whether it's *true*,' said Adamsberg, putting his feet back up on the firedog. 'The key thing is that the Château family believed it. The grandfather must have clung to it through thick and thin, like his predecessors. They were keepers of the flame, priests of the cult. So what does our François believe then? That he's a descendant of some "fanatical Robespierrists" as he put it to me, or that he is really a descendant of Robespierre himself, in flesh and blood? It would change things a lot.'

'Château's been lying through his teeth,' commented Veyrenc.

'If he does believe he's a descendant,' said Danglard, 'and if he is our killer, I'll say it again, why on earth did he write to us?'

'He's acting like his ancestor,' said Veyrenc. 'Robespierre didn't kill people in secret like some "hypocritical" criminal from the stews of Paris. He's doing it out in the open. Because these are exemplary deaths.'

'There really must be a third cork at the bottom of this bottle,' Adamsberg concluded quietly.

XXIII

HAVING BEEN SUMMONED BY ADAMSBERG, FRANÇOIS CHÂTEAU'S two fellow office holders in the association readily agreed to come to the Serious Crime Squad headquarters at 3 p.m. Meanwhile Froissy was looking into the archives of Château-Renard, to trace the descendants of François Didier Château, who had been a local innkeeper there in 1840, and Retancourt and her colleagues were still protecting the president.

NTR, Retancourt had texted. *FC home 22h, supper, bed, lives alone. Now at work hotel 11h–17h. BTW, was assaulted rue Norevin by 3 dumb skinheads, seen as potential lay. Flattered. Justin witnessed. No serious fallout but kids at station in 18th bit worse 4 wear.*

'Quite a lot the worse for wear, rather,' Adamsberg said to himself, as he closed his mobile and called his colleague in the 18th arrondissement.

'Montreux, that you? Adamsberg. You've got three kids there from last night?'

'She come from you, the one that fell on them? A tree or what?'

'A sacred tree – you got it. What shape are they in?'

'They're deeply humiliated. Your girl simply punched them in the stomach, nothing broken, the "tree" knows how to temper her punches. She left their balls intact.'

'She's a gentle soul.'

'Well, one of them's got a squashed nose, another has a torn ear – with three earrings still attached, actually the guy was keener to get those back than the bit of his ear, and the third has a real shiner. She was within her rights, they tried to jump her, they were pissed out of their minds. Her colleague witnessed it all, he gave a statement. Little guy, more like a daffodil than a tree, I'd say.'

'He's a harmless reed, but one that thinks.'

'You seem to have some variety over there. Here I've only got five bloody idiots.'

'Just the one here, I think.'

Adamsberg put down the phone as Estalère ushered in François Château's two associates. One looked fragile and the other burly, like characters in classic buddy movies, but they both wore glasses, and had extensive beards, plus longer hair than would be usual for their age – about fifty.

'I see,' said Adamsberg with a smile as he asked them to sit down. 'You are afraid of people taking clandestine photographs. Estalère, some coffee please. I have already agreed not to ask you your real names.'

'We have to operate in total confidentiality,' said the burly one. 'We just have to. People are so narrow-minded that they easily misunderstand.'

'The president explained the rules of confidentiality. Your beards look very convincing.'

'You probably know we have some excellent make-up artists in the association. Beards are the easy part. They can manage complete transformations.'

'So in that case, you feel safe,' said Adamsberg.

'Has that young man seen a ghost or what?' the thin one asked, when Estalère had gone out.

'Estalère? No, his eyes always look like that.'

'If he had darker hair, he'd make a very good Billaud-Varenne.'

'Is that a Robespierrist?'

'Yes,' said the burly one.

'Estalère's a little lamb.'

'But he's angelic-looking, like Billaud. As for character, that doesn't matter. You saw how François Château subdued the assembly, didn't you? But I can assure you he doesn't produce that effect when he's working at the hotel. As for the man you have on the desk at reception, not very good-looking, if you'll forgive my bluntness, but he would make an excellent Marat.'

'I doubt if he could make his speeches. I wouldn't be able to myself.'

Adamsberg fell silent as Estalère brought in the coffees.

'But François must surely have told you that our assemblies have the facility to loosen people's tongues and change their behaviour,' said the burly one.

'To the point of producing genuine passions and wholehearted identification with the person they're playing,' added the thin one.

'Even if, in real life, the actor doesn't have anything in common with the character, and sometimes it's even the opposite. You find some people with right-wing opinions turn into raging extremists of the left. That's one of the aims of our research: the group effect, wiping out people's individual convictions. But as we change roles every four months, we *are* currently looking for a Billaud-Varenne and a Marat.'

'And a Tallien.'

'But not a Robespierre,' said Adamsberg.

The thin one smiled knowingly.

'And you saw why the other night.'

'Almost too clearly.'

'He is exceptional, irreplaceable.'

'Does he too sometimes fall victim to a "wholehearted identification"?'

The burly one seemed to know something about psychiatry, perhaps it was his profession. One could understand that he wouldn't want his patients to see him in eighteenth-century clothes with a lace jabot.

'Maybe, at the beginning, that might happen,' said the thin one thoughtfully, 'but he's been interpreting the role of Maximilien for twelve years now. It's become a routine. He can do it the way someone else can play draughts. With concentration, and intensity, but no more.'

'One moment,' Adamsberg interrupted. 'Which of you is the treasurer, nicknamed Leblond, and which the secretary, known as Lebrun?'

'I'm Leblond,' said the thin one, with the fair silky beard.

'Thank you, that's helpful. So you're Lebrun,' Adamsberg said to the other man. 'Do you mind if I smoke?' he asked them, feeling in his pockets, having laid in a little stock from Zerk's supplies that morning.

'You're on your home ground, commissaire.'

'Now then, four deaths already in your association: Henri Masfauré, who was your financial linchpin, Alice Gauthier, Jean Breuguel and Angelino Gonzalez. Did you know them by sight?'

'Yes indeed,' said Lebrun, the one with the thick black beard. 'Gonzalez used to wear full costume and make-up, but we've seen your sketch. That was him all right.'

'François Château told me at once I should consult you. Because he says that you keep an eye on the members better than he does.'

'It's worse than that,' said Leblond with a smile, 'we spy on them.'

'Really?'

'You see, we're being open with you. Our "living history" has got out of hand, and it's occasioned some stupefying psychological upheavals.'

'You might even say pathological consequences,' added Lebrun. 'That's certainly what we're seeing at the moment. Which proves to us that we were right to be keeping a close watch on our members.'

'How do you go about it?'

'Most of those who attend behave in classic fashion,' said Lebrun. 'They throw themselves into it. They play their parts, sometimes overdoing it in fact. And that can cover a wide range of behaviour, running from those who are amusing themselves – that was the case with Gonzalez all right, which didn't stop him being a splendid Hébert, did it, Leblond?'

'Excellent. It broke my heart to give the Hébert part to someone else who wasn't too bad, but really nothing like as good. Never mind, by the next meeting Hébert will have been guillotined. Sorry, we're talking shop.'

'So, as I was saying,' Lebrun went on, 'it can run from people who are amusing themselves to people who take themselves very seriously, from those who are just taking on a part to those who are bursting with passion.'

'Yes, and you have the full spectrum of diversity and graded nuances between the two poles.'

'. . . the full spectrum of diversity and graded nuances,' Adamsberg noted. Was Leblond perhaps a physicist?

'And nevertheless, it is all contained within the bounds of "normality", that is to say, our own rather "crazy normality",' said Lebrun, 'especially since we have insisted on taking it in turns to play the parts. But it's the others that my colleague and I are keeping an eye on. About twenty of them. We call them the "infras" between ourselves.'

'Do you mind if I walk about a bit?' asked Adamsberg.

'You're on your home ground,' Lebrun repeated.

'So who are these "infras"?'

'The ones outside the regular spectrum,' explained Leblond. 'Like infrared rays for instance, which our eyes can't see. You have to imagine a comedy show and someone who doesn't laugh. Or a terrifying film that leaves a certain spectator quite cold.'

'Whereas most of the people who attend our sessions "come out of themselves", to put it simply.'

'And we don't just mean the odd moment,' Leblond said. 'It's a constant. An invariant.'

An invariant. He must be some kind of scientist.

'So these "infras",' Lebrun took up the explanation – and Adamsberg noted the harmony of their almost interchangeable double act – 'remain astonishingly neutral, straight-faced. Not unhappy, or absent-minded, but inscrutable. They certainly can't be indifferent – or why would they be there at all? – but distant.'

'I see,' said Adamsberg, still pacing up and down.

'In fact,' added Leblond, 'they *are* there, they're paying attention, but their participation is of a different order from the rest.'

'What they're doing is *observing*,' said Lebrun, 'and we're observing the people who are observing us. Why are they there? What do they want?'

'And your answer to that is?'

'Hard to say,' Lebrun replied. 'Over time, my colleague and I have identified two distinct groups among the "infras". We call one lot the "infiltrators" and the others the "guillotined". If we're right, the infiltrators number no more than ten.'

'We don't count Henri Masfauré, although he also seemed to be watching them. He would talk to one or other, now and then. Victor was there to act as his eyes and ears. And among them were those two other people, who were killed, Gauthier and Breuguel, and another man we haven't seen for some years. So you see that, apart from Gonzalez, the killer has chosen to attack the infiltrators, the watchers in the shadows, the enquirers. Therefore, they can't have been inoffensive.'

'How would you describe the others? The survivors of that group?'

Adamsberg stopped at his desk and, still standing, prepared to take some notes.

'We can only identify four of them with any certainty,' said Leblond. 'A woman and three men. She's about sixty, mid-length straight hair, peroxide blonde. She has strong features and striking blue eyes, must have been a real beauty in her day. Leblond has managed to exchange a few words with her now and then, although the infiltrators are hard to get to know. He thinks she may have been an actress. As for the ex-cyclist – you describe him, you know him better than I do.'

'We call him "the ex-cyclist" because of his huge legs, which he always holds planted slightly apart. As if, ahem, excuse me, he was still a bit saddle-sore. That's just our nickname for him. I'd say he's fortyish, short dark hair, regular features, but devoid of expression. Unless, that is, he's deliberately made his face expressionless to discourage anyone from chatting to him. As all the infiltrators do in their own way.'

'An actress and a cyclist,' Adamsberg noted. 'And the third?'

'I suspect he's a dentist,' said Lebrun. 'He has a way of looking at you as if he's making a judgement about your teeth. And there's a slight smell of antiseptic on his hands. About fifty-five. Brown eyes, which look both inquisitorial and sad, thin lips, well-cared-for teeth, crowns I'd say. There's something bitter about him, and he has dandruff.'

'Bitter, inquisitorial dentist with dandruff,' Adamsberg noted. 'And the fourth?'

'No special distinguishing features,' said Lebrun, frowning. 'He's hard to describe, nothing easy to pick on.'

'Do they stand together?'

'No,' said Leblond. 'But they certainly know each other. They carry out a strange sort of ballet movement. They meet, have a brief word, move off, and so on. Fleeting contacts, but apparently necessary, and I think deliberately discreet. They always leave before the end of the evening. So we've never been able to follow them out, because we are obliged to remain as François's bodyguards.'

Adamsberg added to the list of the 'infiltrators' the names of Gauthier, Masfauré, Breuguel and, lower down, Gonzalez. He drew a line and headed his second column 'The Guillotined'.

'More coffee?' he asked, 'or would you prefer tea, or hot chocolate? Or a beer, perhaps?'

The two men pricked up their ears.

So Adamsberg upped the offer.

'Or indeed some white wine,' he said. 'We keep some excellent stuff here.'

'Beer please,' the two men chorused.

'It's upstairs, I'll take you there. Look out, there's an irregular step on the staircase, always causing trouble.'

Adamsberg was so used to the little room containing the drinks dispenser that he walked in without warning his guests. The cat, accompanied by Voisenet, was eating from its dish of crunchy cat food, while Lieutenant Mercadet was fast asleep on the pile of blue cushions specially arranged for him.

'One of our officers suffers from narcolepsy,' Adamsberg explained. 'He functions in three-hour cycles.'

He took three bottles of beer from the refrigerator, including one for himself, essential in order to make the session more friendly, and opened them at a small bar lined with four stools.

'We only have plastic cups,' he apologised.

'We wouldn't have expected you to have a luxurious bar here. Or that beer was allowed, come to that.'

'Obviously,' said Adamsberg, leaning on the counter. 'Now then,' he said, showing them a drawing of the sign. 'Does *this* mean anything to you? Have you ever seen it before?'

'Never,' said Leblond, and Lebrun followed suit, shaking his head.

'But how would you interpret it? Knowing that this sign has been drawn somehow or other at the scene of all four murders.'

'I don't see what it is,' said Lebrun.

'But in context? Your context, the Revolution?' Adamsberg prompted them.

'Wait a minute,' said Lebrun, reaching out for the drawing. 'It could be two guillotines. The old-fashioned English kind, and the new French one, put together to make a cryptogram? A warning sign?'

'Of what?'

'Well, of execution?'

'But on what grounds?'

'In our context, as you put it,' said Leblond sadly, 'it could be treason.'

'So you think the killer might have identified the infiltrators, the spies?'

'Looks like it,' said Lebrun. 'But the sign would be a royalist one. They say that it was Louis XVI himself who perfected the former prototype of the guillotine, by striking out the curved blade. Mind you, there's no evidence of that.'

'He was certainly a good mechanic,' said Leblond laconically, taking a swig of beer.

'Well, what about your second group, then?' asked Adamsberg, 'the "guillotined" as you called them?'

'Or the "descendants".'

'What do you mean, descendants?'

Voisenet's eyes met Adamsberg's and the commissaire signalled to him not to intervene. The lieutenant picked up the cat who had finished feeding and left the little room.

'He's carrying the cat?' asked Lebrun.

'The cat doesn't like the stairs. And he can't feed unless someone sits with him.'

'So why don't you put his dish downstairs?' asked Leblond, the logician.

'Because he only likes eating up here. And sleeping downstairs.'

'Peculiar.'

'Yes.'

'You're not afraid we'll wake up your lieutenant?'

'No risk, that's the problem. On the other hand, he is super-efficient when he is awake, in the other part of the cycle.'

'Complicated business running a police station,' remarked Lebrun.

'Yes, some people think there's a bit of laissez-aller here,' said Adamsberg, drinking again from the bottle.

He really didn't want this beer.

'And yet you are a successful unit?'

'We don't do too badly. Because of the laissez-aller, I suppose.'

'Interesting,' commented Lebrun, as if to himself.

Lebrun, secretary of the association, perhaps a psychiatrist.

The three men went back downstairs, holding the bottles of beer, and Leblond, in spite of the warning, almost tripped on the odd stair. Once back in the commissaire's office, the atmosphere, previously simply courteous, was more relaxed.

It was Leblond who of his own accord launched the next stage of their session.

'Now, for the "guillotined",' he said. 'These ones are solitary. They don't know each other, so they don't talk to each other. They are regular, assiduous even, but they never volunteer to take the role of a deputy. They sit up in the high seats and melt into the background. They are silent, vigilant and serious, showing no apparent emotion. It's because of their unusual expressions that Lebrun and I have identified them one by one. Three of them always stay till the end and drink a glass of wine in silence at the buffet after the assembly.'

'Whose descendants are they?'

'They're descended from people who were guillotined.'

'But how did you find that out?'

'Because of those three,' said Lebrun. 'We were able to follow them out. Once François is safely back home, we can return for the end of the buffet and we tail them.'

'You mean you know their names?'

'Better than that. Names, addresses, occupations.'

'So you know who their ancestors were?'

'Exactly,' said Lebrun, with a broad and amiable grin.

'But you are not at liberty to tell me their names?'

'We are strictly bound by the rule, we cannot reveal to a third person the identity of our members. Those or any other. But it would not be out of order, for me to point them out to you at a session. Then you would be free to follow them, if that seemed a likely lead for you.'

'You should be clear,' said Leblond, 'that we are not actually *accusing* these people of anything. Neither the infiltrators nor the guillotined. But we don't know why the infiltrators are coming to our sessions, as we said.'

'The motives of the "descendants of the guillotined" are a bit clearer,' said Lebrun, 'because they're inspired by intense hatred, inherited down through the generations, possibly morbid. A feeling of cruel injustice. Possibly seeing Robespierre in person and being able to hate him relieves them a little. Or perhaps they appreciate the implacable course of History, which will lead the Incorruptible to his own inevitable downfall. Culminating in the tumultuous session that closes the Convention cycle, on 9 Thermidor, bringing about Robespierre's painful death next day, 28 July 1794. It always rouses applause and catcalls, a final catharsis – in speeches and witness statements only of course – because we never *ever* re-enact scenes of executions, I hardly need say! We're not perverse or sadistic. But all that said, it's possible that we are unintentionally leading you into some false trails. These infiltrators and descendants of the guillotined may not have the slightest murderous intention. In any case, why would they kill ordinary members and not Robespierre himself?'

'That's the heart of the situation, the heart of the knot of seaweed,' murmured Adamsberg. 'But can you nevertheless give me the names of the *ancestors* of the three you identified?'

'Yes, we can do that, because their descendants have different names.'

'Go ahead.'

'That way, we can at least say we have never let pass our lips a name linked to the association,' said Leblond with a smile.

'Sounds like hypocrisy,' said Adamsberg, smiling back at him.

'Contemptible hypocrisy,' said Lebrun, and he scribbled three names down on the notebook the commissaire had passed him.

He had spent a total of two and a half hours with them, and Adamsberg put on his jacket feeling a bit bemused after they had left. *Sanson, Danton, Desmoulins.* Of the three names he had been given, the only one he recognised was Danton. And that was only because of the colossal statue of Danton at the Odéon crossroads in the middle of the Latin Quarter, with this sentence engraved on it: '*Il nous faut de l'audace, encore de l'audace, toujours de l'audace*' – 'We must have audacity, more audacity, always audacity.' As for knowing anything about Danton's deeds or words, and why he had ended up on the scaffold, that was beyond him.

The many possible leads which this twosome had provided, acting in perfect harmony, neither one dominating the other, Lebrun and Leblond, the psychiatrist and the logician, seemed to add a harmonic note to the chaos of the bundle of seaweed. Which had got bigger, and now obstinately pursued him to the banks of the Seine. He walked past the second-hand bookstalls, astonished to find himself suddenly drawn to ancient volumes. For two days now, he had been living in the eighteenth century, and he was gradually acquiring a taste for it. No, he wasn't acquiring a taste, he was just getting used to it, that was all. He could perfectly well imagine François Didier Château, the humble presumed son, the strangely privileged person who found himself in charge of the stagecoaches of the Loiret, the whole network of post horses, inns and halts. He went down to the river, found a mossy stone bench, and dropped off to sleep on it, as some wayfarer might have two centuries ago. It felt fitting and comfortable.

XXIV

ADAMSBERG WOKE UP AS THE SUN WAS SETTING, SENDING A ROSY glow over Notre-Dame and the dirty river. He called his deputy.

'Danglard, where are you eating?'

'I'm not eating, I'm drinking.'

'Yes, but where will you be eating? The Brasserie Meyer for instance? Between your place and the Seine? I've got three names here, and I've never heard of two of them.'

'What sort of names?'

'People who were guillotined. Whose descendants are haunting the association from the top benches.'

'Twenty minutes,' said Danglard. 'And where are you? They've been looking for you.'

'I was working away from my desk.'

'They tried to reach you.'

'I was asleep, Danglard. On an eighteenth-century stone bench. You see, I'm sticking to the subject.'

The Brasserie Meyer had not changed decor for sixty years. The smell of sauerkraut was all-pervasive and reassured Danglard that the white wine would be of good quality.

Adamsberg waited for his deputy to eat one sausage and drink two glasses of Alsatian wine, before telling him what he had learned from the perfect double act of Lebrun, with his thick black beard, and Leblond, with his silky fair one, and explaining to him their tale of the infiltrators and the guillotined. Then he put the notebook in front of him, with the names of the ancestors of the 'descendants'.

'You only recognise one of these?' asked Danglard.

'Yes, Danton. A name, a statue, a saying in stone. The others are absolutely foreign to me.'

'Well, I appreciate your candour and honesty.'

'Come on, Danglard, out with it,' said Adamsberg, hesitating in front of his dinner. He knew he now had only to listen, and be ready perhaps to ask for the tale to be abridged. He was prepared for that.

'Well, Danton was a friend of Robespierre's from the start, a patriot with a loud voice, and a huge appetite for life, he was a man of passion and faith, but at the same time he was a man of blood, a womaniser, hungry for food and other pleasures that had to be paid for, and he mixed his own finances up with those of the state, even did deals with the court. If there were profits to be made, he was up for it. He was loyal to the Revolution, but corrupt. He wrote letters to Robespierre which are amazing examples of affection. The Incorruptible sent him to the scaffold in April 1794. Robespierre wasn't sensitive to friendship, either to its benefits or to its vices. Towards the end, he could only accept adulation, such as he got from his younger brother and that other acolyte, Saint-Just. Danton's excessive lifestyle must have caused Robespierre unspeakable disgust. This big powerful man could easily dominate the assembly with his voice, whereas skinny little Robespierre had to shout his lungs out to get heard. In four years, any early indulgence Robespierre was prepared to exercise towards others had greatly changed. The execution of the patriot Danton and his friends, after a travesty of a trial, was the first really traumatic shock felt by the people and some of the assembly. The tumbril carrying Danton to the guillotine went along the rue Saint-Honoré where Robespierre had his lodgings. As they went past the house, Danton called out: "Your turn next, Robespierre." And everyone knows his famous instruction to the executioner, as he was mounting the guillotine.'

'Well,' said Adamsberg patiently, 'perhaps not everyone knows it.'

'He said: "Show my head to the people. It's worth it."'

Adamsberg, despite not being oversensitive, or rather avoiding the possible places where sensitivity might hurt, like a bird flying close beside a wall, chose to eat his sausage with his fingers rather than to slice it, piece by piece, head by head, with a sharp knife. And it tasted better that way too. Danglard looked on disapprovingly.

'You're eating with your fingers now? In the Brasserie Meyer?'

'Yes,' said Adamsberg. '*De l'audace, encore de l'audace, toujours de l'audace* . . .'

'Well, that's Danton. It was a terrible execution. Even if Danton was very far from being a man of "virtue".'

'And Dumoulins?'

'Desmoulins, you mean. An even sadder case, if there are degrees of this kind of thing. He'd been a school friend of Robespierre. A fervent republican. Camille Desmoulins had idolised the older pupil. He invited him to his home, he and his pretty young wife thought of him as their friend. Robespierre had played with their baby, or at any rate had held him on his knee. But his school friend Camille was a journalist who had let it be known that he was weary of the Terror and afraid of its repercussions. He was guillotined on 5 April, the same day as Danton. And his wife was condemned to death by Robespierre next day, for plotting her husband's escape. Which left as an orphan the little boy he had once dandled on his knee. Everyone understood then that however long-standing and close your relationship had been with Robespierre, he was a man for whom pity did not exist. Robespierre *had* no close relationships. The guillotining of Desmoulins was atrocious, and at the same time very revealing.'

Adamsberg had finished his Alsatian sausages. He now had to tackle the sauerkraut, which reminded him somewhat of the tangle of seaweed, though it was less dense. This was turning out to be a very peculiar dinner.

'And the third?' he asked. 'Sanson? Was he guillotined the same day too, with Danton's friends?'

Danglard smiled and slowly wiped his lips, appreciating in advance the surprise he was about to unfold.

'No, that very day it was Sanson who guillotined *them*!'

'*What?*'

'As he had Louis XVI, Marie Antoinette and many others during the Terror. Sanson and his son kept the blade of the terrible machine working non-stop, operating it thousands of times in three years.'

'Who was he, Danglard?'

'The famous executioner for Paris, commissaire. "Executioner for capital offences" as he was officially known. Charles-Henri Sanson. He had an awful life, you can be sure of that. I say Charles-Henri, so as not to confuse him with the other Sanson, the son.'

'There's no risk of my doing that, Danglard.'

'Because,' said Danglard, ignoring the interruption, 'the Sanson family were statutory executioners in Paris, and had been from father to son, since the time of Louis XIV, and they carried on into the nineteenth century. The sequence was eventually broken by a later Sanson heir to the name, a homosexual with no issue, who was also incidentally a gambler and deep in debt. Six generations of executioners. But Charles-Henri and his son had the toughest assignment, because they did their service in Paris during the Terror. Over 2,900 heads to cut off. All the executioners of the time complained of the appalling "workload", not on moral grounds, but because they were the proprietors of the machine, and it was their responsibility to clean it, sharpen the blade, get rid of the bodies and severed heads, wash down the scaffold, see to the horses and tumbrils, provide the straw to soak up the blood, and so on. In 1793, presumably because he was worn out, Charles-Henri handed the job over to his son, Henri. Just to add to the horror, another of his sons was killed falling off the scaffold when he held up a head for the crowd to see.'

'Why would a descendant of Sanson be hostile to the Robespierre association?'

'Well, executioners, as you might guess, have never had a very good press, and that was already so, well before the Terror. People wouldn't shake hands with them, or touch them at all, they were paid by having money placed on the ground. They could only marry into other families of executioners. Nobody wanted anything to do with them. But of all the executioner families all over France, only one name has survived in popular memory: that of Sanson. Because he cut the king's head off. And the queen's. And one or other of the Sansons did the same for all the victims of the Terror. Robespierre made their name terribly famous, and transformed it into a symbol of abject cruelty.'

'And one of the present-day descendants can't stand that?'

'Well, it's not an easy weight to bear.'

Danglard let silence fall, while Adamsberg attacked his knot of sauerkraut without much appetite.

'No link with Danton and Desmoulins, then,' he said.

And he felt the knot falling over him again, grasping him with its stinging tentacles, full of traps and dead ends, such as he had never before encountered. He dropped his fork, defeated.

'Let's go,' he said. 'From when this all started, in Le Creux, we have already chalked up fourteen suspects. Fourteen! In nine days. Too many, Danglard. We're all over the place like marbles on ice. We've lost our way. Or rather, we've never really found it.'

'Don't forget that we went skidding over some ice in Iceland, to begin with. That lost us some time. And then we were suddenly propelled into the middle of the Revolution, with this improbable descendant of Robespierre and a string of people wanting vengeance. It's no wonder we're feeling lost!'

It was extremely rare for Danglard, the pessimist, to try to cheer Adamsberg up, since the commissaire's temperament was one of detachment to the point of indifference, something which was one of Lieutenant Retancourt's major grouses about him: his dreamy indolence infuriated her. But tonight, without exactly expressing anxiety, the commandant could see an unusual kind of puzzlement in the commissaire. He was worried by this, chiefly on his own account. Because in Danglard's view, as someone under perpetual assault from worry and distress, which tended to overwhelm him in many threatening forms, Adamsberg represented a sure compass, from which he never took his eyes, possessed of calming virtues which were clinically healing. But the commissaire was right. Since the start of this investigation, they had been as it were lost in a dark forest, exploring paths that led nowhere, organising unsuccessful searches, interrogating left and right, without pause – but without profit.

'No,' said Adamsberg, 'it's not the fault of the facts in the case. It's our own fault. We've missed something. And it's making me itch till it hurts.'

'You mean itching in the Lucionic sense?'

'The Lucionic sense?'

'Like your old pal Lucio's itch.'

'Yes, exactly, Danglard. There's something not quite right about that couple Leblond and Lebrun.'

'I thought you said the interview had gone very well.'

'Very well. Perfectly, in fact.'

'And that means something's not quite right?'

'Yes. Too smooth, too harmonious.'

'Do you mean they'd prepared it? But that would be a pretty normal thing to do.'

Adamsberg hesitated.

'Possibly. And working together, in impeccable harness, they provided us with seven suspects. Four infiltrators and three descendants.'

'And you don't believe them?'

'No, I *do* believe them, they're serious leads, and we certainly ought to question the "guillotined" ones. That's something right up your street, Danglard. I can't see myself being able to discuss historical questions with the descendants of Danton, or of the executioner, or that Dumoulin person.'

'Desmoulins.'

'Danglard, why do you amass such a lot of stuff in your brain?'

'Precisely that, to stuff it full, commissaire.'

'Yes. I see.'

To stuff it full, so that there was little room left to think about himself. A reasonable plan, though the results were generally imperfect.

'Do these seven new suspects bother you?' Danglard asked. 'You think that Leblond–Lebrun are sending them to us just to confuse us?'

'Why not?'

'And perhaps they are trying to protect someone else? Their friend François Château for instance?'

'Does that sound unreasonable to you?'

'No, not at all. But the descendant of Sanson does intrigue me. The fact that descendants of Danton and Desmoulins come along to these sessions is borderline understandable. After all, without having any murderous intentions, they might have some reason to try and find out about the period when their ancestors were involved in dramatic historical events. But what on earth is the descendant of Sanson doing there? He was never mixed up in politics, he just did his job as executioner, and that was that. Anyway, what you're thinking is that Leblond and Lebrun suspect that François Château is the killer?'

'Or possibly that they have doubts about him. Or fears. They might be afraid of him and be protecting him so as not to become his victims.'

'Where's Froissy got to with the innkeeper François Didier?'

'She's working her way through the records. There was some problem around 1848, because of the Revolution that year, the archives are in a mess. She's reached 1912, though, when the Château family was still living in the same place. But the town hall where the registration records are kept shuts up shop at 6 p.m, and nothing's digitised. She'll start again tomorrow.'

'She'll manage.'

'Yes, of course.'

'After the Great War, the family could have dispersed. If she loses the thread at Château-Renard, she might have to look in the nearest big towns that were industrialising after that: Orléans, Montargis, Gien, Pithiviers, or smaller ones like Courtenay, Châlette-sur-Loing or Ramilly.'

'Geography must be good material to stuff your head with too,' said Adamsberg.

'It's like cement,' said Danglard with a smile.

'With cracks though.'

'Of course.'

'That can't be fixed with Polyfilla.'

'Or protected with the droppings of hooded crows.'

'You never know. You could try putting them in front of your door and round the bed.'

'Worth a try.'

XXV

ADAMSBERG DID NOT EVEN GO INTO HIS HOUSE BEFORE SITTING down on the wooden packing case under the beech tree. Three minutes later, Lucio appeared with three bottles of beer held between his fingers.

'I've got something itching, Lucio,' said Adamsberg, accepting a beer. The commissaire got up to open it against the bark of the tree.

'Stay standing,' said Lucio, 'so I can see your face in the light of the street lamp. Ah yes,' he said, returning to his own bottle. 'This time it's really itching, *hombre*. No question.'

'It's really bad.'

'Not necessarily a spider. Could be worse. A wasp, a hornet even. You need to find whatever it was that stung you.'

'That's just it, I can't, Lucio, I'm going round in circles. Fourteen suspects, less the four who have been eliminated. Ten left, plus a possible seven hundred others! All of them spectacular and living in another century, but I can't get a proper grip on a single one of them. Even if I succeed in understanding what's causing the itch, I'll have wasted precious time.'

'No, that's never true.'

Adamsberg leaned up against the tree.

'Yes it is, because the thing that's bothering me has nothing to do with the investigation.'

'So what?'

'I can't allow myself to go roaming around looking for my hornet, when there's some maniac out there killing people left, right and centre.'

'Maybe not, but you've no choice, *hombre*. You haven't found the guy, and your head's empty. So what's the difference? Can you remember when it started itching?'

Adamsberg drank some beer and stood for a while without speaking.

'I think it was on Monday, but I'm not sure. I might be making that up.'

'What else is there to do, in a case like this?'

'No, wait, I think maybe it was before that. I must have been stung in the Hollow.'

'In what hollow? Doesn't matter if you were stung in the armpit or the knee, that's not important.'

'No, no, Lucio, I mean this place called Le Creux, it's the name of a tiny piece of territory in the Yvelines.'

'Oh, *that* Le Creux!'

'Why, do you know it?'

'I worked for four years near there.'

'And do you know why they call this little stretch of land the Hollow, instead of giving it a proper name?'

'Something to do with the bombings in wartime, far as I remember. There was a lot of damage, but they'd lost the official ordnance maps. So when they came to put the road signs back up, it was by guesswork. Botched job. And afterwards they realised that there was about a kilometre between the boundary of one village and the next. So nobody knew who that bit belonged to.'

'Why didn't they just redraw the maps?'

'Not so easy, *hombre*. Because in this bit of land there was a sort of haunted castle, which nobody wanted. Each village would rather have a bit less land than to have to deal with ghosts. Can you credit it? In the middle of a war! As if there weren't more important things to do than fuss over an old wives' tale.'

'Yes, there is a haunted tower. They used to put people in there and leave them to die.'

'Ah, so they're the ones that howl at night, are they? Mind you, I can see why.'

'No, the sounds you hear are hooded crows.'

'You think so? Yes, I cycled past there one night, and the cries didn't sound human to me.'

'The call of a crow doesn't sound human. It's not a songbird. You seem to know the place pretty well, Lucio.'

'Yes, *hombre*, you should add me to your list of suspects, that'd make fifteen. Now, it comes back to me, I remember the name of one of the villages. Sombrevert. Not a cheerful name.'

'And the other's Malvoisine. Did you know the people who lived there?'

'Oh, I was just passing through, and I'll tell you why. There was this inn in Le Creux. I just used to eat there sometimes. And there was this girl who worked there, Mélanie her name was, a beauty. Too tall and thin, but I was mad about her. If my wife ever finds out about it, God protect me.'

'Forgive me, Lucio, but your wife died eighteen years ago, didn't she?' said Adamsberg gently.

'Yes, I told you about that.'

'Then how is she ever going to find out?'

'Let's just say I'd prefer it if she never found out, and leave it at that,' said Lucio, scratching his bristly chin. 'Anyway, the idea of a "hollow" between the two villages just survived. Sometimes the Sombrevert council lops the trees and mends the roads, sometimes Malvoisine. And you think it was in Le Creux that you got stung?'

'Remember this big meeting I told you about? When I was dressed up like in the eighteenth century, in a frock coat? Look, here's a photo.' And Adamsberg showed Lucio his phone.

'You look almost handsome,' said Lucio. 'Maybe you're really good-looking, but nobody realises that.'

'I was rather taken with my costume myself. So I looked in the mirror. And that very moment, I think, there was something wrong. So it must have been related to what happened earlier, in Le Creux. Not when I was walking in the woods and getting burrs on my trousers. No, after that. Céleste in her old cabin with her boar? Pelletier, who smelled of horses? I don't know. Or when I drew on the windscreen?'

Drew what? Lucio didn't care.

'So how long was it between the burrs and the windscreen?'

'About eight hours.'

'That's not long, you ought to be able to work it out. Try. It was a thought that came to you and you hadn't finished thinking it. You shouldn't lose thoughts like that, *hombre*. Have to be careful where you put things. And your second in command, the commandant, does he feel the itch as well? Or that one with the stripy hair?'

'No, neither of them.'

'That means it must be a thought peculiar to you. It's a pity thoughts don't have names, isn't it? You could call them up, and they'd come and lie down at our feet, crawling on their bellies.'

'I think we have ten thousand thoughts a day, or millions we don't know about.'

'Yeah, agreed,' said Lucio, opening his second beer, 'it would be chaos.'

Adamsberg went inside to the kitchen, finding there his son, who was eating bread and cheese, as he worked on the jewellery he had started making to sell.

'Are you going to bed already?'

'I need to look for thoughts I've had and that I've forgotten to think.'

'Oh, I see,' said Zerk, with perfect sincerity.

Lying on his bed, Adamsberg kept his eyes open in the darkness. Lucio's beer had given him a crick in his neck. He forced himself to keep his eyes open. 'Try,' Lucio had said, 'think back, you can do it.'

And he fell asleep without thinking at all.

Two hours later, he was woken by the creaking of the stairs as Zerk
came up to bed. You haven't thought back. Adamsberg forced himself
to sit up. He still had in his head the nagging memory of the perfect
twosome, Leblond–Lebrun, and he was sure that while that bothered
him somewhat, it wasn't the itch. Feeling out of sorts, he went down to
the kitchen and warmed up the remains of a cooked dish: pasta and
tuna, the only thing Zerk had been able to cook when he first arrived.

Adamsberg added some cold tomato sauce, to cheer it up. It was
past two in the morning. The Leblond–Lebrun twosome. And what
else had he called them? The double act. Their improbable statements,
the way their utterances fitted one on top of the other. No, not one on
top of the other, they complemented each other. The ones that fitted
closely were those of Amédée and Victor. Those two had given accounts
of what happened in Iceland separately, but their versions had tallied
almost to the point of being identical. Even the detail of the aggressor
getting his trousers on fire and beating out the flames, even Adélaïde
insulting him, and the other man who said they should heat up the
stones. And they had both used the term 'a monster'. Did that mean
Alice Gauthier had told the story to Amédée in exactly the same way
as Victor had told it to the police? Using the same words? But if you
take ten witnesses of the same event, no two of them will describe it in
quite the same way, pick up on just the same details and pronounce
exactly the same words. Yet *they* had.

Adamsberg put his fork down with care, acting cautiously as he did
whenever a barely formed idea, the embryo of an idea, a tadpole of an
idea, began slowly swimming up to the surface of his consciousness.
At moments like this, he knew, you should not make a sound, because
the tadpole will take fright and dive down to disappear for ever. But it
wasn't for nothing that the tadpole was poking its shapeless head
above the water. If it was just amusing itself, well, he'd throw it back in

the pond. As he sat, not moving an inch, Adamsberg waited for the tadpole to come a little nearer and to start turning into a frog. Amédée–Victor, the same story, like the smooth accounts given by Leblond–Lebrun. As if, like the secretary and treasurer of the association, they had agreed between themselves how to present things.

But that was impossible, because when the three police officers had arrived at Le Creux, the two young men would not have been able to predict that they would be questioned, or have had time to concoct their story.

Yes they had! Still watching the ripples on the water, Adamsberg considered the tadpole idea which now seemed to have grown two back legs. Not enough for him to be able to grab it. Yes, of course they had, they'd been able to talk about Alice Gauthier when they were outside. Céleste had been told about Gauthier, and she had passed the message to Amédée. And Victor had overheard them. Neither Adamsberg nor Danglard had been able to find a plausible reason why Amédée had bolted, riding off bareback on Dionysos, who was a dangerous horse. And why Victor had followed immediately on Hecate. And there, in the forest, they had had a short time in which to compose an agreed story. Then they had acted out the scene of the return: Victor having been unable to catch up with Amédée, Pelletier's whistle to get the frisky stallion back, and a crestfallen Amédée. And, of course, those two understood each other perfectly, they had much closer relations than would be usual between a rich man's son and his secretary. Of course, the pair of them would know of some clearing in the woods. And their parallel accounts of the events in Iceland were the result of an unusual and deep complicity. And if they had felt the need to do that, it must mean that part of the account was untrue, and the truth needed to be hidden.

The double act Amédée–Victor had worked perfectly. And both of them had lied.

*

At last, Adamsberg could pick up his fork and finish the rest of his now-cooled supper. The idea had emerged from the waves, he could see it clearly now, with two front legs as well, sitting beside him at the table, having climbed out of its aquatic sphere to arrive on dry land. There was a complete veil over the Icelandic events, as there was over Amédée's childhood. Where had the boy been before the age of five? Some story about an institution? Or of some disability which hadn't even got a name? And which did not appear to have affected Amédée thereafter at all?

Where the devil had the boy been? A boy without memories? And for that matter, where did the orphaned Victor come from?

He no longer believed the story of the accidental coincidence of surnames. An abandoned child taken in by social services does not come equipped with a surname. Victor had made the choice to call himself Masfauré, which was indeed an unusual name, so as to have an excellent excuse to contact the family. Not only to contact it, but to insert himself inside it, like a cuckoo in the nest of a smaller bird. But with what aim? And to whom did he wish to be close? The great scientist and clean-air hero? The millionaire? Or indeed Amédée?

What was it that Danglard had said about the names of the two young men? Some historical allusion. Yes, the names had been in the family of some duke or other. Adamsberg dismissed this detail, which did not connect with the idea that had made him itch. There'd been two spider bites in fact: the excessively close correspondence between the witness statements provided by Masfauré's son and by his secretary; and Amédée's childhood, lost in the mists of time. Masfauré, the bankroller of the Robespierre association.

Zerk found his father next morning, fast asleep on his chair, legs stretched out and resting on the firedog, having left the remains of a dish of cold pasta and tuna on the table. Indicating that he must have come downstairs to search for some idea and, having found it, dropped off to sleep, content with his success.

He started to prepare coffee quietly, put the bowls on the table without clattering them, moved over to the staircase to start cutting the bread, all so as not to disturb his father's sleep. At the end of the day, he did love him. And he was above all aware that he was not yet capable of leaving this house. Adamsberg, awakened by the smell of coffee, was rubbing his eyes as Zerk came back with the sliced bread.

'Feeling better?' Zerk asked.

'Yes. But it doesn't have anything to do with the investigation.'

'Never mind,' said Zerk. And once more Adamsberg realised that this son was dangerously like himself, and perhaps even worse.

XXVI

SHOWERED, SHAVED, BUT HAVING DONE NO MORE THAN RUN HIS fingers through his hair, Adamsberg shut himself up in his office as soon as he arrived at work. After twenty minutes, he finally managed to get through to the central services of the Social Assistance Board.

'This is Commissaire Adamsberg, Serious Crimes Squad in Paris.'

'Very well, sir,' a conscientious voice answered. 'I must call your switchboard back for verification. You will understand, I'm sure, that we have to check all callers.'

'Good morning again,' she said, after a few minutes. 'So what can I do for you, commissaire?'

'I need information about a certain Victor Masfauré, who was abandoned at birth and fostered thirty-seven years ago. It's urgent.'

'Please hang on, commissaire.'

Adamsberg could hear her keyboard clicking away for quite a long time.

'Sorry,' the woman said after a wait of six minutes. 'I don't have any record of a baby of that name. I've got a couple called Masfauré, who came to adopt a child who had been fostered. But that was *twenty-two* years ago, and the boy's name isn't Victor.'

'But it's Amédée?' asked Adamsberg picking up a pen.

'That's right. He was five years old when these people offered to adopt him. They completed all the necessary formalities.'

'He was fostered, you say? For what reason? Neglect by the parents? Abuse?'

'Not at all, he was abandoned at birth without a father's name being registered. The mother gave him his first name.'

'So can you tell me the name of the foster-family, and their address?'

'A couple called Grenier, Antoine and Bernadette. They were living at a farm called Le Thost, I'll spell that: T H O S T, route du Vieux-Marché, in Santeuil, postcode 28790, Eure-et-Loir *département*.'

Adamsberg consulted his unhelpful watches. Amédée's childhood was within easy reach, an hour and half's drive out of Paris to the west. Nothing to do with the Robespierre investigation, but the commissaire was already on his feet, car keys in his pocket. He wasn't going to go on scratching this itch all his life.

With his jacket already on, he called in Mordent, Danglard and Voisenet.

'I'm going out,' he announced, 'I'll be back later on today. Danglard and Mordent, can you hold the fort here? Voisenet, where are we with the tail on François Château?'

'The report's on your desk.'

'Haven't had time to read it yet, lieutenant, I'm sorry.'

'Well, there's nothing new, no one seems to be following him. He goes home every night at the same time, seems to lead a very orderly life. But he takes precautions. He leaves the hotel, or his office, in a pre-ordered taxi.'

'And you've checked out all the other residents in his building?'

'Yes, sir.'

'If anyone else enters the building, ask for ID. And as usual keep an eye open for anyone acting suspiciously, or looking too casual. Watch out for disguises, spectacles, caps, wigs and beards. If you suspect anyone, follow them into the lift.'

'Right.'

'Where are *you* off to, commissaire?' asked Danglard, in tight-lipped mode.

'I'm going to explore Amédée's childhood. He wasn't in any "institution". He was an abandoned baby, fostered out in Eure-et-Loir. The Masfaurés only adopted him when he was five years old.'

'Forgive me, sir,' said Mordent, rather disapprovingly, 'but are you going back to that business? You're abandoning Robespierre?'

'I'm not abandoning anything. We can't do anything about the "guillotined", well, their descendants, until next Monday, when the assembly meets again, and Lebrun will point them out to us. We've got all we can for the moment out of those three, the Château–Leblond–Lebrun trio. And Froissy is still working on the descendants of the eighteenth-century innkeeper Château. She's looking at the Montargis records at the moment. So yes, I'm going out for a few hours.'

'For a family secret that's nothing to do with us?'

'That's right, Mordent. But we let too many things escape us out at Le Creux.'

'So what, though? These people aren't in the frame any more.'

Adamsberg looked at his three colleagues without replying, and gently pushed past Mordent to the door.

'I'm off now,' he said, followed by the disapproving expressions of all three men.

He was still caught in traffic on the Paris ring road when he took a call from an unknown number, in a hurried and panicky voice.

'Commissaire Adamsberg, this is Lebrun. I'm calling from a phone booth.'

'OK, I can hear you.'

'When I was coming out this morning, I saw Danton walking up and down my street on the opposite pavement.'

'You mean the descendant of Danton?'

'Yes, of course,' said Lebrun, in exasperation, but above all sounding frightened. 'I went back inside and looked out of my window. Two hours, commissaire, he stayed there for two hours solid. He went off in the end, presumably thinking he'd missed me and that I'd gone out earlier.'

'Did you follow him?'

'What would be the point? I know where *he* lives. Do you realise what this means?' the man continued, his voice rising in panic. 'He knows *my* name and where *I* live, he knows what my real face looks like. How did he find that out? No idea. But he's keeping tabs on me now and he could have a knife or God knows what in his pocket.'

'What do you expect me to do, since you refuse to tell me anything at all, either about him, or about yourself?'

'I want protection, commissaire. Four deaths already, and I think I'm in the firing line now.'

'Well, I can't help you without the information, sorry,' said Adamsberg, exiting the ring road and heading back for Paris.

'All right, I agree,' said Lebrun. 'Where, when?'

'About half an hour, in my office.'

'Can't it be earlier?'

'I'm out on call, Lebrun, I'm driving on the ring road. Don't stay in the phone booth, go to our offices at once. In a taxi. And without the false beard please.'

Adamsberg sped up, and was back in his own office twenty-five minutes later. He almost failed to recognise the man who turned round to greet him: short white hair, glasses, a darker complexion than when he was being 'Lebrun', and a more shapely nose. He looked more respectable too, in an immaculate grey suit.

'Good morning, doctor,' said Adamsberg, throwing his jacket over the back of the chair.

'As you see, your Billaud-Varenne has already brought me some coffee. You called me "doctor"?'

'I'm guessing, rightly or wrongly. Psychiatrist perhaps. Who's Billaud-Varenne?'

'The young man with the wide-open eyes – you wonder whether he closes them at night. I told you before he'd make a very good Billaud. Oh, damn it all, we ought to have put a stop to the whole business when we suspected something untoward was happening! Once people started to get worked up. Yes, that's what we should have done. But it was so fascinating to watch the unleashing of these passions. You're right, I'm a psychiatrist.'

'You had a Robespierre who was too perfect. He provided a disturbing replica of your "living history".'

'To the point where the line between reality and illusion disappeared,' said Lebrun gravely. 'And when that happens, commissaire, the consequences can be extremely dangerous. That's where we are now. It means the end of our experiment, of course, but it has already cost four lives.'

'Are you certain that's the man from Danton's family waiting in front of your house?'

'Absolutely. I ought to have gone out and confronted him, talked to him, but I didn't have the guts. Courage isn't my strong point. I'm a man used to sitting quietly in my consulting rooms.'

'This time, doctor, I need his name and address,' said Adamsberg.

The other man thought a moment and nodded.

'My colleagues have authorised me to tell you that,' he said. 'But not for the other two, as long as they haven't done anything to cause concern.'

'What do you think he wanted? He certainly wouldn't have tried to gun you down in the street, it's not his style.'

'After thinking I was in personal danger, I wondered whether perhaps, through me, he was hoping to get to Robespierre. Only the treasurer and I know his home address.'

'And strike at the head of the association? It's too soon, I don't believe in that.'

'Perhaps not to strike yet, but to stake out the place. I think, like you, that Robespierre might be his ultimate target. But before that, he wants to create a climate of increasing terror. He wants Robespierre to feel afraid, in the way that he made others feel afraid. I suppose he imagines, in his delusion, that he is dealing with the *real* Robespierre.'

'Yes, I'd go along with that,' said Adamsberg, lighting a cigarette that had lost half its tobacco in his pocket, and which therefore flared up.

'He's living on the invisible border between illusion and reality, as I said.'

'If you think Robespierre is his target, why do you want protection for yourself?'

'Because I don't feel sure of anything, commissaire. Just limited protection. But perhaps that is asking too much. After all, I haven't been explicitly threatened.'

'Limited to what?'

'To my journeys between the hospital and my home.'

'And your home is where?' smiled Adamsberg.

'From today, I'm going to go and stay with a friend,' said the doctor, smiling back. 'No, commissaire, I'm not going to tell you my real name. Not because it's sacred or untouchable, but just imagine the reaction of my patients if they ever found out. Opening up their psyche to someone who goes around "cutting off heads"! No, I'd have to go without protection, if my name was to appear. Not that I don't trust you, but we all know that secrets left with police will sometimes out.'

'All right,' said Adamsberg with a sigh, 'where do you work?'

'If you can agree to my request, have someone wait for me every evening at six in front of the main gates of the hospital at Garches, I'll be wearing the black beard you've already seen.'

'We could easily find out your name by checking at the hospital.'

'I'm only on temporary detachment there. And if you were to show them my photo, you might be directed to a Dr Rousselet. Which isn't my real name either.'

Adamsberg stood up to walk around and to check how the leaves were coming on, on the tree outside the window. Limes are always late. This Lebrun/Rousselet was a coward, but a well-organised one.

'Danton,' he said, 'the *real* Danton, according to what my commandant said, also had blood on his hands, didn't he?'

'Of course. He was in post during the Terror, before it destroyed him too. He was all in favour of setting up the Revolutionary Tribunal. "Let us be terrible, to prevent the people from being so . . ." – you may have heard this quotation?'

'Nope.'

'". . . and organise a tribunal, so that the people shall know that the sword of justice hangs over the head of all its enemies." And in this new tribunal, verdicts were rushed out in twenty-four hours and followed by the guillotine. So that's what good old Danton contributed to.'

'One week of police protection, renewable,' Adamsberg agreed. 'I'll leave you with Commandants Mordent and Danglard to work out the technical details.'

'Your colleagues will need to know what this Danton descendant looks like. Here,' said the doctor, cautiously putting a photograph on the desk.

'I didn't think you had any photos of your members.'

'I got permission for this one. Judge for yourself.'

Adamsberg examined the portrait of the descendant. It was one of the darkest and ugliest faces he had ever seen.

XXVII

HE DROVE FAST WITH HIS BLUE LIGHTS FLASHING, TO MAKE UP for the time he had spent with Dr Lebrun/Rousselet. The man had tried his hardest to keep calm, but he was eaten up with anxiety. His diction was less smooth than on his first visit, he kept clenching and unclenching his hands, holding his thumbs. Adamsberg had the feeling that there was some make-up involved, even today. Lebrun was still somehow behind a mask, off-centre, on his guard. Ready to recoil at the slightest alert, like those men in the bullring, who goad the bull and then jump back behind the wooden barriers.

'Danglard?' he called, as he drove one-handed, 'Can you speak up? I'm in the car.'

'Good grief, I thought you'd come back.'

'But boats always venture beyond the lighthouse.'

'Still chasing baby Amédée? When I gather the secretary of the association has been threatened and wants protection?'

'Not threatened, watched.'

'Did you see the ugly mug of that Danton descendant?'

'Yes, sinister. Tell me, Danglard, what is the name of those wooden barriers, the ones the guys hide behind when they've been annoying the bull?'

'What?'

'You know, in bullfights.'

'*Burladeros*. And the "guys" are called the *peones* attached to the *torero*. Is this important?' asked Danglard, and there was a caustic edge to his voice.

'Not really. It's just that our doctor – because Lebrun really is a psychiatrist – is someone like that. He's afraid of being gored, so he ducks. Whereas François Château, who we *presume* is more directly threatened, hasn't asked for any protection.'

'After four murders, and with Danton skulking across his street, I can easily put myself in his place.'

'Perhaps we should tell him to cover himself with the droppings of hooded crows.'

'I imagine that will really please him.'

'I think our Lebrun is an active member of this Robespierre association because it means he can watch people being violent and aggressive in ways he's not capable of in real life. He gets his kicks by proxy.'

'So what?'

'Danglard, I'll be back by four. There's no need to get stroppy.'

'So *what*? It's *now* that we're going to question this Danton descendant. And you're waltzing off for a chat with Amédée's family.'

'Look, you'll be much better than me at questioning some guy who's got into ancient history so deep his mind has suffered. To talk to Danton, we need someone scholarly and tactful. But don't do the interview on your own, it goes without saying.'

Adamsberg drove into the modest village of Santeuil and parked near a *bar-tabac*, whose owner agreed to make him a sandwich, although they didn't normally do them.

'All we got is Gruyère,' the man said gruffly.

'Perfect. I'm looking for a farm called Le Thost,' said Adamsberg, pronouncing the s and the t.

'I can see you're not from round here. It's pronounced "Le Toh", you don't say the s or the t. And what might you be doing there?'

'It's to help a child who lived there a long time ago.'

The man wrinkled his nose. All right, if there was a child involved it was different.

'It's about seven hundred metres up the way, the Réclainville road. You cross the route du Vieux-Marché and you're there. But you won't find nothing there no more. Kid's looking for his foster-parents? Too bad. Because they got burnt to cinders, fifteen years ago. The whole building went up in flames, and the couple were killed. Horrible, eh? Seems it was youngsters making a campfire at night near the barn. With all that straw, you can imagine. Went up in an hour. Seemingly they'd taken sleeping pills, the people at the farm, they didn't wake up. A nasty do.'

'Yes, very nasty.'

'Mind, nobody much liked them round here. Shouldn't speak ill of the dead' – the usual opening before people do precisely that – 'but they were proper skinflints. Nothing in their hearts, and everything in the woollen sock under the bed. If they took in orphan children, it was for the money. Dunno how anyone could hand kids over to a pair like that. Cos the littl'uns had to work their socks off, tell you that.'

'Was one of these kids called Amédée?'

'Couldn't tell you, never been up there myself. But you want to know, you should ask Ma Mangematin. Yes, that's her real name, you don't choose your name, do you, but she's a good soul. After you go past where the farm *was* – you can't miss it, it's still in ruins – you go about thirty metres and there's a green gate in a wall on the left.'

'She knew them well?'

'She went over every month to help with the laundry. And took some treats for the kids. She's a good soul, like I said.'

Adamsberg rang the bell outside the green gate a little before four, after brushing the crumbs from his sandwich off his jacket. A large dog hurled itself against the gate, showing its teeth. Adamsberg put his hand on its head, through the bars. After a few growls and whines, the dog settled down.

'Got a way with animals, haven't you?' said a heavily-built woman, who limped out towards him. 'What do you want?'

'I'm enquiring about a little boy who lived at Le Thost, a long time ago.'

'At the Greniers' place?'

'Yes. Name of Amédée.'

'No harm's come to him, has it?' the woman asked, as she opened the gate.

'No, no. But he doesn't remember much about his time there, he needs some help.'

'Well, I've got memory to spare,' said the woman, showing him into her small dining room. 'Can I get you anything? Coffee? Cider?'

Adamsberg opted for coffee, and the woman, whose name was Roberta Mangematin, as he had seen from the letter box at the gate, sponged down the oilcloth cover on the table which was already immaculate.

'You don't mind if I have a glass of cider myself?' she said, now wiping the table with a dry cloth. 'You've come far?'

'From Paris.'

'Member of the family?'

'No, police.'

'Ah,' said the woman, placing the cloth on a radiator.

'It's because Amédée's got himself mixed up in something – no, he hasn't done anything wrong himself, don't worry – and he needs to know more about his childhood at Le Thost.'

'You don't pronounce the s or the t. Some childhood that was, officer.'

'Commissaire,' said Adamsberg, showing her his card.

'And a commissaire's come all the way out here for that?'

'Well, nobody else is interested in Amédée. But I am. So I've come.'

Roberta poured out some coffee respectfully, then served herself a good glassful of cider.

'So how's he now, the kid?'

'He's got film-star looks.'

'There wasn't a prettier little boy in the whole region. Cute enough to eat, he was. And nice with it. You'd of thought that would touch the heart of the old Grenier woman? But no, she thought he was namby-pamby. So she worked him to death. At four years old! To make a man of him, she said. Make a slave of him, more like. Broke my heart, to see that kid with his sad little face. And you say he can't remember anything about it?'

'Just a few bits and pieces. Something about duck's heads?'

'Oh, now then,' said Roberta, putting down her glass with emphasis. 'What a cow, eh? Mustn't speak ill of the dead, but there ain't no other word for it. She got it into her head that one of his chores was he had to kill the poultry when they was wanted. Four years old, ever hear the like? And little Amédée, of course he was too squeamish, he didn't want to do it. She showed him what to do, she grabbed hold of a chicken and crack, she cut its head off with a hatchet. Just like that, in front of him! After that it was crisis after crisis. If he refused to do it, he'd be punished by going without food the rest of the day. And one day, the child had had enough. He was what? Five? Not long before he went away. He got hold of the hatchet, and he went on the rampage. He cut the heads off the ducks, seven, ten of them, all in one go! The doctor told me he was taking revenge for the way he was treated, something like that. The way he was going, doctor said, he'd have cut Ma Grenier's head off too. Not that I believed that.'

Roberta shook her head energetically, chin in the air.

'So what do *you* believe?' asked Adamsberg.

The coffee here was ten times better than in the office, he'd have to have a word with Estalère.

'That he just wanted to show her he could do it,' Roberta replied, 'so they'd stop punishing him and calling him a girlie. He went mad that day, that's for sure. So sad, such a nice little kid. She twisted him, that's what she did.'

'And the husband?'

'No better. Didn't say much. But he did whatever she told him, he never defended the kid. Alcoholic good-for-nothing, *he* was,' she said, filling her glass again, 'though he did heavy work round the farm, I'll say that for him. Doesn't surprise me if Amédée remembers the ducks. Cos you know what she did afterwards?'

'Gave him a good hiding?'

'Yes, of course, but after that?'

'How would I know?'

'Well, all the ducks he'd killed, she made him pluck them and clean them out, and then he had to eat them every meal, breakfast, dinner, supper. Course he threw up all over the place. Thanks be to God, the big boy helped him out. He'd eat up the stuff for him, or hide it and bury it, and give him something else to eat. Otherwise, I don't know what would have become of him.'

'What big boy do you mean?'

'He'd be about ten when Amédée came as a baby. That boy was as ugly as sin, as ugly as Amédée was pretty, but a heart of gold. Protected that kid like a mother hen. Those two lads were really fond of each other, you can say that.'

'So who was this big boy?' Adamsberg asked, suddenly alert.

'She'd taken him in a few years before that, he was another one who'd been abandoned. The mother, she just sent the allowance, that's all. But Amédée, maybe he hadn't really been abandoned after all, because one fine day his parents came to collect him. The woman, she acted like she was a duchess. Never came to see him once, all that time, but she paid up all right, or so Grenier used to say. Masfauré was the name.'

'How do you know that?'

'Through the postman, everyone knew. Should have seen it when they turned up! I was doing the laundry. And Amédée, he was clinging on to Victor, the big boy, hard as he could, didn't want to let go. Victor was murmuring to him, with the kid hanging round his neck like a monkey, couldn't make him get off. In the end, old man Grenier, he pulled them apart, and they put Amédée into this big car, he was screaming his head off, mind. Three-quarters of an hour, whole thing was over.'

'Did this boy Victor have fair hair?'

'That's right, curly blond hair, like an angel. That was the only thing about him that was pretty. And his smile. But I didn't see him that often.'

'Madame Mangematin, you talked about an allowance.'

'You don't think people like those Greniers would have taken them in out of the kindness of their hearts, do you?'

'No, of course not. Do you know whether there was one a month, or two separate ones?'

'Oh, I couldn't tell you that. The postman used to talk about the Masfauré money, no other name. I can ask him if you like. But he's getting on a bit, he might not remember.'

The woman went into the next room to phone. The fierce dog had crept in and now lay down between Adamsberg's legs. The commissaire scratched the creature's neck without thinking, his mind on the two little boys in Le Thost. Or 'Le Toh' as the locals called it.

'You're gifted with animals, monsieur,' said the woman, returning. 'That dog, he killed a duck on me, one day. But of course that's different. It's natural for a dog to kill.'

'Yes,' Adamsberg said, wondering whether killing had entered Amédée's make-up, when the Grenier woman had 'twisted' him.

'Just one envelope every month,' Roberta said, picking up her glass of cider once more, 'he'd swear to that. Except before Amédée it was a different name, not Masfauré. She must have got married in between.'

'But how did he know it was the allowance?'

'Well, he told me that at the time, we had a laugh. A postman can spot when there's banknotes in an envelope, just by the feel. So it came in cash, she didn't want to leave any traces behind, seemingly.'

'So that would mean that Victor and Amédée were *brothers*, or maybe half-brothers, wouldn't it? If one envelope arrived to cover both of them.'

'Gracious, I never thought of that,' said Roberta, corking up the bottle. 'But it wouldn't surprise me, because they were together all the time. But what I can tell you is when the Masfauré woman came to fetch Amédée, she didn't so much as look at Victor, he could have been a piece of shit, pardon my language. Even a bad mother wouldn't be like that, would she? And if she *was* his mother, why wouldn't she fetch the two boys together that day?'

Adamsberg leafed through his notebook, where his jottings were in no sort of order.

'Can I trouble you to call the postman again, and ask him whether, before Amédée arrived, the envelope wasn't sent in the name of Pouillard? Marie-Adélaïde Pouillard? That was Amédée's mother's maiden name.'

'No trouble, I always like talking to the postman.'

The reply came quickly, in the affirmative: yes, Pouillard was the name. Roberta had taken the opportunity to invite the postman over for supper.

XXVIII

Adamsberg joined them in the middle of the interrogation. It was a small room, tucked under the roofs of Paris, untidy and airless. The man – a former bookbinder, Danglard told him – had been unemployed for four years. Danglard's hair was ruffled, and on end, perhaps out of anger, and Justin was standing with head lowered, arms nervously folded.

'Welcome, monsieur le commissaire,' said the descendant jovially. 'Glad to have you with us, your colleagues are keeping me entertained. As you can see, I don't have a chair to offer you.'

'Never mind, I prefer to stand.'

'Like horses, eh? It might do you good, but the main drawback is that you can't see past the end of your nose. Which makes you imagine that a descendant of Georges Danton would have *killed* someone to defend his ancestor's honour!'

The man burst out laughing. Unprepossessing and repellent he undoubtedly looked, with his hollow cheeks, long, irregular, discoloured teeth and widely spaced dark eyes.

'Yeah,' he said, still laughing, 'fat old Georges Danton. Described by some as a sincere patriot, warm-hearted, loving and generous. But in *my* book, he was totally fucking corrupt, an opportunist, arrogant,

232

impressing everyone of course, with his bulk and his booming voice. But he was greedy and debauched, he had blood on his hands – and he was a traitor. At least Robespierre, villain that he was, wasn't for sale. Like I told your colleagues here, I'm a royalist! That's the least I could do, eh, to make up for the atrocities committed by my rotten great-great-something-grandfather. He voted for the death of the king, so he can't complain if he lost his own head.'

'And is he complaining?'

The question seemed to unseat the loquacious descendant of Danton for a moment.

'And anyway, if you're a royalist,' Adamsberg went on, 'what are you doing joining an assembly like that?'

'I'm keeping *watch*,' the man replied, now in deadly earnest. 'I observe, I follow. I keep a tally of all their follies, all the vices of its members, a bunch of men that wear disguise and run around like rats in a sewer, they don't even have the courage of their convictions. They think they're anonymous, do they? Not to me they're not! Swindles, unpaid taxes, crooked deals, pornography, arms trade, homosexuality, paedophilia, any weakness, it's all grist to my mill. So I don't think I come away empty-handed, oh no. Those republicans, they stink to high heaven. You needn't waste your time looking for my records, they're tucked away somewhere safe. And I've got plenty of them. Just a bit more evidence and I'm ready to light the fuse. Put the boot into that nest of pitiful insects. Exactly what you'd expect from descendants of the despicable fanatics who ruined France with their pathetic democracy. And if I destroy *them*, I'll bring down the whole Republic.'

'I see,' said Adamsberg. 'And how are you managing to carry out such a huge investigation all on your own?'

'On my own? You're way off beam, commissaire. The royalist network is much more extensive than you think. It has tentacles reaching into the legal profession, and even into your own police force. And there are quite a lot of us in the association. Do you really believe the French Republic is destined to last for ever?'

The man laughed again, and then with a dramatic gesture, flung open the twin doors of a small cupboard. Pinned up on the inside panels were reproductions of portraits of Danton and Robespierre, bespattered with dirt, their eyes defaced with red paint which had sent rivulets dripping down their cheeks.

'Like them like that, eh?'

'Violent piece of work,' commented Adamsberg. 'Violent enough to make you a killer, while you wait for the big night.'

The man lovingly closed his cupboard.

'As if I'd waste my time picking them off one by one, when I can soon be done with the lot of them.'

Adamsberg signalled to his colleagues that it was time to leave.

'And you can tell that chinless wonder François Château, and his two stuck-up pedantic acolytes,' the man shouted after them, 'that their pigsty is doomed!'

'Aggressive guy,' said Adamsberg, when they were back in the street.

'Danton must be fed up with him,' said Justin.

'It's always your own folk who betray you.'

'Is he having us on?' asked Danglard.

'No, I don't think so,' said Adamsberg. 'Those posters were old, he hadn't just laid them on. He really does hate them.'

'Makes him a credible suspect,' said Justin.

'I think he's aiming higher,' said Adamsberg. 'He wants to fling the mud of scandal at them, and he thinks if he can destroy the reputation of the association, he can destroy that of the Revolution, and bring down the whole Republic, no less! What did he say to explain why he was spotted outside the psychiatrist's house?'

'That the secretary was just one of the people he was spying on. He's looking for a chink in his armour.'

'And has he found one?'

'Don't know. His "files" are in a secret place, he kept saying.'

'I don't think either of the stuck-up and pedantic acolytes are at much risk from that Danton descendant. If the killer wants to decapitate the association, he'll go for Robespierre. And for the time being, the murderer is setting off his wave from a long way off, by eliminating the "occasion-als". Why? Because a storm you can see approaching gradually is much more frightening than one that falls on you out of the blue. He'll pull in his net little by little, deliberately, because he wants to be seen coming over the horizon. We can reduce the protection for Lebrun, just see that he gets into a safe taxi at the hospital gates. Same for Leblond. Call him in too, try to find where he lives. He's a bit more slippery than the secretary, I think.'

'Lebrun will whimper with fear,' said Danglard.

'If he's as scared as all that, let him resign.'

'He'd lose face. A psychiatrist hiding behind a *burladero*.'

'A what?'

'The wooden barrier in the bullring,' said Danglard in exasperation. 'You asked me what it was yourself, not six hours ago.'

'So I did.'

The angelus sounded at 7 p.m. in St François-Xavier's Church. Adamsberg stopped in the street.

'Time for a coffee,' he said.

An aperitif rather, thought Danglard. Given the time.

'Should you be interested in following up on "it's always your own folk who betray you",' said Adamsberg, 'it's possible that the two Icelandic murders are not quite what we thought.'

'We said we'd finished with Iceland,' said Justin, rather plaintively.

'Yes indeed. But that doesn't stop us taking a little trip there, if you're tempted.'

Neither the commandant nor the lieutenant was tempted, and they didn't move. Adamsberg smiled at them, gave a little wave and left them. The two men watched him walk off and go into a cafe. A few minutes later, they were sitting at his table.

'It's not Iceland we're going to, in fact, but a farm in the Eure-et-Loir *département*.'

'Where you went today?' said Justin.

'And which meant you missed the first part of our questioning of Danton,' added Danglard sourly.

'Was it interesting?'

'No.'

'Well, there you are, Danglard. Half an hour's enough for people like him. A farm with an odd name, Le Thost, pronounced "Le Toh" by the way, occupied in the past by a couple named Grenier who took in foster-children.'

'Where Amédée Masfauré lived until he was five, yes, you told us that.'

'Where he was imprisoned, more like. Ill-treated in every way, until the kid went berserk with this business of chopping the heads off ducks.'

'He mentioned something about ducks when we were at Le Creux,' said Danglard, who was suddenly much more relaxed, now that his glass of white wine had appeared.

Justin turned his head from left to right during the entire story about the seven or ten ducks, trying to shake off the images like flies. A child with a hatchet, the blood, the duck meat put non-stop on the plate for days afterwards. And the big boy who helped get rid of the pieces of meat.

'Easy to see why he's buried his memories then,' he said.

'I don't think he's buried anything,' said Adamsberg. 'I think he's lying. And the big boy who looked after him during those five night-mare years, another foundling like himself, I'm sure Amédée hasn't forgotten him either. He was, and probably is, still, the only person he's ever loved, his saviour.'

'And?'

'And he was ten years older, not good-looking, that is except for his fair curly hair and a big smile. Someone who wasn't seen very much by the neighbours.'

Danglard had his eyes fixed on some faraway place, but automatically held out his arm as the waiter passed.

'*Brothers*, you mean? They're brothers?'

'I don't get it,' said Justin.

'Amédée and Victor,' said Adamsberg. 'Brothers. Half-brothers. Abandoned, ten years apart by the same mother.'

'Where's the evidence?' asked Danglard, his arm still outstretched.

'Only one letter arrived every month at the farm, containing the allowance. Not two. Once Amédée was there it came from Madame Masfauré. But before that, it had come from Mademoiselle Pouillard, Marie-Adélaïde Pouillard, who later married Henri Masfauré.'

The waiter filled up the glass Danglard was holding out, and the commandant turned his head suddenly to thank him, breaking out of his brief daze.

'And one fine day, she came to fetch Amédée, when he was five years old?' asked Justin. 'Out of remorse? But if so, why did she only take the one child?'

'Because if it had been up to her, she'd never have come at all.'

'OK,' said Danglard. 'Let's suppose that Henri Masfauré learned somehow or other that his irresistible wife had given up a baby for adoption some time in the past. According to the dates, not long before they married. Perhaps she was afraid she'd lose Masfauré?'

'Because he didn't want children?'

'I'm not sure that's it,' said Adamsberg. 'More likely she preferred to get rid of the child, rather than see the Masfauré money get away. Same scenario ten years earlier, with some theatre producer. Remember, this woman was a man-eater, nothing stopped her.'

'Of course,' said Danglard. 'Brothers, Amédée and Victor, names of the dukes of Savoy.'

'Precisely,' said Adamsberg. 'You were spot on with that.'

'But I can't see it makes much sense,' Danglard said, shaking his head. 'Even when she gave them away to unknown people, she gave them names attached to the aristocracy.'

'When Masfauré learned of the existence of this abandoned son,' said Adamsberg, 'either he felt a pang of conscience, or perhaps it was a matter of morality. At any rate, he obliged his wife to go and fetch the child. I think our philanthropist saw a different side of his wife that day. Perhaps he was horrified by her. Or perhaps he forgave her? But in any case, it was out of the question for Marie-Adélaïde that Masfauré should learn there was actually *another* child, abandoned fifteen years before. So she didn't say a word about Victor, and when she went to the farm, she didn't so much as look at him. Deliberately.'

'Contemptible,' said Danglard, 'a contemptible hypocrite.'

'So now we're getting somewhere,' said Adamsberg quietly. 'Aged about fifteen or so, Victor was certainly old enough to have poked about in the Greniers' paperwork and found out what his mother's name was: Pouillard. And then he could have seen the same writing on the envelopes, but in her new name of Masfauré. So imagine what this teenager must have felt when the beautiful Marie-Adélaïde Masfauré turns up at the farm to pick up little Amédée, and doesn't give him a glance. Then she snatches from his arms Amédée, the only person under the sun for whom he had any affection. The big car goes off, with the little boy sobbing his heart out, and leaves the other boy to his lot.'

'Abandoned twice,' said Justin.

'Quite enough to turn Victor into a bundle of rage and hate,' said Danglard.

'To the point of killing her, commandant?'

Adamsberg tipped his chair back, thoughtfully.

'Well, he may have *wanted* to,' said Justin.

'But why then, ten years later, did he turn up at the Masfauré house?' asked Adamsberg. 'Having appropriated their name for himself, in order to attract their attention? Why didn't he just say he was Marie-Adélaïde's son? Why didn't he create a scandal? Why did he enter the family in disguise, and then become entrenched there? What could have been his purpose, if not to kill her, Justin?'

'Because if he made himself known and she died, he'd be the first suspect,' said Danglard. 'Nobody was to know she was his mother.'

'So he bided his time,' said Justin, 'until the right moment came along.'

'In Iceland,' said Adamsberg.

'In Iceland,' Danglard repeated. 'So does Amédée know that Victor is his brother?'

'I think,' said Adamsberg hesitantly, 'it must be because his parents expressly told him to keep quiet that Amédée told us nothing about his early childhood. He must of course remember Victor, his hero at the farm. But he didn't recognise him when he turned up years later. After all, he was only five when they were split up, so he might well not recognise a grown man of twenty-five. But perhaps, unconsciously, he *does* know who he is. Nothing else can explain why he's so devoted to him, just like a kid. As for Victor, I'm convinced he's kept his secret, even from his dear Amédée. If he hated his mother, their mother, enough to want to kill her, he would have to keep it quiet.'

'So the whole story about Iceland and the man with the knife . . . ' Justin began.

'. . . would be false,' Adamsberg finished the sentence.

'But they didn't have time to concoct a story before we questioned them,' Danglard objected.

'Yes they did. Remember the way Amédée went dashing off on horseback, completely pointlessly, and then Victor went after him? Victor ordered Amédée to do that, the minute Céleste mentioned the name of Alice Gauthier.'

'But how could Victor have guessed that Gauthier was on the Iceland expedition? He didn't know the people's names.'

'Because Amédée had already shown him the letter. He didn't have any secrets from Victor.'

'I see,' said Danglard. 'So they had time to get their story together when they were out in the woods.'

'Remember the description of the killer that Victor gave us? An ordinary sort of face, no distinguishing features. He gave a vague impression of him, a sort of invisible man. But he insisted – and so did Amédée – on the man's savagery. He was "a monster", abominable, a real killer. As if Victor was leading us down a dark passage with a torch. Look over there, you cops, for the monster without a name or a face. And you can keep on looking till the end of time.'

'What about the death of the legionnaire?' asked Justin.

'A cover-up for the murder of the mother?'

'And what about Masfauré? Did Victor kill Masfauré too?'

'No. Why would he kill his benefactor? Ten years later? No, no motive. Masfauré belongs with the Robespierre case. Two cases, two different murderers. Which we thought were one and the same. That's why the seaweed seemed so tangled. Danglard, you can tell them all about this tomorrow. I'm not sure I want to come along.'

'You're not totally satisfied, are you, commissaire?' said Danglard in a low voice. 'About Victor.'

Adamsberg turned towards his deputy, with a faraway look in his eyes: it was one of those moments when he was off in some inaccessible zone, and his eyes had darkened so that the iris and the pupil were one.

'Satisfied, perhaps,' he said. 'But I'm not happy about it.'

XXIX

THERE WAS AN OUTBURST OF EXCITEMENT IN THE COUNCIL CHAMBER WHEN Danglard had finished his report. Appreciative whistles and the clicking of fingers signalled approval of Adamsberg's 'cloud-shovelling' trip to the farm at Le Thost, from which he had brought back interesting data.

The commissaire's reputation for being a 'cloud-shoveller' – conferred upon him by a police officer in Quebec during a previous case – had long divided his squad, which was split between 'believers' and 'positivists'. The believers went along with the commissaire's meandering thoughts – often unspoken or hard to read – out of loyalty or, as in the case of the devoted Estalère, blind faith. The positivists were those officers who were wedded to Cartesian logic for conducting investigations, and were exasperated or disorientated by the commissaire's wayward approach. Retancourt was the pragmatic leader of this faction. Yet to everyone's surprise, the statuesque lieutenant had not criticised Adamsberg's expedition to the farm the previous day. 'Just like a woman,' Noël had commented, 'soon as a kid's involved, their brains turn to mush.' To which Kernorkian had replied tartly that at least if Noël was regarding Retancourt as a woman, that must be some kind of progress.

Mordent and Voisenet, who had indicated disapproval of their boss the day before, kept their heads down, in embarrassment.

'Bullseye,' Mordent admitted, stretching his long neck.

'Definitely,' said Justin, 'it throws a different light on those murders in Iceland.'

'Murders whose statute of limitations ran out four months ago under French law,' Veyrenc pointed out. 'If Victor Grenier-Masfauré *did* knock off the legionnaire and his own mother, it can't come to trial.'

'So we're still wasting our time with the Icelandic business after all,' Voisenet concluded.

'Yes, but we've got more information now,' said Danglard.

'Pity we don't know how many ducks got their heads chopped off,' said Mordent. 'Seven, ten? It would make a good folk tale: "The Seven Ducks of Le Thost".'

Mordent did in fact depart from conventional procedures himself, from time to time, but only in relation to myths and legends, and not for long. His gaze never became vague like Adamsberg's. He always maintained the fixed and accurate expression of a bird watching for prey. So his moments of fantasy were just temporary lapses, whereas the commissaire's often entailed long marches without a compass through a mist.

'One,' said Retancourt, sticking up her thumb, 'Victor is perfectly capable of committing murder. Two,' and her index finger went up, 'he is a man who acts on his desires. Three, Victor accompanied Masfauré to the Robespierre assembly. Four, we can't rule him *out* from the murders of these revolutionary play-actors.'

'No, no,' Danglard objected, 'Victor's murders – if they happened at all – would only have been prompted by the shipwreck of his childhood. You don't just go killing people left and right, for want of anything better to do.'

'The Icelandic murders are a closed file,' said Voisenet, 'but the Robespierre series is still going on, and our investigation is still stuck. We've hit the buffers, and we can't see which way to move now.'

'On Monday night,' Mordent reminded them, 'we'll be able to follow and identify the two other "descendants". The ones from the families of the executioner and that other man that was guillotined.'

'Sanson and Desmoulins,' said Veyrenc.

'Yeah, but for now,' said Voisenet, 'we're going round in circles, guarding Château and his henchmen, and we're no nearer identifying the other members of the "occasionals" group.'

Voisenet was someone who liked action: waiting, standing by and getting nowhere got on his nerves. He was hasty by nature, something apparently incompatible with his interest in freshwater fish. Adamsberg guessed in fact that his fixation on fish provided Voisenet with a vital counterweight. Which was why he always let his lieutenant read his specialist periodicals in the office.

Mercadet, who had interrupted his sleep cycle too early, so as not to miss the meeting, asked Estalère for another coffee.

'They'll *all* get knocked off, while we spend our time riding round in police cars and hanging about in doorways,' he said.

'Who's still alive?' Estalère asked.

Veyrenc chose to take on the peacekeeping role that was normally Adamsberg's.

'From the "occasionals" group, at least four, Estalère.'

'Four, OK, so who are they?'

'A woman, someone Lebrun and Leblond call "the actress".'

'Right.'

'And a sporty type they call "the cyclist".'

'Right,' said Estalère again, concentrating hard.

Even when he was concentrating, Estalère's eyebrows remained raised and his eyes even wider open, if that was possible.

'There's one man who seems observant or watchful, Lebrun–Leblond think he's a dentist. There's a slight whiff of antiseptic about him. And lastly a man with no particular distinguishing features.'

'That's all then,' said Estalère, as he went out to fetch another – extra-strong – coffee for Mercadet.

'If there's some miracle, we might get to see them at the session on Monday night. We'll need extra people if we have to keep tabs on the two descendants and the four infiltrators.'

'Yes, we could,' Mordent agreed. 'But now, since four people from their group have been killed, I doubt whether they'll turn up. What's Robespierre up to?'

'He's working late,' Justin replied. 'Probably preparing his speech for Monday'.

'Which will be?' asked Veyrenc.

'The sessions of 11 and 16 Germinal, year II, edited and cut down,' said Danglard, who had found this out. 'Or in other words, the speeches Robespierre made on 31 March and 5 April 1794.'

'The ones in which he called for the arrest of Danton, Desmoulins and their friends,' Veyrenc added.

'Precisely so.'

This information went over the heads of all the other members of the squad. At that moment, Adamsberg entered the room, his head bent as he consulted the screen of his phone, and he greeted his colleagues with a brief wave. Estalère leapt up on his coffee mission.

'Froissy has completed her research,' Adamsberg told them, without sitting down. 'She's traced the entire line of descent from village to village, as far as Montargis. Our François Château is indeed a descendant of the innkeeper François Didier Château, the presumed son of Robespierre. Which makes him more suspicious to us. Danglard, fill them in about this strange innkeeper from 1840. And remind me to ask you later what Robespierre's "painful death" was. It was Lebrun who mentioned it. Meanwhile, Retancourt, I'd be glad if you could come to my office.'

Adamsberg closed his door carefully, while Retancourt sat down on the chair for visitors, one manifestly not meant for someone of her size, and which disappeared under her. But then, no chair was built with Retancourt in mind.

'You can call off the guard duty on François Château.'

'Good,' said Retancourt warily.

Because that vague look in Adamsberg's eyes, noticed the previous day by Danglard, had not disappeared. And everyone in the squad knew what that meant: meandering, mist, cloud-shovelling, in three words.

'As you will have gathered,' said Adamsberg, accepting the cigarette Retancourt offered him, 'what happened in Iceland was different from what the brothers Amédée and Victor told us.'

'Yes.'

'Something much more serious.'

'Matricide.'

'Even more serious, Retancourt. Do you remember, Victor told us that the killer reduced all the members of the group to total silence, on pain of death? And indeed they all kept quiet for ten years. Can you imagine *Victor* terrorising nine men and women, all older and more experienced than himself? At the age of twenty-seven? That's how old he was at the time.'

'Old or young, what does that matter? It's nothing to do with age.'

'According to Victor, the killer told them that his "network" or whatever he called it, would pursue them, even if one of them got him put in prison. How could Victor have a "network"? Brought up on the farm, self-taught? Where would he get such power and such strength of conviction?'

'It's beyond prosecution now, commissaire, in any case,' said Retancourt, shrugging her shoulders.

'Never mind.'

'"More serious" than what? What's this all about?'

'I don't know, Retancourt. How can I? We need to find out.'

Retancourt pushed her chair back noisily, her suspicion growing with every second.

'And where will we do that?' she asked.

'In Iceland. I'm going to the warm rock.'

'That is illogical, commissaire, it makes no sense.'

'Never mind,' Adamsberg repeated. 'But it all depends on an inter-view today. I'm going back to Le Creux to talk to Victor and Amédée.'

'What for? To tell them they're brothers? Just like that, without taking any precautions? It'll be a big shock, they'll react, they'll be devastated.'

'Yes, indeed. And I don't like the idea.'

'So why do it?'

'To find out. One of them may tell the truth perhaps.'

'And then what?

'And then nothing, I'll know, that's all.'

'And what about the Robespierre murders?' asked Retancourt, by now indignant. 'The four infiltrators who are under threat? Are you going to abandon them just to "know" what Victor got up to on the warm island?'

'I'm not abandoning anything. The Robespierre chessboard is frozen at the moment. But things will move eventually. Nothing ever stays the same, fixed. Sooner or later something budges. Someone once said "Animals move", I don't remember who. Anyway, it'll shift of its own accord, trust me.'

'Yeah, right, with another four people getting themselves murdered!'

'Do we know that?'

'And if the interview today gets you nowhere?'

'Well then, I'll go to the warm rock, there are twenty-three officers here, all perfectly well informed, and all capable of sticking to the Robespierre affair.'

'Twenty-three you say? So you're not going alone?'

'That's right. It's not that I'm afraid of the icy wastes, but it's the way I operate. Watching other people allows me to stay – how would you put it? – on the straight and narrow.'

'From which you've totally departed, commissaire,' said Retancourt, standing up and signifying that she was about to leave. 'You're off on a wild goose chase. If the divisionnaire finds out you're dashing off on a closed case, and leaving the current investigation behind, you'll be disciplined.'

'Would you do that, Retancourt? Inform on me?'

Adamsberg lit another cigarette and walked over to the window, turning his back on his colleague.

'You can't do that, Violette,' he said – he liked every now and then to address her by her first name. 'Because you're coming with me. Unless, as I say, the truth emerges this afternoon, which I very much doubt.'

'No way,' said Retancourt, moving to the door. 'No way am I leaving the team in the middle of a mess.'

Now they were both standing, two obstinate creatures facing each other, the two most dissimilar animals one could imagine.

'OK,' said Adamsberg, still facing the window, and letting his ash fall to the ground. 'I'll take Justin.'

'Justin? Are you mad? He can't even lift five kilos.'

'And how much can you lift, Violette?'

'From the ground or shoulder?'

'Which is the hardest?'

'From the ground.'

'OK, how much from the ground?'

'Seventy-two kilos,' said Retancourt, blushing slightly.

Adamsberg whistled in admiration.

'That's nothing,' Retancourt said, 'the world record for a woman in my category is 148 kilos.'

'I don't need the world record holder. You will be quite capable of hauling me out of icy water if I fall in.'

'It's April. Not the same conditions as when those twelve cretins went off in November.'

'Don't be so sure. At this time of year, there are five short hours of sunlight if you're lucky, the temperature's between 2 and 9 degrees, risk of snow or Arctic storms, plenty of mist and icebergs floating round on the frozen water.'

'Well, not Justin,' Retancourt insisted. 'He can stay here. He's good at tailing people, he's as shifty as a cat.'

'You and Veyrenc. Not Danglard of course. Even the plane trip would destabilise him for a couple of months, remember Quebec?

Danglard can stay here to coordinate things with Mordent. Danglard has the knowledge and Mordent the judgement.'

By now, Adamsberg was walking up one side of the long desk in his office, while Retancourt was pacing about on the other. Trying not to get her feet entangled in the huge pair of stag's antlers lying in a corner, a souvenir from a dark forest in Normandy which Adamsberg hadn't thought to move anywhere else. Two creatures prowling up and down, two metres from one another, separated by the symbolic *burladero* of the wooden desk. Unaware that behind the closed door, Estalère was standing transfixed, carrying the coffee he had made for the commissaire, which was now cold. He could hear the sound of quarrelling, and this argument between the two people he admired the most left him distraught.

'If you won't get this idea out of your head, commissaire,' Retancourt said, in a conciliatory move, 'at least postpone it. Let's finish with this Robespierre business and go after that. You can enjoy the warm rock to your heart's content then.'

'I've already booked three tickets for Tuesday. Open tickets, in case the animals move.'

'Are they booked in our names?'

'For me, yes. For you and Veyrenc, no. Or else I'll take Voisenet – he might like to see some northern fish. Mercadet would be good but we can't let him drop off to sleep for three hours in the snow. Voisenet and Kernorkian. Or Noël.'

'You wouldn't be able to stand three days with Noël.'

'Of course I could. What he says goes in one ear and out the other for me. He's strong, and he'd be good at life-saving. You haven't forgotten that, Retancourt?'

'No, I haven't.'

'And the cat. Snowball. He'd be better than a hot-water bottle.'

Retancourt stopped in her tracks. Adamsberg did too, and smiled at her.

'Have a think, Retancourt. Answer by tomorrow afternoon at latest.'

XXX

ADAMSBERG HAD POCKETED HIS PHONE AND CAR KEYS AND CAUGHT up with Danglard in the corridor.

'Coming with me, commandant?'

'Where to?'

'To Le Creux. To find out what these two brothers have been concealing from us.'

'They don't know they're brothers, well, Amédée doesn't. You'll trigger a trauma, a catastrophe perhaps.'

'Or something good, a necessity.'

'It's past two o'clock and we haven't had lunch.'

'We can eat a sandwich in the car.'

Danglard pulled a face, and hesitated. But since the previous day in the cafe, the story of the farm at Le Thost and its consequences had, despite himself, begun to preoccupy him.

'We'll have dinner tonight at the Auberge du Creux,' Adamsberg added. 'That'll make up for it.'

'Maybe we can order a menu ahead. Even get some of those potato cakes?'

'We can try.'

As they crossed the main office, the commissaire stopped at the desk where Veyrenc was working.

'Questioning session out at Le Creux, followed by dinner at the inn, that suit you?'

'Count me in,' said Veyrenc. 'There's something about those two . . .'

'Have you done something to your hair?'

'I tried to dye it last night.'

'Didn't really work, did it?'

'Nope.'

'Looks worse. Kind of purple.'

'Yeah, I know.'

From her office, Retancourt, holding herself as tight as a clenched fist, watched the three men walk out.

Adamsberg glanced at his stopped watches when Céleste came to open the large wooden gates to them.

'It's four o'clock,' Veyrenc told him.

Céleste seemed quite glad to see them, and smiled as she shook hands, her eyes fixed on Veyrenc.

'She's taken a shine to you,' Adamsberg whispered to his childhood playmate. 'What was it Château said about you? Why you wouldn't be appropriate for the revolutionary assembly? Oh yes, something about looking like an ancient statue.'

'Alas, Roman rather than Greek,' said Veyrenc.

Adamsberg took a step to the side, so that he could walk in the grass and find the dried-up burdock from before. Céleste had gone in search of Amédée and Victor, who both arrived from the stables. Smelling of horses and looking concerned. If the cops had caught Henri's killer, surely they would have telephoned before this? So what the hell were they doing coming out in person again?

'Sorry to turn up without warning,' said Adamsberg.

'No, you're not sorry,' said Victor. 'That's what the police always do, turn up without warning. Take people by surprise.'

'True. Can we sit down somewhere?'

'Will this take long?'

'It might.'

Amédée pointed to a wooden garden table and chairs in the middle of the lawn.

'It's still sunny,' he said. 'If you're not too cold, we can stay outdoors.'

Adamsberg was aware that people being questioned always felt happier outside than in a confined space. His intention wasn't to crush them, so he headed for the table.

'This is a delicate matter,' he began, once they were all seated. 'It's tricky to tell you why we've come.'

'Why have you?' asked Amédée.

'Because both of you have lied to us. Sorry, but there's no other way to put it.'

'Does this have to do with my father?'

'No, not at all.'

'What's it about then?'

'Your private lives.'

'Which we have no obligation to tell you about,' said Victor, standing up. 'If you arrest someone for poaching, you don't have the right to know who he's sleeping with.'

'Well, sometimes we do. Anyway, this is nothing to do with who you sleep with. Sit down, Victor, you're going to alarm Céleste unnecessarily.'

Céleste was hurrying towards them, holding in shaky hands a tray laden with every possible kind of drink and biscuits. Veyrenc got up at once to help her and distributed the bottles and glasses on the table, while Victor took his seat again, not without a heavy frown on his face.

'Amédée,' said Adamsberg, turning towards the young man who looked concerned, 'you told us you couldn't remember anything except a few images from your first five years in some institution.'

'That's right.'

'No it isn't, it's wrong. You *weren't* in any institution. You were fostered at a farm. At Le Thost, with a brutal family, and your parents came to fetch you when you were five.'

Amédée locked his fingers together like spiders' legs and was unable to speak. Victor immediately moved on to the attack.

'Where did you go digging all that up?'

'With the social security authorities, and at the farm, or to be more precise, by visiting a neighbour, Madame Mangematin. Roberta. She used to come and help with the laundry on washing days for the Grenier couple. She remembers Amédée. Who had been abandoned at birth, and whom a couple called Masfauré came to take back five years later.'

Adamsberg was speaking as slowly and gently as he could, but he was conscious that his words would be startling for the younger man.

'Don't you remember *anything*, Amédée, when I say those names?'

'No.'

'Do we have to talk about the ducks? You said you remembered some ducks.'

'Yes.'

Placing his hand on the table, Victor had bent back the two top joints of his index finger. Amédée did the same. A signal of complicity, a warning not to speak.

'One day you chopped the heads off seven or ten of them. And then you were forced to pluck and clean them, and eat them day after day, morning, noon and night. A big boy on the farm, who was older than you, helped you out.'

'I remember that big boy, I told you that before.'

'And the ducks, you remember them? The hatchet? The blood?'

'Yes, he remembers,' said Danglard, speaking as softly as Adamsberg.
Amédée uncurled his index finger.

'What's the point of all this?' he said, sweat beginning to form on
his forehead and upper lip. 'Yes, I was fostered. But my parents told me
never to talk about it. I don't like remembering it, and I don't like talking about it. And anyway, what does it *matter*? What possible interest
can it have for you?'

'The boy who helped you eat the ducks,' Adamsberg insisted, 'you
remember him?'

'If there's one person in the world I do want to remember, it's him.'

'He protected you, right?'

'I'd have died a hundred times over, if it wasn't for him.'

Victor had now bent all his fingers back, but Amédée seemed not to
notice, or not to be able to receive the signal, as he was propelled back
into the dark memory of the farm at Le Thost where there had been
only one bright spot, the 'big boy'.

'And when your parents arrived, these unknown parents, they
snatched you away from him. I was told you were hanging on to him,
and he didn't want to let you go.'

'I was too little to understand. Yes, they did snatch me away, it was
for my own good, they told me afterwards. But *he* whispered in my
ear: "Don't worry, wherever you are, I'll be there. I'll never leave you.
Wherever you go, I'll go."'

Amédée was gripping his thighs. Adamsberg took a deep breath, looked
up and let his eyes wander over the treetops. The worst was yet to come.

'But he'd disappeared,' said Amédée in a choked voice. 'Of course he
had, how would he ever have found me? But I only realised that much
later. For years I waited for him, I used to look out over the park every
evening, but he didn't come.'

'Yes, he did,' said Adamsberg. 'He came all right.'

Amédée leaned back in his chair, his hands over his forehead, like
an animal who has been beaten for no cause.

'He kept his word,' Adamsberg went on, as Victor unbent his fingers and tightened his lips. 'And you really didn't recognise him?' he asked, leaning towards Amédée. 'Him!' he said, pointing to Victor with a slight movement of his hand. 'That other Victor, also known as Victor Masfauré.'

Amédée turned his head towards his father's secretary, extremely slowly, like a man with frostbite, unsure how to use his body.

'When you'd last seen him, he was a gawky teenager with an ugly mug, but when you met him ten years later, he was a grown man, a muscular man with a beard. But what about his curly hair, Amédée, and his smile?'

'I've still got an ugly mug,' said Victor, aiming to lighten the tension of the moment.

'I'm going to take a walk with my colleagues. I'll leave you two alone for a few minutes.'

Crouching down on the grass at a distance, Adamsberg could see the two men grabbing each other's hands, and interrupting each other, trying to talk at the same time. He watched as Amédée leaned his head on Victor's shoulder, while Victor patted his hair. A quarter of an hour later, the situation seemed to have calmed somewhat. He gave them another five minutes, then signalled to his colleagues, who were sitting on a bench to the side – on account of Danglard's English tweed suit, which was not intended to make contact with the damp ground.

'Watch their fingers,' Adamsberg said, as he took his time approaching the table. 'When Victor bends his index finger, he's telling Amédée not to say anything.'

'And you really didn't recognise him?' Adamsberg asked Amédée once more.

'No,' said Amédée, his hand still gripping Victor's arm, and a quite changed expression on his face.

'But subconsciously, you *did*, didn't you? You recognised him emotionally, and you adopted him and loved him, although he was just your father's secretary.'

'Yes,' Amédée admitted.

'That takes us to you, Victor, and your secrets. What is your real name?'

'You know that, it's Masfauré.'

'No, it isn't. A child abandoned at birth is normally given three first names and the last one becomes a surname. So what was it.'

'Laurent. The Greniers knew me as Victor Laurent.'

'But you gave yourself the name Masfauré, to get Henri's attention. You entered his house under a false name, and you got settled in there, without telling Amédée that you were his old companion from the farm.'

Pretending to be drowsy, one of his hands holding on to Amédée's, Victor explained in a tired voice.

'I didn't want to shock him. Amédée seemed to have recovered, he was well cared for here, if a bit melancholy, but, well, he was living his life, and I didn't want to upset everything. Just being here was enough for me.'

'That's all very fine, and indeed I quite believe you,' said Adamsberg. 'But coming back like that, without telling him, keeping him in the dark for twelve years, what sense was there in that?'

'What I just told you.'

'No,' said Veyrenc firmly.

'No,' Adamsberg echoed. 'Amédée would have welcomed you with open arms as his saviour from Le Thost. It wasn't from *him* that you really wanted to hide your origins.'

'Yes, it was,' Victor insisted, looking more grim, and frowning under his incongruous thatch of blond curls.

'No. It wasn't from him you were hiding, it was from *her*.'

'Her? Who?' Victor made an attempt at a rebellious movement.

'Marie-Adélaïde Pouillard, Madame Masfauré.'

'I don't know what you're talking about.'

'You snooped into the Greniers' correspondence as soon as you were old enough. And you knew what was going on, before Amédée left.'

'There wasn't any correspondence,' cried Victor, 'or else it had all been destroyed. I did look for it, but I didn't find anything.'

'Destroyed? When it could have been used for all kinds of blackmail? People like the Greniers? I don't think so. You did find it. How else would you have known the address of Amédée's new home?'

There was a pregnant silence, and Danglard proposed that they all have a glass of port. Or something of the kind. He bestirred his long flabby legs over to the house in search of Céleste. 'Can you give us something strong?' he asked. And for once this wasn't for himself. Everyone waited in silence, as if the drinks would resolve everything, or at any rate hold things still.

'All right,' Victor finally said, after two glasses of port, 'I *did* look through the papers in the Grenier house. They were hidden in a crack in a rafter, behind a rusty scythe. But there were only a couple of letters.'

'Look, we're agreed, aren't we, that you made this discovery before Amédée was taken away?'

'Yes,' Victor conceded, taking another glass. 'I was thirteen.'

'There weren't just a couple of letters, there were about a hundred. And you learned quite a lot.'

Victor bent back his index finger, this time as a message to himself. Amédéc had long since given up trying to understand. He was still staring at Victor with that amazed, puzzled but almost beatific expression sometimes seen in Estalère.

'It was just his mother's name and address,' Victor summed up curtly. 'When I came of age, I left the farm, I went from one job to another, but once I got a motorbike, I would go to look at him, through the woods. Until I found a way of getting taken into the house.'

'With a new CV and a new name.'

'Where was the harm in that? I'd promised him.'

'True. But then living here for *twelve years* without saying anything that might "upset" him, I can't buy that. It was for another reason that you kept quiet.'

'I don't know what you're talking about,' Victor repeated automatically.

His voice was both tired and excited: he was by now slightly drunk, as Adamsberg had intended, pouring him out some more port. The more you drink, the faster you drink, which is what Victor did, knocking back his fourth glass in a couple of mouthfuls. Amédée still said nothing, as he gripped Victor's arm. Danglard, on this occasion, took care to remain sober.

'Yes, you do,' Adamsberg insisted. 'It was the same envelope that came each month, containing the allowance for *both* children. And you found that out.'

'No, *my* mother never paid anything.'

'Not true, Victor. The envelopes had dates and handwriting on them. Adélaïde Pouillard's handwriting in the early years. Then Adélaïde Masfauré's. The same first name and the same handwriting. It was easy enough to grasp what was happening.'

'They were all destroyed,' Victor muttered.

'You can't destroy people's memories. The postman's for example. He remembers.'

Fuddled with the generous amounts of port Adamsberg had poured him, Victor, the good Samaritan, uncoiled his fingers.

'All right,' he said simply.

'You weren't just companions of misfortune, were you?' said Adamsberg as quietly as possible. 'You're brothers.'

Adamsberg left the table again, and plunged into the woods, where Marc the wild boar confronted him with his snout. His colleagues had taken up positions on the clean bench. Adamsberg sat down on a pile of dry leaves: Marc lying beside him, allowed the policeman to scratch his soft furry muzzle, well away from the emotions which were presently being unleashed at the table. Adamsberg had inherited from his mother an extreme reticence about expressing feelings which, she said, wore away like soap and dispersed if you talked about them too much. He looked up, and so did Marc, when he saw Veyrenc standing in front of him.

'That's another twenty-five minutes gone,' Veyrenc said. 'If we wait for these two brothers to work through all their emotional baggage, we'll be here a couple of years.'

'And that would suit me just fine.'

Adamsberg stood up, brushed down his trousers with his hand and gave a last stroke to Marc's snout before returning to the table of revelations and confessions. The tough bit was coming next, and he chose to go at it quickly. He spoke without sitting down now, pacing up and down on the grass, as the others followed him with their eyes.

'Victor comes back, like a ghost, secretly, twelve years ago, under a false name. Why? Because he doesn't want anyone to find out that Adélaïde is his mother. Very odd behaviour. Which makes sense only from one point of view: he intends to kill her.'

'What?!' yelled Victor.

'You'll get your chance to talk in a minute, Victor. Let me finish,' Adamsberg ordered him. 'And I'll make it the worst-case scenario. Victor has been nursing this intention for a long time, ever since he was a child at Le Thost. It gets even worse when he sees her turn up, his own mother, and she contemptuously and completely ignores him. He sees her take the little boy away and leave him there. Every day, every night, he nourishes his hate, his anguish and his plan. She's going to pay for this. So when he's twenty-five, he manages to get taken into the Masfauré establishment under a false name. He waits for his chance. It's vital that no one should actually know she's his mother. But *she* will know all right, just before he attacks her. In Iceland. He encourages the idea of the trip to the warm rock. In an isolated place like that, anything might happen. A hole in the ice, or perhaps he can lure her to one side on the island, she slips on the frozen ground, her head strikes a rock, he calls for help, too late, she's dead. He swears to himself that she's not going to return alive from the island. But then they get caught in the fog, and the "legionnaire" is stabbed by this violent individual in their group. Let's assume for the moment that it wasn't Victor who did that. But he seizes the opportunity it gives him. In the night, having taken the man's knife, he aims for the heart and kills his mother as she sleeps. And the second murder is immediately attributed to the violent man, and his vengeance is accomplished. But ten years later, danger looms up. Amédée receives this letter from an Alice Gauthier and shows it to him. And the day after Amédée's visit, Alice Gauthier is found bleeding to death in her bath. But why draw the sign?'

'I don't know anything about that sign!' said Victor furiously.

'Wait. Later,' said Adamsberg, pouring him another glass. 'Second danger. The cops turn up to question Amédée about his conversation with Alice Gauthier. Who had told him the truth: Adélaïde Masfauré was indeed killed on the island. But as for the monstrous man and his actions, the only evidence we have for that comes from the statements made by . . . Amédée and Victor. Why would that monster have killed Adélaïde? In the first case, the legionnaire, one might imagine a quarrel between two panicking males. But why her? After the first murder, it was possible her husband might have taken the chance to eliminate his wife. Or perhaps it was his devoted secretary, Victor? Alice Gauthier could have conveyed her doubts to Amédée. Victor sees there's a risk he might be suspected, especially since now Masfauré has also been killed. The cops are going to ask questions, they won't go away. So Victor gives Amédée his version of what happened. That's why there was that chase on horseback, to get their story straight between them: Adélaïde Masfauré being sexually attacked, the man falling backwards into the fire – it's a realistic detail, but it sounds a false note if it's given such prominence – the man's humiliation, and then the stabbing in front of everyone. "If we don't say this," Victor tells Amédée, "your *father* might be suspected. What are the police going to conclude? That after killing his wife and then Gauthier, he finally committed suicide? Is that what we want?" Amédée, who always obeys Victor's instructions, because for him Victor can do no wrong – but also believing that his father must be guilty – backs up his story. There you are, I've finished.'

Victor poured himself another glass – Adamsberg had lost count by now. Arms folded and cheeks inflamed by alcohol, Victor made an effort to speak calmly, holding his back as straight as Robespierre's. The attitude of a man who is very drunk and extremely shocked, but trying to maintain his equilibrium.

'No, commissaire, you're wrong. It happened the way Amédée and I told you. Otherwise why would the killer have threatened us? Why would everyone have kept quiet for ten years? If it was me that killed her? Tell me that.'

'That is indeed the problem. The long silence.'

'But on the other hand, commissaire,' Victor said resolutely, 'your version is quite plausible, I recognise that.'

He stood up unsteadily, then with a violent gesture swept the glasses off the table. He caught up the bottle of port, and drank a few mouthfuls straight from it. Then standing legs apart, and swinging the bottle from his hand, he shouted aloud:

'And I'll tell you why it's so plausible! Because yes, I *did* want to kill her! Yes, I'd always wanted to! Yes, when she took Amédée away, and yes, I promised myself one day I'd do it. Yes, when I came here to be close to my brother. And yes, I said nothing, so that no one would know I was her fucking son. The son of my fucking mother, I mean!

Kill her and get away with it, yes! And Iceland was a golden opportunity. So of course, I backed the idea of going to the godforsaken rock! But yes, that guy *did* kill the legionnaire, believe it or not! And I did have the idea that I could stab her and make it seem like it was him! Yes, you reconstructed it all quite correctly! Only I *didn't* kill her. It was that bastard who stole my murder! *My* murder!'

Victor drank again and this time lost his balance and keeled over on to the grass. He tried to get up but failed, and stayed sitting on the ground, hugging his knees, head down between his legs. Then came a free flow of hiccups, sobs and cries of distress. Adamsberg raised his hand to stop anyone intervening.

'Leave me be, Amédée,' said Victor between hiccups. 'I don't wanna get up.'

'A blanket, shall I get you a blanket?'

'I wanna be sick. Bring me something to make me sick.'

'What?'

'Some horse manure.'

'No, Victor.'

'Please, fetch some horse manure. I want it now.'

Amédée, at a loss, looked up at Adamsberg who reassured him with a glance.

'But then when we were safe back in Grimsey,' Victor began again, in his husky voice, tears and mucus streaming from his face, 'I realised that the killer had saved my – what would you say, saved my soul? I wouldn't really have wanted to do it. No, that's not it. I could have done it, I *was* going to do it, kill her, murder her. No, I understood something else.'

Victor laid his head on his knees, as if it weighed too much. Adamsberg supported his chin.

'Don't go to sleep, I'm holding you. Rest your head on my fist. Carry on.'

'Wanna be sick.'

'You will, don't worry. What did you realise?'

'Where?'

'When you got back safely to Grimsey.'

'That I could never have done it. I saw my mother again, dead, among the rocks and the snow, and I would have hated being the one who'd done it. Whereas, in another few hours, if that bastard hadn't done it, that horrible thing, *I* might have. And then I'd have killed myself.'

'That's what you realised?'

'Yes. Bring me some horse manure. And if you want to charge me, go ahead, see if I care. I don't give a shit any more.'

'Charge you with what? I don't have any evidence one way or the other.'

'But you're going to look for it.'

'No, the time's run out on those murders, Victor. They're beyond the statute of limitations.'

'Well, *look* for some evidence, for God's sake, look for it! Or Amédée will always wonder whether I stabbed his mother to death!'

'How are we supposed to look for evidence, if you won't tell us any more about that man?'

'I dunno *where* he is, I dunno *who* he is! *I. Don't. Know. Who. He. Is!*'

'You're not telling the truth, Victor. But you can lean over and throw up now, it's over.'

What, there on the grass, by the table? Danglard shook his head. It had happened to him, rarely, but he'd always taken trouble to be discreet about it.

'Help me, Amédée,' said Adamsberg, as he caught hold of Victor's shoulder. 'We need to make him kneel, head down. You press his stomach, I'll bang his back.'

Ten minutes later, when Amédée had thrown a few spadefuls of earth on the grass, Veyrenc and Danglard helped Victor up, took him to the lodge and put him to bed, followed by the others. Adamsberg leaned up against the bedroom wall thoughtfully, his arm up and his index finger extended.

'What are you doing?' asked Danglard.

'What?'

'With your finger?'

'Oh, that. A fly. It had fallen into the bottom of a glass. I rescued it.'

'Yes, but what are you doing now?'

'Nothing, Danglard, just waiting for it to dry off.'

Veyrenc had removed Victor's shoes and dropped them on the ground.

'You don't need to stay,' Adamsberg said to Amédée, who was sitting like a servant at the end of his brother's bed. 'He'll sleep like a log now until the morning. He just drank himself into a state. He fell into the bottle of port, and he needs to dry out, that's all.'

'Dry out?'

'Yes,' said Adamsberg, watching the fly rub its wings together. 'He'll be fine by tomorrow afternoon.'

Now the fly was rubbing its front legs together. It tried moving a centimetre on Adamsberg's fingernail, wiped itself again, and took off.

'Takes longer for a man,' he remarked.

XXXI

THEY DINED AT THE AUBERGE DU CREUX, WHERE MÉLANIE HAD AGREED to put on a special menu. Danglard tested the *pommes paillasson* for texture with his fingertip, just as Bourlin had.

'Perfect,' he said. 'I mean the dinner. As for the events of this afternoon, hard to say.'

'You can't test an investigation with your fingertip,' Veyrenc said.

'Quite.'

'It would be practical if you could: is it medium rare, just right, overcooked, spoiled, fit to chuck out?'

'This isn't an investigation,' said Adamsberg. 'We're off-piste, as Retancourt very sharply informed me. We have no business stirring up this story, and whatever happened on that warm rock, it's beyond the statute of limitations, we can't handle it.'

'So what did we come out here for?' Danglard asked.

'To learn something, and to liberate some ghosts.'

'That's not our job.'

'Still, we did it,' said Veyrenc. 'As to how successful we were, that's another matter. Did we liberate any ghosts, Jean-Baptiste?'

'Yes, we did do that, we really did. It means there's one more who won't go and wail in the haunted tower. But it's a lot harder to work out whether we actually learned the truth.'

'You don't believe Victor?' asked Danglard.

'He was very convincing,' said Veyrenc. 'He went as far as he could. He confessed in front of his brother that he had intended to kill their mother. That was more than brave, it was crazy.'

'Port does make you crazy,' remarked Danglard knowingly. 'His need to confess was stronger than his fear, so he broke down the barriers.'

'Well, the barriers were already well damaged by the port,' said Veyrenc.

'It's like I said. Sweet alcohol reaches the brain with the speed of an acrobat on a trapeze.'

'But in the end,' Adamsberg went on, 'a miracle "saved his soul". Another killer got in first, and committed the "monstrous act" instead of him. So Victor comes out of it all as white as the driven snow in Iceland.'

'*In vino veritas,*' said Danglard.

'No, I don't agree, Danglard. I've never thought alcohol led to speaking the truth. To pain, yes, it does cause that.'

'So why did you keep pressing the drink on him?'

'So he would take the brakes off, and career downhill as far as he could. But that doesn't mean he's reached the end of the road. Even when he's drunk himself silly and the barriers are badly damaged, the unconscious will be guarding its most precious property, the way Marc guards Céleste. We won't get any more out of him. I was waiting for the results from that stream of emotion and half-truths. I hinted as much to Retancourt at midday today. And she is violently against.'

'Against what?' asked Danglard.

'She just says all this is nothing to do with us, full stop.'

'She's right.'

'Yes. So she won't come along. I thought of her, and you, Louis, to come with me.'

Neither Veyrenc nor Danglard asked 'Where?' There was a silence, one of those pregnant silences in which even the sound of cutlery on plates seems inappropriate. Veyrenc put his knife and fork down. He picked up the wanderings of Adamsberg's mind faster than anyone else, perhaps because he came from the same mountains in the Pyrenees.

'When do we go?' he asked, in the end.

'Tuesday. I've booked three tickets to Reykjavik, or however you pronounce it. Takes three and a half hours. Then forty minutes to . . .' Adamsberg pulled out a notebook from his inside pocket. '. . . to Akureyri,' he read out slowly. 'Then a short flight to the little island of Grimsey. And opposite the harbour, from the end of the jetty, you can see the islet with the warm stone. At this time of year, the pack ice will be breaking up, so we'll need to find a fisherman to take us. It won't be easy, what with the local superstitions about the little island. Even to get someone to hire a boat from.'

'To find what?' asked Danglard. 'Rocks, a few snowdrifts? Unless you plan to lie on the warm stone so you can live for ever.'

'No, I'm not interested in the stone.'

'Well, what then?'

'How should I know, Danglard? I haven't started looking yet.'

Danglard put his knife and fork down in turn.

'Well, you said it yourself. This isn't an investigation, and it's none of our business.'

'Yes, I did say that.'

'And you could be hauled over the coals for this.'

'As Retancourt already warned me. She practically threatened to go and inform on me to the divisionnaire.'

'Retancourt isn't a grass,' said Veyrenc.

'No, but she's furious, and she might do anything to stop me going.'

'Well, she's completely in the right,' said Danglard very firmly.

'What time Tuesday?' asked Veyrenc.

'You're coming?'

'Of course,' said Veyrenc in his habitually calm way. An 'ancient Roman', as Château had called him.

'What do you mean "of course"?' cried Danglard, suddenly finding himself isolated, facing his two colleagues.

'He's going, so I'm going,' said Veyrenc. 'It interests me too. I agree with Jean-Baptiste, Victor hasn't finished telling us everything. He's lying, and very well too. Hard to detect.'

'So how *did* you manage to detect it?'

'By watching Amédée's face. Something else happened in Iceland. It would be interesting to find out what.'

'*Interesting*! But plenty of things are interesting!' Danglard exploded. 'I'd like to visit all the Romanesque churches in France, that would be "interesting", but can I get to do that? I'd like to go and see the woman I met in London, because she's going to dump me if I don't go over there. And have I got time to do that? With four murders already and more to come?'

'You didn't tell me about that, Danglard,' said Adamsberg, 'about your girlfriend with the red glasses.'

'None of your business,' said Danglard aggressively. 'But you, oh no, you're swanning off to Iceland, not on any mission, quite illegally. Why? Because it's "interesting"!'

'Yes, very,' Adamsberg agreed.

'You're saying that, commandant, because you're jealous,' said Veyrenc with a smile, that smile which was attractive to women, but which left Danglard quite cold. 'You envy us, but you're too scared of flying to come with us. The trip, the cold, the mist, the gloomy volcanic rocks. But at the same time, you're sorry to miss out on the little inn opposite the warm rock, and the glass of *brennivín*.'

'That is fucking nonsense, Veyrenc, and you know it. And, I may say, I am quite familiar with *brennivín*, also known as the "black death". You're going off without any agenda, any logic, without any rational excuse whatever.'

'Well, you're pretty much right,' said Adamsberg. 'But look, Danglard, wasn't it you who said not so long ago that it's always good to bring more grist to the mill of human knowledge?'

'Leaving us with this disastrous Robespierrist imbroglio on our hands?'

'Exactly, Danglard, it's the right moment to go. The Robespierre business is at a standstill. All our pawns are waiting on the chessboard, but nothing's moving. You see what I mean? Not a pawn is moving. Can you remind me who it was that said "animals move"?'

'Aristotle,' muttered Danglard crossly.

'Who was an ancient sage, yes?'

'Greek philosopher.'

'And you admire him, don't you?'

'What the fuck has Aristotle got to do with this?'

'He can help us with his wisdom. Nothing stays long without moving. The Robespierre chessboard is abnormally motionless. *Abnormally* so, Danglard. Sooner or later, a piece is going to move. And we'll have to spot it. But it's too soon, so now is a good moment to go. Anyway, I don't have any choice.'

'Why?'

'Because of this itch.'

'A Lucio-type itch?'

'Yes.'

'Have you forgotten, commissaire,' said Danglard, by now thoroughly furious, 'that we *do* have a move to make on that chessboard, on Monday, at the next session of the assembly? We have to identify the descendants of Desmoulins and the executioner Sanson.'

'But I'll be *there* Monday night, just like you, Danglard, plus the eight officers who are on surveillance duty. Which is why I'm not leaving till Tuesday.'

'There'll be a mutiny in the squad. They won't like it.'

'It's possible, but I'm counting on you to keep it under control.'

'No, certainly not.'

'Your choice, commandant. After all, you'll be in charge.'

Danglard stood up, bursting with exasperation, and walked out.

'He's going to wait in the car,' said Veyrenc.

'Yes. Pack your bags this weekend. Warm clothes, hip flask, currency, compass, GPS.'

'I don't think we'll be able to get a signal on that little island.'

'No, probably not. Perhaps the fog will roll up and we'll die of cold and hunger. Do you know how to skin a seal?'

'No.'

'Neither do I. Who should we take with us?'

Veyrenc thought for a moment, twiddling his glass on the table.

'Retancourt,' he said.

'I told you, she's against it. And when Violette is against something, she's harder to budge than a concrete pillar. Well, too bad, we'll have to go on our own.'

'She'll come,' said Veyrenc.

XXXII

THE WEEKEND HAD NOT IMPROVED DANGLARD'S TEMPER, AND HE didn't open his mouth as he sat in the back of the car taking them on the Monday evening to the weekly session of the General Assembly of the Convention, an amalgam of the sittings held on 11 and 16 Germinal, in the spring of 1794, the ones covering the arrest and trial of Danton.

Adamsberg had spent the intervening two days packing his bags for Iceland. He already possessed survival blankets, pitons and an ice axe, being a seasoned mountain-dweller who had climbed peaks in the Pyrenees where the temperature could drop to minus 10. He had checked the weather forecast for late April in Reykjavik (which he still couldn't pronounce) where it should be 9 degrees Centigrade – but minus 5 in Akureyri, with wind, swirling mists and possible snow. He had recruited an interpreter via the embassy, a man called Almar Engilbjarturson. Right, they'd call him Almar.

The car was stuck in traffic near the Gare Saint-Lazare. Danglard's anxiety got the better of his wish not to speak.

'We're going to be late, we'll miss the session.'

'We'll get there all right, we'll even have plenty of time to get into costume.'

The prospect of putting on his fine purple frock coat and his lace jabot slightly mollified the commandant.

'Danglard, now I think of it, you never filled me in about Robespierre's "painful death".'

Expecting of course that this information would take a long time to deliver. In spite of his determination not to speak, Danglard could not resist the enquiry.

'He was arrested on 9 Thermidor,' he began, rather grumpily, 'at four in the afternoon. Along with his younger brother Augustin, and the archangel Saint-Just, and a number of others. Then after being moved from place to place, when a Parisian uprising in their favour had failed to materialise – I'm keeping this short, you understand –'

'Yes, fine, Danglard.'

'– Robespierre ended up at the Paris City Hall. At about two in the morning, a hostile armed column forced the doors of the chamber they were in. Augustin threw himself out of the window and broke his leg. Couthon, the one who was paralysed, fell down the stairs, and as for Robespierre himself, there are two hypotheses. The more likely one is that he shot himself through the mouth, in a suicide attempt, but succeeded only in destroying part of his jaw. The other is that a gendarme by the name of Merda, I'm not kidding, that was his name, fired a shot at him. Whichever it was, Robespierre was laid out on a table, terribly wounded, his jaw hanging loose. He was stretchered to the Tuileries, where two surgeons tried to deal with him. One of them put his hand inside his mouth to extract the fragments, and brought out two teeth and some bone splinters. There was nothing they could do for him, except bind up his jaw to hold it in place. And it was only next day, at five in the afternoon, that they were all ferried to the guillotine. When it was Robespierre's turn, Henri Sanson, that's the son of that Charles-Henri Sanson we talked about, ripped the bandage from his face. His entire jaw came off, blood poured from his mouth and Robespierre uttered a terrible cry. A witness wrote: "What we could see of his features was terribly disfigured. He was as pale as death, a dreadful sight." He adds that when the executioner held up his head to the people, "It had become a monstrous, repulsive object."'

'Was the executioner *obliged* to take the bandage off?'

'No, there's no way it would have been an obstacle to the blade.'

'Do we know what the Sansons looked like – any portraits?'

'There's one of the father, Charles-Henri. Big fat man, large head, drooping eyes under threatening brows, very long prominent nose and large blubbery lips.'

'Apparently he liked to dissect the corpses he had decapitated,' Veyrenc added. 'Should be charming to meet a descendant of his tonight.'

Lebrun met them in the cloakroom, almost with open arms. He was wearing a grey wig and his neck emerged from a froth of lace over his dark red coat. He was sitting on a Louis XVI type of chair, fixed on to a trolley with two large wooden wheels. Holding a cane in his hand, he had taken on the role of the paralysed politician.

'Citizen Couthon, good evening,' said Danglard, who had recovered his serenity, or perhaps he had simply managed in a few minutes to escape from the troubling present by being projected back into 1794.

'I don't really look like him, you know,' said Lebrun, showing amusement in turn. 'Come now, Citizen Danglard, do I look fierce enough to be Georges Couthon, Robespierre's "second soul"?'

'No, not really,' said Danglard, 'but you'll do.'

'Get your costumes, leave your phones here, you know our rules. I reserved the same costumes as last week, so that you can feel you're in character.'

The three police officers reappeared shortly, clad in black, purple and dark blue, Veyrenc rubbing his white stockings to make sure they were quite clean.

'Are you ready to join in, Citizen Veyrenc?' asked Lebrun.

'Why not?' said Veyrenc, adjusting his wig in front of the mirror.

'Who's presiding at the assembly tonight?' asked Danglard.

'Tallien.'

'Nasty piece of work,' said Veyrenc.

'Yes indeed, citizen. Tonight, we'll be seated with the Mountain, at the higher level. My wheelchair would be too conspicuous in the centrist Plain, and you'd be spotted too easily. Don't forget that this is when Robespierre launches his accusations at Danton. Even if you are alarmed and frightened, you don't dare oppose him, you must cravenly applaud. Fear starts to spread among you. If they dare attack Danton, where will it end? But nevertheless, everyone carries on trying to keep on the right side of Robespierre. That's your role, understood?'

'Perfectly,' said Danglard, laughing at Lebrun's imitation of the worried deputies of the Mountain.

Adamsberg was starting to realise that Lebrun was amusing. Because people who are frightened make a comical impression.

And now a man with a long thin face, his eyes half closed under very prominent eyelids, like a frog, with dry lips, came in silently and unobtrusively.

'Ah, I almost failed to recognise you,' Adamsberg said to Leblond. 'What a striking disguise.'

'Citizen Fouché, I presume,' said Danglard. 'This is a good evening for you, isn't it? You'll be observing from the shadows, without saying a word.'

'Yes, it's a good get-up, isn't it?' said Leblond, with a slight bow. 'But it's actually impossible to imitate Fouché's lantern jaws and his reptilian expression.'

'Still, you do look like a disturbing person,' said Adamsberg, addressing Leblond as 'vous', despite Danglard's whisper that it was customary to use the familiar 'tu' during the Revolution, to show that everyone was equal.

'Not disturbing enough,' said Leblond/Fouché, pulling a face. 'What you should know, commissaire, is that Fouché is the most repulsive character in all the Revolution. A thoroughgoing cynic, devilishly cunning, twisted but smarmy, a bootlicker, who watches everyone, and moves this way and that with events, a snake in the grass compared to the idealist Robespierre, who gets carried away by his unworldly purity. Fouché is ferocious, and he's terribly bloodthirsty. He has just – *I* have just – come back from Lyon, where I deemed it more efficient to massacre suspects by lining them up and firing cannon at them. I came back on orders from Robespierre, who was furious and told me that "nothing could justify the cruelty of which I was guilty". That's me, this evening, fellow citizens, in the hot seat,' Leblond concluded, giving a sly and self-satisfied grin. 'I'm pretending to bow down to the Incorruptible, in order that my excesses should be pardoned.'

His smile made Adamsberg feel suddenly uneasy.

'And were you guillotined along with Robespierre, Citizen Fouché?' Adamsberg asked him.

'*Me?*' replied Leblond, exaggerating his treacherous expression. 'Me, the man nobody can lay a glove on? Oh no, on the contrary, I will already be plotting his fall, visiting deputies at night and persuading them that they are next on the list of those to be guillotined. False, but effective. I'll sweep Robespierre away: in four months, he's a dead man. And now, citizens, time for me to go onstage.'

'He's very good, isn't he?' said Lebrun, watching his friend disappear.

'Almost too good, he sends shivers down the spine,' said Adamsberg.

'But that's Fouché for you,' Lebrun said. 'He does send shivers down your spine.' He punctuated his words by banging the floor with his cane. 'And now Citizen Lieutenant, if you would be so good as to push my chair, we need to move.

Adamsberg let the other three go ahead of him and made a quick call to the office before leaving his phone in the cloakroom.

'Kernorkian? Put two more men on duty tonight. I'd like someone to keep an eye on the treasurer, the man we're calling Leblond.'

'That's impossible, sir. He and Lebrun just seem to melt magically away when they've accompanied Robespierre home.'

'That's what I mean. Check out the cellars, the roofs, the courtyards, see if there are back doors, other discreet escape routes.'

There was a large attendance that night for the 11–16 Germinal session. The deputies crowded together, in their dark or brightly coloured coats, each looking for a place to sit in the cool, dimly lit hall. Lebrun sat near Adamsberg and his colleagues, sliding the wheelchair between two benches, while Leblond/Fouché was surveying the assembly from his perch high up in the Mountain.

'See up there,' whispered Lebrun, 'the right-hand public gallery, a man in black with a red scarf, next to a woman waving a flag.'

'The fat man?'

'That's right, he's got a hat pulled down over his eyes. That's him.'

'The descendant of Sanson?'

'How do you know I'm not pointing to Desmoulins?'

'Because that man looks as if he's trying very hard to project the character of an executioner.'

'He's just playing a part. Everyone here is playing a part. You saw Leblond just now, one could almost think he was really dangerous.'

'Whereas he spends his life solving equations?'

'More or less. Please be discreet. Couthon is so recognisable that everyone looks hard at him, so as to work out how to follow his lead.'

'Understood.'

Adamsberg switched on the microphone behind his ear, perfectly disguised by his long black wig.

'Sanson's present,' he whispered.

'Roger.'

Robespierre, having been called by the president of the session, Tallien, was now walking down the steps from his seat in order to climb to the rostrum. As before, the room fell silent, a silence made up of veneration and fear. True or false?

Adamsberg watched the participants: it was hard to make out whether their expressions – concentrating, fawning or nervous – were part of their play-acting, or prompted by genuine feelings that had overcome them for the evening. And he understood the interest of the study undertaken by Lebrun–Leblond on the frontier between truth and fiction, when people are readier to chase after an illusion than after reality. The illusion cast that night was a great and dark one, arising from the feverish and bloodstained days of the Terror. It was enough to make one lose one's bearings entirely, and he could see that it was affecting Danglard and Veyrenc, who were absorbing Robespierre's rhetoric open-mouthed, and seemed to have entirely forgotten their mission. Robespierre was very intense this evening, at this difficult session when he had to convince the deputies to put to death the great bull Danton, the very image of vital revolutionary power. In a near-mystical silence, Robespierre's creaky voice could be heard even in the furthest seats:

'We shall see this day whether the Convention will be able to shatter its so-called idol, corrupt for so long, or whether in its fall that mighty idol will crush the Convention and the French people!'

Applause came from the ranks of the Mountain, though some deputies kept their fists clenched on their knees. The Plain meanwhile hesitated, whispering in excitement and alarm. Adamsberg remembered what he was supposed to be doing and clapped prudently, imitating his colleagues for the evening. At his side, Lebrun/Couthon was banging his stick on the floor to orchestrate and accompany the applause. The atmosphere was tense, edgy and emotional, the disturbance palpable in the combined scents of face powder and sweat, condensed by the cool air. Everyone knew what the event was that they were re-enacting this evening, but they were all experiencing it with anxiety, as if they did not know in advance how it would end. Adamsberg himself, despite his ignorance of the historical facts, wondered how Robespierre, such a weak and stiff-looking individual, with about as much vitality as a wooden plank, dared to attack Danton, a figure bursting with energy.

'In what way is he superior to his fellow citizens? Is it because some mistaken individuals have rallied round him?'

Adamsberg watched as Danglard, in his purple jacket, looked on tensely: familiar with these famous speeches, he was following the crescendo of rhetoric. Well, at least it would distract him from Iceland. Even thinking about his departure tomorrow seemed to Adamsberg incongruous, inappropriate, almost trivial, in this hall. Why Iceland, and where the devil was Iceland anyway?

'Look out,' Lebrun whispered, 'listen carefully to the next bit.'

Robespierre had paused briefly to finger his jabot.

'I tell you that anyone who is trembling at this moment is guilty. Because innocence never fears the public gaze.'

'That's atrocious,' Adamsberg whispered back.

'The most terrible of all, in my view.'

Robespierre was continuing with his speech, taking care over the rhythms of his interminable sentences, fixing his blank gaze on one or another deputy, attentive to the least tremors within the assembly, taking off his spectacles now and then, and adjusting them with a gesture that was always delicate. He was forcing his weak voice, making calculated appeals to emotion, yet this impulse brought no colour to his own pale cheeks.

'The second target has appeared now,' said Lebrun. 'Right-hand gallery, last but one seat. Between two men wearing brown. Long auburn hair, girlish mouth, grey coat.'

Adamsberg alerted Danglard, who was still concentrating on the orator, since he would be coordinating any further action concerning the descendant of Desmoulins. The commandant took about ten seconds to respond and, looking embarrassed, switched on his mike.

'Yes, the Desmoulins descendant, I've got him in sight.'

'Roger, commandant.'

'My life is dedicated to the fatherland, my heart is free from fear, and if I were to die, it would be without reproach and without ignominy.'

The assembly rose as one man, and clapped feverishly, though with various degrees of enthusiasm. Once more, Couthon's cane beat the ground, punctuating the applause.

'There's going to be a break now,' Lebrun explained. 'As I told you, we'll have a suspension before moving to the session of the 16 Germinal.'

Hundreds of deputies now crowded round the buffet, but the presence of food and drink did not turn the atmosphere into one of a convivial gathering in the twenty-first century. No, the roles they were playing had penetrated them to the bone, in the cold air and candlelight. The conversations and gestures continued to refer to the revolutionary period.

'Amazing, don't you think?' said Lebrun, approaching Adamsberg in his wheelchair, which was being pushed by the subtle Fouché, the latter currying favour with Couthon in order to make up for the massacres in Lyon. 'Even Leblond/Fouché, as you see, is still playing his part of a traitor to every cause but his own. He'll end up one of Napoleon's ministers, in charge of the police, of course, and will be made a duke.'

'The least they could do for so much service to the state,' remarked Leblond caustically.

'Sanson's moving,' Adamsberg reported suddenly.

'Desmoulins is eight metres behind him,' said Danglard.

'They're making for the exit,' said Lebrun. 'You'd better hurry.'

Voisenet, Justin, Noël and Mordent moved into position. The receiver crackled four minutes later.

'Got them in sight,' said Mordent. 'They came out together but they're going in opposite directions now.'

'The big one is Sanson,' said Adamsberg. 'Voisenet and Noël, you take him. The baby-faced one is Desmoulins, go after him yourself and take Justin.'

'Sanson's on a motorbike, Desmoulins in a car.'

'Get the registrations. In fact,' said Adamsberg, turning to Lebrun, 'those two seem to know each other. Which might make the situation more serious.'

Twenty minutes later, Sanson had been followed to the rue du Moulin-Vieux. Fifteen minutes later again, they had Desmoulins localised in the elegant rue Guynemer, near the river. The two men were to be told to report to the squad next day. Adamsberg was regretting not being there to hear what they had to say. But he had arranged with Mordent to be able to listen in to the interrogations next day from Iceland, if that proved possible.

Rebellion was simmering among members of the squad.

Adamsberg wondered once more what he was doing, setting off on this distant trip.

'Iceland seems a long way off,' he said to Veyrenc.

'Well, it *is* a long way off,' Veyrenc replied.

'I mean far away in thought, in time, two centuries away. This living assembly can make your brain spin. Talking to you now, I'm not sure I can imagine what air transport is.'

'Yes, I understand. You have to admit Robespierre was exceptional tonight. Blood-curdling.'

'Less than Fouché though.'

'Did you notice that too? He seemed quite at home in his ghastly role.'

'What the devil are we going to do in Iceland? If it exists?'

'Sow the seeds of Revolution.'

'That would be an idea,' Adamsberg agreed. 'Bring along some eighteenth-century speeches. They can keep us company when we're stuck on the island in the fog.'

'Then we can declaim them.'

'Liberty, Equality, Fraternity. As we freeze to death.'

'Precisely.'

XXXIII

'SEEMS YOU'RE OFF TO THE NORTH POLE,' LUCIO CHALLENGED HIM
from his usual position in the garden.

The street lamp had lost its bulb, and Adamsberg hadn't seen his
neighbour in the gloom.

'Not the North Pole, Iceland.'

'Same thing.'

'But I don't know now why I'm going.'

'To finish scratching the itch. The one you picked up at Le Creux.
Simple as that.'

'But it's all wrong, Lucio,' said Adamsberg, reaching out to take a
bottle of beer.

'It's already open. That way you won't demolish the tree.'

'It's all wrong, I'm abandoning the investigation and my team, just
to go and scratch an itch in the land of ice.'

'You've got no choice.'

'Right now, I've no idea where Iceland is, or the aeroplane either. It's
because of these assemblies, I told you about them. I'm still back in
April 1794. Do you understand what I'm saying?'

'No.'

'What do you understand then?'

'That it must have been some pretty damn tough insect that bit you.'

'I've still got time to cancel.'

'No.'

'Nearly all my officers are against this. Tomorrow, when they see that I've really gone, there'll be a rebellion. They don't understand.'

'It's never possible to understand someone else's itch, *hombre*.'

'I'm going to cancel,' said Adamsberg, standing up.

'No,' said Lucio again, gripping his wrist in his remaining hand, which, because it had to do the work of two, had become almost as strong as both hands together. 'If you cancel now, it'll get infected. And end in tears. When the trunk is packed, the traveller has to go. Want me to tell you something?'

'No, I don't,' said Adamsberg, irritated at the old man's display of superpowers.

'Drink up your beer. In one go.'

Wearily, Adamsberg obeyed, under the stern gaze of his Spanish neighbour.

'And now, *hombre*,' said Lucio firmly, 'go to bed.'

He had never said that before.

Then he heard the old man clear his throat and spit on the ground. Lucio had never done that before either.

XXXIV

ADAMSBERG JOINED VEYRENC AT THE CHECK-IN FOR THE 14.30 flight to Reykjavik. Not much of a queue, since April was not a popular month for tourists. Several businessmen and many blond heads, hair that was almost white it was so fair – Icelanders evidently, going home for Easter. They were travelling light, unlike Veyrenc and Adamsberg, who were weighed down with their heavy backpacks, in preparation for the ice and snow. But then the island where they were going was not like the other ones.

There was an empty seat alongside them, Retancourt's, which Veyrenc had refused to cancel.

'I saw her back in the queue,' he said, as he settled down. 'She didn't try to join us, her face is as closed as an oyster. One of those oysters, you know, that you just can't open, and you end up throwing it away or banging it with a hammer to finish it off.'

'I see.'

'Which means she's saying, "Don't ask me why I'm here, whatever you do."'

'And why *is* she here then, in your opinion?'

'Either because she thinks two guys like you and me will never survive this expedition, and that she has a duty to protect us from the hostile elements . . .'

'Or because, in spite of everything, she's interested in the mysterious warm island.'

'The stone. Do you think she wants to get some strength from the stone?'

'No, no, certainly not,' said Adamsberg. 'That would make her too strong by half. She'd explode. She'd better go nowhere near it.'

'Or maybe it's because she's not actually joining the rebels – although she has taken their side – because she wants to tone down the revolt. Without her, the opposition's going to lack solid backing. Right now, back at headquarters, they must be baffled and confused: "Why has Retancourt followed them to Iceland?" "Who's right, who's wrong?"'

The last passengers were now boarding the plane, and Retancourt was approaching, but without looking at them. Adamsberg pushed up the armrests and moved closer to Veyrenc, so as to leave room for the large lieutenant, the narrow seat being ill-suited to her muscular bulk. None of the three uttered a word during take-off, Retancourt having thrust her nose in a magazine, without reading it.

'Blue skies over Iceland, I read in the paper,' said Veyrenc.

'Yes, but it only takes a sneeze to make the weather change there,' Adamsberg replied.

'You're right.'

'We won't even get to see Rejkavik.'

'Reykjavik, you mean.'

'I can't even pronounce it.'

'Seems the houses there are painted all colours, red, blue, white, pink, yellow . . .' Veyrenc went on. 'There are masses of lakes and cliffs, and mountains either pitch-black or covered with snow.'

'Sounds beautiful.'

'Yeah, sure.'

'I've learned how to say "goodbye" and "thank you",' said Adamsberg, taking a little card out of his trouser pocket. '"*Bless*" and "*takk*".'

'Why didn't you learn to say "hello"?'

'Too difficult.'

'We won't get very far then.'

'We'll have our interpreter from the embassy. He should be waiting for us when we get to Akureyri, holding up a notice.'

'We can get a bite to eat in Reykjavik airport first.'

'Yeah.'

'What do you think they'll have?'

'Smoked fish.'

'Or just international food.'

Nothing. Not a twitch. The laborious efforts of the two men to make conversation and draw Retancourt out of her silence were completely in vain.

Landing at Reykjavik and eating from the international menu was quickly accomplished. Retancourt swallowed her meal, still without a word.

'This is going to be fun, isn't it?' whispered Veyrenc. 'We'll be dragging her round like a statue for days.'

'Looks like it.'

'We could leave her behind. Sneak away.'

'Too late, Veyrenc.'

Adamsberg consulted his phone.

'The interrogation of Sanson's descendant is due to start at 1900 hours,' he said. 'The time difference is two hours, it's nearly five now, we should go online.'

Something seemed to have changed in Retancourt's expression. Looking a little less sullen, she followed the two officers to a table, where Adamsberg set up the connection.

'We've only got sound,' he warned them. 'And the volume on this *tölva* isn't that great. So we should try not to make any comments during the interview.'

'I don't think Lieutenant Retancourt will make any difficulty about that,' Veyrenc dared to say.

'No indeed,' Adamsberg followed suit. 'Violette is on a pilgrimage through the Stations of the Cross. But Iceland's very beautiful.'

'Very beautiful.'

'Great trip.'

'Great.'

'And unusual.'

'Very unusual.'

The interview of the executioner's descendant was late starting. The man, whose name was René Levallet, was facing a trio of interrogators, Danglard, Mordent and Justin.

'So are you going to tell me why the fuck you've called me in?'

A gruff voice with a working-class Parisian accent.

'As you were informed,' Danglard told him, 'you are here as a witness.'

'A witness to what?'

'We'll get to that. What's your occupation, Monsieur Levallet?'

'I'm a slaughterman, Meursin Abattoir, Yvelines *département*.'

'And what kind of animals are slaughtered there?'

'Cattle, what do you think? And it's humane killing, don't get any wrong ideas, it's all done legal.'

'And that means?'

'First you got to stun them with an electric shock, so they're unconscious when we slit their throats. Doesn't always work, though, got to say.'

'And you like your work?'

'Got to make a living, haven't you? Someone has to do it. People like to have a nice steak to eat, they don't ask where it comes from. So you get on with it.'

'The way some people used to get on with the job of executioner.'

'What's that got to do with anything?'

'It's got to do with your ancestry: you are descended from the illustrious Sanson family of executioners during the French Revolution.'

'And what the fuck is *that* to you?' Levallet retorted. 'Some poor devil had to make the guillotine work properly too. We'd be more professional these days. Stun 'em first, like the animals.'

'The death penalty's been abolished now, Monsieur Levallet.'

'So what am I supposed to be a witness of?'

'The re-enactments of the revolutionary assemblies by the Association for the Study of the Writings of Maximilien Robespierre.'

'So what? It's legal, isn't it?'

'Yes, indeed it is.'

'Yeah, right, well, that's me out of here then.'

'Not yet. *Why* do you go along every Monday?'

'Why shouldn't I? Some people go to the theatre, don't they? Same thing then.'

'It's like going to the theatre for you, is it?'

'You want to put it that way, go ahead. I don't care.'

'*Your* theatre, or rather a theatre in which there are actors who gave your ancestor Charles-Henri Sanson a nasty reputation in days gone by.'

'Well, so what?'

'Four members of this assembly have been *murdered*, Monsieur Levallet. Here, take a look.'

And there was the sound of photographs of the victims being put down on the table.

'Never seen any of 'em,' said Levallet.

'Our concern is,' Mordent told him, 'that there's a killer out there. He's started to pick off members of the association, but he's working up to strike at its head: Robespierre, or rather the actor who plays Robespierre.'

'Yeah, well, he thinks he *is* Robespierre. Bit sick if you ask me.'

'And on that account, we're interviewing a lot of your members,' Mordent went on, untruthfully. 'That's why we need to know what *your* motive is for going to the sessions.'

'Just to watch, what do you think? Anyway, I'm not the only descendant turns up there.'

'That's true,' said Danglard, 'and we have reason to believe you are friendly with the descendant of Camille Desmoulins.'

'Yeah, nice fellow he is.'

'Nice', the kind of thing children say, Adamsberg thought. Divide the world into two, nice and nasty.

'But he's not a *friend*, more a kind of acquaintance.'

'And what do you talk about, or do with this acquaintance?'

'We have a bit of a moan, right? We tell each other our troubles. Because of that lot. We're on the same side, see.'

'What kind of troubles does Desmoulins have?'

'That's not his name, for starters. And I don't have to tell you anyway. But what gets his goat is that they guillotined old Camille, who was decent enough, and then his wife too, afterwards. Because they had this little boy, only two years old, and he was an orphan after that.'

'Yes, I know about that,' said Danglard.

'So that wasn't humane, no way, was it?'

'No, agreed. But what are *your* troubles? Nobody in your family was guillotined, were they?'

'So now we're supposed to tell the cops all about our troubles, are we?'

'On this occasion, Monsieur Levallet, I'm sorry but yes, you do need to.'

'You're *sorry*, are you? Then I can go after that?'

'Yes.'

'Well, I'll tell you then, my troubles are a lot worse than Desmoulins's. As I've told him. And all because of those guys down there, poncing about in their fancy clothes. I wouldn't mind seeing them all dead, the lot of them.'

'You'd kill them, would you?'

'No need. Don't you cops ever think? Cos at the end of the show, they're all dead anyway. Heads taken off by Charles-Henri, and then by Great-Uncle Henri. And good riddance. Good to see them all get their comeuppance, and it's us, the Sanson family, giving it to them. So next in line, Danton and all those other bastards are going to cop it.'

'Including that "decent" Camille Desmoulins?'

'Yeah, but look, he wasn't as white as the driven snow either, let me tell you, that's what I tell his descendant. There was others got taken off before it was his turn, did he stand up and protest? No, he did not. *And*, from what Desmoulins tells me, he did something very stupid, Camille. His pal Robespierre had lodgings in a house where there was a lot of young girls. Right? And he liked them. Not what you're thinking, he looked out for them, he helped them to get an education. Right? And Camille went round there a lot too, welcomed in. And one day he gave this book to one of the girls, very young she was. And Robespierre twigged right away that this book wasn't proper. Adult pictures, know what I mean?'

'Pornography?'

'That's right. And Robespierre saw red, he snatched it away. After that, Camille was never in his good books. And Robespierre wasn't someone you wanted to be on the wrong side of, know what I mean?'

'So,' said Danglard, after a brief silence, 'you were saying that now "Danton and all those other bastards are going to cop it"?'

'Do you think Danglard knew that story about the book?' Veyrenc whispered.

'Can't have, or he'd have said something.'

'That'll have rattled him then!'

'Sure to have.'

'Exactly,' Levallet was saying. 'And it's Great-Uncle Henri that's going to do it. Because the old man, Charles-Henri, his strength was failing, or something. And the time's coming – only nine more sessions to go – when Henri gets the order to cut Robespierre's head off too. And he hurt him an' all, pulling off the bandages. Mind you, there, I don't hold with that. He was out of order that day. But they didn't know about humane killing, back in the olden days. I promise you, the beasts I slaughter, they don't suffer. Still makes you feel really bad sometimes, though.'

'I understand what you're saying,' said Mordent, who from his tone of voice really meant it.

'And what are *your* troubles?' Dangard insisted, almost gently. 'The ones you tell Desmoulins about.'

'That's not his name.'

'We know his name. He's called Jacques Mallemort.'

'Bad enough having a moniker like that, eh?'

'Yes, I'm sure it hasn't helped him. But we're talking about you right now.'

'Shit, do I have to tell you my whole life story?'

'Sometimes we need it. But for now, tell us just whatever it is that they've done to you.'

'No, I can't.'

'Why not?'

'Cos it makes me blub, that's why not, and I'm not going to start crying in front of some cops.'

A long silence followed. Retancourt had forgotten to maintain her closed expression, and had been attentively following the story of the man who executed cattle.

'Well,' broke in Justin finally, '*I'm* a cop, and I cry sometimes.'

'What, in front of the others, kid?'

'It did happen once, when this girl walked out on me.'

'Women, eh? Nothing but trouble.'

'Agreed,' said Justin.

'And what about you others, you captains or whatever you are? You ever blubbed in front of the men?'

'It happened to me once too,' said Mordent.

'So you won't tell anyone, if it happens to me?'

'Absolutely not,' said Danglard. 'Look, what about a glass of wine, would that help? I've got a very good bottle of white, 2004.'

'You have a high old time, don't you, in the cop shop? This isn't a trap, is it?'

'No, I'll have a glass with you.'

'What, on duty?'

'It's aperitif time. And look, see the recorder? If it should, er, happen ... well, I'll switch it off.'

Another silence.

'It was six years back. I wasn't so big then and I was a lot better-looking, though you might find that hard to believe.'

They heard the sound of glasses on the table and a bottle being opened.

'Danglard's taking advantage,' said Retancourt suddenly, with the ghost of a smile.

'No, Violette. I think he's really doing it to help.'

'His case of 2004 is pretty good,' said Veyrenc.

'Correct,' said Retancourt.

'Hey, this wine's a cracker,' said Levallet, as if echoing the views of the listeners-in at Reykjavik airport.

'I go and fetch it myself from Sancerre. It's not expensive, I get it from this little vineyard.'

'Give me the address?'

'All right, why not?'

'Bucks a man up, it does. So, right, there was a time, I didn't look too bad, I had a girlfriend, three years we were together, and she was expecting, so we were going to get married.'

'She was pregnant?'

'Yeah, five months. And I was really pleased. This kid wasn't going to work in abattoirs, no way. Specially since we knew it was going to be a girl, know what I mean? Anyway, my girlfriend, she had an auntie, horrible old bigot, come visit and she came right out with it, told her I was a Sanson, and it was in my blood, because I was working at the slaughterhouse. As if that had anything to do with it, like I said, you got to earn a living, haven't you? But see, the thing was, *I* hadn't told her, I hadn't told Ariane.'

'Why not?'

'Well, she's a girl, girls don't like it, do they? They get upset, she'd be put off by an executioner, *and* by a guy that spends all day slaughtering animals, normal, yes? So I told her I worked for a firm making shoes, only way out in the same suburb in the Yvelines, because I didn't want her trying to come and see me at work. I found out all this stuff about shoes. Leather, fake leather, soles, laces, Velcro, whatever. Specially Italian ones. Told her I worked in the slipper department. More reassuring, like.'

'Yes, you're right, I'd have done the same thing.'

'So of course then the sky fell in. Specially the bit about the executioner. Ariane said because of all the lies I'd told her, she was going to have this baby who'd be an executioner's daughter. And she'd never live with a man who had it in his blood.'

There was a short silence.

'It's OK, it'll pass,' said the man, after Danglard had interrupted the recording. 'If you press hard on your eyes, it pushes the tears back in. I begged her, I said everything under the sun, but no, she left me. When she looked at me, her face, it was full of disgust. And she went as far away as she could – to relations in Poland – so I'd never get to see my daughter.'

Another silence.

'He's pressing his fists into his eyes,' said Adamsberg.

The recorder sprang back to life.

'After that, I put on weight, I got fat as a pig, my hair started falling out, everything went wrong, see what I mean? I could have murdered that old aunt, but the fact is, she died in a car crash and good riddance. And whose fault was it that people know about the Sansons, eh? Those revolutionaries in Paris, that's who. Isn't that the truth? Because there was plenty of executioners in the provinces, but nobody knows *their* names, do they? I could have murdered them, see, those guys, I wanted to kill everyone anyway. So this doctor, cos I had to go to the doctor for my heart, kept getting these palpitations, it was him told me about this club, where you could see them acting out the Revolution, and in the end, he said, they *all* get their chips. And I thought it would do me good to see that. But when we get through to July, I'm quitting, I'm going on a diet. Find another woman, like Desmoulins tells me to. I hadn't even thought about that.'

The flight for Akureyri was being called in Icelandic and in English. The travellers picked up their bags and Veyrenc led the way to the right gate.

'It's not him,' said Adamsberg.

'No, I don't think so either,' said Veyrenc.

They waited to hear what Retancourt would say, not being sure whether, after the pause, she would come back to life or revert to being a statue.

'Sad,' she said. 'Sad, but harmless.'

'When do we get there?' asked Veyrenc.

'Seven fifty p.m. local time.'

Adamsberg took his phone out of his pocket.

'It's Danglard,' he explained. 'He wants to know what we think. He's being very distant.'

'Sad case, no danger to anyone. Let him go,' said Adamsberg into the phone.

'Already done,' said Danglard.

'When are you seeing Dumoulin?'

'*Des*moulins,' said Danglard. 'Ten o'clock tomorrow. That'll be 8 a.m. on your fucking island.'

Adamsberg spent the short flight to Akureyri pondering the sad story of the descendant of Sanson, and his strange presence in the assembly.

Lebrun had told them that there were a number of doctors of all kinds among their members. Perhaps Levallet had told him the story too. The association's secretary was a good listener – maybe he had even given him some professional advice.

The Icelandic interpreter was waiting for them, energetically waving a notice above his head. Small, plump and dark-haired, unlike Adamsberg's expectations, he was quite elderly, about sixty, and seemed restless. But good-humoured with it. He was acting like someone who has been waiting impatiently for some dear friends to arrive, and he greeted them volubly, speaking French with a strong accent.

'Can we call you Almar?' asked Adamsberg, as they shook hands. 'I can't pronounce your last name.'

'Hey, man, no problem,' said Almar, throwing up his short arms. 'Here we don't use surnames, we're all "son of X", or "daughter of Y", see?'

Veyrenc guessed that Almar had picked up his colloquial French in some rather informal milieu. That might explain why Adamsberg had been able to get hold of him so easily at the last moment. Almar did not seem like the sort of interpreter who would be chosen for international conferences or university work.

'So *my* son's called Almarson, son of Almar. Cool, eh? Where are we going? I wouldn't want to hang out here, Akureyri's pretty rubbish. Well, for anyone who's seen the world a bit. I'm from Kirkjubæjarklaustur, so you can see where I'm coming from.'

'Not really.'

'Never been here before?'

'No, we're here for a police investigation.'

'Yeah, that's what they said. It'll be a gas.'

'Not necessarily,' said Retancourt.

And the little man suddenly seemed to become aware of the enormous lieutenant looming over him: he scrutinised her carefully.

Adamsberg meanwhile was thinking about the descendant of Desmoulins. Bad luck for him having a name like Mallemort, Evil–Death, when you think what his ancestors had gone through. A little boy left an orphan after his parents' 'evil death'. Was this man too coming to the sessions as a kind of therapy, to watch while those responsible were sentenced to death as well? Or indeed to avenge the evil death?

'Where do you want to eat?'

Adamsberg explained that they had to be up early in the morning to listen in to another interrogation at eight o'clock, while their flight for Grimsey would be taking off at eleven.

'You can listen to an interrogation from *here*? Cool,' Almar whistled. 'I'll take you to a hotel south of town near the airport. No hassle. The pad's friendly, the grub's good – if you like fish? The rooms aren't the Ritz though. OK with you?'

It was OK with them.

'Wrap up warm before we go out. It's not that cold today, just a bit nippy, minus 3, that's 20 degrees colder than in France, but nothing dramatic. The cold in Iceland is fine, it's bracing, you'll see. Not all cold places are the same.'

'No, indeed,' said Adamsberg.

They put on sweaters and anoraks, and Almar took them to a small hotel with a red-painted facade, south of the centre of Akureyri. There were still traces of snow on the roofs around.

'Well, at least we can say we got to see a red house,' remarked Veyrenc.

'And sightseeing was the main point of this trip, wasn't it?' said Retancourt.

'Precisely, lieutenant,' said Adamsberg.

'It's called the Bear Inn,' said Almar, pointing to a flashing pink sign. 'Mind you, bears? Haven't seen them in Iceland in years. And with the melting of the ice cap, they'd never get this far.'

'Why is everything painted in such bright colours?'

'Because Iceland's all black and white: volcanic rock and ice and snow. So we need some colour. Everything goes with black, don't you French say that? But wait till you see how blue the sky is. You'll never in your life have seen a blue like it!'

'How much daylight is there, this time of year?' asked Retancourt.

'About the same as France. Not that we see the sun a lot. It rains quite a bit.'

Almar saw them settled in their rather chilly rooms, ordered their dinner and arranged for their early breakfast. He was not going to spend the evening with them, as he was taking the chance to meet up with some friends in Akureyri whom he had not seen for seven years.

'It'll be a gas,' he said again. 'I've ordered beer for you – whatever you do don't ask for wine, it'll cost you an arm and a leg. Meet up at ten tomorrow morning. That'll be plenty of time to get the little plane – this time of year there aren't many tourists wanting to go to the Arctic Circle. Who do you want to question on Grimsey, anyway? There are only about a hundred people there.'

'No one,' said Adamsberg. 'We want to visit another island offshore, where there's a warm rock.'

Almar's good humour seemed suddenly to melt away.

'Fox Island you mean?' he asked.

'Yes, I think that's what it's called – it has two pointed rocks that look like ears.'

'Ba-ad idea,' said Almar. 'You know there was this scandal ten years ago? Bunch of idiots went over there and two of them died of exposure.'

'That's exactly why we're going', said Veyrenc. 'That's what the investigation's about.'

'There'll be nothing left now,' Almar insisted. 'Looking for clues? Don't fool yourselves. There've been hundreds of blizzards since then, snow and ice. There's nothing left on Fox Island.'

'Well, we have to go and look,' said Adamsberg, 'we're under orders.'

'Respect to your chiefs, but your orders are bloody silly. What's more, you won't find anyone willing to take you over there. They all think there's a monster on the island.'

'Who do?'

'Some people believe it hundred per cent, others don't but they'd rather not tempt providence. They're not hotheads like you French. That's what they say round here – a Frenchman will go chasing off at the drop of a hat. Not us, no sirree.'

'Well, we'll have to hire our own boat then, and take ourselves over there. It's only a stone's throw from the harbour.'

'A stone's throw here, commissaire, can last for ever. Blow your nose and the weather changes here. Call your chiefs, don't go.'

'But *you'll* know we're there, Almar. If you don't see us coming back, you'll launch a rescue party.'

'A rescue party?' said Almar, getting worked up, and waving his arms around more than ever. 'A *rescue*? In the fog? How's the chopper going to spot you? How's the pilot going to land if he can't see anything? *Skit!*' he said, heading abruptly for the door.

'I think he said "Shit!"' suggested Veyrenc, as they watched their interpreter walk off, still gesticulating in the air.

'I think he has every reason,' said Retancourt.

The hotel proprietor, who was satisfyingly blond, with an austere face carved out of material to face any weather, brought them their food without speaking: thin slices of salt herring on rye bread, followed by smoked lamb (according to Veyrenc) with a dish of vegetables.

'It's a bit like sauerkraut,' said Adamsberg, sampling it.

'Yes, but it's red.'

' Well, it's red sauerkraut, they like bright colours here.'

'You heard what Almar said?' asked Retancourt, who ate twice as fast as the others.

'We'll hire a boat.'

'We'll hire nothing of the sort and we're not going anywhere. You heard him, he knows the country. Ten years of storms will have swept everything away. What are you expecting to find? A knife with fingerprints? A scrap of paper under a stone, with a confession?'

'Retancourt, I want to take a *look*. I want to see if it fits what Victor told us. I want to see if they lit a fire. Even ten years later, that would leave traces on the rocks. I want to see if they really did get timbers from the old rack for drying fish. I want to get an idea, imagine it. See if the warm rock actually exists, or if it's all been invented to stop us going anywhere near it.'

Retancourt shrugged her heavy shoulders and twisted round her finger the blonde curls at her neck, her sole delicate feature.

'The lamb was very tender,' said Veyrenc, trying to create a diversion. 'Will you have some more?'

'You can stay behind, if you want, Retancourt,' said Adamsberg. 'I'm not going to force anyone to do anything.'

'You're going off the rails, commissaire. And all for what?'

'Because I've got this itch, as Lucio says. Tonight, Violette, look out of your window at the lights of the town with the mountains around and the brightness of the ice. It's fantastic. It's soothing.'

'So that's why we're here, right?' said Retancourt.

XXXV

THE PROPRIETOR HAD SERVED THEM A BREAKFAST OF WHICH IT WAS apparently obligatory to sample every item: unlimited coffee, sour milk, pâté, ham, cheeses, rye crackers. They made their way to Veyrenc's room, feeling somewhat full, and carrying refills of coffee. His was the only bedroom with a little table, and where Adamsberg could get a signal. He opened the window and looked out at the black and white mountains. Almar was right, the sky was a dazzling blue, outlining the relief so clearly that it trembled.

'It's starting,' muttered Retancourt, 'and Danglard's in charge.'

'Perfect weather,' remarked Adamsberg, shutting the window.

They heard the four photographs of the murder victms being put down on the table once more.

'Yes, there was a rumour going round at the buffet that there had been murders,' admitted Desmoulins's distant descendant. 'But no, I don't recognise any of those people.'

Jacques Mallemort's voice was calm and confident, no sign of irritation.

'But *that* one there, now I come to think of it . . .'

'He was an occasional visitor, who became a participant. His name was Angelino Gonzalez.'

'He got hooked, did he?'

'Here's a picture of him in costume,' said Danglard.

'It's a good drawing,' said Mallemort. 'Ah, now I see who you mean. He played Hébert, he was unbelievable, cursing and swearing like a trooper. And when Robespierre looked shocked in reply, that was very convincing too.'

'Do you have any information about him?'

'We've never exchanged a word. When we're there, you know, we tend not to talk about ourselves, that's not the point.'

'What we want to know is why *you* have been attending these assemblies.'

They heard a familiar sound, the creak of a chair-back which they all knew well, from among the little ritual noises in the station, such as the cat jumping off the photocopier when its desire to play with papers in the wastebin got the better of its natural laziness. So Mallemort/Desmoulins was leaning back in the chair.

'I see,' he said. 'It's a criminal investigation. Someone's attacking members of the assembly. And since I'm a descendant of Camille Desmoulins – though I don't know how you found that out – perhaps I'm a likely suspect. I'm supposed to be consumed with bitterness, two hundred years later, at the atrocity of my ancestors being executed, I'm out to avenge the honour of the inoffensive Camille by going round killing people. Do you know how many of us there are? Almost seven hundred. It would be a monstrous programme, it would be a better plan to block the exits and set fire to the hall, wouldn't you think?'

His voice was still perfectly calm, no trace of panic. This man seemed simply to be thinking aloud, rather than defending himself from any accusation.

'It would be more likely,' he went on, 'from the police point of view, that is, if the target was Robespierre. I say Robespierre, because the man who takes this role is spectacular. Bordering on disturbing. But before getting to him, perhaps the murderer is aiming at unsettling him, with a few other murders, showing him that death is creeping up on him. I presume you have managed to meet him? The actor?'

'Yes,' admitted Danglard, reluctantly.

'He's less at ease with this one than with Sanson,' whispered Adamsberg. 'He's not sure how to proceed with this man with his girlish looks.'

'And is Robespierre afraid for his life?' asked Mallemort.

'We don't think so. He's worried about the membership above all. Can you please answer my question, Monsieur Mallemort?'

'I hadn't forgotten.' They could hear a smile in this reply. 'This is my second cycle of assembly meetings. Four years already.'

'You're attending all the sessions twice over?'

'Yes. But my motives have changed over time. So I have two answers to the question of why I go.'

'Two?'

'That's right. The first one, why I joined the association in the first place, is simple. I'm a historian.'

'Yes, we know, you're professor of modern history at the University of Nanterre.'

'Correct. I wanted to find out how it was that Robespierre came to order the beheading of Camille, who venerated him, who'd been his faithful and affectionate companion. I was thinking of writing a little article on the question. I know Desmoulins might have been a good husband and father on the whole, but he wasn't as perfect as all that. It's said he gave a licentious book to a young girl, Robespierre found out and snatched it away. And that was when Camille's death warrant was signed.'

'We heard that story,' said Danglard, without elaborating.

'So after all those years, as you said,' Mordent asked, 'does the beheading of Desmoulins and his young wife still revolt you?'

'In the dark depths of my soul?' asked Mallemort, and this time, they could clearly hear amusement in his voice. 'At first perhaps. Family tradition, you'll understand. But it faded somewhat. The sessions I attended gave me a clue, I think.'

'And that was?'

'Robespierre's total abstraction from murder. You see, the executions were always out of his sight, they were dematerialised as far as he was concerned. As if he wasn't guillotining men, but concepts: vice, treason, hypocrisy, vanity, lies, money, sex. Did Camille, who could love a woman, and be an affectionate friend, but possibly also had perverse tastes, represent the "vice" Robespierre couldn't allow himself to indulge? Sorry, I'm going on rather.'

'That's all right,' said Danglard. 'But what about the second reason? Why did you go back? Why did you attend a second cycle?'

There was silence, and once more they heard the chair creak.

'Ought to do something about that chair,' said Veyrenc.

'Well, much as the first reason is simple – a historian's curiosity doubled up with the family history, pretty classic – the second reason is all the more embarrassing. Let's say that the first time round, I think I was guessing what had happened to Robespierre. And the second time, I understood what Camille had experienced.'

'Do you mean,' asked Danglard hesitantly, 'that you fell under Robespierre's spell?'

'Thank you for saying it instead of me, commandant. I suppose we're not allowed to smoke in here, are we?'

There was a rustle, the sound of a glass ashtray being put down, the click of a lighter.

'It happened so gradually. I wasn't coming for Camille any more, I was coming for *him*. It really disturbed me. Why was I so fascinated? What was behind this virtual hypnotism? Then I watched the other members. And all of them, or near enough, were spellbound too. I've been told the association's secretary is writing a study on this, the psychological slope Robespierre is making us all slide down, an addictive whirlwind that swallowed up my ancestor.'

At this point Danglard and Mallemort started to leave the parameters of the investigation, and to discuss historical points about the

Revolution: the infamous law of 22 Prairial, paranoia, the Feast of the Supreme Being, Robespierre's childhood, Desmoulins's amorous ambiguity, and the reaction against Robespierre on 9 Thermidor.

Adamsberg shook his head.

'You see, Retancourt, I'm not the only one who goes off-piste,' he said.

'Danglard's thrown in the towel,' Veyrenc concluded. 'A few more minutes and they'll be strolling arm in arm over to the Brasserie des Philosophes.'

'So,' said Retancourt gloomily, 'these three descendants haven't led us anywhere at all?'

'It's a knot of tangled seaweed, I've said so since the start,' said Adamsberg. 'It's not moving. But the descendants ought to be kept under observation, they've had plenty of training in role-playing and lying.'

'But if we're off-piste, the piste we ought to be following isn't clear at all,' said Veyrenc.

'No, very opaque,' Adamsberg agreed. 'In this association, everyone goes round in period costume, masked, made up, no names, no identities, individuals yet not individuals, pretending not to know each other. Images, appearances, deceptions, illusions, fantasies, and not an ounce of solid truth you can count on. They can say anything they like: that there's a group of "infiltrators", so-called occasionals, and descendants of those who were guillotined. So what? They can serve us up any number like that. Who are we to believe and what's our next move? There could be seven hundred of them with a wish to kill seven hundred.'

'Hush,' said Veyrenc. 'They're starting again. Maybe Danglard was just creating a diversion.'

'Creating the complicity of scholars,' agreed Adamsberg.

Danglard's voice was now good-humoured, curious, ceasing to be inquisitorial.

'But your surname, Mallemort, is very rare, isn't it? And it means "evil death". There's actually a place called that in the south of France, near Marseille. How does it come to be a surname?'

They heard the historian give a little chuckle.

'Ah, now you're putting your finger on the intimate wounds of history, commandant. In 1847, one of my ancestors, who was obsessed with Camille Desmoulins's fate, and who had the very ordinary name of Moutier, applied to the mayor of Mallemort, the place you mentioned, for permission to bear the name. It was, he said, so that the "evil death" of his ancestor would never be forgotten by his descendants. And in the atmosphere of '47, just before the Revolution of 1848, it was granted.'

'Charming idea.'

'And if that was all – '

'But you have his *first* name as well, don't you? Your name is Jacques Horace.'

'Ah no, Camille wasn't called Horace.'

'I don't mean Camille, I mean the child who was left an orphan, little Horace Camille.'

The laugh this time was a little more strained.

'I can see I have nothing to teach you, commandant.'

'And in spite of the weight of this name – Horace Mallemort – you are not haunted, you have no phobia, no desire for vengeance?'

'I've already explained. What about you, commandant, what family secrets do you have?'

'Half my ancestors died from silicosis in the mines of northern France.'

'So do you feel a great desire to kill all the coal owners?'

'Not necessarily. Shall we go and have some lunch?'

Adamsberg stood up.

'It's going to end with a glass of white wine,' he sighed. 'Let's meet downstairs, fifteen minutes. The blue sky will do us good.'

'Just a sneeze and the weather can change,' Retancourt reminded him.

XXXVI

THE SMALL PLANE, HALF EMPTY, WAS CIRCLING ABOVE THE RUNWAY
of the little island of Grimsey. Adamsberg looked down at the tiny area
of land, with its dark cliffs and patches of snow, and the stretches of
yellowed grass, not yet renewed after the thaw. Toy houses, painted
white and red, lined the edge of the harbour and the only road.

'Why aren't we landing?' Veyrenc asked.

'Because of the birds, thousands of birds,' Almar explained. 'You
have to circle for a bit to scatter them. Or if not, they use tractors.
There,' he said, pointing out of the window, 'that's the village of
Sandvík, by the harbour, about fifteen houses, one of them's where
we'll be staying.'

Once they were on the tarmac, Adamsberg watched as the flocks of
birds regrouped.

'A hundred inhabitants and a million birds on this island!' said
Almar. 'Cool, eh? But watch out, don't tread on any eggs, the terns can
be ferocious.'

They left their luggage in the guest house, which was painted red
and yellow with white windowsills, as clean as a child's toy. This doll's
house must have been where the group had lodged ten years ago,
including Victor and Henri Masfauré. The dining room smelled of
baking rye bread and smoked cod.

'The woman who runs it's called Eggrún,' said Almar, 'I checked last night. Her husband Gunnlaugur is down at the harbour, he's a fisherman, like three-quarters of the men here. We can start with him, that'll show you what you're up against.'

Adamsberg jotted down the names as best he could in his notebook, as he followed Almar down to the harbour. The interpreter talked for a while to Gunnlaugur, who was unloading his catch from the boat. From here, looking straight ahead along the jetty, they could see perfectly clearly the two ears of Fox Island, with its warm stone. Their tips were still white with snow, but the coastline was black. Three kilometres away at most. Retancourt looked impassively at the island.

'The Frenchies are tired of life, are they?' Almar translated.

Then to all Almar's questions, Gunnlaugur replied by shaking his head, finally throwing them a glance of pity and scorn. All the other fishermen at the quayside, young or old, had much the same reaction, negative and dismissive, until it came to Brestir, one of the younger ones, more talkative and less anxious.

'Hire my boat? So how many kronur do these idiots of yours have?'

'They're offering two hundred.'

'Two fifty, plus five hundred deposit, in case I don't see my boat again.'

'He's not wrong,' said Almar, 'I'd want paying in advance too.'

'OK, tonight, back at the guest house,' said Adamsberg.

'No, now.'

'I haven't got that much on me.'

'In that case, no dice, end of discussion,' reported Almar, folding his arms.

Adamsberg scribbled a few words on his notebook, tore out the page and gave it to the interpreter.

'Here's the name, address and phone number of my senior deputy, with my signature,' he said. 'He'll pay all right, he wouldn't want me to leave this world in dishonour.'

Then Adamsberg opened his anorak and took out 250 kronur from the inside pocket.

'Tell him he'll get the five hundred deposit when we're aboard,' he said.

'It'll be high tide at about 1400 hours,' said Brestir, pocketing the notes, 'and I'll wait here. But they should go and talk to Rögnvar. I don't want it said that I'm a bad Christian who let a bunch of ignorant people go to their death.'

'And where's he?'

'On the jetty, gutting cod. He has to do something.'

'Where are we going?' said Veyrenc swinging round. 'To get extreme unction from a priest?'

'Icelanders are Protestants,' Almar said. 'No, it seems Rögnvar once went over to the island.'

One of the fishermen with whom they had talked, or tried to, beckoned Almar over. A short conversation, and the interpreter returned.

'What did he say?' asked Veyrenc.

'Do I have to translate everything?'

'It's your job, Almar,' Adamsberg reminded him.

'Right. Well, he asked if in the soft countries there were a lot of guys with stripy hair. I said it was the first time I'd seen one.'

'Soft countries?' said Retancourt.

'He means Western Europe. Where men don't have to fight the elements. Where they just talk.'

'And they don't ever talk more than he does?'

'Not to strangers. Icelanders are said to be as severe as their climate, but as kind as the grass is green.'

'Will you come to the island with us?' Retancourt asked him.

'Not on your life!'

'But you're only half-Icelandic, you should be immune to superstititon.'

'My mother's Breton, that only makes things worse. Here's Rögnvar, the old man sitting on that chair, he's only got one leg. Rögnvar, Brestir sent us to you. These foreigners are going to Fox Island, and Brestir thinks you should have a word with them before they go.'

Rögnvar stared for a long while at the faces of the three newcomers.

'French?' he asked.

'Yes, why?'

'Because it was Frenchies who died over there.'

'That's exactly it, they're doing an investigation into that, they've got orders.'

'No need for investigations, how many times did we tell them that when they got back? They were more dead than alive.'

Rögnvar put the bleeding codfish he was cleaning across his knee and took a deep breath. Adamsberg offered him a cigarette which he accepted eagerly.

'You know,' he muttered, 'they say that in ten years' time only the volcanoes will be allowed to smoke on this island. They want to ban cigarettes. Already, to get a drink you gotta pay an arm and a leg. You could say I've paid with a leg, ha ha. As if men haven't always had to drink if they wanted to survive. Well, when they've ended up banning everything, tell you what, it's quite simple, I'm off. To France,' he said with a wink, 'where a man can have a chat in winter outside a cafe on the pavement. Anyway, you go to the island, you better smoke some cigarettes, the beast doesn't like the smell of humans.'

'Tell them about it, Rögnvar.'

'It won't take long. It was thirty-seven years ago, I was young, there was this girl, she said she'd marry me if I'd go to Fox Island and bring her back a piece of the hot rock. I couldn't give a damn about all their old stories, of course, so off I went in my father's little boat. I can tell you there's nothing there, no birds, nothing, no moss, not a seagull, weird. It was calm, yes, but a funny kind of calm. You could hear sounds of blowing, but there was no wind, and like something crawling, but no animal to be seen. It was eerie. The island's no bigger than a pocket handkerchief. Just the front and the back, a smooth platform between the two ears, where once there was a guy did some herring drying, but that's it. He'd gone over there so no one would steal his fish. He came to a bad end, is all I know about him. And the girl too, the one who sent me off there? The next year, she slipped on some puffin eggs and she fell off the cliff.'

'And that's the story, is it?'

'What's your name?'

'Almar.'

'Well, Almar, let me have a smoke in peace, I'll finish my story when I want.'

After drawing a few times on his cigarette with closed eyes, Rögnvar went on.

'See, the stone, you couldn't break a piece off it. So I picked up a bit of rock from nearby, she wasn't going to know, was she? And I went back to the boat. But when I started the engine, I felt a terrible pain in my left leg. As if someone had set light to my bones. So I'm screaming, I'm clinging on the side of the boat, and rolling on the bottom, clutching my leg, and it doesn't seem calm no more. Like as if there was this growling, and puffing, and there was a horrible smell. It smelled of decay, death. So I grab my leg with one hand and with the other I hold on to the rudder, I go back as fast as I can, nearly crash into the jetty, Dalvin and Tryggvi come running along. And after that everything went very fast. They whisked me off to hospital in Akureyri, and there, what they did, they just cut my leg right off! I woke up to find that. Not a wound, nothing, the leg had just started decaying all on its own, no reason, it had gone blue and green. There was even an article in the paper about it. Another hour, and I'd have had it. It was the *afturganga*, he'd tried to kill me.'

'What's the *afturganga*?' asked Adamsberg.

'The living dead, the demon that owns the island. Now you've got the whole story, Almar.'

308

'It's not for me, it's for them.'

'Yes, I gathered that,' said Rögnvar, looking sharply with his blue eyes at Adamsberg, who offered him another cigarette and lit one himself. 'And what's your name?' he demanded, still through the interpreter.

'Adamsberg.'

'Could almost be a name from round here, like Berg. And you're the one wants to go to the island?'

'Yes, that's right.'

'But *she* doesn't,' said Rögnvar, pointing to Retancourt.

'No.'

'Then why has she come?'

'Orders,' said Adamsberg, spreading his arms in a gesture of impotence.

'Orders, my foot. And that one,' he said, pointing to Veyrenc, 'he's come because he's your friend.'

'Yes, that's right.'

'But that woman, even if she's furious as a killer whale, she could be useful. Because they say that only unusual strength can overcome an *afturganga*. Or some great spiritual force. But I don't get the sense of any great spiritual force round here.'

Adamsberg smiled.

'You don't really have orders to go, do you?' Rögnvar went on.

'Nope.'

'You just wanted to come?'

'Yes.'

'That is to say, you *thought* it was you that wanted to come. But really it was him.'

'The *afturganga*?'

'Yes, he was calling you from far away.'

'Why?'

'Maybe he's got something to say to you. How would I know, Berg? But you can be sure of one thing, when an *afturganga* summons you,

you'd be wise to obey. Good luck, Berg, don't know if we'll meet again.'

'In that case,' said Adamsberg, 'I'll leave you my cigarettes,' and he put the packet on the old man's knee, alongside the cod.

After the conversation with Rögnvar, a certain unease reigned in their little group, at whom the fishermen were now looking as if to bid farewell. Unfinished sentences, questions unanswered, desultory conversation, and it lasted until lunchtime.

'Eat up,' Adamsberg said finally.

'Feeling uncertain about it?' asked Veyrenc with a smile.

'No, I'm *sure* about it, because the *afturganga* has summoned me in person. It's an honour. It reassures me.'

'Yeah, right, he'll have a smoke with you, commissaire,' said Retancourt, 'with his grey scaly back and his death's head, and he'll tell you all about it. How he gobbled up the legionnaire, and Madame Masfauré, and how he'd have gobbled up the lot of them if the fog hadn't lifted.'

'So that proves, Retancourt, that he can't command a fog for more than two weeks.'

'That would be plenty long enough.'

'Danglard has sent me a text, saying that Lebrun came to the office,' said Adamsberg, looking at his phone. 'He wanted to see me. Personally.'

'And?' asked Veyrenc.

'And nothing. They told him I was away on family business. He wouldn't speak to anyone else.'

'And is Danglard wondering how we're getting on?'

'No. He doesn't want to know. Where is the Arctic Circle, Almar?'

Almar burst out laughing and waved his arms.

'It runs right through the marriage bed,' he said.

'What do you mean?

'It's what they say. The pastor here one day discovered that the Arctic Circle ran right through the middle of his house, and the middle of his bed, what's more. Cast a bit of a chill over their sex life, because he didn't want to cross the line unknowingly. Big laugh, eh?'

'But where is it? Does the house exist?'

'Jean-Baptiste,' Veyrenc said, 'the Arctic Circle moves every year.'

'All right, and where is it now?'

'Apparently, there's a fence showing you where it is. Do you really want to set foot in it?'

'If we make it back, why not?'

XXXVII

BRESTIR WAS READY AND WAITING, AND ADAMSBERG HANDED HIM the promised five hundred kronur. This time, the Icelander's blue eyes did not express the ironic indifference of the morning, but the respect owed to foolhardy hotheads who might never be seen again.

'This is the starter, this here's the gear lever,' Brestir said. 'You'll be heading into the wind, it's blowing from due west.'

In the strengthening breeze, the official temperature was minus 5 degrees, but with the wind-chill factor, more like minus 12. The three French police officers were warmly clad, Adamsberg a little more lightly than the others, with his anorak over his old Pyrenean sheepskin jerkin, which had been washed so often it was as stiff as a tortoiseshell. He looked at the sky, which as far as the eye could see was bright blue, dazzling the eyes.

'Once you're out at sea, don't steer straight ahead,' Brestir warned them. 'The bow waves will be too strong for the boat, you might get into trouble, and above all it could affect the engine. You'll have to tack. Who's steering?'

'I am,' said Veyrenc.

'Okay,' said Brestir, after looking hard at the compact build and strong face of the lieutenant. 'Get the balance right, have the woman in the middle,' he advised, without beating about the bush. 'She shouldn't lean to one side or the other.'

Almar translated all this, a little awkwardly. Veyrenc started the engine and they left the little harbour, steering south to start with. The fishermen had paused in their activity, and a little group of men was watching their departure with fatalistic expressions. Only Rögnvar raised his arm to wave them off.

'Can you manage it all right?' Adamsberg shouted from the bow, loud enough for Veyrenc to hear him in the teeth of the wind.

'Yes, it's a good little boat,' Veyrenc shouted back, 'it's well balanced and it responds well.'

'Tack north now.'

The boat took its zigzag course towards the island with the two white ears.

'Sure you don't know how to trap seals?' shouted Adamsberg, pulling his hood tightly round his own ears to protect them from the freezing wind.

'Never had to,' laughed Veyrenc, who was as unperturbed as if he were driving an ordinary police car.

There was something extremely solid about Louis Veyrenc, and Adamsberg felt it forcefully during this crossing. Meetings in an office are not very revealing of true solidity.

'South now.'

'Is this really the time to worry about hunting seals?' asked Retancourt.

'Now or never, lieutenant! North again, and come in gently. It's not sand, it's dark shingle.'

'I don't want to rip the boat open,' said Veyrenc, as he carefully steered the boat, sideways on, towards the beach.

They hauled the boat up on to the shingle, Retancourt alone taking the bows. Adamsberg asked Veyrenc for a cigarette – having left his as a last bequest to Rögnvar – then took off his gloves and sheltered behind the hull of the boat to light it, which was not easy.

'Old wives' tale!' said Retancourt, whose shapely nose and blue eyes were all they could see emerging from her bright yellow hood.

'We should do whatever Rögnvar says,' said Adamsberg.

'The creature will be waiting for you in any case,' observed Veyrenc, 'whether you smoke or not.'

'Just as well not to offend it with the smell of humans. You should smoke one too, Louis, as a matter of courtesy, I'm sure Danglard would approve. I'll take the first steps up the beach, and I think our meeting place will be the warm rock.'

Adamsberg pointed up at the plateau where the remains of some wooden sheds could still be seen.

'It can only be there,' he said. 'The other side is a steep cliff.'

As they crossed the long windswept beach, the shingle gave way to flat rocks which sloped upwards about twenty-five metres towards the ruined sheds. The snow and ice still remaining in places made progress difficult. Retancourt alone reached the plateau without an increased heart rate.

'Well,' puffed Adamsberg, 'they certainly did use up three-quarters of this old building for firewood. Let's look for the famous rock now, but we'd better not get separated.'

'Yes, we *should* separate,' said Retancourt, 'because it's stupid to waste time. The whole place is only a hundred metres long by forty across. We'll still be able to see each other.'

'As you like, lieutenant.'

A few minutes later, Veyrenc, who was near the fox's left ear, signalled to the others. The famous rock, in fact just part of a rock, was no bigger than a child's cot. Smooth and worn to a silky sheen by many hands, it was covered with carved inscriptions.

'Since I got the summons, I'll go first,' said Adamsberg, and he knelt down and took his glove off to feel the black and slightly shiny surface of the rock with the palm of his hand. 'Yes, it *is* warm,' he confirmed.

'Good thing we came all this way, then,' commented Retancourt. 'To find out something we already knew.'

'What's this writing? What do you make of it, Louis?'

'Old Norse, must be runes. Do you want me to copy some for Danglard?'

'Why not?' said Adamsberg. 'It would make a nice present for him. A respectful offering.'

'No way!' said Retancourt abruptly, as she scanned the western horizon. 'We mustn't waste any time.'

'You're right,' said Adamsberg, to mollify her, and stood back up. 'We have to look for where they bivouacked. That's what I'm after.'

'It must be down there,' said Veyrenc, pointing back towards the beach. 'In that niche, where the two ears would have shielded them a bit from the wind. Just before the ground rises. That's where I'd have camped.'

'Good,' said Adamsberg, 'we'll go back down, I suggest backwards like on a ladder, we don't want to take a tumble here. And he didn't even come,' he added in a slightly disappointed voice.

'Don't worry,' said Retancourt, 'he'll come all right.'

Their feet skidded on the slippery rocks which sometimes fell away under them, and their hands slipped on the patches of gleaming ice.

'What idiot ever said down was easier than up?' said Veyrenc, as at last they reached the beach.

'Danglard said something like that,' said Adamsberg. 'But he meant downing wine, I think. Let's see if we can locate their fireplace. Fourteen days continuously burning, it ought to have left some trace. Let's move forward like in fingertip searches.'

The two men walked slowly, carefully examining the surface of the rocks, while Retancourt, manifestly thinking it a waste of time, and with much ill will, looked vaguely left and right.

'And when we find the fireplace,' she said eventually, 'we'll know what? That they made a fire. Which we also knew already.'

'What are these holes?' asked Adamsberg, stopping still. 'Here, there, and over there?' and he walked on again.

Small orifices, about as large as ratholes, regularly spaced about fifty centimetres apart.

'They must have been for posts,' Retancourt pronounced. 'Look, they make two parallel lines.'

'So what do you conclude, lieutenant?'

'I think that guy who didn't want anyone to steal his fish must have had his herring smokery here. Because lighting a fire up on the top wouldn't make sense. You don't smoke fish inside a wooden shed, unless you want the whole thing to go up in flames. He put it here, out of the wind, just a light structure, so he could hang up his fish.'

Retancourt stopped speaking to follow the line of holes.

'Twenty-eight posts,' she said. 'A structure of about four metres by two. Well, big deal. We've discovered an old herring smokery.'

'But how did he manage to make these holes?'

'Like anyone else, used a crowbar and put a small stick of dynamite down.'

'OK then,' said Veyrenc. 'So it must be here that the group camped. If the fisherman thought this the best place, they must have too, basic animal instinct.'

'But there's no sign of a fire,' said Retancourt. 'No brown or black stains on the rocks. The ice has eaten it all away. Journey's end.'

Retancourt was right, and Adamsberg looked down at the ground in silence. A smooth surface, telling them nothing, which the frost and polar wind had scoured clean of any traces, as if with a wire brush.

'What about *in* the holes though?' said Adamsberg. 'Down inside them?'

He put down his backpack and quickly took out his blanket, rations, tools, compass and gas burner, until he found a spoon and some plastic sachets. Without noticing that Retancourt had turned to face the west and was sniffing the wind deeply.

'Get a spoon out too, Louis, and help me. If you find anything, put it inside these sachets. The erosion won't have got right inside these holes and they may not be frozen at the bottom.'

'What are we looking for?' asked Veyrenc, as he pulled out his own picnic canteen.

'Seal blubber. Dig.'

The post holes were no more than ten centimetres deep, and both men could easily reach to the bottom of the hollows in the rock. Adamsberg examined the contents of his first spoonful: a mixture of charcoal, with bits of black or reddened rock.

'If it *isn't* black like soot,' he said, 'leave it, it means the fire wasn't there.'

'Right.'

'There were twelve of them, they surely didn't make a tiny little fire, it was probably about a metre and a half across. You look there, I'll look here.'

'Finished,' said Veyrenc, standing up. 'No charcoal in the other holes, the fire must have stopped here.'

'And here,' said Adamsberg, closing his last sachet. 'Louis . . .'

'What?'

'What do you think this is?' he said, holding out a little white pebble.

'Retancourt's disappeared,' said Veyrenc, standing up. 'I'm sorry, I know she's a goddess for you, but her bad temper is really starting to get on my nerves.'

'Same here,' said Adamsberg, while nevertheless looking anxiously around for her.

'Up there,' said Veyrenc, pointing at the plateau. 'She's gone way back up there, what the fuck's she up to?'

'Getting away from us. Look, what is this?' he repeated, showing him the white stone. 'Be careful, take your glove off.'

He spat a few times on the pebble, then rubbed it with his sweater before putting it into Veyrenc's palm. Then he sat down and waited in silence.

'Not a stone,' said Veyrenc.

'No. Test it with your teeth, don't swallow it.'

Veyrenc bit a few times on the object with his canines.

'Solid and porous,' he said.

'It's a bone,' said Adamsberg.

The commissaire stood up, without speaking, put the little fragment, about the size of a marble, inside the sachet, and looked at it through the plastic.

'That didn't come from a seal,' he said. 'It's too small.'

The wind carried towards them words being shouted by Retancourt, who had gone up on to the plateau. Now she was skidding down the slope, on her back, feet in the air ahead of her, arms outstretched to catch at handholds, sliding from time to time on a patch of ice in order to move faster. Adamsberg was still rolling the little bone between his fingers, through the plastic, while Veyrenc watched with interest the astonishing descent of the sturdy lieutenant.

'In her yellow oilskins, like that, she looks like a snowplough.'

'You know, don't you, that Retancourt can convert her energy into anything she likes, depending on the circumstances,' Adamsberg explained. 'So if she wants to be a snowplough, that's what she becomes, quite simple.'

'Do you think she sat on the warm rock? Or maybe she saw the *afturganga*?'

'Maybe. Louis, this didn't come from a seal,' Adamsberg repeated.

'A bird then, a tern or something that died here.'

'It's too big for a tern.'

'Well, a puffin then.'

*

And now Retancourt was running towards them. Adamsberg stuffed his six sachets into the inside pocket of his anorak just in time, before Retancourt grabbed them both by the arm, without slackening her pace.

'To the boat, *now!*' she shouted, pulling them along.

'Oh shit!' Veyrenc protested, wrenching himself away and kneeling down to try and stuff his things back inside the rucksack.

Retancourt gripped the stolid Veyrenc by the collar, and shook him violently.

'Never mind your damn bag! Or yours, commissaire! I'm telling you to run for your lives!'

In a way, the two men had no choice. Retancourt had got behind them and was propelling them forward with all her might.

'Faster, for God's sake, can't you run?'

Adamsberg realised that although the sky was still just as blue, the air had changed consistency, bringing a damp smell with it. He turned his head and could see forming on the plateau a white layer of mist, as threatening as a lava flow, already wiping out the sight of the old sheds.

'It's the fog, Veyrenc, run!'

They reached the edge of the shingle just as the site of the herring smokery, where their bags were still lying, had already become half enveloped in mist. As he ran, Veyrenc twisted his ankle on the uneven pebbles, and fell full-length. Retancourt hauled him upright and, putting her arm under his shoulder, carried on, dragging the lieutenant with her.

'No, commissaire! Don't try to help, I can manage. Get to the boat, start the engine, for God's sake!'

And now they could no longer see the site of the smokery, or the shingle beach. No, the mist didn't advance at the speed of a galloping horse, it was bearing down on them like an express train, or a monster, or an *afturganga*.

Adamsberg couldn't 'start the engine'. On his own, he was not strong enough to heave the boat off the shingle and into the water. He glanced towards the harbour on Grimsey, which was still in bright sunlight. Even so, they had already switched on the lighthouse. It must be to guide them. But through the bright sky, it was hard to spot the yellow flashing light. Adamsberg could still see ten metres behind him. Retancourt let Veyrenc drop to the ground so that she could help the commissaire launch the boat. Adamsberg jumped in, started the engine and helped drag Veyrenc over the gunwale, as Retancourt, standing in the water, hoisted him up by the waist.

'Give it everything,' said Veyrenc, holding his ankle in both hands, 'the fog's gaining on us.'

Adamsberg set a course towards the port and put the engine at full throttle. With the wind behind them, they had no need to tack, and he steered straight for the jetty, keeping first about fifteen metres ahead of the fog, then ten, then seven. It was about three metres from their stern, when they grounded rather roughly on the slipway, and several hands helped them back on to terra firma.

Brestir moored the boat, then with Gunnlaugur guided them to the guest house. Rögnvar followed on his crutches.

XXXVIII

IN THE DINING ROOM OF THE GUEST HOUSE, GUNNLAUGUR INSTALLED them peremptorily near the largest radiator, while his wife Eggrún placed small glasses in front of each of them. Almar was waiting for them there, pacing round like a captive bull, and revealing his emotion by waving his arms in the air.

It was a long table, with benches on either side, and the Icelanders had settled themselves without a word around the little group of foreigners. Veyrenc had requested a stool to rest his foot on: it was turning blue like Rögnvar's leg. Eggrún filled the glasses and Adamsberg dipped a finger in and tasted it.

'*Brennivín?*' he asked.

'Doctor's orders,' said Eggrún. 'As they say, better the black death than the white one. Sometimes.'

'We might not have died,' said Adamsberg, looking round at several pairs of blue eyes which were examining them as if they had escaped by some miracle. 'The fog might only have lasted ten minutes.'

'Ten minutes – or a month,' said Gunnlaugur.

'It'll last two weeks,' Brestir forecast. 'Now that the wind has dropped.'

The fog was now thick around all the windows of the house. It would in fact hang around Grimsey longer than predicted, almost three weeks. For now, Adamsberg nodded, and drank off his glass of *brennivín*, which brought tears to his eyes.

'Good,' said Eggrún, approvingly. 'You drink up too,' she ordered Veyrenc and Retancourt, who both obeyed.

Silence fell once more, and Adamsberg understood that everyone was waiting for them to tell their tale. It was only proper. A stranger had no right to carry away secrets brought back from Fox Island.

'You saw him?' asked Rögnvar.

As the man who had been crippled by the *afturganga*, Rögnvar was deemed by all entitled to open the conversation.

'Saw him, no,' said Adamsberg. 'I went to greet him on the warm stone. But I didn't sit on it,' he explained prudently.

'Greeted? How?'

'I put my hand on the stone. Like this,' he said, putting the palm of his hand flat down on the table.

It immediately reminded him of the photographs of people's hands used as identification at the Robespierre meetings.

'Well, all right,' commented Rögnvar. 'And what did he do?'

'He sent an offering.'

'Show us,' Rögnvar demanded.

Adamsberg went to look for the sachets in his anorak, hoping that the islanders would not want to keep them as national treasures. After all, it was to him that the *afturganga* had vouchsafed them. And he had paid dearly. He put them on the table, slightly reluctantly.

'Open them up,' commanded Rögnvar.

'They're not very clean.'

'The *afturganga* doesn't offer diamonds. Open up.'

Adamsberg emptied on to the table the contents of the six sachets in six little piles. While he was doing so, Retancourt dropped off to sleep, sitting upright, without swaying, on the bench. Almar looked at her in amazement.

'She's capable of sleeping standing up too,' said Adamsberg, 'leaning against a tree, without falling. She needs the rest.'

'Naturally,' said Rögnvar. 'It was her, wasn't it?'

'It was her that what?'

'That saved your lives.'

'Yes,' said Veyrenc.

'Because of her strength,' said Rögnvar, 'like I told you. She was strong enough to hold off the *afturganga*'s fog at a distance, before it swallowed you up.'

'Will it bother her if we talk while she's asleep?' asked Eggrún in concern.

'Not in the least,' Rögnvar replied, instead of Adamsberg who was carefully sorting out the six little heaps of black dust with his finger.

It was not only the first sachet that contained a little white stone. Sachets 3 and 6 did as well. A total of five white stones – like the ones Tom Thumb used, Mordent would have commented.

'And this stuff?' Brestir asked.

'Is what remains from the camp of those twelve French people, ten years ago,' Adamsberg replied.

'No, it can't be,' said Gunnlaugur. 'Nothing would be left on that place.'

'We found these materials in some holes,' Veyrenc explained. 'They were post holes, made for the herring smokery, long before. And this stuff was down inside them.'

'The *afturganga* has his own hiding places,' said Rögnvar.

Adamsberg did not dare suggest that, in his view, the twelve French travellers had camped and eaten on the site, and that the remains of their meals had simply fallen down inside the holes, like golf balls.

'And this was what you were looking for?' asked Rögnvar.

'More than we bargained for, actually.'

'I don't understand.'

'Can I take these over there and give them a wash?' Almar asked, with a frown. 'The little white things?'

'Yes,' said Adamsberg, 'but be careful.'

'What is it you don't understand?' Veyrenc asked.

Rögnvar respected the man with the fiery locks, who had come from another world.

'Why did the *afturganga* try to kill you?' he said, shaking his head and scratching it in perplexity. 'You must have done something stupid, Berg.'

'I explored the holes with a little spoon,' said Adamsberg, spreading his hands to show he couldn't see where he had gone wrong. 'And Veyrenc did the same. And we put what we found carefully in sachets. I did spit on one little white thing to clean it a bit.'

'What else did you do?' asked Rögnvar, still not satisfied.

'I examined it, I showed it to Veyrenc, took it back to have another look. And while we were doing that, she –' he pointed to Retancourt still sleeping like a column in a cathedral – 'she came running towards us.'

'Ah, that must be it,' said Rögnvar. 'You *hung about*!'

'That's right,' Gunnlaugur confirmed.

'The *afturganga* calls you from very far away,' Rögnvar went on, 'he offers you all that, and what do you do, you *hang about*!'

'But what difference does that make?'

'It means you made yourself at home. He receives you and right away you take it easy, you think you can treat it as your place. Conquered territory. So, of course –'

'Of course,' Gunnlaugur added.

'– he's going to destroy you. He calls up the white cloud and swallows you up.'

'You mean it was discourteous of me?' Adamsberg asked.

'Call it that, if you like,' said Brestir. 'An offence. No one stays on the *afturganga*'s territory a minute longer than he allows.'

Almar had finished washing the little white objects, turning his head to translate from time to time, and he placed them back carefully alongside their respective piles of soot. He signalled to Adamsberg to come and join him at the bar. It was a sober sign, not one of his excessive gestures.

'What'll you have?' asked Adamsberg.

'A beer.'

'It's on me.'

'Have one yourself as well.'

'I've had enough with that *brennivín*. My whole jaw is still burning.'

'You'd do better to have a beer then. Or a coffee. Have a coffee, with plenty of sugar.'

'All right,' Adamsberg agreed. Allowing Almar to pass the request to Eggrún, and understanding that here, in these circumstances, it was better to go along with what was proposed. Just as it had been, he remembered, in a cafe in the Normandy village of Haroncourt, on a previous case.

'So what do you think they are, your little white things?'

'Puffin bones?'

Almar drank off half his beer, and suggested that the commissaire drink up his coffee. Adamsberg felt a wave of fatigue settle on his shoulders. At the table, Veyrenc seemed to be quailing similarly, while Retancourt was still asleep. He put the empty cup down and stirred the brown sugar with his spoon.

'They are the small bones at the end of a limb,' Almar said. 'I studied anatomy in years gone by. In Rennes.'

'Yeah, right,' said Adamsberg, his eyes ready to close.

'They don't come from puffins,' Almar said. 'These are human bones.'

XXXIX

ADAMSBERG WENT OUT OF THE GUEST HOUSE WITHOUT BEING ABLE
to distinguish its wall from those of the neighbouring buildings, even
though they were painted red and blue. He breathed in the damp,
iodine-laden smell of the fog, now sitting still on top of the village, the
same smell he had noticed on the warm island, and above all the one
that Retancourt had recognised, well before the others, leading her to
go up to the plateau a second time to see what the west wind was
bringing. Retancourt, who had overcome the *afturganga*'s cloud. He
pulled up his anorak sleeve to consult his watches. He could see their
dials, but not clearly enough to say quite where the hands were pointing. Even with the compass, now lying somewhere near the post holes
on the island, they would have been unable to steer the right course,
still less avoid floating blocks of ice.

In the dining room, Eggrún was bandaging Veyrenc's ankle with professional care, after applying a strong-smelling ointment, not unlike the one
Pelletier had put on Hecate's hock. Rögnvar was stooping over the injured
leg, looking preoccupied. He beckoned Almar over to translate.

'Are you sure you twisted your ankle as you ran on the shingle?' he
asked Veyrenc.

'Yes, sure. It's just a sprain, Rögnvar.'

'But it hurts a lot, doesn't it?'

'Yes,' Veyrenc admitted.

'And when you fell, did you feel a sharp pain? As if it went right through to the bone?'

'Yes, after a bit. Probably a torn ligament.'

Rögnvar picked up his crutches and headed over towards Gunnlaugur who was playing a game of chess against himself.

'I know what you're going to ask,' said Gunnlaugur.

'Yes. Call the airport and get them to have a plane on standby to go to Akureyri hospital. We need to check the ankle once an hour. If the purple goes above the bandage, we'll need to fly him out.'

'How can anyone take off in this fog?'

'I'd put my hand in the fire that it's not reached the runway, or not so thick anyway. It's just settled over Fox Island and on us.'

Gunnlaugur pushed a pawn forwards and stood up.

'I'll go and phone,' he said. 'Don't touch the pieces.'

Behind his back, Rögnvar examined the chessboard. Then he moved the black castle. He was the best player on Grimsey, an island famed for proficiency at chess.

Adamsberg helped Veyrenc walk to a small bedroom Eggrún had prepared for him on the ground floor.

'What about her?' Eggrún indicated, pointing to Retancourt.

'Just leave her be,' said Adamsberg. 'She can recover five times as fast as the rest of us.'

Eggrún glanced at the chessboard where her husband had just discovered Rögnvar's underhand move.

'By the time they've had a game and a return match,' she said, 'dinner won't be before eight thirty. Go and get some rest for three hours.'

At seven, Rögnvar left Gunnlaugur puzzling over a crucial move that threatened his queen, to go and take a look at Veyrenc's leg, while the lieutenant slept. For the moment 'it' wasn't bad enough to cause more concern. Nevertheless, his toes were swollen. And a purple patch about the size of a krona coin had appeared above the top of the bandage.

'Tell them to stay on standby,' he said, sitting back down, dropping his crutches on the floor.

Retancourt, who had been awake for half an hour, asked in sign language if she could sit alongside them to watch the game. From the corner of her eye, she could see Eggrún laying the table and bringing in dishes: herring, cod and salmon, fried, smoked or salted, in thin slices, accompanied by beer and even a bottle of wine. And that was just the first course. A banquet, to indicate that the successful assault on the *afturganga*'s island had broken the ice, so to speak.

Sitting on his bed, Adamsberg had nodded off only for a few moments. He was waiting for the clock to chime the quarter hour at 8.15 before going to help Gunnlaugur move Veyrenc to the table. Retancourt joined them and sat down solidly, her features looking perfectly rested. Adamsberg poured out the wine and raised his glass.

'To Violette,' he said gravely.

'To Violette,' Veyrenc echoed.

'Your fall on the beach could have meant the end for us,' said Retancourt, clinking glasses with Veyrenc.

'It wasn't *my* fall, Retancourt. It was the *afturganga* that caught me. Rögnvar is convinced of that. He's not going to leave me until he's sure my leg isn't going to develop gangrene.'

'He's right about one thing,' said Retancourt. 'Nothing and nobody could possibly live on that island. There weren't even any seabirds' eggs on the cliff. No sign of any seals poking their noses out of the water. I couldn't see any movement in the sea. Those tourists were lucky if they managed to catch seals, very lucky.'

This would be the moment, thought Adamsberg, still feeling dazed by the shock of his discovery, and yet what else had he been expecting, when he went off to gather the remains, supposedly, of a campfire and seal blubber?

'Almar had a word with me earlier,' he said, as he brought out a tin box for cough sweets, now holding the five little bones, and placed it on the table. 'These were down inside the holes,' he explained, for the benefit of Retancourt, who had been fast asleep when Almar had washed the bones.

'They're bones,' said Retancourt, picking one up.

'Must be from puffins,' said Veyrenc. 'So they did at least find something to eat.'

'No, Louis, they're not from puffins. They're human.'

Adamsberg stood up, in the silence that followed, to go and fetch Almar from his room. The little guide had just woken up, and was struggling into a thick blue sweater.

'Come and explain to them,' Adamsberg asked. 'I can't remember the right names, I won't be credible.'

'They're the carpals,' Almar said, pointing to his own wrist, 'between the forearm and the hand, the wrist bones if you like. There are eight of them, and they fit together in two rows. Have you got a piece of paper, commissaire? Thank you. It's easier to show you this way,' he went on, drawing the two bones of the forearm, then the eight smaller carpal bones and finally the hand bones, or metacarpals, as he called them. 'So on the upper row we have the scaphoid, the lunate, the triquetral, and the delicate little pisiform, which looks like a squashed chickpea.'

'Pretty names,' said Veyrenc in a carefully neutral voice.

'And the lower row consists of the trapezium, the trapezoid, the capitate and the hamate.'

'Are you a doctor, then?' asked Retancourt, still chewing automatically on her meat.

'No, but I work part-time as a physiotherapist in Lorient. I have this second job as an interpreter from time to time. That's why I can tell you you've just got a bad sprain,' he said, turning to Veyrenc. 'Nothing's broken, but perhaps there is a torn ligament and a bruised metatarsal. We won't be able to tell for sure till the swelling goes down. I'll give you an anticoagulant injection before the flight, and we can get a boot to hold the foot once we're in Reykjavik. I'll organise that for you. Six weeks resting the foot.'

Veyrenc nodded slowly, his eyes on the tiny bones Almar was handling.

'And they're old, are they, these bones?' asked Retancourt.

'No. They can't come from the man with the herring smokery. Anyway, in his time, there would have been posts in the holes. Look at this one,' he said, holding it up to the light, 'you can still see a bit of ligament on it. I'd say between seven and fifteen years old.'

Retancourt's blue eyes looked up at Adamsberg.

'We didn't hear that any of the tourists was injured, or lost a hand.'

'No, lieutenant.'

'What is worrying,' said Almar, 'is that *these* two, a triquetral and pisiform, fit together perfectly. See? Their indentations correspond exactly. And the triquetral fits on to the lunate. Try.'

The bones passed from hand to hand as they tried to fit them together like a Chinese puzzle, while Adamsberg made signs to order another bottle of wine. Almar was a fast drinker.

'It's not so easy when you're not used to it,' said Almar, taking them back. 'Then these two, the trapezoid and the capitate, also fit together. But their upper grooves don't fit with our lunate and triquetral.'

'So you conclude?' said Adamsberg, who already knew what was coming, and was filling up their glasses.

'You ordered wine? But I told you it cost a fortune here,' said Almar.

'Eggrún let us have the first bottle on the house, so I ordered another out of courtesy.'

'By the way, did Brestir give you back the five hundred kronur? His boat came back safe and sound.'

'Yes, Almar. Can you go on please? The grooves that fit and the ones that don't.'

'Yes. So what we have are bones from two different wrists. That I can say for sure.'

'Right and left then?' asked Veyrenc.

'No, two right hands. From two individuals, I would guess,' he went on, spreading the little bones into two piles, like poker chips, 'a man and a woman. The triquetral, the pisiform and lunate come from a woman, the trapezium and the capitate from a man. So if it comes from your group, I can tell you that something *fucking* out of the ordinary must have happened.'

'So what *did* happen, for God's sake?' asked Veyrenc.

Almar took two long sips of wine.

'You'd better finish the story, commissaire,' said Almar, raising his hands. 'I've done my bit. I don't want to carry on.'

Adamsberg took the two male bones and put them under the light.

'Here,' he said, 'you can see the mark of a knife, and there, two other marks. The bones were cut at the point where the wrist joins the hand. And the cut edges are black. It's not dirt, they were burnt by the fire.'

Adamsberg put the bones on the table at the very same moment that one of the chessplayers behind him moved a piece on the board.

'Check and mate,' said Adamsberg heavily. 'They were cut up, cooked and eaten. The legionnaire and Adélaïde Masfauré. They were eaten.'

Eggrún had come over to clear the dishes from the silent table and put in front of each of them a pancake with rhubarb jam. Almar thanked her enthusiastically.

'If you don't eat your dessert, you'll be the ones who get eaten,' he said. 'Force yourselves.'

'Matter of courtesy,' muttered Veyrenc.

'So, as gifts go, this was one all right,' said Adamsberg, attacking his pancake.

'You mean from the *afturganga*?'

'Yes.'

'Now we know why he called you from so far away. It wasn't a detail. And it was polluting his island.'

'Yes. Catching seals my foot,' said Adamsberg, raising his voice. 'They killed them *in order to* eat them! I'm going to have a smoke outside,' he added, picking up his anorak.

'Finish your pancakes first,' Almar told him.

'They're excellent,' Retancourt murmured in an even voice. 'Almar, please thank Eggrún for this dinner. Warmly.'

'Shall we tell Danglard about this?' Veyrenc asked Adamsberg. A rare spark of anger flashed across the commissaire's vague gaze.

'No,' he said.

While Adamsberg and Retancourt were putting on their anoraks, Veyrenc picked up the rustic wooden crutches which Gunnlaugur had given him. 'No, we don't need them,' he had been assured. There were a dozen pairs of them in the house, tourists were always having falls, Almar had translated.

'Berg,' said Gunnlaugur, looking up from the chessboard, a pawn in his hand. 'Stay in front of the house. Don't go more than three metres away. There's a bench in front of the second window on the right, a red one. Try and find that and don't leave it.'

They found the bench, especially since Gunnlaugur had opened the window to guide them in this extraordinary fog. Adamsberg had never seen anything like it. Pure cotton wool.

'We need to put some more ice on that sprain,' said Almar who had followed them out, holding his glass.

'We'll find some, doc,' said Veyrenc. 'No shortage of snow round here.'

'It's a beautiful place,' said Adamsberg, lighting everyone's cigarettes. 'I can't see more than a metre ahead, but I know it's beautiful.'

'Horribly beautiful,' said Almar.

'I think I'd like to stay here,' said Adamsberg.

'With Gunnlaugur and Eggrún fussing over us as if we're their chicks, I'll stay too,' said Veyrenc. 'I need an Icelandic first name. Almar, what should it be?'

'Easy, you can be Lúðvíg.'

'Perfect. And Retancourt?'

'What's her first name?'

'Violette, like the flower.'

'Well, Víóletta then.'

'Easy really, Icelandic, isn't it?'

'Horribly easy.'

'I didn't say *I* was going to stay,' remarked Retancourt. 'Do they play a lot of chess here?'

'It's a national sport, practised with passion,' said Almar.

'We didn't have time to copy the runes on the stone for Danglard,' said Veyrenc after a silence. 'It probably said something like *stranger who treads this isle beware . . .*'

'*. . . of the monstrous vices of contemptible hypocrites*,' said Adamsberg. 'We could sit around making up stuff like this all our lives, without mentioning it. Never tell anyone about the warm island and the bones. It wouldn't be so bad. We'd chat about this and that and go over it again and then drink up, and then go to sleep.'

'What time's the plane tomorrow?' asked Veyrenc.

'Midday on the tarmac,' said Adamsberg, 'and by the time they've got rid of the million birds, we'll be at the airport in that town on the other side by about one o'clock.'

'Akureyri,' said Almar.

'Then take-off for Reykjavik's at 14.10, arrival in Paris 22.55, local time.'

Paris.

There was an almost stormy silence.

'We'd chat about this and that, and go to sleep,' said Adamsberg.

XL

'GO GENTLY WITH RETANCOURT,' VEYRENC SAID TO ADAMSBERG AFTER breakfast next morning. 'I don't think she can take this business of them eating the bodies.'

'Well, who can, Veyrenc? Can you stomach the idea of Victor eating his mother? Or the great philanthropist tucking into his wife?'

'Did they *know*? Or did they believe in the seal all along? Anyway Violette can't stand the idea, she really can't.'

'She's a sensitive soul,' said Adamsberg, without irony.

Retancourt joined them, bringing more coffee.

'This is how I see it,' she said, filling their cups. 'They really did die from the cold. And the others then ate them, in order to survive. Like those people in the plane crash in the Andes.'

Retancourt was trying to tone down the drama, to make it almost acceptable to her revolted imagination.

'In that case,' said Adamsberg, 'why would Victor have invented his story of people being stabbed to death?'

'Because by comparison, two stabbings would seem less serious,' said Veyrenc. 'At the same time, they could explain why Alice Gauthier had issued her summons to Amédée, which they had to tell us about.'

'Fair enough,' said Adamsberg. 'But then, why invent this story of the killer threatening them all for ten years?'

'To justify their silence? Whereas, in reality, nobody was threatening them. Their silence was instinctive and understandable. Who would go round boasting on their return that they had eaten their companions? They all agreed to keep quiet, for ever, there doesn't actually have to be some imaginary murderer tormenting them.'

Adamsberg went on stirring the sugar into his coffee.

'Not how I see it,' he said.

'Because?'

'Because what Victor told us, even if it's not true, was a story full of fear. The way he described "the monster", even if he was exaggerating, had something convincing about it. And that scare he had at the Auberge du Creux. Remember, Louis, when he suddenly stopped talking, because he thought he'd recognised "the man" in the mirror? If that wasn't genuine fear, why would he want to make us think the killer had appeared at a neighbouring table? Pointless.'

'I didn't know about that bit,' said Retancourt. 'So who was that man?'

'A tax inspector, we were told. Who may have had some resemblance to the killer.'

'So you think there *was* a killer?'

'Yes.'

'All right, give us your version, Jean-Baptiste.'

'It's even worse than the other possibilities.'

'Just get on with it,' said Retancourt, swallowing the last of her coffee.

'Right. Although we don't know a lot about this group, we do know there was a doctor among them. Victor said they called him "Doc". It wasn't important for his made-up story, so it must be an authentic detail. And that's the essential point. I think there really *was* a fight between the murderer and the legionnaire. But not a genuine fight, I suspect. One that was deliberately provoked, in order to kill the man, but which could be disguised as a fatal accident. Then the murderer

335

goes away with the corpse, to dispose of it, as he says. Once out of sight, he cuts up the body before it has time to freeze. He cuts off all the recognisable parts, head, hands, feet, bones, and slices off the meat.'

'Hurry and get this over with,' said Veyrenc.

'Sorry, but I have to stress one detail. The killer only has a knife, an ordinary sheath knife. Not strong enough to cut through the solid bones of the arms, for instance. So he cuts the easiest place, the joint, the wrist, and the little carpals, as Almar showed us, stayed connected to ligaments. He gets rid of the remains of the corpse among the ice floes, and he freezes the pieces of meat he's prepared. He lets some time go by, so as to make it seem realistic, and then look what happens, he manages to trap a seal! He brings the meat back to the camp. Was it when they were eating the so-called "seal" that the doctor, as he ate his share, came upon a bone? We may find out later. The same scenario is enacted for Adélaïde Masfauré. I don't believe the cock-and-bull story about the attempted rape, the fall on to the fire, the burnt trousers and the stabbing. I think when it was his turn to be on duty at night, the killer simply smothered her, by pressing her face in the snow. She's found dead in the morning, apparently of hypothermia. Once again, the killer gets rid of the body, brings back meat to the camp a few days later, a second miraculous seal, this time "a young one". The doctor pulls a bone from his mouth, and identifies it straight away.'

At this point Adamsberg stopped short and his eyes previously resting on Retancourt suddenly went blank. Retancourt immediately recognised this absent gaze, something she always feared.

'Commissaire?'

Adamsberg put his hand up to request silence, took out his notebook slowly, and wrote down the last sentence he had pronounced: *The doctor pulls a bone from his mouth.* Then he reread it, following it with his finger, like a man who cannot understand what he is seeing. He put the notebook away, and his eyes reverted to normal.

'Sorry, I was thinking,' he said, by way of apology.

'About what?'

'No idea. And the doctor then identifies this bone,' he repeated. 'What does he do? Throw his meat on the fire? Tell them the truth? Well, yes, probably. And they all suddenly realise what these life-saving meals that they've been eating for days actually consisted of. Did they, *all the same*, go on and finish eating Adélaïde Masfauré? Or had they *already* known the truth, about the legionnaire? Did they just accept it? Then when the fog finally lifts, the killer gives them orders and threatens them, without meeting any resistance. None of them wants to go telling the world about what they've done, and now we know why. But afterwards, anything can happen. Someone becomes ill, gets depressed, has a religious conversion, or perhaps is just smitten with terrible remorse. There's always the risk one of them will confess, and we saw what happened with Gauthier. So the killer keeps an eye on them. All of them. Because yes, he has eaten two human beings like everyone else, but above all he had killed them, *knowing* that it was in order to have something to eat.'

Adamsberg at last drank up his coffee, which had been well and truly stirred.

'Well, so what?' said Retancourt, becoming distant once more, returning almost to her attitude of the previous day. 'All right, now we know the true story about this desperate group of tourists on the warm island. But where does that get us in the end?'

'We know there's still a murderer haunting them.'

'But a murderer who didn't kill either Alice Gauthier or Henri Masfauré or Breuguel or Gonzalez. A murderer who isn't *our* murderer, the one we're after. A murderer who had nothing to do with the attacks on the Robespierre society.'

'I think,' Adamsberg murmured, 'I know why the Robespierre chess game isn't moving.'

'Tell us then.'

'I don't know.'

'You just said you thought you did.'

'It was a manner of speaking, Retancourt.'

Retancourt leaned back heavily in her chair.

'Whether they died and were then eaten, or whether some guy deliberately killed them and then they were eaten, we still reach the same conclusion: it gets us nowhere. We've come all this way for nothing.'

'*Veni vidi non vici*: I came, I saw, I didn't conquer,' said Veyrenc.

At the neighbouring table, Rögnvar was indiscreetly getting Almar to translate their conversation for him. The story belonged to him, it was his right. He hoisted himself on to his crutches, told Gunnlaugur not to touch the chessmen, and came to stand in front of Retancourt, Almar behind him, to interpret.

'Víóletta,' he said, 'one cannot but respect a woman who has held the *afturganga* at a distance. Such that even your comrade's leg will be all right. If it wasn't for you, Víóletta, he would have . . .' and he pointed eloquently to his own missing leg. 'And Berg would have died. Because he made a mistake and lingered on the island. Whereas you understood that was the wrong thing to do. You understood that from the start, didn't you, Víóletta, long before you saw the fog?'

Retancourt frowned, and without apparently realising it, moved her chair a little closer to Rögnvar, the local madman, Rögnvar, the local wise man, and looked at him.

'Yes. That's true,' she said.

'When?'

'When we got there,' said Retancourt, after thinking. 'They wanted to write down the runes engraved on the rock. I said – well I think I shouted – not to do it or we'd waste time.'

'You *see*,' said Rögnvar, seating himself on a stool, which Eggrún had hurriedly brought up. 'You *knew*. And you'd known for a long time, since you left your own town, Paris, where you can sit on cafe terraces in winter. You didn't want to come, but you knew. So you came.'

Rögnvar was leaning forward, his long, still-blond hair almost touching Retancourt's forehead. Adamsberg watched this sight in amazement. Retancourt, the leader of the positivist faction in the squad, the materialists, caught in the toils of Rögnvar. Retancourt captured by the spirits of Iceland. No, they certainly hadn't come here for nothing.

Then Rögnvar put his large hand on the lieutenant's knee. Who would have dared to do that in the squad?

'But you are *wrong*, Víóletta,' he said.

'Why?' asked Retancourt in a whisper, unable to look away from Rögnvar's piercing blue eyes.

'You just said –' and here Rögnvar pursed his lips – 'that you'd come all this way for nothing. You said, brave Víóletta, that it didn't get you anywhere.'

'Yes, I did say that, Rögnvar. Because it's the truth.'

'No.'

'But, Rögnvar, you don't know anything about the case we're working on in Paris.'

'No, I don't know about it and I don't care. But listen to this, Víóletta, listen carefully.'

'All right,' Retancourt agreed.

'*The* afturganga *never summons in vain. And his offering always points out the way to go.*'

'But look here, Rögnvar, the *afturganga* took your leg. Was that pointing in any direction?'

'That's different. I wasn't summoned. I violated the island. Berg though, he was summoned.'

'Say that sentence again.'

'*The* afturganga *never summons in vain. And his offering always points out the way to go.* No, don't write it down,' said Rögnvar, gripping Retancourt's wrist. 'Don't worry, you'll always remember it.'

Looking out of the plane window, Adamsberg watched the island of Grimsey disappear, still partly wreathed in fog, with a feeling of nostalgia he had not foreseen. Tall Eggrún had kissed him au revoir, and on the harbour, the local men had all stood together to wish them farewell. Gunnlaugur, Brestir and Rögnvar, of course, raising their hands, along with the other fair-headed fishermen whose names he didn't know.

Tonight, Paris. And then tomorrow. Tomorrow, he would have to explain to the squad about his escapade, which had not, it was true, made the Robespierre chessboard budge one millimetre. He wasn't bringing back the killer, only a bottle of *brennivín*, presented to them by Gunnlaugur. But he would still have to give an account of himself. Argue, synthesise, organise his presentation, all the things he hated doing. And he would be facing a sea of hostile faces, except for those of Froissy, Estalère, Justin and Mercadet (whose own handicap made him sympathetic to other people's).

'Veyrenc,' he said, 'would you do the report back tomorrow to the squad? I know it won't be much fun. But since Château said you have the physique of a Roman senator, I'm sure you'd do it better than me. And Retancourt will back you up.'

'They're going to be hopping mad.'

'Obviously.'

'I'll tell them,' said Veyrenc calmly: he was sitting with his leg outstretched in the aisle, having had an anticoagulant injection administered by Almar. 'But you try to win over Voisenet and Mordent on to our side. Voisenet because he likes anything related to fish, and Mordent because he's a folk-tale buff. He'll really relish the story of fighting the *afturganga* and Víóletta the Brave.'

'I don't want to "win them over", Veyrenc. They have to work out their own ways, which aren't the same as mine.'

'That's why they're mad at you. And you can understand why they haven't followed you.'

'Not really,' said Adamsberg softly.

*

Shortly before they landed at Roissy-CDG, Adamsberg drowsily opened his notebook at the page where he had written down that morning in the guest house: *The doctor pulls a bone from his mouth.* Underneath it, he noted the remark Veyrenc had passed about Château: 'He's lying through his teeth.' Then he drew an arrow and wrote: 'Robespierre. He *is* him. And he's got them.'

The lights had been extinguished, the seat belts were fastened, the seats returned to the upright position. The plane had begun its descent and they could already see the headlights of cars on the motorway. Adamsberg woke Veyrenc and showed him the page in the notebook. Veyrenc shook his head without understanding.

'It was you that said it,' Adamsberg insisted. 'After our first visit to the assembly. You said "That was him".'

'Robespierre, you mean?'

'Yes, and you were right. He *was* Him.'

XLI

THE MEMBERS OF THE SQUAD WERE SITTING IN UNACCUSTOMED places at the long table in the council chamber that Friday morning – a public holiday as it happened, the first of May – and Estalère's coffee round was thrown into confusion. Instinctively, as they waited for Adamsberg to arrive, different factions had formed and were sitting together. At the top of the table, at the far end of the room, Danglard and Mordent had not changed their positions, as befitted those holding temporary responsibility. But instead of the usual seating arrangements, Retancourt had taken a chair at the other end, as if facing Danglard, with Froissy and Estalère on one side, Mercadet and Justin on the other. To his own right, Danglard noted, sat the hesitant dissenters, including Voisenet and Kernorkian. To his left, the determined opponents, of whom Noël had become the leader. Brigadier Lamarre, only just back from leave in Granville, and unaware of the situation, had sat down between two empty chairs and was quickly reading the reports for the last two weeks.

It wasn't unlike the Robespierre assemblies, Danglard thought, with its Jacobins, its Girondins, its Dantonists, and its 'Plain' in the middle. He sighed. Something was rotten in the kingdom of Adamsberg, and he had a sneaking suspicion that some of this was primarily his fault. Sulking in his tent, he hadn't sent a single message to Iceland to ask how the fruitless expedition was going, and yet he had believed the mission would be a dangerous one. True, he had received nothing either. But he was under no illusion: Adamsberg would not be bringing back anything in his bags, not even a bottle of *brennivín* for him.

Veyrenc made a rather impressive entry on his crutches and sat on a chair that Retancourt had saved for him, next to her. He turned sideways and asked Estalère to fetch a stool to rest his ankle on.

Danglard gave a start. So Veyrenc had been injured! How had that happened? And looking at the faces of both Veyrenc and Retancourt, which seemed paler and more drawn than usual, he realised they must have been through some misadventure. And he, Danglard, normally the loyal deputy chief, but now entrenched in his dogged and contrary irritability, had not asked for their news. He expelled from his mind this attack of remorse, and prepared to listen to Lieutenant Veyrenc's report. Which would of course lead nowhere. And that was what hurt most.

'Are we going to wait for Adamsberg?' he asked, glancing at his watch.

'No,' said Veyrenc, looking round at the hostile faces or bowed heads, and meeting the commandant's eyes.

'Injured, lieutenant?' asked Mordent.

'A rather risky fight on the deserted shores of the warm island.'

'Who were you fighting?' asked Danglard, in surprise. 'If the island was deserted?'

'Ah well,' said Veyrenc. '*He crept up behind us, hiding well out of sight/The shingle was black, and his body was white./He gave us an offering we took for our own./In place of his payment, he bit to the bone.*'

Vyerenc made a sweeping gesture with his arm, which to him indicated the *afturganga*, but which Danglard read as: 'You couldn't possibly understand.' Not that there was a great deal of difference.

'So you reached the island,' said Danglard, 'and then what?'

'If you'll allow me, I'll tell you what happened in order, at my own pace.'

'Feel free, go ahead,' said Danglard curtly.

*

How long had it been, he asked himself in an access of melancholy, since a meeting of the squad had taken place in such an icy atmosphere? And he was well aware that the tone of his own voice was making a major contribution to this. A thought ran rapidly through his head, and made him shudder. Had Adamsberg's disappearance, not to say desertion, leaving him, Danglard, temporarily in charge, been to his personal advantage? Did he really, subconsciously, want to replace Adamsberg as chief? And if so, since when? Since he had put on that flashy purple silk frock coat, which made him look so impressive, since he had felt – and enjoyed, admired – Robespierre's power of dominating the assembly? But as the new chief by default, what in fact had he done or discovered that had in *any* way advanced the Robespierre investigation? Apart from providing encyclopedic knowledge when asked. And what about Noël, Voisenet and Mordent? Had any one of them brought even a grain of sand to the inquiry?

Grains of sand. By a simple and rapid association of ideas, Danglard saw once more Céleste's paintings, that is to say her single painting with its dots of red. Which you had to look at with a magnifying glass, to see that they were ladybirds. Was that it, Céleste's obscure message? Was she drawing attention to the smiling dignity of small things, minuscule and neglected? Had he been going forward without a magnifying glass, unable to pick out even a single ladybird?

Feeling on the brink of some nameless distress, Danglard poured himself a large glass of water and drank it off, which was unusual for him, while Veyrenc began his presentation, starting at the point they left the harbour of Grimsey for the island, with none of the local men to accompany them. Veyrenc left out Rögnvar's warnings, and his leg lost to the *afturganga*.

When he reached the point about identifying the human bones and what they signified about that long-ago drama – namely cannibalism – Veyrenc's account inevitably caused shock waves of revulsion and astonishment, exclamations, indignation, questions and horror. For a short while, this exceptional information overcame the factions and moods. Adamsberg had not been wrong: what had happened on that island had been completely different from the story they had heard before.

Veyrenc remained aloof, watching the turbulence in the squad, and proceeded next to tell them about Retancourt's decisive action, which had rescued them from the lethal fog, without lingering over it in any attempt to inspire pity. There were a few appreciative whistles and nods. That was until they had settled down, and Noël could launch into an attack on the actual significance of the expedition.

In the end, what precisely *had* it brought them?

Precisely? However astonishing the results, in what way did it advance their current investigation?

There was confusion, various opinions were voiced, inconclusive discussion followed.

'Kernorkian,' Danglard interrupted, 'what about your report on the way Lebrun–Leblond slipped between our fingers? What was the result of checking the network of back alleys, cellars, roofs, courtyards? The commissaire did ask you to do that.'

'Yes, commandant, it's done.'

'Done, but you didn't tell me what the conclusion was?'

'Sorry, commandant, I thought I was supposed to report directly to the commissaire on his return.'

A vague bitterness once more flooded Danglard's mind, a bitterness he had never experienced and did not like. He filled his glass of water and took a few gulps to dilute it.

'In the commissaire's absence, I'm replacing him. So was there some escape route through the cellars?'

'No, commandant, there wasn't any kind of back entrance via cellars or courtyards. But you can get out across the roofs. The zinc sheets are flat and there are easy slopes. Between the two buildings, there's a gap of only thirty centimetres, protected by an anti-pigeon grid, so you don't have to be an athlete to get across. Then there's a skylight, through which you can get into number 22, and then exit via the car park into a side street. And that's probably how they managed to come away from François Château's place without us spotting them.'

'Right, well, on Monday night, stick to Leblond via this exit, and find out where he lives. Take Voisenet and Lamarre. A car and a motorcycle.'

'Yes, sir.'

'And what else?' asked Noël. 'Sweet FA! Four deaths! And we're still chasing these puppets, Château, Lebrun, Leblond, Sanson, Danton and the rest of them, out of *seven hundred* people! Because we haven't a clue what we're doing. While the commissaire goes swanning off to solve a tourist mystery in Iceland.'

'At his own expense,' Justin pointed out quietly.

'But he's not *here*,' said Noël firmly, to approving grunts from the seven uniformed officers of the squad.

'If the investigation's at a standstill, it isn't his fault,' said Mercadet. 'So if you've got any bright ideas, Noël, we're all agog.'

'Is Adamsberg the only person who's supposed to do any thinking?' asked Retancourt.

'Is he even doing that?' retorted Noël. 'The investigation's stuck because he's not doing anything, and he's not doing anything because he keeps running off to Le Creux or the North Pole. And his inaction affects the rest of us, it pins us down. It, er, saps our initiative.'

'Nobody asked you to be so sensitive to his influence,' observed Mercadet.

'I can't see what's so wrong,' added Froissy. 'All the interviews and interrogations have been done, everything's been followed up.'

Adamsberg, who had arrived late on purpose, was leaning against the door listening to the last exchanges.

'And they still haven't led us anywhere,' said Mordent. 'Like throwing sand into the sea.'

'And why was that?' asked Justin, eyeing Danglard.

'Yes, his mind *was* on Iceland,' said Danglard. 'But that episode is closed now.'

Adamsberg chose that moment to push open the door, causing total silence to fall.

First he examined Veyrenc's leg, on Almar's orders, to check that the journey home had not caused any complications. In his mind's eye, he saw once more Brestir, Eggrún, Gunnlaugur and Rögnvar waving goodbye from the harbour. While facing him were a group of colleagues looking sullen and in semi-rebellion, frustrated by this investigation that was going nowhere, exasperated by their own lack of inspiration, and unable to admit that the tangle of seaweed they were dealing with was dark and impenetrable. And in their feeling of powerlessness, they needed a scapegoat. Himself. He met the shifty gaze of Danglard and Mordent, who had given up expecting him, and went to stand behind Retancourt and Veyrenc, while Estalère slipped a cup of coffee into his hands. He looked round at the room, noting the changes of seating, the rancour, hesitations, lowered brows and the strange ambiguity in Danglard's attitude, with one shoulder up and one down as if he were torn between revolt and distress.

Danglard, the future chief of the squad? Why not? He had a clear mind and a fund of knowledge far superior to his own. Detached, almost indifferent. Adamsberg surveyed his team without knowing quite whether it was still 'his' team. He chose his words carefully.

'As Veyrenc has told you, the expedition to Iceland has blown out of the water the lies we were told by Victor and Amédée Masfauré. It points towards a killer ready to do anything to keep secret the two murders and the cannibalism.'

'Ready to do *anything*?' asked Noël. 'But who hasn't done anything at all in ten years? So what business is it of ours?'

'It's our business, because out of the twelve original travellers, six are still in mortal danger, and we should add Amédée to the list.'

'But they're not dead, and they haven't been threatened.'

Noël was braver than others, such as Voisenet who was keeping his head down, or Mordent who was fiddling with his papers. It was courage that came from his naturally violent character, but courage all the same.

'Simple information, lieutenant,' said Adamsberg. 'As for the Robespierre chessboard, it's still not moving. But animals have to move. So there must be some reason for this immobility, it isn't fate, it isn't bad luck. I think I can sense it somewhere, but I can't express it. Got that, Danglard?'

'Yes,' replied Danglard in a dull voice. 'But it still gets us nowhere.'

'Nowhere?'

Danglard interrupted his note-taking, alerted by a slight change in the commissaire's voice, a new sharpness. Rare on his part, and always accompanied by a particularly penetrating gaze. He looked up and saw it, that look, boring into him, a hint of fire from Adamsberg's usually mellow eyes. It was for him perhaps and for him alone that that brief flash had come and already gone.

'But where then?' asked Danglard.

'Towards movement. We have to go to where the animals are moving. Not hang about, as Retancourt understood when the fog threatened to maroon us. I'm going out this afternoon. Danglard, you're still in charge of the squad. I get the feeling you don't dislike it.'

Adamsberg drank off his cold coffee, then, holding a plastic bag, went round the table to stand by his senior deputy. He took the pencil from his hands and wrote underneath his notes: 'Nowhere, Danglard? *The* afturganga *never summons in vain. And his offering always points out the way to go.*'

Then he brought out the bottle of *brennivín* and put it on the table with a friendly expression.

'Come on,' he said to Veyrenc, as he passed behind his chair. And Retancourt, although not invited, rose to follow them. A strange conversion, Adamsberg thought. But when you've been lost in the fog, you've been lost in the fog, as Rögnvar would have explained.

XLII

'SO WHAT IS IT WE WANT TO GET THEM TO SAY?' ASKED RETANCOURT.

They had eaten lunch at the Auberge du Creux, which was open despite the public holiday, and had warned the Masfauré brothers that they had arrived. But without mentioning the trip to Iceland. On the phone, Victor, although ignorant of the reason for this new visit, was already on the alert. Because Adamsberg had asked him if they could meet in one of the lodge houses at the gates, out of Céleste's hearing.

'Well, first, we want to be able to end this, draw a line under what happened,' said Adamsberg, thinking of Lucio. 'And then we want to stir something into movement.'

'Victor won't tell us about the killer,' said Veyrenc.

'You don't knock a door in with the first blow from your shoulder. Today we're just going to shake it.'

Retancourt refrained from asking what all this was for.

And now, in Amédée's pavilion, the two brothers were eyeing them in silence, very much on their guard.

'The three of us got back from Iceland last night,' Adamsberg said. 'More precisely from the island of Grimsey, and more precisely still from the island of warm rock, Fox Island. We had a bit of trouble,' he went on, pointing to Veyrenc's leg, 'which matched the troubling information we gathered there. Information which – unlike the last time – won't tell you anything you don't already know.'

'I don't see . . .' Victor began in a low voice, 'I don't see what you could have "gathered". There's nothing left on that Fox Island.'

'There are some holes in the rock, which once held wooden posts. On the site of your camp. You did pitch it at the top of the beach, sheltered a bit by the fox's ears?'

Victor nodded.

'You wouldn't have been able to see the holes when you were there, they were buried under snow. And then, Victor, the snow melted. And any debris lying on top of them fell down inside. Sheltered from the icy winds.'

'That doesn't make sense!' said Victor. 'You went all that way, to dig around in some post holes? That you didn't even know existed?'

'True.'

'Looking for what?'

'Seal blubber, why not?'

'And you found some?'

'No. We found charcoal but no blubber. I'm sorry, I'm really desperately sorry. Can you come outside with me, Victor.'

Adamsberg leaned against the wall of the house, protecting himself from the rain that had started to fall. He brought out of his pocket the little tin for cough sweets and slipped the five small bones into the palm of his hand.

'Lie after lie, but we've almost reached the end of the road. These are human bones, wrist bones. Belonging to one adult male and one adult female. Cut up, cooked and eaten. You can see the traces of the fire and the cuts from a knife.'

Adamsberg returned the bones to the tin and slipped it back in his pocket.

'DNA analysis from both you and Amédée will prove that three of these bones belonged to Adélaïde Masfauré. And Eric Courtelin's sister's DNA will prove that the others came from the legionnaire, as you called him. *That's* what Alice Gauthier told Amédée, wasn't it? That they had been eaten? He already knows?'

'Yes,' said Victor in a hoarse voice. 'That Gauthier bitch. He wasn't supposed ever to find out.'

'How has he taken it?'

'Very badly. He's on medication for it. I've been sleeping in the same room, ever since he got back from seeing that woman. He cries out in his dreams, and I wake him and calm him down.'

Adamsberg went back into the room and sat down facing Amédée.

'So Alice Gauthier told you the whole story, did she?' he asked.

'For the sake of her immortal soul, yes,' said Amédée through his teeth.

'What else did she say? That they died of exposure or that they were killed?'

'That that man had killed them.'

'By accident, during a struggle? Or deliberately, in order to . . . consume them?'

'Deliberately, to consume them,' Amédée whispered. 'That's what they all understood afterwards.'

'Understood, what do you mean?'

'The one they called "Doc". He spat out a small bone. Belonging to the legionnaire. After their third meal. And the doctor told them. What it was. Too late, they'd already . . .'

'Consumed him,' Adamsberg supplied.

'And one morning they found my mother dead.'

'Stabbed?'

'No, probably smothered in the snow, before dawn, was what Gauthier said.'

'So when, a few days later, the killer brought in some more meat to help them survive, a so-called young seal, everyone understood. That he intended them to do the same again.'

'Yes.'

'That's enough now,' Victor intervened. 'Yes, we understood. All of us.'

'And you did it again? Consciously this time?'

'Yes. All except me. Because I knew she was my mother.'

True or false? Adamsberg wondered.

'That's the truth,' said Amédée. 'Alice Gauthier said "the young man didn't eat it".'

'So how did you survive, Victor?'

'I don't know. Perhaps because I was the youngest.'

'And why didn't you stand up to him?'

'There were nine of them, nine against me.'

'Henri Masfauré too?'

'Yes.' Victor breathed in deeply. 'He was sitting next to me. He was very weak, and shivering with cold. I begged him not to. But he said this way she would always be in him. So he did it.'

'And now,' Adamsberg said, 'we can truly understand the seriousness of the silence that has been imposed on you. The threat hanging over you. And why you have all been so obedient. It was unspeakable. But not when death is approaching. That's what Alice Gauthier did, egotistically, she spoke out at the end. And any one of you might do the same, in a moment of great weakness, or remorse, depression, religious conversion, illness, despair . . . And I believe,' said Adamsberg, standing up and walking to and fro in the little dining room, 'in fact I'm *certain*, that he is watching you, he is observing you, and that he calls you together. You all see each other, and he regularly quizzes you about it.'

'No!' cried Victor. 'We keep our mouths shut and he knows that. He doesn't need to see us and "observe" us.'

'You *do* meet,' insisted Adamsberg, raising his voice. 'And *you* know who he is. You may not know his name, but you surely know his face. Describe him, help me to find him.'

'No, I don't know what he looks like.'

'You're not the only one in danger, Victor. Amédée is too. Because he knows. Like the others.'

'I'm protecting him. Amédée won't say anything.'

'No, I won't,' agreed Amédée, who was looking both feverish and exhausted.

'What about the others, then? You don't care about them?'

'No, I don't.'

'Why, because they consumed your mother?'

'Yes.'

Adamsberg made signs to his officers, and they prepared to leave.

'Victor, *think* about the consequences of your refusal to talk.'

'I've thought about them.'

They left the two brothers sitting in silence, Amédée with his head in his hands, Victor rigid and resolute.

'He won't crack,' said Veyrenc, as they got back in the car.

'Amédée might,' said Retancourt.

'But Amédée doesn't know what the killer looks like.'

They returned to Paris in the rain, now beating hard against the windscreen.

'Just as well you didn't show the bones to Amédée,' said Veyrenc.

'The least I could do,' said Adamsberg with a shiver – either the effect of his wet clothes or of a fleeting image of someone showing you the bones of your mother who had been eaten.

'I'll drop you off at headquarters,' he said, 'but I won't come in.'

'Are you leaving the field free then?' said Retancourt with a snort.

'Why provoke them? They're all exhausted because of our failure to resolve this case, they feel defeated and they're retreating into their shells. What do you think about Danglard?' he asked with a smile. 'Think he'd like the position for good?'

'Danglard's behaving oddly,' said Veyrenc. 'Something's worrying him.'

'I think it's Robespierre,' said Adamsberg.

Zerk moved about quietly. His father had dropped off to sleep before supper, his feet on the fender. Zerk knew what had happened in Iceland and he was watching over Adamsberg as he slept. The fact that Violette had saved him from the *afturganga*, as she had once saved a pigeon whom they had rescued, had increased even more his admiration for her. When the phone rang at ten past ten, he was infuriated. Adamsberg opened his eyes and answered it.

'Commissaire,' Froissy announced, 'there's been another one.'

XLIII

ADAMSBERG JUMPED TO HIS FEET AND WOKE UP PROPERLY.

'Where? When?' he asked, picking up his notebook.

'Place called Vallon-de-Courcelles, about eight kilometres from Dijon. He isn't dead, he escaped by some miracle.'

'Who reported it?'

'The Dijon gendarmerie. The man took himself to hospital for emergency treatment. The killer tried to hang him, but the victim managed to undo the knot.'

'What does he say?'

'He can't speak yet. His trachea is damaged, he's on a respirator until the swelling goes down. But he's OK, he'll survive. He can communicate by signs and he can write, but not much yet. The gendarmes examined the scene. It was in a garage, where our killer had forcibly dragged his victim.'

'Why is he *our* killer? Why didn't they think it was a suicide?'

'Because they found the sign, in felt pen, on a petrol can. Red this time.'

'Blue, white, red. The tricolour flag, the Revolution. This bastard's playing games.'

'Yes. According to the gendarmes, the victim, who's a strong man, managed to reach a chain hanging from the ceiling. They found traces of it on his skin. By hauling himself up a bit, he succeeded in loosening the rope, then he was able to get his foot on a shelf, and undo the slipknot.'

'His name?'

'Vincent Bérieux. Forty-four, married, two children, works in computers. I'm sending you a photo. He's got tubes everywhere, he's lying in a hospital bed, not necessarily his usual appearance. But it gives a general idea.'

Adamsberg received the photo on his mobile. The man might correspond vaguely to the person Leblond had called 'the cyclist'. Square head, regular features, quite good-looking, no particular expression, brown eyes looking blank, as well they might after such a shock. He called the number that François Château had given him for emergencies – 'but don't try to trace the number, commissaire, it's not in my name' – and forwarded the photo to him, telling him to send it on to Lebrun and Leblond, whether they were asleep or not.

Meanwhile, Zerk had warmed up the supper and poured out two glasses of wine. Adamsberg signalled his thanks as he next called the Dijon gendarmerie. He was put through to Brigadier-chef Oblat, who was handling the case.

'I was expecting your call, commissaire. I've just been questioning the victim,' said Oblat in a strong Burgundian accent. 'We're trying to understand what he says in sign language, and he can write a little. He was certainly attacked at about 7 p.m., and taken to the garage, where the rope and a chair had been prepared.'

'Was the garage forced?

'It wasn't locked. It just has ordinary tools inside, DIY stuff.'

'And does he know his attacker?'

'He swears not. He said the attacker was a fat man, bordering on obese. Something like one metre eighty, or maybe less. That's all we've got. He was wearing a mask and a white wig.'

'White?'

'Yes, and on the floor, under the rope, we found a lock of artificial white hair.'

'Straight or curly?' Adamsberg asked, at the same time obeying Zerk's sign to start eating his potato omelette, before it got cold.

'I didn't ask. But the man was fat, that's all we have really. Oh, another thing, under the mask he was wearing glasses. So a fat man with glasses. In a grey suit, totally nondescript.'

'And nobody has noticed an unfamiliar car in –' Adamsberg glanced at his notebook – 'Vallon-de-Courcelles?'

'We asked any residents who were still up. In these villages, if you haul people out of bed they won't be very cooperative. We'll see if we can get any witness statements in the morning. But of the thirteen people who weren't asleep, nobody had noticed a strange car. I don't think the attacker would have been so stupid as to park in front of the church, would he? He could just have left it somewhere out of the way and walked into the village. Here they all eat supper early and go to bed early, there isn't a cat in the streets.'

'A fat man with glasses, who's prepared to walk a bit.'

'Not much to go on, eh? We did look for fingerprints, but some guy who wears a mask and false wig is surely not going to forget to put gloves on. Shall we do the preliminaries or do you want to take it yourself?'

'You have my full confidence, chief.'

'Thanks, commissaire. Because, not meaning to criticise, but Paris tends to grab all our cases. Still, this is you, not Paris, right? Shall we get the felt pen analysed?'

'Don't bother. But do send me a photo of the sign, and some pictures of the crime scene.'

'They've already gone off to your HQ, because we'd received your circular, so that's why we were on the lookout. Disguised as a suicide, I thought, better look and see if there's a sign. That's when we found it on the petrol can. Not really hidden, but not that obvious either.'

'Excellent work, chief. But send all that to me as well, on my personal email. I'll spell it out for you. Is the victim under guard?'

'Twenty-four/seven, yes, commissaire, for now. His best protection is if we can keep it out of the press. That way the killer won't know that his attempt failed, and he won't be back.'

'It'll give us a bit of breathing space, yes.'

'But what does the sign mean? It looks like a sort of capital H.'

'It's a guillotine.'

'Oh, right. Bit gruesome. Like in the Revolution then?'

'Exactly.'

'Is this some loony? A mad revolutionary or something? Or the opposite perhaps, if you see what I mean.'

'That's what we're trying to find out. We've been investigating an association that studies the revolutionary period. We think the killer is operating inside that club, and that he's choosing his victims. But there are seven hundred members, and they all join it anonymously.'

'Ah, you've got a proper tangle there. How are you going to solve it?'

'We're waiting for the false move.'

'So he'd have time to kill another forty or fifty of them, if he's clever.'

'I realise that, chief.'

'Sorry, commissaire, didn't mean to depress you.'

'No harm done. He may well have made it tonight, the false move. The victim's wife and children, where were they?'

'Weekending with the grandmother in Clamecy.'

'A fat man, with glasses, prepared to walk, and who is well informed.'

'Good luck, commissaire. When a case stalls, nothing you can do, no good trying to bash your head against a brick wall. If it's not coming right, it's not coming right. A pleasure to talk to you. I'll let you know if we find anything tomorrow.'

'Chatty fellow but not stupid,' said Adamsberg to himself, as he ended the call. 'Good-hearted.'

'I'll warm up your omelette again.'

'Don't bother, I'll eat it cold like they do in Spain.'

'You're going to Dijon?'

'No, he's sending me all the info.'

'So why does he put a mask on, this killer? Sorry, but I could hear everything from your mobile. Why doesn't he put a stocking over his head, like everyone else?'

'That might be his false move, Zerk. But he couldn't have guessed that his attempt to kill the man would fail. Second mistake, leaving too quickly after trying to hang the man. The chair would have made a noise, falling over, so perhaps he thought he'd better get out fast.'

'You're not going to tell Danglard?'

'Froissy is on duty with Mercadet. They'll tell him.'

'You don't want to do it, do you?' said Zerk. 'Why do you think he's being like this?'

'Not the first time he's got mad at me.'

'But it's the first time he's persuaded other people to join him. What's got into him?'

'What's got into him is that we're really stuck on this case. And when Danglard's stuck, he gets bored. That's his worst enemy, boredom. Because when Danglard's bored, he gets desperate, and when he's desperate, he goes to pieces and starts lashing out. But I also think meeting Robespierre didn't do him any good. He's got kind of hooked. He'll calm down, Zerk, don't worry.'

'How come he gets bored?'

'You know, one of the most valuable things I've passed on to you, Zerk, is that even when you're not doing anything, you're not bored.'

A text message came in from François Château on Adamsberg's mobile.

Leblond sure of ID. Man he calls cyclist. From occasionals or what's left of them. Infiltrator.

Name Vincent Bérieux, Adamsberg texted back. *Lives Vallon-de-Courcelles. Ring a bell?*

No, but V-de-C charming place on mountainside, been there.

'Is he taking the piss, or what?' Adamsberg asked, showing Zerk the message.

'No, I don't think so.'

No mountains Dijon area, Adamsberg texted back.

Locals call it mountain. We all make our own Mountain, commissaire. Goodnight.

'Yes, he bloody *is* taking the piss.'

Adamsberg called Froissy.

'Who was guarding François Château tonight?'

'One second, commissaire. Lamarre and Justin. But he didn't come home tonight. Whereas he usually gets in at the same time every evening. So Noël went to the hotel. Because sometimes Château stays late. They've got an audit coming up in a couple of weeks, so we thought, as their accountant, he was working overtime. But he wasn't in his office either.'

'And no one saw him enter or leave?'

'No, commissaire. Château goes in through the gardens, he has direct access to his office. He could have been there without us seeing him.'

'And he could have left as well, Froissy. *And* had time to come back from Dijon by now.'

Adamsberg composed another text message for François Château.

Château, where r u?

Home in bed. It's late!

23.15. My men didn't see you.

Poor watchdogs! Bit worrying. Worked late on audit + home 20 mins ago.

'Oh shit!' said Adamsberg, banging his phone down on the table.

'But the gendarme said the attacker was fat,' said Zerk.

'He's in that association, they all know how to disguise themselves. If he looked fat, it means he was thin. And Château's thin.'

'But he's little. And they said he was one metre eighty, didn't they?'

'Or maybe less.'

'And anyway, why would Château shoot himself in the foot like that, knocking off his own members?'

'Same way Robespierre did, knocking off his.'

Adamsberg looked at the phone again before going upstairs. Oblat had worked fast: photos of the sign and the crime scene. He pulled up a chair and examined the images more closely. Zerk leaned over his shoulder.

'So you *are* going to Dijon,' he said simply.

XLIV

BRIGADIER-CHEF OBLAT DROVE HIM FROM THE STATION TO VINCENT Bérieux's garage in Vallon-de-Courcelles.

'Nothing's been touched?' Adamsberg asked, as they went in.

'No, nothing, commissaire, because of the sign. We were waiting for you.'

'Why didn't the killer centre the rope, in your opinion? Why is it hooked to one side?'

Oblat scratched his neck, in his too-tight uniform collar.

'Petrol cans in the way, maybe?'

'Maybe. And it's a heavy chair, the one he used. Can you go outside and listen?'

Adamsberg put the chair upright and let it fall over again.

'So, did you hear anything?'

'Not a lot.'

'Would the neighbours have heard that, do you think?'

'Too far away, I'd say, commissaire.'

'So why did he run away so fast, and too soon?'

'Panic is all I can think of. After committing four murders, you might not have nerves of steel.'

'Can we take down the rope?'

'It's all yours,' said Oblat, climbing up on the chair.

Adamsberg fingered the rope, as if he were testing fabric, letting his hand run along the coarse fibres and sliding the slipknot, then handed it back to the gendarme.

'Can you take me to the hospital?'

'Right away,' said Oblat. 'You'll see. He's not saying much.'

'Nerves,' said Adamsberg.

'Shock, most of all. Looks like he wants to wipe out the memory, I've seen it happen before.'

Adamsberg went into the Dijon main hospital at one thirty, when the patients had just finished lunch. A smell of cabbage and overcooked veal hung in the air. Vincent Bérieux was not expecting him, but looking vaguely at the television from his bed: he was on a drip, with various tubes attached to him. The commissaire introduced himself, and asked how he was feeling. In pain. Here, the throat. Hungry. Tired. In shock.

'I won't stay long,' Adamsberg said. 'Your case is connected to those of four other victims.'

By blinking, the man indicated: 'Why? How's that?'

'Because of this,' said Adamsberg, showing him a drawing of the sign. 'It was painted on a petrol can in your garage. And we found it with the other victims too. Does it mean anything to you?'

Bérieux shook his head several times: firm denial.

Adamsberg hadn't realised how difficult it can be to read the expression on a man who is lying open-mouthed under a breathing mask, his features twisted in pain. He couldn't tell whether Bérieux was telling the truth or not.

'The white wig, can you tell me anything about that?'

The patient motioned for a pad and pen.

'*Old-fashioned. Like in olden days,*' he wrote.

'And you've no idea who your attacker was?'

'*Not at all. Quiet life, me.*'

'Not as quiet as all that, Monsieur Bérieux. Because what makes you leave Vallon-de-Courcelles now and then, where you *do* have a quiet life with your family, to go to meetings of the Association for the Study of the Writings of Maximilien Robespierre?'

Bérieux frowned, obviously surprised and disturbed.

'We know all about it,' said Adamsberg. 'The other victims used to attend as well.'

The man picked up the pen again.

'Don't tell my wife, she doesn't know. She wouldn't like it.'

'I won't tell. But why, Monsieur Bérieux?'

'Curiosity.'

'I'm afraid that's not enough for me. You're a great reader of history books?'

'No.'

'Well then?'

'Always keen on stuff about Robespierre. Wanted to take a look, dammit. Don't tell my wife,' he wrote again, underlining the last sentence this time.

'Well? After you'd taken a look?'

'I was hooked, dammit. Went back. Like people go to casinos.'

'How often?'

'Twice a year?'

'Since when?'

'6 or 7 years.'

'Henri Masfauré, Alice Gauthier, Jean Breuguel, Angelino Gonzalez, recognise any of those names?'

A shake of the head: no.

Adamsberg pulled out photographs of the four victims.

'What about when you see their picture?'

Yes, Berieux nodded, after looking hard at the photos.

'Ever speak to them?'

'Nothing to say. You don't go there to chat. You just attend.'

'I've been told you *were* acquainted. Perhaps not well, but a bit. That you exchanged a few words and gestures.'

'Just being polite, like with other people.'

Adamsberg looked at the man's eyelids, which were drooping, indicating that he was tired. He wouldn't say any more. He did know the other people. But in what connection? At whose request? And what were they after, to have carried on meeting for so many years?'

The patient rang for the nurse. Tired, shaky, he indicated.

'You're exhausting him,' the nurse said. 'His cardiac rhythm has accelerated. Can you please leave it for now and come back another time if you need to? He's had a bad shock, you have to understand.'

His cardiac rhythm has accelerated, Adamsberg said to himself, as he ate a meal on the square outside the Cathedral of Saint-Bénigne, near Dijon central station. Adamsberg thought again about François Château's two text messages the night before. The president hadn't sounded shocked, or anxious, on learning that another of his members, the *fifth*, had been attacked. His tone had been ironic, detached. Last night, Château was being Robespierre, indifferent to other people's fate.

He called Justin.

'What the hell were you up to with Lamarre last night?' he asked sharply. 'Château says he got home at 10.55, but you didn't see him.'

'Perhaps he came back via the roof,' said Justin.

'No, because the way through the car park is being covered. Like I say, what the hell were you doing?'

'We didn't budge from the spot, commissaire.'

'That doesn't mean you didn't do anything. Lieutenant, I'm not threatening you with the guillotine, but think hard, it's important.'

'All right, there was a moment or two when we were having a bet, playing heads or tails. And the coin rolled away a bit. Fetching it and looking at it, could have taken about a minute. Well, it was a two-euro coin.'

'Plenty of time, then, for Château to have entered the building.'

'Yes, sir.'

'While you were playing a game.'

'Yes, sir.'

'What was the bet?'

'Whether he'd come home.'

'And what did the coin say?'

'That he would.'

From the train, Adamsberg sent a text message to Danglard: *Rope pulled over to side, coarse texture, white hairs from wig on floor, victim not talking.* He sent the same message to Veyrenc and Retancourt.

How is he? Veyrenc texted back.

Like a cat crouching. V. muscular cat.

Are u coming into squad?

No. How is it?

Grumbles, murmurs, whispers. Your place 6pm?

OK.

Veyrenc put his phone down. It was so unlike Adamsberg not to come into his office during an investigation that he felt the need to go and visit him. Not that he thought the bad mood in the squad would deeply affect the commissaire. He was not sensitive to this kind of nervous tension, which slid across the surface of his indolent nature. But Danglard's opposition was something else again, and one way or another, the commissaire would be affected by that.

Veyrenc and Adamsberg spent an hour and a half going over all the elements of the case in vain, but the ends led inconclusively in countless directions. For example, Leblond had called the office desk earlier to ask for an update. He sounded a bit tense, but not overly so. Lebrun was another matter. He had called at the station in person, wearing a beard and wig, much alarmed by the latest attempted murder.

'He was sweating,' said Veyrenc. 'Made his make-up run.'

'I suppose he wanted more protection?'

'Yes, he asked us to watch *all* the access points of the hospital at Garches. But that's impossible.'

'And anyway, what would we be watching out for? A man we know nothing about, we don't know what he looks like, easy to lose in the crowd of staff and visitors to a hospital. We just know he wears glasses and walks on his own two feet and that's all. So what did Danglard decide?'

'He suggested that Lebrun take some leave, and stay home with the friend he's lodging with, or just leave town. But he said he couldn't do that, because of his work and the association. So Danglard agreed to assign an extra man, to calm him down. He also asked for a gun licence so he could defend himself if he's attacked.'

'People are getting very jumpy. All over the place.'

'You don't seem too disturbed by that.'

'No, I'm not, on the contrary I'm pleased. When people get jumpy, it means there's some movement. Do you understand, Louis? We've been needing something to budge. That wig, those white hairs in the garage, that's something moving. Because they're over the top. As my son said, why didn't the attacker just put a stocking over his head like anyone else? The gendarme from Dijon called me again. The white hairs were long and curly at the end. Therefore they came from a wig – of a kind you can well imagine. It doesn't take us far, but the killer was taking a risk. Why was he wearing it?'

'To get into character?'

'You're thinking of Château. But I don't think he needs to dress up to get into character or vice versa. For the historical character to enter him and possess him, he knows what to do. He's got the key. Much more powerful than some miserable wig any fool could put on.'

Veyrenc served himself a second glass of port.

'Do you remember the death of Robespierre?' Adamsberg said, looking more animated. 'The story Danglard told us in the car? How he was carried on a stretcher, shot in the jaw and wounded, and two surgeons came to see him?'

'Yes, of course.'

'And one of the doctors put his hand into Robespierre's mouth. He pulled out a mass of bloody tissue and two of his teeth. OK, say you're that surgeon. Just think. You've got Robespierre lying in front of you. Until today, he was the madly worshipped master of the country, the idol of the Revolution, the great man. What would you do with the teeth, Veyrenc?'

'What do you mean?'

'The teeth you're holding in your hand? Teeth belonging to the great Robespierre? You don't give a damn, perhaps? You just chuck them on the floor, like a bit of rubbish? As if you were gutting a duck? Think.'

'I see what you're getting at,' said Veyrenc after a moment. 'No, I wouldn't throw them away. I couldn't do that.'

'Don't forget, you're not a fanatical Robespierrist yourself, you're just a doctor. So?'

'Even so. I still wouldn't throw them away.'

'You'd keep them,' said Adamsberg, slapping the table with his hand. 'Of course you would keep them! If only not to commit the sacrilege of throwing them to the dogs. But next, citizen surgeon, when Robespierre is dead, and his body has been covered with quicklime so that he can never be seen again, what do you do with them *then*? His teeth?'

Veyrenc thought quickly, sipping his port, and shifting his injured leg.

'OK, I'm just a surgeon, I'm not a Robespierrist,' he said, as if to himself. 'So, a few months later maybe, I'd give them to someone. Someone for whom they might have great importance, and who wouldn't get rid of them.'

'Who? Help me, because I've no idea who that might be.'

Veyrenc thought again, at greater length, counted on his fingers, shook his head, seemed to be weighing up the various candidates, keeping some, rejecting others.

'The woman who loved him fondly all her life. Actually there were two of them. Madame Duplay, his landlady, and one of the daughters, Éléonore. But Madame Duplay hanged herself in prison after Robespierre's death. That leaves Éléonore. Yes, I'd take the teeth to Éléonore Duplay. He was her god.'

'What happened to her?'

'She escaped by some miracle from the repression that followed, and she survived another forty years. But without him, her life had no meaning. She lived on for years as a recluse, with another sister, I think. They never stopped mourning.'

'So she didn't have any children?'

'No. Obviously not.'

'OK, so now, you're Éléonore.'

'All right.'

'Concentrate.'

'OK.'

'Are you going to die, Éléonore, after over forty years worshipping this man, without bothering to do anything about Robespierre's teeth?'

'No, absolutely not.'

'So who will you pass them on to, when you're an old woman?'

'My sister? She's got a son.'

'What happened to the son?'

'He became a Bonapartist, I believe.'

'Look it up on the *tölva*,' said Adamsberg, passing his laptop across.

'Yes, that's right,' said Veyrenc after a few minutes. 'Éléonore was still alive when *her* nephew actually became tutor to Bonaparte's nephew, the future Napoleon III.'

'So that wouldn't work, Éléonore. You couldn't give mementoes of Robespierre to someone with Bonapartist connections. Who *can* you give them to?'

Veyrenc hoisted himself up on his crutches, and poked the fire – it had turned cool in these early days of May – then came back to sit down. He tapped the floor with his wooden crutch, while he thought.

'Right. What about the man rumoured to be Robespierre's actual son?' he decided. 'The innkeeper Danglard told us about, François-Didier Château.'

'That's got to be it, Louis. When did Éléonore die?'

'Pass me the *tölva*. 1832,' he said after a few moments. 'Thirty-eight years after him.'

'And by then, our innkeeper, François-Didier Château, is forty-two. So before she dies, she gives him the teeth. Would that work, Louis? If you were Éléonore is that what you'd do?'

'Yes.'

'How would she have kept them? Like our Icelandic bones? In a little box for sweets?'

Veyrenc banged again on the floor, this time a regular beat.

'That noise is annoying, Louis.'

'I'm thinking.'

'Yes, but I don't know why, it gets on my nerves.'

'Sorry, just a reflex. No, in those days, the teeth would surely have been put inside a locket of some kind. Under glass, with a gold case. Or silver.'

'The sort you can wear round your neck?'

'That's what they're for.'

'And after François-Didier, where do the teeth end up, from descendant to descendant?'

'With our François Château.'

Adamsberg smiled.

'There you are then,' he said. 'Does that seem possible to you? Correct?'

'Yes.'

'So there really is a relic of Robespierre.'

'Well, they have a lock of his hair in the Carnavalet Museum.'

'But teeth are very different. Have you noticed that François Château, when he's playing Robespierre, has this compulsive gesture?'

'He blinks a lot?'

'No, I mean with his hand. He is always fingering his lace jabot, on his chest. He's touching the locket, Louis, I'd put my hand in the fire on it.'

'Agreed, though perhaps that isn't the happiest turn of phrase.'

'Yes, you're right. And when he puts this locket round his neck, he becomes Robespierre, with the great man's teeth against his skin. I'm sure he doesn't wear it when he goes to work at the hotel. But I'm sure he *was* made to wear it as a child. The teeth, like a talisman, are a means of making him become one, physically, with his ancestor. He really becomes another person, he becomes Him.'

'And when he murders someone, if he does murder anyone, does he have the teeth then?'

'Of course. It wouldn't be Château doing the killing, it would be Robespierre, carrying out a purge, executing. *That's* why I think that wig in the Dijon case is too much. He wouldn't need that. He owns something much more important than a disguise.'

'But Robespierre never appeared in public without his wig, You can't imagine Château pulling a stocking over his face, can you? Robespierre wouldn't have a woman's stocking over his face.'

'You've got a point there,' agreed Adamsberg, sitting back, arms folded.

'Is he so absolutely inhabited by Robespierre?' Veyrenc asked, looking up at the ceiling and tapping his crutch again on the tiled floor.

There was a long silence, which Adamsberg didn't break. He opened his eyes on to the void, and all he could see was thick fog, the fog of the *afturganga*. Suddenly, he grabbed Veyrenc's wrist.

'Go on,' he said, 'go on, but don't say anything.'

'Go on what?'

'Banging the floor. Go on. I know why it was getting on my nerves. Because it was waking a tadpole.'

'What tadpole?'

'The beginning of an idea, still vague, Louis,' Adamsberg said quickly, afraid of getting lost in the fog again. 'Ideas always come up out of the water – where else would they come from? But they go away again if we talk about them. So say nothing, but go on tapping.'

Although he was well used to the improbable meanderings of Adamsberg's mind and the confusion of his thoughts, Veyrenc eyed the commissaire's face rather anxiously: eyes wide open, pupils all but disappeared, lips pursed rigidly. Veyrenc went on tapping the floor with his crutch. After all, he supposed, the rhythm might be helping the thoughts along with its vibration, like when you are on a march, or hearing the sound of a train going over the rails.

'It reminds me of Leblond,' Adamsberg said. 'The smooth and silky Leblond. You know, last time we went, he was playing the snake in the grass. Who was that?'

'Fouché.'

'That's the one, Fouché. Carry on.'

After a few minutes, Veyrenc was tempted to stop the game, but Adamsberg with a circular gesture of his hand signalled to him to carry on. Until suddenly, he jumped up, pulled on his jacket, still fitted with his holster, and ran out across the garden. Veyrenc hobbled after him, and saw him hurry down the road and get into his car.

'I'll be back!' he shouted.

And Veyrenc saw him changing gear quickly, first, second, and then disappearing out of sight, at the corner of the little street.

XLV

ADAMSBERG WAS DRIVING DOWN THE ROUTE NATIONALE, TOO FAST. *Slow down, there's no rush, slow down.* But his speed, rare for him, matched the turmoil of thoughts, sentences and images running through his head. As if going faster could bind them all together, like beating eggs. The cynical Fouché, the fog, the teeth, the wig, the rope in the garage with its rough texture, the carpal bones, Robespierre, the *afturganga*, Bérieux's mutism. Fear, the sound of the wooden stick on the floor, movement. The chessboard on which no pieces had moved.

The *afturganga*. And astonishingly, as he thought of the creature on the island, the description of Robespierre came back to him in fragments: *. . . a reptile rearing up, with a frighteningly gracious gaze . . . make no mistake . . . it is painful pity . . . mixed with terror.* The images blurred, Robespierre mutated into the *afturganga* of the Revolution, the one who kills, and the one who gives – on condition you never seek to know him, on condition you never penetrate into his sacred territory.

Then he saw in his mirror the lights of two motorcycles approaching, and one passed him, the rider signalling to him to pull over. God in heaven, fucking traffic cops!

He jumped out of the car.

'OK, OK,' he said, 'I was going too fast. Urgent case, I'm a police officer.'

He showed the gendarmes his card. One of them smiled.

'Commissaire Jean-Baptiste *Adamsberg*,' he read out loud. 'Well, just fancy that!'

'Urgent, is it?' said the other, legs straddled as if he were still on his bike. 'No siren going?'

'I forgot to set it,' said Adamsberg. 'Look, I'll come and see you tomorrow to sort this out. You're from which gendarmerie?'

'Saint-Aubin.'

'Right, got it. I'll see you tomorrow, officers.'

'Not so fast,' said the first gendarme. 'For a start, it's Sunday tomorrow, and anyway, that'll be too late.'

'Too late for what?'

'The breathalyser,' he said, while his colleague found the kit and held it out.

'Breathe into this, commissaire.'

'I'll say it again,' Adamsberg said, as calmly as he could manage, 'I'm on an urgent case.'

'Sorry, commissaire, you were driving very erratically.'

'Yes, indeed, erratically,' the other one agreed gravely. 'You were very tight cornering the bends.'

'I was driving fast, that's all. How many times do I have to tell you, it's urgent?'

'Just breathe in here, sir.'

'Very well,' said Adamsberg, 'give it here.'

He sat down in the driving seat, and breathed into the bag. His engine was still running.

'Positive!' said the gendarme. 'Follow us please, sir.'

Adamsberg, already in driving position, slammed the door shut and took off at high speed. Before the two men had had time to run back to their motorbikes, he had taken a right turn and escaped along minor roads.

Ten thirty, pitch dark and a fine rain falling. He braked at ten past eleven in front of the large wooden gates to the Haras de la Madeleine. Lights were still showing in both the lodge pavilions. He banged hard on the gates.

'What's all that racket?' called Victor, stepping out on to the drive.

'Adamsberg. Open the gate, Victor.'

'Commissaire? Are you going to keep bugging us for ever?'

'Yes. Open up, Victor.'

'Why didn't you ring the bell?'

'Not to wake Céleste, in case she's still up at the house.'

'Well, you must have woken Amédée,' said Victor, as he opened the gate with a clanking of chains.

'His light's on.'

'He sleeps with it on.'

'I thought you were sleeping over with him.'

'I will do, when I've finished working. Ah see, now you have woken him.'

Amédée was crossing the drive towards them, wearing jeans and a thick jacket pulled on over his bare chest.

'It's the commissaire,' said Victor. 'Yet again.'

'Quick,' said Adamsberg.

Victor took him into a small ground-floor room, containing very little furniture: a battered leather sofa, an old armchair and a low table. No family heirlooms here, obviously.

'Want some coffee?' said Amédée, looking rather alarmed.

'Yes please. The very first scene, Victor, describe it again for me.'

'What scene, for God's sake? What do you mean?'

Victor was right, he could afford to slow down now. It wasn't urgent.

'Look, I'm sorry, I'm on edge, I broke the speed limit getting here, I was pulled over by some traffic cops, and the bloody idiots breathalysed me.'

'And?'

'Positive.'

'So how did you get here?' asked Victor. 'Special commissaire's privilege?'

'Absolutely not. They were rubbing their hands, thinking they could take me to the station. So I jumped back in the car and drove off.'

'Ooh, leaving a crime scene. Bad mark,' said Victor, looking amused.

'Yes, very,' said Adamsberg patiently. 'Just please describe to me, again, the scene when the twelve of you, all French, were sitting round the table at the guest house on Grimsey. The day before you went to the island.'

'Well, all right,' said Victor, 'but what more is there to tell?'

'The killer, just describe him to me.'

Victor stood up, gave a sigh and waved his arm dismissively.

'I've already told you.'

'Tell me again.'

'Well, ordinary, average sort of fellow,' said Victor wearily. 'Except for his hair, he had plenty of that. He had the kind of face you don't really notice, a short beard, but no moustache, glasses. About fifty perhaps, but he could have been less. When you're young, everyone looks old.'

'And his stick, Victor, you mentioned he had a stick.'

'Is that important?'

'Yes.'

'OK, yes, he had a stick, to test the ice with when you walk on it.'

'And you said he was doing something with the stick?'

'Yeah, right, he was tapping it up and down on the flagstones. Tap, tap, tap.'

'Fast or slow? Try to remember.'

Victor looked down, searching his memory.

'Slow,' he said in the end.

'Good.'

'I don't get it. God knows why, but you're determined, aren't you, to get to the bottom of the Iceland story, whatever it takes?'

'Yes.'

'And now you have. But you're not supposed to be looking for the Iceland killer, you're looking for the one in the Robespierre club. The one who draws those signs.'

'True.'

'So why are we going back over Iceland again?'

'Because I'm looking for *both* killers, Victor. Give me some paper, a few pieces, and something to draw with, pencil preferably.'

Amédée brought him some drawing materials and a tray to rest on.

'We've just got a blue pencil, will that do?'

'It's fine,' said Adamsberg, sitting down to work. 'I'm going to make a few sketches of faces, Victor. I'll start with the killer on the island.'

Adamsberg worked in silence for several minutes. Then he passed his first sketch to Victor.

'Does that look like him?' he said.

'Can't say it does, no.'

'Please don't give me any more lies, Victor, this time we really are reaching the end of the road, and we're up against the wire. We're not going to use port to make a breakthrough this time. Or else,' he went on, 'did he look like *this* one?' and he passed across a different sketch. 'Is this one any better?'

'If you're going to keep fiddling around with a whole set of portraits, I'm not prepared to play this game.'

'I'm not fiddling with anything, I'm making deductions.'

'From what?'

'From a face as it is today, that I'm trying to make younger by ten years. Which isn't easy, because the face isn't remarkable in any way, just as you said. No big nose, no bushy eyebrows, no striking eyes, no prominent chin, nothing like that. Neither handsome nor ugly. Neither Danton nor Billaud-Varenne. So, now, look at this one.'

Victor observed the second portrait, then let it fall on to the low table, and pursed his lips.

'Go on,' said Adamsberg. 'Say.'

'All right,' said Victor, breathing heavily as if he had been running. 'Like that.'

'That's him?'

'Yes.'

'The killer in Iceland.'

Adamsberg took out some battered cigarettes from his pocket and offered them. Amédée took one, but looked at it carefully.

'This a spliff?'

'No, no, just some cigarettes of my son's.'

Adamsberg lit his cigarette, picked up the pencil and went back to work. A sound from outside alerted him, and he stopped to listen for a moment. Holding the sheets of paper, he approached the uncurtained window looking on to the park. The night was dark, and the street lamp out on the road lit up only a small portion of the drive between the two pavilions.

'Perhaps it's Marc,' said Victor. 'He's a bit noisy when he prowls around.'

'Would he leave Céleste at night though?'

'Normally, no, he wouldn't. Perhaps he's come to greet you. Or maybe it was just the wind.'

Adamsberg came back to sit down and resumed the drawing. Three new portraits, which took him about fifteen minutes.

'What are you drawing now?' asked Amédée.

'Now I'm drawing the other one, the killer in the Robespierre circle. I know you've seen him, Victor. When you accompanied Henri Masfauré to the assembly.'

'I didn't look at everyone.'

'But you *did* look at him. Of necessity.'

'Why?'

'You know very well why.'

'Why three drawings?'

'Because this man has several faces, and I don't know which one would be most familiar to you. Wearing make-up, white powder, with dark shadows, add a little silicone to the cheeks, take a wig, a lace collar that covers the neck, and the illusion is complete. That's why I'm making several sketches. Because with all the make-up in the world, you can't disguise the shape of the eyes, the placing of the mouth, the cheekbones. There,' he said, putting his new sketches on the table.

Adamsberg looked towards the window again. A rustle, a twig snapping? A cat? But they don't make any noise. A hedgehog, a hare? Hedgehogs are quite noisy. Victor put his finger down on one drawing, then another.

'That's him, and maybe that one is. But not exactly in that get-up.'

'But it *is* the man you saw close to Masfauré?'

'Yes.'

'And near to you as well.'

'You think so?'

'Victor, give it up! Now,' he said, placing the first sketch alongside the others, 'look at the killer from the island and the killer at the Robespierre meetings.'

Victor had quickly bent back his fingers on the table, but Amédée, totally absorbed by Adamsberg's sketches, and possibly a bit dazed by his medication, once more failed to notice. Amédée had had to suffer too much recently to be completely in control of himself.

'Oh, it's the same man!' he said spontaneously.

'Thank you, Amédée. And you can see that just as well as him, Victor. But of course you actually *know*. It *is* the same man. The island murderer. Who made regular arrangements to meet you.'

'He *didn't* arrange to meet us!' Victor began angrily.

Adamsberg lifted his hand to impose silence and listened again to the sounds of the night.

'We're not alone,' he said quietly.

They all listened hard.

'Can't hear anything,' said Victor.

'Someone's footsteps,' said Adamsberg. 'Very quiet. Put out the light. And move back.'

Adamsberg took out his pistol and loaded it, then approached the window carefully.

'Did you shut the main gate, Victor?' he whispered.

'Yes.'

'Then he must have come through the woods. Is there a gun here?'

'Yes, two shotguns.'

'Fetch them. Give one to Amédée.'

'I've never handled a gun,' said Amédée weakly.

'Well, you're going to now. You just press the trigger. And watch out for the recoil.'

'Maybe it's someone who heard you banging the gate fit to wake the dead and has come to take a look,' said Victor.

'No, Victor,' said Adamsberg as he peered out into the night. 'It's your "monster" out there.'

Victor, head down, went into the kitchen to fetch the two shotguns and gave one to Amédée.

'You're sure?' he asked.

'Yes.'

'Where is he?'

'He's going along the side of Amédée's pavilion,' said Adamsberg. 'The night's as black as soot, I can hardly see him. Did *you* tell him, Victor, that I'd travelled to Iceland, and found the bones?'

'Of course not – are you crazy?'

'Well, how come he's here then?'

A brief gleam of moonlight shone out then it was dark again. *Shit, a sub-machine gun, an MP5? Or some other fucking hardware.*

'Oh God,' breathed Adamsberg, moving towards the door. 'He's armed to the teeth.'

'What?' said Amédée.

'He's got a sub-machine gun. He could take out ten men in a few seconds.'

'Have we got a chance?' asked Amédée, trying to shoulder his gun.

'Just one. Not ten, not even two. Turn the sofa round with its back to the door. Kneel down behind it, one each side. It's a solid bit of furniture, it'll protect you for a while. And don't move.'

'What about you?'

'I'm going out. Does the door squeak, Victor?'

'No.'

Adamsberg opened it cautiously.

'When he crosses the drive,' he whispered, 'he'll show up a bit under the street lamp. But I won't. He'll be a target and that's our one chance.'

'The lamp goes out at midnight,' whispered Amédée, sounding defeated.

'What's the time now?'

'Three minutes to.'

Adamsberg swore again under his breath and slipped outside, moving along the left-hand wall for three metres towards the trunk of a plane tree. The man now ventured a step on to the drive, making the gravel crunch. Unlike himself, the killer was not dressed entirely in black. Adamsberg could glimpse the pale triangle of his shirt, and fired four times. There was a cry of pain, and the street lamp went out.

'Just my arm, you sonofabitch,' yelled the man, 'and the left hand's perfectly good. Went to the island, did you, you dimwitted cop? And what did you find there?'

'The bones of your victims!'

Adamsberg aimed again, before the man could shift the MP5 to his uninjured arm. Three seconds' grace, and he aimed for the knee. The man fell to the ground and his shots went harmlessly into the foliage of the plane tree. His weapon was heavy, too heavy, three kilos in his left hand, and it was hard to hold the handguard with his injured right hand. It's not so easy to manipulate an MP5.

'You can just give me those fucking bones, Adamsberg,' he yelled, 'or I'll kill your two kids when I'm done with you.'

The man was bursting with rage, and his voice had become high-pitched, screaming hoarsely. Solid and determined, uncrushable, he had struggled upright, his right arm dangling, and Adamsberg saw his shadow approach slowly, dragging one leg. He ran back inside the pavilion and double-locked the door – an illusory form of defence.

Another couple of seconds' grace, time to join the brothers in the shelter of the sofa. How many shots did he have left? Two, possibly.

A burst of fire smashed the lock, and was followed by a second salvo, the bullets going into the wall or into the frame of the sofa. The two brothers fired their shotguns at random, but without connecting. In the flares from the shots, Adamsberg could see the barrel of the MP5, which was shaking and barely under control, but which was pointing straight at them.

'Come out, Victor!' the man shouted. 'I'll give you one chance to save them. Céleste and her fucking piglet, they're bleeding in the woods. They tried to stop me.'

'Don't move, Victor,' ordered Adamsberg.

He emptied his magazine, but the man had moved towards the window now and Adamsberg missed him. It was all over. The monster was going to wipe out all three of them. Could he have guessed this would happen? Could he have predicted this? With one last effort, the commissaire picked up the coffee table and hurled it towards the killer, who stood upright again, amid the debris of the table, dazed perhaps, but unsinkable. When suddenly, two torchbeams lit him up from behind.

The windowpanes exploded as two shots hit the indestructible gunman in the legs, without warning. Gun in hand, Adamsberg saw the two traffic cops who had stopped him earlier, holding torches. The one who walked bow-legged then pinned the man to the ground, while his colleague seized the MP5. Good thing I drank that port, Adamsberg thought. And absurdly in this scene of carnage, he heard Rögnvar's deep voice saying: '*The* afturganga *does not abandon those he has summoned.*'

Victor had switched the lights back on. Adamsberg put his hand on the shoulder of one of the gendarmes.

'Two casualties in those woods, call the emergency services.'

Then he followed Victor at a run towards the cabin. The boar was lying on the ground panting: it had been wounded in the belly. Céleste, one hand in the animal's fur, the other gripping her pipe, was groaning. Adamsberg examined her. She had taken more than one bullet in the thigh. But it looked as if she had escaped more lightly than Marc, since the artery did not appear to be touched.

'Should I give her some water?' asked Victor.

'Don't move her, just talk to her, keep her awake. Pass me your shirt.'

Adamsberg rolled up the cloth to make a tourniquet and tied it tightly round the wound. Then he took off his T-shirt and passed it to Victor. 'Press that against Marc's belly, he's lost a lot of blood.'

Bare-chested under his jacket, Adamsberg ran back to guide the paramedics, whose siren he could hear. He made them take their ambulance to the edge of the wood, then the two men and two women followed him down the path. Céleste was placed on the first stretcher and carried rapidly away.

'Where's the second casualty?' asked the woman who had stayed behind.

'There,' said Adamsberg, pointing to Marc.

'Are you taking the piss?'

'Bring up the other stretcher!' Adamsberg shouted.

'Calm down, sir, please.'

'It's commissaire, Commissaire Adamsberg! Bring up the other stretcher and save this poor animal, for God's sake!'

The woman raised her hand, in a gesture of conciliation, nodded, and made a call for emergency veterinary services. Ten minutes later, Marc had also been transported away. Adamsberg knelt down and picked Céleste's pipe off the ground, then stood back up and looked at Victor. There was no need to say anything, both men were dripping with sweat and looked shattered.

Back in the pavilion, a doctor was attending to the wounds of the killer, who had taken bullets in his arm, one knee and both calves, and lay groaning on the ground.

'Your name, brigadier?' Adamsberg asked.

'Drillot. A priori, when we saw the scene, we thought the individual had to be floored fast. You're a commissaire, he had a machine gun. That was our operational view. But note, a priori. Don't go telling us now we shot without issuing a warning, we didn't have time.'

'I'll state that you warned him before you broke the window.'

'Thank you, but we can't take him in, until we know what it's for.'

Adamsberg sank into the armchair, which had somehow survived the shooting. Rather like the bottle of wine Angelino Gonzalez had been carrying.

'He's killed six people,' he said in a toneless voice, then pulled out a cigarette and lit it. 'Two of them ten years ago in Iceland, four more in the course of the last month. He attempted to murder someone else last night. And this evening, he has injured a woman and her companion, and he *intended* to kill all three of us.'

'What's his name?' asked the bow-legged gendarme. 'I'm Brigadier Verrin,' he added.

'No idea. Did you get our circular, all gendarmeries should have done, about a murderer who left a sign at the crime scene? This sign,' he added, and he drew it quickly on one of the sketches which he had picked up from the floor.

Verrin nodded.

'Yes, we did, commissaire.'

'Well, he's *that* man.'

Verrin hurried out on his bandy legs. Victor walked into the room, now strewn with plaster from the walls and the ceiling. He held out a clean shirt to Adamsberg.

'I've given him a sleeping pill,' he said. 'He's gone off now.'

'Who do you mean?' asked Brigadier Drillot, who had his notebook out.

'Amédée Masfauré, the son of one of the victims.'

'Well, you'll all have to give me your identities properly,' said the gendarme stiffly.

The paramedics had now taken the wounded man away. Brigadier Verrin hurried back in.

'Found his ID in the car,' he said. 'Name's Charles Rolben! I phoned the gendarmerie. And do you know who that is, Charles Rolben?'

'No idea,' said Adamsberg.

'A judge. A high-up judge. *Very* high up. That's what the station just told me: "Don't make waves, no waves, you'd better be bloody sure." Got any evidence? Because someone like that, we have to handle him with kid gloves. The commanding officer is having kittens.'

'Look, brigadier,' said Adamsberg, 'you just saw this very high-up judge wielding an MP5, right?'

'Yes.'

'You will find bullets from that gun in the body of Céleste Grignon, who was shot in the woods with her companion. And embedded in the walls of this room. And in the leather on the sofa. Yes, brigadier, that man is a merciless killer. I can even tell you he *likes* killing. He's killed without the slightest compunction. His first two victims were among a group of tourists who got stranded on an island off Iceland. You might remember the case?'

'Yes, vaguely. But perhaps there was some serious motive?'

Victor looked imploringly at Adamsberg.

'No motive whatsoever,' Adamsberg lied. 'He's completely insane. He stabbed the first victim, then he attempted to rape a woman and killed her afterwards. Let's all go home now, brigadier, you know where to contact me. You'll get a preliminary report on Monday. Or rather Monday night. Because it'll be long, very long.'

'That's as may be, commissaire, but we haven't finished with you.'

'What's that supposed to mean?'

'Speeding, driving under the influence, refusing to accompany officers, evading arrest.'

'Ah. That. So you followed me, did you?'

'No, we lost you. But we found you by tracking your mobile phone.'

'Of course,' said Adamsberg slowly, 'your commanding officer will be obliged to report upstairs: *you* fired on a high-up judge, from behind, without any warning.'

'Fuck that,' growled Drillot. 'You said you would cover us.'

'And *I* say drop the charges of being drunk in charge and evading arrest. The situation was urgent, as I told you several times when you pulled me over. A cop can't know, when he's just had a couple of glasses of port with a friend, that he could get called out urgently within the hour.'

'Three glasses, I'd say,' remarked Drillot.

'Two, brigadier. I couldn't have been positive.'

'If I understand you right, commissaire,' said Drillot, screwing up his eyes, 'you're casting doubt on our account.'

'Indeed I am.'

Verrin made a sign to his colleague and nodded.

'So how are you going to explain why we followed you?' he asked.

'For speeding. You didn't pull me over, but because I was certainly driving too fast, you chased me here.'

'All right. That'll work.'

'Accepted,' said Drillot.

'Where have they taken Céleste? The woman who was wounded in the woods.'

'Hospital in Versailles.'

'And Marc?'

'Who's Marc?'

'The wild boar.'

'What wild boar?'

The SOC team was now all over the pavilion, and Adamsberg walked out. Victor came to the car with him and leaned in at the window.

'You didn't tell them anything about what happened in Iceland?'

'No. You were right to be scared of him. We'll meet again. With Amédée.'

'What for?' asked Victor, looking anxious again.

'To have a meal at the inn. You can order the menu, and we'll invite Bourlin.'

'And that man I saw in the inn that day? The so-called tax inspector?'

'Yes, you're right, that was him too. He must have already decided to keep on *my* tail.'

'Commissaire,' called Victor, as the car started away. Adamsberg braked, and Victor ran a little way to catch up.

'You *do* believe me, don't you, that I didn't eat my mother?'

'I believe you all right, Victor. Someone who eats ducks to help his brother certainly doesn't eat his mother.'

Once back home, Adamsberg took the time to send a very curt email to Danglard:

Meeting of squad tomorrow at 1500 hours. Please see everyone attends.

Then another to Brigadier-chef Oblat in Dijon.

Murderer under arrest. Protection of Vincent Bérieux can be lifted.

And finally to Brigadiers Drillon and Verrin.

Many thanks!

XLVI

DANGLARD PARKED IN THE COURTYARD AT SQUAD HEADQUARTERS, feeling highly anxious. Adamsberg had sent his message just after 4 a.m., asking for the whole team to be called to a meeting on a Sunday. He knew that Adamsberg had been to see the fifth victim in Dijon the previous day, and that the statement from Vincent Bérieux had left them none the wiser, once again. A fat man, masked, wearing a wig and glasses.

Danglard feared the worst as he shambled across the yard, and indeed it would be only logical. Adamsberg was going to exact reprisals. For lack of respect, insubordination: he would be within his rights to challenge several of them and ask for them to be transferred. Starting with Danglard himself. Then Noël, Mordent and even Voisenet, although the latter had been more circumspect. Danglard felt the mist of guilt stifle his breathing. It was he who, with his sarcasm and disapproval, had encouraged the others, except for Noël, who needed no encouragement to be aggressive. But all the same, he told himself, standing up straighter as he opened the door, when the ship springs a leak, someone has to bring the captain back to his senses, and tow Adamsberg to the land of the living: facts, logic, coherent courses of action. Was it not symptomatic, and seriously so, that the commissaire had gone off, against all reason, to explore the Icelandic fogs which had almost swallowed him up? And wasn't it his, Danglard's, responsibility to keep the ship on an even keel?

Yes, of course it was. Cheered by the clear thought of his duty and his obligation to carry it out, however difficult the task, the commandant entered the council chamber with a confident tread. He immediately noted on the faces of the malcontents among the squad similar signs of apprehension. Adamsberg, as everyone knew, only very rarely had recourse to confrontation. But this time, they were all aware that a red line had been crossed. And the commissaire's reactions could, on those exceptional occasions, be as rapid as they were hostile. Many of them could remember the day he had smashed the top off a bottle, when faced with the bone-headed Brigadier Favre. In this atmosphere of fear, they, like Danglard, were looking for justifications for their behaviour, to reply to the commissaire's attack.

As Adamsberg walked slowly into the big room, he did not look in the least combative, but in his case, that meant nothing. Each officer, depending on the side of the table where he or she was sitting, examined the chief's face with pleasure or anxiety. He by contrast seemed clear-eyed, as if purified from some kind of trouble, which had in the past altered his features and veiled his smile. His colleagues were unaware that the infernal knot of seaweed had at last been disentangled.

Adamsberg stayed standing, and observed that the new seating arrangement – with those for and against, the moderates and the don't-knows – had not changed since their last meeting. For once, Estalère was rooted to the spot and Adamsberg had to make an encouraging sign for him to rush off and prepare the twenty-seven coffees. The commissaire had not planned out his speech in advance and, as always, things would emerge in their own time.

'The murderer in the Robespierre circle was arrested last night,' he announced, folding his arms. 'He's taken several bullet wounds and is in hospital in Rambouillet. The arrest took place after a shoot-out in Le Creux.'

Without knowing why, Adamsberg looked down at the palm of his right hand, the one that had fired nine shots at a man. At a man who had killed two people on the island, drowned Gauthier and slit her wrists, shot Masfauré, stabbed Breuguel, pushed Gonzalez down the steps, tried to hang Bérieux and wounded Céleste.

'The wounds he sustained to his arm and knee were from my gun, and the bullets in his calves were fired by two gendarmes from Saint-Aubin, Drillot and Verrin. I should say that the man was armed with an MP5, and was spraying it at three of us: Victor and Amédée Masfauré and myself. Before that, out in the woods, he had shot up Céleste and her pet boar, badly injuring them.'

'What on earth was he doing at Le Creux?' asked Froissy, who had no guilt feelings to prevent her speaking up.

'He had followed my car, quite simply. As had the two gendarmes from Saint-Aubin.'

'So why were the gendarmes following you?' asked Retancourt, who had no obstacle to enquiring either.

'I was speeding,' said Adamsberg with a smile. 'I refused to stop and drove away from them.'

Mercadet looked at him in amusement.

'But why did you act like that with the gendarmes, commissaire?' asked Voisenet, in a slightly subdued voice. Since, in the end, the arrest of the killer had changed the whole situation and low profiles seemed to be called for. Although, so far as he understood it at present, the arrest appeared to have been the product of pure chance.

'So that they *would* follow me, Voisenet.'

'Really?'

'No! But their arrival saved the day. I was faced with an MP5, and had only my service pistol, and the Masfauré brothers had a shotgun each. But a sub-machine gun's heavy, and the killer was having to use his left hand, and couldn't aim it accurately. It slowed him down, he missed several times, and that's what saved us. Without the gendarmes of Saint-Aubin turning up, I'm not sure we would have survived,' Adamsberg concluded calmly.

Estalère had now served the coffees, and they all welcomed the diversion. For once, nobody stopped making noises with their spoons and saucers, which went on for quite a long time.

'So was all this pure chance then?' asked Noël. 'The fact that the killer came after you?'

'You'll have to speak up, Noël,' said Adamsberg, pointing to his ear, 'I'm still a bit deaf after the gunshots.'

'Pure chance? That the killer was out there?' repeated Noël, more loudly.

'No, not at all, lieutenant. I had gone out to see Victor, in order to draw the murderer's face for him to view. After all that time when he was just lurking away in my mind, sheltering behind his masks, it was only last night that he really *appeared to* me.'

'You had some clues?' asked Danglard, feeling he could not remain silent after the fairly brave interventions of Voisenet and Noël.

'Yes, plenty.'

'And you didn't tell us about them?'

'I did nothing *but* that, commandant. You were in possession of all the same elements as I was –' and at this point Adamsberg did raise his voice – 'as was the entire squad you have been leading since I left for Iceland. I told you that the Robespierre chessboard wasn't moving, it was at stalemate, whereas "animals move". I told you to go looking for movement. I told you that the Sanson, Danton and Desmoulins leads were unimportant. And there were plenty of other clues too. Why was it the "occasional" people, who only came sometimes to the assemblies, who were being attacked, if the point of it all was to reach Robespierre? Why was the guillotine sign sometimes so inconspicuous? And yet so obscure? Why were those brand-new books on Iceland left at Jean Breuguel's flat? Why was Victor keeping determinedly silent? Why was there all this fear everywhere? Was it genuine? False?

Why would someone wear a wig to hang Vincent Bérieux? You all received the photographs of the scene of crime, like I did. Why was the rope not suspended from the middle of the garage? Why was it hooked to one side? I even told you about that yesterday in my text message: white wig, victim not talking. You had all these elements to hand the same way I did. But for some time now, you haven't wanted to see or hear. And yet, commandant, didn't all those things add up to something rather consistent?'

Danglard had had neither the time nor indeed the desire to note down all these scattered facts, that is if something like 'animals move' counted as a fact. Justin and Froissy were attempting to do so quickly, while all Danglard could see for the moment was a cloud of red ladybirds, which he must certainly have missed, scattered across the valley of the Chevreuse.

'So they weren't *my* elements, Danglard,' Adamsberg went on, 'they were yours too, and everyone else's.'

'Agreed.'

'Agreed? What's agreed? Which one of you, Danglard, Voisenet and Mordent, you who know such a lot, told me that seal meat doesn't taste of fish? No one. You've all read the statements made by Victor and Amédée about the tragedy in Iceland. According to Amédée, the man came back one night *dripping with blood and stinking of fish*, hauling along a dead seal. He also said that Alice Gauthier had retained a memory of that evening as a delicious meal tasting like a *giant salmon*. Then Victor told us afterwards of the same miraculous fishing expedition: *kilos of fish*. And he said that when they got to Grimsey, *they stank of seal blubber and rotten fish from head to toe*. I did tell you that the two brothers had had time to coordinate their version of events before they spoke to us. That there were too many coincidences between their accounts, like the "monster" and the trousers in flames when the murderer fell on the fire. I told you, Danglard, that this story was far from being the truth. So did you go back and study their statements? No, because at that stage, nobody wanted to hear any more about Iceland or that place out at Le Creux. But we hadn't finished exploring Le Creux. We'd left it open, we'd missed a path somewhere, and we'd walked away from it.'

He heard once more Lucio's hoarse voice saying: *'There's a pathway you haven't seen. This guy's playing games.'*

'So did *you* read their statements again, commissaire?' asked Kernorkian, in a non-committal voice.

'Yes, I did, to note down the similarities between what they said. *Why* were they lying, and what was it they were actually lying about? *Salmon, fish, stinking fish*, these kept cropping up insistently in both accounts. Now you, Danglard, and you, Voisenet, know better than I would that seals are mammals, not fish. In fact I only knew that because you told me.'

'But surely,' Estalère ventured, 'seals eat tons of fish. So wouldn't their meat smell of it?'

Adamsberg shook his head.

'Doesn't alter the fact that their meat does not smell of fish. Any more than beef smells of grass.'

'I see,' said Estalère thoughtfully. 'So what does seal meat taste like?'

'Something between liver and duck, with overtones of salt and iodine.'

'How do you know that? Did you eat some in Grimsey?'

'No, I *asked* someone.'

Adamsberg walked a few paces back and forth.

'Well, anyway,' he said in the end, 'I did tell you, several times, that this investigation had been from the start like a huge tangled knot of seaweed.'

Which isn't a 'fact', Danglard said to himself, while Justin noted it down all the same.

'And that you can't just plunge into a thing like that. We were pulling out tiny little broken fragments, and getting drawn into other traps. We had elements, clues, but they were floating, dozens of them, just under the surface without any apparent connection between them, in a sort of fog. The whole thing had been drowned in confusion by this twisted and determined killer. We needed some serious event to trigger a movement and bring the mass up into the air. So as to be able to draw his face.'

'The face of the killer?' asked Estalère conscientiously.

'Of the killer, yes.'

'And to show it to Victor before showing us?' said Danglard.

'Correct, Danglard. Because Victor knew perfectly well who the killer was.'

'How was that?'

'Because he attended meetings of the Robespierre association, with his employer Masfauré. I needed his witness statement, and in the end I got it. No, in fact it was Amédée who gave it away. I'm not sure Victor would ever have talked. But Amédée was feeling trusting, he had rediscovered his childhood friend and brother.'

'So it wasn't a waste of time, after all,' said Veyrenc, 'to make that expedition to the farm at Le Thost.'

'What was the trigger event then?' asked Mordent, his long heron-neck shrunk down inside the grey feathers of his sweater. 'The one you needed to bring the mass up to the surface?'

'The sound of a wooden stick hitting the floor. Which you might also have noticed, Danglard, because you were there with me that evening. But you weren't really concentrating, you were angry about my leaving for Grimsey.'

'*What* did you say?' asked Voisenet.

'Veyrenc kept tapping his crutch on the floor at my house yesterday evening. And it all came up into clear water. It had to. Although, at first, I had thought it was Fouché. I just had to extend the field a little.'

Danglard felt completely lost. Adamsberg's words conveyed nothing to him. He needed a clear, organised answer. He suspected that the commissaire was enjoying wrapping them in the mists of his personal island.

'This murderer, who was at large in the Robespierre society,' he spoke up firmly, 'who is he then, commissaire?'

'The same person as the killer in Iceland.'

There was an oppressed silence, some intakes of breath, the sounds of cups being fidgeted with, pencils being put down or chewed, and Estalère felt it might be the right moment for a second round of coffee. Whatever many of his colleagues thought of him, Estalère had been following, with all its combinations of the serious and the trivial, the complex construction of the opposition mounted against Adamsberg.

'A killer,' Adamsberg continued, 'that we went looking for on Fox Island. Where it all began. Where, as I said to you, something was still budging. Because I *did* tell you, didn't I? A movement that went on creating waves, until the attempt on Vincent Bérieux and then on us, last night.'

'What's his name then?' asked Danglard, who could perfectly well hear the muffled reproaches beneath the surface of Adamsberg's calm voice.

'Charles Rolben, he's a "high-up judge", I'm told. Nothing less. Six murders, five attempted murders.'

'Who counts in the six?' asked Noël, pulling down the zip of his leather jacket, possibly as an unconscious sign of opening up.

'On the island, Eric Courtelin and Adélaïde Masfauré. Back here, Alice Gauthier, Henri Masfauré, Jean Breuguel, Angelino Gonzalez. Attempted murders: Vincent Bérieux, the Masfauré brothers and me. Plus seriously wounding Céleste. And Marc,' he added.

'Quite a tally,' Mercadet commented.

'But apart from you, Céleste, Amédée and the ones on the island,' Danglard said, 'they *were* all members of the Robespierre association.'

'But that isn't the fucking point, Danglard,' Adamsberg said in exasperation. 'You *still* don't want to understand. They were all members of the tourist group that got marooned in Iceland. Jean Breuguel was the "civil servant" Victor told us about, the one who laughed when he sat on the warm stone. Angelino Gonzalez was the specialist on little auks. Vincent Bérieux was the one Victor thought was a ski instructor. All members of the group! And they'd all eaten the bodies of their companions. Is that something trivial, Danglard? Isn't that something pretty colossal? A colossal lead that you didn't think I should be following up.'

Danglard pushed his notes away from him, and poured himself a glass of water. The commandant was giving in, as they all understood. Adamsberg was waiting for this shift before he gave them a clearer account, if he could manage it.

'If it was Iceland all along,' asked Mordent, 'how could you manage to draw a portrait of the killer from the island? This Charles Rolben, whoever he is?'

'Because we *did* know him, Mordent. He was a member of the Robespierre association, like all the others.'

'François Château?'

'Not Château, commandant, but the one who was afraid. The one who asked for police protection.'

'Lebrun!' said Retancourt.

'Lebrun, the bloodthirsty, egotistical, violent killer, so well disguised under his make-up, his beards and wigs. And with his nondescript features which could be modified as he wanted. The "monster" as Amédée called him. Remember when he took the role of Couthon, Danglard? Was he so insignificant then? And wasn't he openly enjoying the ferocity of his colleague Leblond playing Fouché?'

Danglard nodded curtly.

'You may remember then, that evening, in his role as the paralysed Couthon in his wheelchair, how he kept tapping his cane on the floor. And remember that we were told the killer on the island had a stick with which he tapped the ice? Only one of the founders of the association would have come up with the idea of instituting *compulsory* meetings there for the survivors from the island. To watch them, looking out for any weaknesses, or failings. It was an idea of genius: he could see them repeatedly at his beck and call, but in an assembly where everyone was wearing costume and make-up, and to cap it all anonymous. Who would ever be able to notice them? And if any of them were to die – any of these "infiltrators", even several of them – why would the cops go poking around in Iceland for the explanation? Much more likely that they'd go for *Robespierre*, the name that still arouses so many passions. Yes, they'd head for Robespierre. And that's where we all went running, and I led the way.'

'But if he wanted to get us *away* from the Icelandic lead, and move us in the other direction,' asked Veyrenc, 'why didn't he make the sign clearer, more readable?'

'That was where he showed another stroke of genius, Veyrenc. If you give the cops, or anyone else for that matter, a clue that's too obvious, they're going to be suspicious. "It's too good to be true", "it's a trap", we're being pushed in a certain direction, and it's suspect, But if you force them to think, and bring them to believe that they, the cops, have worked out through their own wits the meaning of the clue, then they'll be totally committed to their discovery. The more effort has gone into it, the greater one's attachment to it. If by any chance we *hadn't* worked it out, then François Château's letter, which was authentic and sincere, would have taken us straight to the Robespierre path. Everybody we showed it to denied that they knew the sign, except Lebrun, who had invented it. Just for us, exclusively for us. Neither too clear nor too obscure. And of course, once three murders had appeared in the papers, Lebrun pushed Château to get in touch with us. Better than that. Just in case we were still tempted to go looking in Iceland, he put the three *brand-new* books in Jean Breuguel's flat. Which said to us that, aha, the killer wants us to keep thinking in terms of the Iceland business. He's slipped up, we thought, like the idiots we were. But the slip-up was deliberate of course. What better way to make us give up on Iceland? Which we did. All of us. We were drawn into the orbit of the Robespierre circle where – and I'll say it again – nothing was moving. Why? Because nothing was *happening* there. Lebrun had forced us to play on this chessboard with over seven hundred other players on it, but the pawns weren't moving. Because the real pawns were moving somewhere else. And we'd have stagnated on this stationary chessboard till the end of time without any result, because there wasn't one to be found there.'

'Until all the members of the Iceland group had been killed off,' said Mercadet.

'Without our getting near guessing the identity of the killer,' Voisenet admitted.

'Right, lieutenant. Lebrun? The amiable Lebrun? The one who helped us by pointing out the group of descendants. A group that led precisely nowhere. And also pointing out to us, playing with fire perhaps, but there was no risk, like when you put your finger through a candle flame, the group of "infiltrators" whom, as he confided in us, he distrusted. The infiltrators' group, which was in fact none other than the Icelandic group, that he summoned twice a year to the assembly, in order to check them out and warn them once more to keep their mouths shut.'

'I don't get it about the candle,' said Estalère.

'I'll show you sometime,' said Adamsberg. 'How to do it without getting burned. "Who were these infiltrators?" Lebrun was asking us. Perhaps anti-Robespierrists out for vengeance? Royalists? Spies? And maybe Robespierre himself was eliminating them. In his madness? And why not? Poor Lebrun ended up "fearing" for himself. And we believed him.'

'Oh shit,' said Voisenet, returning to his normal self. 'We've been played for fools from start to finish.'

'Not to the finish, Voisenet. Until too much immobility started to appear abnormal or suspicious. Until, once we'd gone round in circles, we started to wonder if there wasn't some other lead to follow. Or one that had been abandoned and lost from view. But there was only one.'

'Iceland,' Noël admitted.

And once more Adamsberg recognised the courage of the usually thuggish Noël, since he was surrendering without shame.

'There is one thing,' said Adamsberg. 'When Lebrun came round here, in my absence, to ask for more protection, did he discover somehow or other that I was in Iceland? I thought we'd told him I was away on family matters.'

Danglard slowly raised his arm, in silence.

'It was my fault,' he said. 'When I was arguing with him about the protection, I let something slip.'

'What kind of "something", Danglard?'

The commandant summoned up the courage to look Adamsberg in the eye, feeling like Danton, he told himself, marching towards the sacrifice.

'I told him we'd do what we could while you were away, because you'd gone off on holiday to Iceland.'

'It wasn't a small "something" then, Danglard.'

'No.'

'It was that information he'd come to find out, because he'd seen my car was still outside my house. He'd been spying on me since the very beginning of the investigation. And you gave him the information, because you were irritated with me. So you can imagine his reaction. I was going back to Iceland. Following up a lead he had taken such trouble to destroy, because he wanted us to concentrate on the unfathomable Robespierre circle. So then he attacked Vincent Bérieux. Bérieux was the anonymous "cyclist" of the association, the "ski instructor" on the Icelandic trip. And he hangs him, taking care to dress up first in an eighteenth-century wig. Why? To send us back to Robespierre at all costs. And he does better than that. He fixes the rope to the side, near a chain which Bérieux might grab hold of, and near a set of shelves where he could get a foothold. The rope was in any case very coarse, a slipknot wouldn't work too well with it. And he knew perfectly well that Bérieux, given his physical strength, might manage to extract himself. As he in fact did.'

'He hangs him, but he spares his life?' said Kernorkian. 'What sense does that make?'

'Just so that Bérieux can tell us that his attacker was wearing a white wig, from the revolutionary period. So we'd never move away from Robespierre.'

'I see,' said Estalère, concentrating hard and chewing the inside of his cheek.

'Yeah, I get it,' sighed Mordent.

'And Lebrun, thinking ahead, even leaves a lock of white hair on the ground, just in case his hanged man does actually die. But Bérieux survives. He tells us about the wig, but that's all. He does it for the same reason as his attacker: to keep us thinking "Robespierre society" and not Iceland. So that nobody ever finds out that he too had eaten the bodies of his fellow travellers, like all the others. He told me he went to the assemblies because he'd always been "keen on Robespierre", but he was lying of course. He went because he was summoned, like the others.'

'Of course,' said Mordent, with an even deeper sigh.

'It was all working like clockwork for Lebrun, the wig sent us towards someone crazy enough to go around killing people while dressed in eighteenth-century costume. And which crazy individual might we think of? Someone who regularly puts on a white wig?'

'Robespierre,' said Retancourt.

'Whom we'd probably have arrested sooner or later. A descendant of the Incorruptible himself, a man whose childhood was blighted by a grandfather fanatical about the legend, a man who played the role in the assembly as if he really was inhabited by his ancestor, yes, he had everything to make us think he was unbalanced, out of his mind, and a killer. That's where Lebrun/Charles Rolben was leading us, I'm quite sure. Don't forget he hanged Bérieux one night when he knew François Château would be working late at the hotel, alone, so without an alibi.'

'He was sending his friend to the guillotine!' said Froissy.

'People like him don't have friends, Froissy.'

'But why,' she asked, looking up from her laptop screen, 'did he attack Masfauré after Alice Gauthier? Why not Gonzalez or Breuguel?'

'Because once we started to investigate the Robespierre circle, we'd discover that Masfauré was their financial backer. So we'd think it was the association that the killer was trying to wipe out, not some former visitors to Iceland.'

'Yes, of course,' repeated Mordent, breathing out heavily. 'But to attack you was very risky.'

'Not more than anyone else. What he really feared was that Amédée, the weak link in the chain, would end up giving in to my questioning him. And after I returned from Iceland, I *had* visited the two brothers again. So I must have come up with something there. And found out, somehow or other, what really happened on the island with the warm rock. So when I went off by car last night, he followed me. I started heading for Le Creux, which fulfilled his worst fears. This time, he can't afford to let us survive. He's ready. He goes straight there by main roads and gets there first, because I was driving along side roads to try and get rid of my gendarmes. He goes through the holes in the fence between the big house and the woods, he immobilises Céleste and her pet boar on the way, and he arrives at the pavilion where we are.'

'And you didn't hear him shooting in the forest?' asked Voisenet.

'It was over a kilometre away, and the wind was blowing to the west. If Lebrun hadn't learned about my trip to Iceland, Danglard, he would have stayed his hand, hoping to get us fixated on the Robespierre circle and perhaps arresting François Château. We could have picked him up quietly on Monday night, when he went out via the car park. He wouldn't have injured Céleste, and he wouldn't have shot at us. I should remind you *all* that no private information about the movements of any member of the squad should be divulged to an outsider. Not even if someone goes out to take a leak or feed the cat. Not even if the outsider seems friendly, cooperative and frightened. Sorry, Danglard.'

Danglard took a moment, then stood up, regaining his sober and dignified elegance. Adamsberg, who had no taste for grand gestures, especially when announced with solemnity, flinched slightly, but Danglard's expression gave no hint of bombast.

'I wish,' he said calmly, 'to offer you my congratulations. I on the other hand, have committed a very serious mistake, one which might, and indeed *ought* to have led to the death of four people, of whom you could have been one. Consequently, I will give you my resignation in writing this evening.'

'No, impossible this evening,' said Adamsberg, as if he were declining an invitation to dinner, 'because it's Sunday, and I don't read things on a Sunday. Impossible tomorrow, because we have to tackle the report, and I'll need your drafting skills. Impossible after that, because I've put in a request for three weeks', leave. Consequently you will be heading the squad in my absence.'

Where's he going? wondered Danglard. To the Pyrenees of course, to soak his feet in the green water of the Gave de Pau.

'Is that an order?' asked Mordent, whose neck had re-emerged from his shoulders.

'It is indeed,' Adamsberg confirmed.

'That's an order,' Mordent hissed to Danglard.

'You can all leave now,' said Adamsberg gently. 'It's Sunday.'

Veyrenc caught Adamsberg by the arm as he made for the door.

'All the same,' he said, 'if it wasn't for those gendarmes, you'd have had it.'

'Not necessarily. Because an *afturganga* never abandons those he has summoned.'

'That's true, I'd forgotten.'

'Looking at it that way,' Danglard muttered softly, following them out, 'the *afturganga* also *summoned* the gendarmes from Saint-Aubin.'

'Looking at it that way,' said Adamsberg, 'that's an excellent observation from you, commandant, after recent days. I'll be able to go off happily.'

XLVII

AFTER DINING TOGETHER, ADAMSBERG AND FRANÇOIS CHÂTEAU WERE strolling in the almost deserted garden at the end of the Ile de la Cité, walking around the statue of Henri IV. François Château was still struggling with the horror and intense anger into which he had been plunged by Adamsberg's information about his secretary, Charles Rolben aka Lebrun.

'Imagine! A magistrate turning cannibal! Charles! Charles stabbing people in order to eat them! No, I can't visualise that, I'm quite unable to absorb it.'

It was about the twelfth time Château had repeated that sentence in one form or another. This evening, he was certainly Château, not Robespierre. He wasn't wearing the locket, Adamsberg felt sure of that.

'Has he said anything?' Château asked.

'No, he's refusing to say a word. The doctor has diagnosed a state of some kind of fury . . . hang on, Château, I'll have to look it up . . . "a state of destructive fury", ' Adamsberg went on reading from his note-book, '"with extreme signs of frustration and execration, no doubt emanating from a psychopathic personality." He's smashed everything he could find in his hospital room, television, phone, window, bedside table, he's been put under sedation. Such violence, and you never noticed it in him?'

'No,' said Château with a shake of his head, 'no. Except . . .' He hesitated.

'What kind of a judge was he?'

'The kind they call "pitiless". I didn't want to pay too much attention to that kind of gossip, it bothered me.'

'Why?'

'Because of the extreme fondness he had for Robespierre's Revolutionary Tribunal. It was rather upsetting. He sometimes said that, by comparison, our law courts were very lukewarm affairs.'

'You were friends?'

'Colleagues. He always kept his distance. He did have a very clear sense of social distinctions. I was just an accountant, and he was a judge. In the circles he moved in, he was on good terms with bigwigs, personalities from politics, high finance and so on. He used to entertain very lavishly, so Leblond told me, at his villa in Versailles, where all the best people met. Or you could say all the worst.'

'Was Leblond invited?'

'He's a distinguished psychiatrist at the hospital in Garches.'

'That's where *Lebrun* asked us to come, to provide him with police protection.'

'Well, that's complete nonsense,' Château said, with a shrug. 'Charles was never a psychiatrist. Is that what he told you?'

'Yes.'

'I suppose in a way that makes sense, because he was interested. He wanted to be able to "diagnose" people, he pestered Leblond with questions: could you tell, by such-and-such signs or expressions, or tone of voice, if a person was in a fragile state? Depressed, suffering remorse? Other people's weaknesses, that's what fascinated him. And when he invited Leblond to his soirées, he would give him a mission. Observe such-and-such politician or banker or industrialist and report back. Leblond was uneasy about this, he said he was a doctor not a spy on people's souls, but Charles was very persuasive when he wanted to be. People did what he said. But sometimes,' said Château with a smile, 'it was *me* he was frightened of, or worse, forced to admire.'

'When you were Robespierre.'

'Yes, commissaire. He was a passionate Robespierrist. He had only one criticism of him, and that was his famous belief in virtue. The fact that Robespierre never wanted to be present at an execution. His distaste for blood. He said that was contemptible hypocrisy. "That, my friend," Leblond used to say, "is an amateur analysis." But Charles wouldn't have it. He wanted Robespierre to be a man of action, not a man behind a desk, he'd have liked to see him cutting off heads, hoisting them on the ends of pikes, running through the streets with the people, going up on to the scaffold in person to operate the guillotine. I see now what that was about. Charles loved all that, blood, executions, massacres. And he loved himself. What did those two lives in Iceland matter if *he* could survive? But why did he start killing them all so many years later? Was he suddenly overcome with a murderous urge?'

'More likely an urge for self-protection, Château. Alice Gauthier had confessed, and that threw into imbalance the whole equilibrium of the Iceland survivors. Amédée Masfauré might tell people after that, as might his father, or Victor. Control of the group was likely to escape Rolben. He decided he'd better get rid of the whole lot of them, once and for all.'

'I just can't conceive it,' said Château for the thirteenth time. 'Six murders, and he could have gone on to do eleven. And how is that woman, the one he tried to mow down with a machine gun in the woods, like the horrible Fouché in Lyon?'

Adamsberg stood still.

'Not out of danger yet,' he said.

'I'm so sorry. After the final assembly, the ones of the 8 and 9 Thermidor, I'm going to wind up the association.'

'You told me that your finances – paid out by Masfauré, but on orders of Charles Rolben of course, as you may imagine – would allow you to complete your research.'

'Never mind, commissaire, it would be indecent to carry on now. The curtain must fall. And when people learn who Charles was, what he's done, and the name of the association of which he was secretary, we shall be swept away by scandal in any case, whatever happens. The page is turned.'

Château sat down on a bench, his legs out in front of him, but his back still very straight, and Adamsberg lit a cigarette in the gathering dusk.

'Why not?' said Adamsberg. 'But why not live him a different way?'

'Live whom?'

'Robespierre. You're not wearing the teeth tonight.'

'What teeth?'

'His teeth. Retrieved by the surgeon on the night of the 9 Thermidor and given to Éléonore Duplay, passed on to François-Didier Château, and handed down from one male descendant to the next, till they reached you. You are descended from the presumed son of Robespierre.'

'You're inventing stories, commissaire.'

'There,' Adamsberg said, putting a finger to Château's chest. 'You wear them there, in a locket. And then He enters you. He expels François Château, body and soul, and comes back to life, he alone exists then, not you.'

Château put out his hand to ask for one of Adamsberg's cigarettes, no longer surprised at their tattered appearance.

'Why go on holding out?' Adamsberg asked as he gave him a light. 'The story's coming to an end.'

'What does that matter to you? Whether the teeth exist or not? Whether I'm wearing them round my neck or not? Whether HE enters me or not? What interest can it possibly hold for you?'

'I suppose my interest's in "François Château, body and soul". Who might end up being devoured by Him, why not? But this evening, I guess, I can't bear the thought of anyone being devoured.'

'There isn't a solution,' said Château gloomily.

'Get a DNA analysis. Of the teeth and then of yourself. You'll have your answer. You'll know then whether you really are descended from him, or whether, back in 1790, some unmarried mother merely boasted that the great man was the father of her unborn child.'

'Never.'

'Why? Because you're afraid?'

'Yes.'

'Afraid of being his descendant, or of not being?'

'Both.'

'Fears that spread inside doubt, like mushrooms in a cellar, can only be dealt with by having certain knowledge.'

'That sounds so simple, commissaire.'

'It does. But then you'll know, and it will make a big difference.'

'But what if I don't want there to be a big difference?'

'What will be different will be the historical facts,' Adamsberg went on. 'Whatever the result is, you can still go on acting in the persona of Robespierre if you like. But you'll know which is *him* and which is François Château. And that's not nothing. As for the teeth, you can put them where they ought to be: with the people, as Robespierre might say. Give them back to the people. Offer them to the Carnavalet Museum, where all they've got is a measly lock of his hair.'

'Never!' said Château. 'No, never, do you hear me?'

Adamsberg stubbed out his cigarette and stood up to take one more turn around the statue of Henri IV.

'Well, I'm off now,' he said at last, returning to the bench.

And Adamsberg walked away, leaving Château to his heavy destiny, crossing the bridge over to the Left Bank, breathing in the smell of the Seine as he went. He paused, leaning on the parapet, to watch it flowing past, dirty, polluted, but still powerful. A quarter of an hour passed, more perhaps. Suddenly Château appeared at his side, by the wall, not looking exactly happy, but perhaps a little relieved, with a slight smile on his face.

'I *will* do it, commissaire. The DNA test.'

Adamsberg nodded. Then Château stood upright, with his ramrod back – which he would always have – and held out his hand.

'Thank you, Citizen Adamsberg.'

This was the first time Château had ever addressed him by his name, and not his rank.

'May life be good to you, Citizen Château,' Adamsberg replied, shaking his hand. 'And may all your descendants be girls.'

Adamsberg walked all the way home. Before he opened the little gate, he looked down at his palm. It's not everyone who gets a chance to shake hands with Robespierre.

XLVIII

ADAMSBERG HAD WAITED TO HEAR BETTER NEWS ABOUT CÉLESTE before he left, and Danglard had driven him to the airport. They separated at the departure lounge. Next day, the commandant would have to start interrogating the killer, Charles Rolben, on his own.

'How to tackle him, which way to get at him, what tactics to adopt – the whole thing is perplexing me.'

'Don't worry about it, Danglard. Rolben is a cruel man with no conscience, so there's no point working out a tactic for him. He'll never give in, whether you try kindness, wit, intimidation, or even your white-wine trick. He's a master of violence, don't expect to get anything out of him. Just line up our evidence and the witnesses. There's just one thing that might make him go berserk. If you don't seem to pay him much attention, if you act as though he were someone of little significance. Keep me posted. Are you going to see Céleste?'

'Yes, this afternoon.'

'Well, you can give her this then,' said Adamsberg, taking her pipe out of his pocket. 'That'll cheer her up. And tell her Marc is safely back home again at the stud farm.'

Once Adamsberg had gone through the departure gate, Danglard waited in the big lounge, holding tightly the pipe and the ladybirds that went with it. He wanted to wait for the plane to take off, before leaving the airport. It would be spring there now, the grass would be growing up again tall and green. The commandant looked at his watch.

9.40. Danglard nodded. The plane was taking off: ultimate destination the island of Grimsey.